LIFE AND DEATH ON MARS

BOOKS BY EDWARD M. LERNER

Novels

- Probe
- Moonstruck
- Fools' Experiments
- Small Miracles
- Dark Secret
- The Company Man
- On the Shoals of Space-Time
- Life and Death on Mars

Marcus Judson novels

- Energized
- Déjà Doomed

InterstellarNet series novels

- InterstellarNet: Origins
- InterstellarNet: New Order
- InterstellarNet: Enigma

Fleet of Worlds series novels (with Larry Niven)

- Fleet of Worlds
- Juggler of Worlds
- Destroyer of Worlds
- Betrayer of Worlds
- Fate of Worlds

Collections and nonfiction

- Creative Destruction
- Countdown to Armageddon / A Stranger in Paradise
- Frontiers of Space, Time, and Thought
  (mixed fiction and nonfiction)
- A Time Foreclosed (chapbook)
- Trope-ing the Light Fantastic:
  The Science Behind the Fiction (nonfiction)
- Muses & Musings
- The Sherlock Chronicles & The Paradise Quartet
- The Best of Edward M. Lerner

LIFE AND DEATH ON MARS

Edward M. Lerner

ISBN: 978-1-64710-088-9

First Edition. First Printing. December 2023
1 2 3 4 5 6 7 8 9 10

An imprint of Arc Manor LLC

www.CaezikSF.com

To the crew of *Apollo 11*—and the entire NASA team that made their mission possible:

The heroes of the *first* Space Race

CONTENTS

Dramatis Personae. 1

DESPAIR 5

DESCENT. 11

DECISIONS 31

(MIS)DIRECTIONS 65

DEPARTURE. 99

DIGGING IN. 141

DEFIANCE 203

DESPERATION. 231

DISCOVERIES. 299

DESPONDENCY. 363

DIAGNOSIS. 387

EPILOGUE (Diaspora). 455

Acknowledgments 469

About the Author. 471

Dramatis Personae

(Also see explanatory notes and acronym definitions that follow the character list)

Crew of United States-led Ares One mission

Meriwether Lewis

Alexander (Xander) Hopkins	computer engineer; presidential confidant; NASA
Katrina (Cat) Mancini	pilot and medic; mission commander; NASA
Sun Ying (Sonny)	physician and biologist; CSA

William Clark

David Berghoff	pilot and robotics engineer; ESA
Giselle Delacroix	geologist and paleobiologist; ESA
Ito Hideo	manufacturing and mining engineer; JAXA

Crew of PRC-led Chìdì (Red Dragon) One mission

Zheng He (all CMSA)

Zhao Jin (Gene)	pilot and power engineer; mission commander; colonel in the PLA Strategic Support Force
Wu Mingmei (Myra)	mechanical engineer and copilot
Chen Xiuying (Brittney)	physician and biologist/biochemist
Wang Kai (Carter)	systems and computer engineer; major in the PLA Strategic Support Force

Yuri Gagarin

Nikolai (Kolya) Mikhailovich Antonov	pilot and industrial engineer; RSSC; colonel in the Russian Aerospace Force
Ivan (Vanya) Borisovich Vasiliev	chemical engineer and biochemist; RSSC

1

Maria (Masha) Kozlovna Petrova	hydroponics engineer and botanist; RSSC
Oorvi Bhatt	mining engineer and geologist; ISRO

Crew of New Earth One commercial mission
(American, unless otherwise indicated)

Bradbury

Jacob (Jake) Walker	pilot and aeronautical engineer; married to Teri
Islah Massaley	chemical and geological engineer; Liberian
Julio Silva	construction and power engineer; Brazilian
Maria Theresa (Teri) Rodriguez	mission commander; mechanical engineer; married to Jake

Burroughs

Reuven (Reuben) Ben-Ami	pilot and aeronautical engineer; Israeli
Paula Kelly	physician and biologist
Keshaun Johnson	power and computer engineer
Maia Phillips	botanist and gengineer; New Zealander

US government, non-astronaut

Dale Bennigan	presidential science advisor; physician; molecular biologist
Lance Kawasaki	White House press secretary
Rebecca (Becky, Becks) Nguyen	NASA Associate Administrator, Human Exploration and Operations
Arthur Schmidt	Director of National Intelligence
Matthias Van Dijk	NASA administrator; ex-senator
Carla DeMille	president

Other

Wu Lingyun	PRC president
Blake Wagner	IPE owner; NEP partner; American
Ira Coleman	Reporter, with a source within PPL; American

2

Notes

1. In addition to indicated disciplines, the Mars mission crew all receive extensive cross-training in second and third specialties.

2. Dates reflect Earth's calendar (unless otherwise indicated, in the United States Eastern Time Zone). The Martian year is almost twice as long as Earth's; the Martian day is closer to 25 hours than to 24.

3. Personal names:

   Per customary usage, Chinese and Japanese identifications are shown with family names first.
   Many Chinese professionals take an additional, Westernized name.
   Identifiers in parentheses are nicknames or Westernized names.
   Russian names include patronymics.

4. Organization acronyms (American, unless otherwise noted)

   CMSA: China Manned Space Agency
   CSA: Canadian Space Agency
   DNI: Director of National Intelligence
   DSN: Deep Space Network (several spacefaring countries operate their own DSN)
   EPF: Earth Protection Front (international radical protest movement)
   ESA: European Space Agency
   FSB: Federal Security Bureau (Russia); successor to the KGB
   IPE: Interplanetary Enterprises (privately held company based in the United States)
   INSERM: National Institute of Health and Medical Research (French acronym)
   ISRO: Indian Space Research Organization
   JAXA: Japan Aerospace Exploration Agency
   LTEE: Long-Term Evolution Experiment
   MSS: Ministry of State Security (PRC)
   NASA: National Aeronautics and Space Administration
   NEP: New Earth Partners (international consortium)
   NSA: National Security Agency

OSTP: Office of Science and Technology Policy
PLA: People's Liberation Army (PRC)
PPL: Planetary Protection Legions (international protest
            movement)
PRC: People's Republic of China
RSSC: Russian State Space Corporation, aka Roscosmos
UAE: United Arab Emirates

"Today, rock 84001 speaks to us across all those billions of years and millions of miles. It speaks of the possibility of life. If this discovery is confirmed, it will surely be one of the most stunning insights into our universe that science has ever uncovered."

—Statement of Bill Clinton, President of the United States, regarding meteorite ALH 84001, of known Martian origin (August 7, 1996)

"Despite vigorous efforts from the scientific community, there is no accepted evidence that ALH 84001 contains traces or markers of ancient Martian life—all the purported signs have been shown to be incorrect or ambiguous."

—"Uninhabitable and Potentially Habitable Environments on Mars: Evidence from Meteorite ALH 84001," Alan H. Treiman, Ph.D., Lunar and Planetary Institute, USRA (April 15, 2021)

DESPAIR

5

September 8, 2035

The face scarcely seemed human. Scarcely seemed a *face*.

Bloated, purple-mottled flesh, the swollen lips almost black. Oozing pustules. Tissues peeling and flaking, even to scattered glimpses of muscle and bone. The nose little more than naked, pitted cartilage. Eyes, except for anime-sized black pupils, all blood-red. Had it not been for the snaky, sweat-soaked tresses, languidly adrift like some somnolent Medusa, even to speculate at a gender would have been impossible.

Yet there could be no question who, or where, this was.

Not given the distinctive copper hue of that hair. The precise bearing in the sky from which the signal arrived. The fraction of a microwatt remaining in that signal, evidence of the great distances it had traveled.

No ambiguity at all.

The video could only have originated aboard *Meriwether Lewis*, the NASA vessel on its triumphant return—alone from among three recent missions—from Mars. Except, somehow, in the few days since *Lewis*'s previous routine reporting window, triumph had morphed into ... something unimaginable. And as surely as basic physics, geometry, and the faintness of the signal established the video's origin, those long, coppery tresses identified Katrina Mancini: *Lewis*'s pilot and the Mars mission commander.

7

Beneath that gargoyle-ish visage, a bit of polo shirt, just collar and shoulders, came within the bridge-camera's view. That garment might have once been white. Sweat-sodden, blood-spattered, vomit-encrusted, it was difficult to know.

"W-we don't know wha-what it is," the apparition began. (Such, anyway, was the eventual reconstruction. Before digital enhancement, the slurred, faltering audio automatically recorded had been all but unintelligible. And no wonder—in the struggle to enunciate, she revealed bleeding gums, missing teeth, a swollen, purple tongue, and glimpses of a pus-coated throat.) Loud pounding on the hatch behind her didn't help. "We don't know w-w-which ..."

A mystery whose completion dissolved into a mucousy gurgle.

She broke into a violent shudder. Fresh sweat beaded on her face; more, shaken off, wafted in droplets. With jaws clenched and cheeks spasming, the seizure went on and on.

By hawking up gobs of bloody phlegm, she regained a measure of control. "W-we don't know which sample e-e-escaped confinement. Or c-can't be con-confined. Or was mishandled. We j-just know that it happened. S-something is loose aboard. R-revived from dormancy. Or mutated." Her apparent stab at an ironic smile was ... grotesque. "As you can see."

Behind the bridge hatch, the tumult only got louder.

"Whatever *it* is? We ... we have no immunity. From the f-first symptoms, I, w-we all, got this way in *hours*." Teeth chattering faster than ever, she struggled to describe symptoms. An impossible list, as if every part of her body were under attack at once. Maybe, every *cell* at once.

"The m-medic AIde knows of n-nothing to remotely match it. It sn-sneers at broad-spectrum antibiotics. And at broad-spectrum antivirals." She offered, once more, that frightful rictus. "I doubt I could l-last even another hour.

"But whatever is killing us? Has already killed Hideo? It survived, even if d-dormant, the hard r-r-radiation and near-vacuum and the bitter c-cold of Mars. Maybe f-for eons. It will outlast *us*. It thrives ... *in* u-us. It can't ever g-get to Earth. Ever g-g-get near other people.

"So, I'm making certain that w-won't happen. I've only waited this l-long"—till the Deep Space Network was scheduled to aim one of its biggest dishes at *Lewis*—"so y-you'd know."

A quick sideways-and-back dip of her head seemed to suggest the hatch that flexed and boomed behind her. "Even though opinions differ." Exposed muscles fluttered, whether in a spasm or in another failed attempt at an ironic smile. "Call this my final command decision."

A hand—mottled flesh sloughing from bone; tendons twitching; knuckles swollen—rose into the camera's view. Awkwardly clutching a serrated galley knife.

To begin, as the comm session ended, sawing at her throat.

Thereafter, radio silence.

No updates from *Lewis*. No response to NASA's repeated urgent pleadings. Not even the routine trickle of telemetry from shipboard sensors.

Houston tried to contact the shipboard AI. They failed. Tried to access and remotely control the spacecraft. They failed at that, too.

All the while, Earth's most powerful radar telescopes probed but saw nothing. Until—on a trajectory rapidly diverging from *Lewis*'s precisely calculated return orbit and last known position—a spreading cloud of debris was detected.

With more spacecraft and their crews already outbound to Mars ....

DESCENT

[About 23 months earlier]

"I've said I want to die on Mars, just not on impact."

—Elon Musk, CEO of SpaceX, SXSW talk
(March 9, 2013)

October 6, 2033

The ship—after almost six months hurtling through empty space—encountered the first faint wisps of air. Still at its long-range cruising speed, it plummeted toward Mars at almost 13,000 miles per hour. In round numbers, four times as fast as a high-speed rifle bullet.

International crew and scientific conventions be damned, Teri Rodriguez thought in miles per hour. Also, apparently, in bullet speeds.

Backing in heat shield first, that velocity was but a number. At that, one numeric abstraction among many: projected translucent readouts filled the bridge canopy. Together, the virtual instruments bleached the stars from the pitch-black sky.

Even the singular, brilliant blue dot that Teri sought in vain.

The next few minutes could decide if she'd live to see Earth again. Minutes during which she had no control. Zero.

Only that wasn't quite true.

No matter her dread, she might act otherwise.

No, she *would* act otherwise.

"Piece of cake," she called out. Because mission commanders said things like that. Especially when scary stuff was imminent. Especially when any sane person would be scared shitless. Especially anyone aware of how hastily thrown together and jury-rigged this expedition had been—which she, more than anyone, *was*. If her voice quavered?

She assured herself the ship's growing vibration explained it. "Enjoy the ride, people."

Behind her, in the main cabin: twin grunts of acknowledgment. Those quavered, too.

"Commencing EDL," Reuben Ben-Ami announced. Entry, descent, and landing. *His* voice was steady, crisp and clear, with that flat, unruffled delivery pilots cultivated—but there was no mistaking the glint in his eye. Pilots loved their firsts. First pilot to land on another freaking *planet*? Love was too inadequate a concept.

But the emotionless aspect? If Teri knew such monotones all too well, her aversion was not Reuben's fault. Anyway, this was the worst possible time to be dwelling on what was ....

Whether or not that monotone persisted, crisp and clear wouldn't. Couldn't. Didn't. In seconds, the whistle of their atmospheric entry had risen to a piercing wail. If not for their headsets, no one would have heard Reuben's updates.

Not even on this cozy bridge—pretty much a broom closet, though normally one with a view—which, shoulder to shoulder, she shared with the pilot.

If *pilot* even remained the suitable term. Chasing their moving target on an arcing course for the past almost 300 million miles? Yes. Sure. For that entire way, Reuben had had the con. But for the next few minutes? No matter the hands positioned on the flight console's narrow shelf, fingers itching to poke or swipe or grasp *something*, events came too quickly now for even the most trained human reflexes. Computers, triply redundant, must be, and were, in charge. Should those fail? Well, at that point, Reuben would do his best.

First people to die on another planet? That would be one for the record books, too.

Deceleration was squeezing the air from her lungs, mashing her brain against the back of her skull, blurring her vision. As the accelerometer readout climbed past four gees, her cheeks sagged into a teeth-baring grimace.

Wisps, had she just thought? This was like slamming into a wall!

"Aerobraking," came a calm, euphemistic, pilot-speak update. "Altitude, a hair above a hundred klicks."

Metric: likewise pilot-speak.

Approaching straight on, they'd have punched right through this tenuous, poisonous joke of an atmosphere, would have augured themselves into the ground. All within *seconds*. And yet, lugging enough fuel to shed the massive vessel's interplanetary velocity was impossible. Which was why, shuddering and jinking on final approach, Reuben had tweaked their course into the nearest of near misses. Barely grazing the atmosphere, flying damned near sideways, while friction transmuted velocity into heat.

A *lot* of heat.

Brighter by the second, fire—their heat shield burning off!—enveloped the ship. Flames streamed well past the canopy. In theory, those were harmless. In theory, entry was supposed to work this way. Okay, it wasn't fire, couldn't *be* fire, for the lack of oh-two to oxidize anything. Rather, superheated gas as the heat shield vaporized ....

Within a minute, the shield's temperature had leapt by more than a thousand degrees. In that same minute, they'd shed a chunk of velocity—

But still far from enough. Teri's heart pounded. Her mouth had gone bone-dry.

You've done this before, she reminded herself. A dozen times, at least.

Except *this* was nothing like a shuttle reentry from orbit through Earth's deep, dense, beautiful, wing-buoying atmosphere. The two maneuvers had about as much in common as skiing the Alps did with gliding down a bunny slope. Maybe less.

Except commanders *didn't* say shit like that. Commanders kept a stiff upper lip. Women commanders, more so. Her, most of all. Especially since—

No. *Not* the time.

Meanwhile, her molars ground. Clenched jaws *ached*.

"Ninety-five klicks."

Eyes, guts, brain ... what part of her *didn't* bounce and quiver like Jell-O on some psychotic carnival ride? Teri more felt than heard the seemingly random firings of attitude thrusters that—somehow, despite the turbulence and ceaseless buffeting—maintained the ship's orientation. Because if the heat shield didn't stay pointed *just* right ....

"And up."

Her apparent weight eased, and the shaking abated as they swung up and out of the atmosphere. To dip a tad lower, shedding a bit more speed, on their second entry. A third. A fourth. Porpoising up and down, arcing side to side, the encapsulating flames ever hotter and brighter, for what seemed an eternity ....

And so, slowed by each fiery, brain-rattling encounter, they skipped across the tenuous atmosphere like a stone across a pond. At the top of each arc, flames winked out and black sky reappeared. At each re-emergence, Phobos, the nearest moon—seeming a third the size of *the* Moon, if in a deflated-football sort of way—presented itself in a new phase. Until, on the deepest dip yet, their headlong pace diminished at last from hypersonic to merely supersonic, the vaporization of their heat shield all but complete, Reuben's warning came: "Deploying—"

A *bang!* masked any specifics, the ship twitching as a ring of explosive bolts ejected the charred remnants of their heat shield. Stern-facing cameras, uncovered at last, provided a first glimpse of the onrushing ground.

Onward, downward, they plunged. With flames no longer licking the canopy, the sky morphed from black to deep blues to, dropping to altitudes into which windblown dust could reach, a succession of dark pinks.

She oriented herself by the rising sun. Retreating below the southern horizon as they fell was a vast chasm. To her west and northwest, huge mountains loomed. The Grand Canyon, by comparison, was a dimple, and Everest a pimple.

"Twenty klicks."

Except not even. *Twenty* denoted their height in kilometers above the imaginary sphere designated to serve this world as its "zero elevation." Their landing zone was at an elevation three klicks above that "sea level."

"Brace yourselves."

At ten kilometers above zero elevation, slowed almost to a mere thousand miles per hour, the ship shuddered: devices—cannons in all but name—blasting out their payloads. Gigantic parachutes, each bigger than a football field, snapped open. Maroon sky vanished behind swirls of pure white.

The ship bucked like a wild stallion, and Teri's breath whooshed out of her.

Only the fisheye lens of a forward-facing camera could capture the six blink-of-an-eye chute deployments—or one of those chutes bursting apart. The next shock marked explosive bolts jettisoning those flapping tatters before they could foul the intact chutes. Aerodynamics rearranged the surviving parachutes but couldn't quite rebalance their load.

Leaving the ship suspended at an angle, swinging, swaying ....

Behind Teri, from the main cabin: loud retching. And stronger by the second, that stench! Her gorge rose. Jaws clamped tighter than ever, she focused on the bridge canopy and its HUD.

If she could control nothing else, she *would* control her own stupid, spasming gut.

Reuben's gesture toward the canopy and the remaining, straining chutes morphed into a quick shrug. As if to say, *these things happen.* As if citing the simulations that predicted they could handle a single failed chute. Because nothing *but* simulations had anything to offer about their situation. No wind tunnel existed large enough to have tested deployment of even *one* of their chutes. Much less all six together or the permutations if one or more failed.

She knew how *she* didn't want to make it into the record books.

Nine klicks ... eight ... seven ....

Still, they fell. Their pace slowed to a "mere" seventy-plus miles per hour: interstate highway speeds. More than fast enough for impact to crush their hull like an eggshell.

"We have a terrain match," Reuben said.

The virtual display rearranged itself, instrument readouts shrinking to recede to an edge of the canopy. A rear-facing camera's panoramic view claimed the vacated space.

As red and pink blurs resolved into a rippled, cratered, rock-strewn plain, Reuben said, "Resuming manual control. Switching altimeter to local reference. Landing indicators are ... on."

The plummeting altimeter readout switched from black to green—and its value dropped to scarcely four! Pale dashed contour lines and two Day-Glo icons manifested over the terrain view. The green stylized rocket fixed at center image was them. The yellow circle near the image's eastern edge—jittering about a small, somewhat trapezoidal expanse of the undulating plain—highlighted their landing zone. Attitude thrusters pulsed, nudging bright icons together.

She saw boulders, crevices, and craters ... everywhere. Teri shivered. Fear or excitement? She couldn't tell. Or wouldn't admit.

"Three klicks," Reuben advised. "More bumps coming up."

A firecracker-y barrage parted the harness lines of the remaining parachutes. The seat dropped out from under her. Her stomach leapt into her throat. As wind snatched the acres of untethered fabric, the sky—turned light pink, dotted with gauzy white clouds—barely registered.

"And we're *flying* again," Reuben announced.

With rockets howling, they braked to a hover a scant hundred yards above a vast, foreboding, rutted, rocky expanse. Lunae Planum, on Mars maps. Plain of the Moon, at least if she'd retained the Latin the sisters had long ago drummed into her. Somehow, throughout the tedium of the long flight, it had never occurred to her to track down the English translation.

Somewhere nearby was NASA's *Viking 1* probe. Alighting close to the first successful Mars landing ever? She liked to believe that was a good omen—as though such superstitious nonsense mattered. Anyway, *close* was a relative term, and she caught no glimpse of that artifact. Antique. Relic.

Focus! she ordered herself.

Reuben, humming tunelessly, sidled the ship about. Eyeballed the ground below. Eyeballed the radar data. Squinted at the fuel gauge. Frowned. And repeat—

Until, inside a cloud of crimson dust, and with the gentlest of bumps, they settled, with a slight tilt, onto an almost flat area among massive boulders.

They'd made it with, gulp, six percent descent fuel to spare.

With a low-pitched growl, the engines fell silent. Hydraulics in one of the landing legs brought the ship level. The HUD went blank.

"Tango delta," Reuben announced. Pilot-speak for touchdown. He nodded modestly as, from the rear cabin, both passengers cheered. (The tremulous acclamation? That would be whoever had puked.)

Teri, keeping relief to herself, offered a soft, heartfelt, dignified, "Well done."

The dust raised by their landing glacially settled. What emerged was ....

Words failed her.

She let out the breath she had not consciously been holding. How was it Buzz Aldrin had described the lunar landscape? Right. *A magnificent desolation.*

18

So was this.

The morning sun, casting long shadows, was brighter than she had imagined. Earth-bright, almost. The joke of an atmosphere was too tenuous to attenuate the light—and yet, over the eons, wind-blown grit had abraded each rock and stony ridge almost to smoothness. But the colors! Salmon, rose, carmine, coral, cordovan, maroon, and countless hues between. She lacked the vocabulary for so many shades of pink and red.

Three minutes later, perhaps two hundred meters toward the stunning sunrise, their sister ship set down. Its bridge lights blinked twice, signaling a safe landing—because, barring some emergency, the mission's first broadcast from the surface had been scripted. *Her* broadcast—for which half the big dishes on Earth must be listening, and half the people on that planet would be waiting. They'd done it! More than anyone (a thought she'd never speak aloud), *she'd* done it. Won the Great Mars Race. No matter her qualms about the tradeoffs that had been necessary ….

Reuben handed her the mic. "Commander."

The furthest thing from Teri's mind was the triviality expected of her. Except, clearly, that it wasn't. She only *wished* she could, somehow, sidestep it. That she would rise to the occasion. That she'd express thoughts apt to the occasion. After everything they'd been through, her designated, self-serving pronouncement had all the gravitas of a mutt lifting a hind leg to mark its territory. Which, in a way, was kind of the point.

She followed her script anyway.

"NEP Mission Control, this is Mars mission actual. *Bradbury*"—this vessel—"and *Burroughs*"—its companion—"have arrived safely." Moreover, they'd done it, if Mission Control's latest data were correct, eight days ahead of the Chinese expedition. Ten days before the NASA, et cetera bunch. She was patriotic enough to feel ambivalence over the latter.

"We hereby declare this New Earth Partners Base One"—ignoring, for the moment, the small matter of first constructing that facility—"from which we are proud to open this new frontier for New Earth Partners and humankind."

But forget that pretension. Among themselves, they would damn well call this place something, anything, else. Lowell Base, perhaps, after the century-earlier, Mars-popularizing astronomer. She liked Wells Base, though some might find a reverse invasion a tad too ironic. The troops could pick a name.

She hung up the mic and sagged, emotionally drained.

Her transmission would be eleven minutes on its way to Earth. Mission Control's acknowledgment, undoubtedly just as stilted, would be as slow to return. They had at least that long before any go-ahead, before suiting up to first venture onto the surface. *She* had at least those twenty-two minutes until the next phase of her job began.

Which was why the response seconds later made Teri flinch.

"Well, howdy, pardners," said a woman with an unmistakable Texas twang. Casual greeting? Or deniable snark at the consortium's billionaire principals? To have any doubt vanquished in the next breath. "Well, if it ain't the B Team. Greetings from international base Asaph Hall on Phobos." (That name took a moment to click in: the astronomer who had discovered Mars's two moons.) "Welcome to the neighborhood.

"If you don't mind me asking, what took y'all so long getting here?"

October 6, 2033

"**W**ell, howdy, pardners," Cat drawled.

Well, nobody smug here, Xander Hopkins thought—even though *here* only gazed down upon the Red Planet.

Yet *here* was spectacular in its own right. Stickney Crater, at the center floor of which he stood (boot tips tucked beneath the guide wire to which two safety tethers were clipped) was a good nine kilometers across. Phobos itself was a mere twenty-two klicks from end to end on its long axis. The marvel was that the impact forming this bowl hadn't shattered the little moon. But it hadn't, and Stickney sat on the side of Phobos tidally locked to Mars. All in all, this natural amphitheater had been a natural landing site and would be an ideal base for long-term operations.

Not to mention that *here*, after tedious months cooped up inside a flying tin can, was luxuriously spacious.

"Well, if it ain't the B Team," the mission commander continued.

Had the latest arrivals been aware of Xander's bunch's presence? Doubtful, judging by the pomposity they'd just belched into the ethers. Likely the grand poobahs Earthside had kept NASA's late-breaking news to themselves. If so, fair enough: preparing for their fiery landings, the NEP crews hadn't needed any distraction or disappointment.

Cat was relentless, clearly enjoying herself, "Greetings from international base Asaph Hall on Phobos."

From orbit a scant few thousand miles above Mars, that planet … loomed. No other verb would do. Oh, Xander had long ago done the math. He'd known that from where he now gawked, the orb overhead would span a seventeen-degree arc of sky. *The* Moon, *Earth's* moon, occupied a mere half degree.

But those calculations had been mere fun with numbers. Far more tangible was that standing in Xander's yard back home, a quarter held at arm's length would hide the Moon. Here, to cover the mottled red globe, then at full phase, rather than a coin he'd need a dinner plate.

But home, like any decent meal, had likewise become an abstraction. Best not to dwell upon for how long ….

Cat's gloating, patched in to everyone on-or off-ship, rolled on. "… don't mind me asking: What took y'all so long getting here?"

To be fair, the NASA-led team *had* arrived first. Entire hours ago. Per the mission clock, operating—as did most international efforts—on Greenwich Mean Time, Zulu time, a whole four minutes before midnight of the previous day. Bragging rights ensued. Or, as Cat had radio-trumpeted Earthward upon their arrival. "This day, *Lewis* and *Clark* have made landfall on a new, far shore."

Doubtless, the president had been delighted. Xander pictured her still chortling at the sleight of hand, no matter its drawbacks, by which the NASA-led mission could claim to have come in first. Then he imagined her more gleeful still at Cat's twisting of the metaphorical knife. At least the prez would be (Xander checked the clock in a corner of his HUD) in about ten minutes.

"Thanks, Phobos." The response lacked some of the calm, the self-assurance, of moments before. "For now, we Martians"—counter-swagger?—"are busy, as you might imagine. We'll be in touch. Till then, NEP base … out."

A staccato *tap-tap* on Xander's counterpressure-suit sleeve demanded focus on the here and now. Again, somehow impatient, *tap-tap*.

After the long months aboard *Lewis*, its three crew pretty much living out of one another's pockets, any new face was beyond welcome. Even, somehow, a face hidden by a reflective helmet visor. On this side of Phobos the sun had set, but full Marslight put any full Moon to shame. Against that intense, ruddy glare, everyone off-ship wore their "sun" shields down.

Still, a new face.

Their personalized vacuum gear spanned a psychedelic rainbow, the six suits ranging in hue from neon red to, in Xander's case, an eye-popping shade of purple. (Forget *violet* and *indigo*. Both were purples.) Even before turning, from the mere glimpse of a red suit sleeve, Xander knew. Returned from his latest excursion, this had to be David Berghoff. An old ESA hand. German. Gruff. Taciturn. Formal ("Dave" had been a frostily received nonstarter.) Pilot of *Clark*. Throughout the prelaunch phase, in the team's rare downtime, a poker-faced card shark. If not the IT whiz Xander (ever so humbly) deemed himself, David was nonetheless good with computers and robots and Xander's designated backup. Certainly more expert at matters tech than Xander was at piloting.

Tap-tap. Somehow, it conveyed, "Enough rubbernecking. Back to work."

By the book was commendable in a pilot. Even by the footnotes, end notes, afterword, and glossary. The thing was, they were done piloting. They would be for a long time to come.

Xander sighed.

Only then, on the ground team's common channel, did he propose, "Perhaps we should savor the moment."

Because while two of their teammates—Hideo and Giselle, *their* suits respectively road-stripe yellow and lime green—continued to unfold and stake the first of their inflatable structures, Xander and David had already accomplished their primary task. More than theirs, the *mission's* principal, immediate-upon-arrival task. The first of their several landers offloaded. Checked over twice. Battery charges topped off. Fuel and oxy tanks filled from *Clark*'s reserves. A full complement of rovers likewise prepped and then secured inside the lander. Sent on its way.

Lander One had touched down—remote-controlled by David, the first teleoperated touchdown on Mars a consolation prize after Cat landed *Lewis* first on Phobos—and phoned home an entire forty-two minutes earlier. Not from any of their highest priority research targets, to general chagrin. The lander had resisted networking with the nearby comsat constellation, so they'd switched their goal to someplace with a direct line of sight to Phobos and *Lewis*'s high-powered transmitter. (Not even a full day here, and already Xander had a glitch to troubleshoot. The shape of things to come? Well, sorting this out could be a learning opportunity for his understudy. Networks weren't David's strong suit.)

The landing capsule's fiery descent, relayed from *Lewis*'s telescope to Xander's HUD, had seemed nothing short of spectacular—

Until *Burroughs* and *Bradbury* followed. Whereupon, words had failed him.

A trace of envy did not.

Perhaps for the physics-impaired, to deliver a little robot or to land a couple-hundred-tonne spacecraft differed only as a matter of degree. For them—realistically, most people—the Phobos rendezvous, coupled with Lander One's descent to the planet, proclaimed, *See, we could've sent people down. We* chose *not to.*

Only the last half of that implication being true.

Rightly or wrongly, by fair means or otherwise, to win the Great Mars Race had become … everything.

David laughed. "You misunderstand. I wished only to ask if you were enjoying the view." He gestured toward their future habitat, still flat as a pancake. "But when we are done playing tourist, perhaps we should help …."

Done? It was hard to believe this mission had happened at all. Harder still to believe he was a part of it. Standing on freaking *Phobos*.

And hardest to accept that through every stage of planning, decisions about this mission had been made for all the wrong reasons.

October 24, 2033

His breath loud and rasping in his helmet, Wang Kai swept his gaze across the barren—yet somehow spectacular—terrain.

What a landscape this was!

Kai and his fellow explorers, in two facing rows of four, stood on hallowed ground. Here on Utopia Planitia, in 2021, the People's Republic had landed its little *Zhurong* rover. Zhurong: the legendary rider of fire-breathing dragons. As that little pioneering robot, trailing fire, had streaked to its epic landing, so, hardly a decade later, had the two ships behind him arrived among far greater flames.

NASA's 1976 *Viking 2* lander also stood somewhere on this vast plain. But as with their Apollo missions to the Moon, the Americans had squandered their lead here. China would not make that mistake.

None of which eased this day's sting of coming in a distant third. Of coming in *last*.

Zhao Jin—*Colonel* Zhao, still, at his insistence—bounded forward. Cleared his throat. Began perorating. "Today, the empire is truly celestial."

That opening line might have been dramatic. Had this mission arrived here *first*. Had anyone outside their country even known or cared that China once styled itself as the Celestial Empire.

What followed was no less stilted and formulaic.

As the mission commander stiffly recited his Party-preapproved arrival speech, Kai continued studying the scene. Behind his sun visor, with only his eyes moving, that disrespect would go unnoted. It was nothing personal: Zhao, with allowances made for his ingrained, rigid formality, was a decent guy. Nor was it as though Kai hadn't heard this speech rehearsed, again and again, and again, in Mandarin and English. Nor could even the most talented oratory have undone the shame of their last-place finish.

Rote and ceremony paled amid such glorious, unaccustomed *novelty*.

In every conceivable shade of red, the rock-strewn plain seemed to stretch forever. Here and there were craters, none smaller, he estimated, than thirty meters across. The thin atmosphere offered *some* protection against meteors. A silent current of that rarified atmosphere raised traces of the powder, finer than dust, covering much of the ground. In the distance, a dust devil whirled.

The dome of cloudless sky was at once glorious and strange, the thin atmosphere and its ubiquitous dust scattering sunlight so differently than at home. (But was Earth still home? The odds were he'd never see that world again.) From near the horizon, where the sky was a delicate rose, the vault of heaven darkened overhead almost to a golden brown—except, incongruously, for the narrow blue-white rim around the distance-shrunken sun. Phobos had set. Yet tinier Deimos was but a dimly visible point.

Scant minutes had elapsed since their arrival, entry and descent tossing them around like the dice in some madman's mahjong cup. They had disembarked onto ground hardly cooled. Wisps of steam yet swirled beneath the ships, perhaps portending underground ice at accessible depth and in exploitable amounts. Oxygen, they could wring from the carbon dioxide of the tenuous atmosphere. Water, in the form of buried ice, they must *find*. If not here, how far might they have to search?

Zhao prattled on, his tone formal, his voice thick with emotion.

The horizon was closer than on Earth—but after so long aboard *Zheng He*, one bulkhead or another ever within arm's length, that open vista … beckoned. Kai wished—oh, *how* he wished—he could run, and run, and run some more. For weeks now, he'd dreamt of running. If he'd never been a first-tier competitor in the annual Beijing Marathon, he'd always achieved a respectable finish. He'd even twice broken two hours, forty-five minutes.

After the many months in space, *could* he still run? Yes. Without a doubt. Capsule and booster, tethered together through most of the long flight, lazily revolving around their center of mass, had simulated half of Earth's gravity. Mars's gravity was less, a mere 38 percent of standard. For all the awkward bulk and sheer mass of his vacuum gear, he felt *powerful*.

But more insistent than the urge to run free, more intense than *anything*, Kai wished he could share this moment with Li. Or share anything at all with her.

Zhao's wooden speech, meanwhile, had reached a melodramatic pause. Four bounding steps took him to *Zheng He* and an open cargo-hold hatch. He returned bearing a long metal rod, the one end pointed, the other wrapped in crimson fabric. With a flourish, the colonel unfurled and waved the banner. Bold red, with five bright, golden stars: a flag as fitting to a Mars mission as to the proud nation that had sent them. Bold, too, as their vessel's eponym. Admiral Zheng He's great expeditions had visited Southeast Asia, Indonesia, India, Arabia, and far down the eastern coast of Africa—before Columbus was even born.

A firm thrust drove the pole's tapered end past fine dust, through the brittle, crunchy layer beneath, deep into the Martian ground. The pitiful excuse for an atmosphere struggled to stir the cloth, but that had been anticipated. Stiff wires soon held the flag extended for the cameras.

As Zhao offered his final accolades to the glorious Party that had envisioned and made possible this grand adventure—

Colonel Antonov, ranking officer among the *laowai*, broke ranks to stride back to *his* vessel. He had also brought a flag. The lightweight fabric, with its three broad stripes of white and blue and red, even rippled in the feeble Martian breeze. "The proud peoples of Russia …"

This was not part of the script!

That three Russians had flown aboard *Zheng He*'s companion vessel? No matter its name, *Yuri Gagarin* was Chinese-designed and-built. For even a Great Power, a mission to Mars was expensive. And so, rubles had been welcomed. Rupees, too, to fill *Gagarin*'s final seat. Even the frequent recourse to English, their single shared language, could be excused.

Not so Russian bravado.

Kai had had a recurring fantasy throughout the mission training. The daydream always began with some cosmonaut's tiresome nostalgia about a Russian space accomplishment decades past—and ended, much more pleasantly, as *he* reminded the *laowai* who had invented gunpowder in the ninth century. Who had used gunpowder in rockets by the eleventh.

Alas, good manners kept this a fantasy.

There would be consequences for Antonov's disrespect. His disregard for protocol and politeness. His flaunting a banner that, all had agreed, would be left at home. (That this was ostensibly an international mission? That the agreement had been for *no* flags? China, surely, was the more deserving nation to take credit.)

Zhao could, with the wave of a hand to *Zheng He*'s watchful AI, cut off the transmission to Earth. But he wouldn't, Kai knew. The damage was done. He didn't doubt the Russians were recording; one way or another, their video *would* find its way to Antonov's masters and then into worldwide distribution. But worse than futile, for Zhao to react would be an error. Would reveal to everyone that the Russians had defied orders—and gotten away with it.

Better, then, for Colonel Zhao to bide his time. To show his displeasure, reassert his authority, in other ways. Which, as certain as the sun rising in the east, would happen. His role as mission commander, his honor, demanded there be consequences. The question was … when?

Meanwhile, Kai wished all the posturing would give way to *practical* matters. They had cargo to unload. Equipment to uncrate and assemble. Shelters to inflate—and to cover, with sandbags yet to be filled, against the ceaseless, sleeting radiation. Chemical plants to start, to separate oxygen and reclaim carbon dioxide. Solar panels to deploy, to power it all.

A city, Fire Star City, to build ….

For neither of his questions did Kai wait long for answers, as Zhao set everyone to work—pointedly, demeaningly, tasking the three Russians to fill sandbags.

Unseen behind a sun visor, Kai smiled. His father's father, he of the proverb for every occasion, had a favorite well-suited to this moment.

A sharp tongue or pen can kill without a knife.

He smiled again at the string of Russian curses. The menial assignment had delivered its message.

As Kai labored at offloading and deploying solar panels, he found the time to wax philosophical. Disappointment might have made some squabbling inevitable. China *had* lost the Mars race the president himself had so confidently initiated. As Russia *had* lost its race to the Moon—never mind that the Americans then abandoned that world for more than a half-century.

Now another generation of Americans, their plutocrat stooges among them, had won a different sprint. In the long run, that accomplishment would mean nothing. Because the conquest of Mars would be a marathon.

DECISIONS

"The time has come for humanity to journey to the planet Mars.

"We're ready. Though Mars is distant, we are far better prepared today to send humans to the Red Planet than we were to travel to the Moon at the commencement of the space age. Given the will, we could have our first crews on Mars within a decade."

—*from the Founding Declaration of the Mars Society, August 1998*

"While the probability of returning a replicating biological entity in a sample from Mars ... is judged to be low and the risk of pathogenic or ecological effects is lower still, the risk is not zero. Therefore, it is reasonable that NASA adopt a prudent approach, erring on the side of caution and safety.

"Recommendation. If sample containment cannot be verified en route to Earth, the sample, and any spacecraft components that may have been exposed to the sample, should either be sterilized in space or not returned to Earth."

—*"Mars Sample Return Mission: Issues and Recommendations" Task Group on Issues in Sample Return; Space Studies Board; Commission on Physical Sciences, Mathematics, and Applications; National Research Council, 1997*

March 12, 2032

Xander stood rigidly. Pondering the surreal. At a loss for what to do with his hands. Trying his best not to stare. Clueless why he was here.

Here: the White House. The West Wing. The freaking Oval Office! Plaster ceiling medallion overhead bearing the presidential seal. Great Seal of the United States woven into the plush carpet. On a small table to his left, a Frederic Remington bronze. All around, framed portraits. Ahead, seated at the freaking *Resolute* desk itself, scowling, radiating … intensity? Anger? Impatience? … the president herself.

"Quit gawking," came the hiss/whisper from Xander's right.

Matthias Van Dijk was the administrator of NASA. That made him, at a couple removes, Xander's boss. From a curt comment on the short ride from NASA headquarters, Van Dijk didn't know why *he* had been summoned, nor understand the diktat to bring along the agency's head of manned spaceflight.

Someone Xander, emphatically, was *not*.

An hour earlier, Xander had been behind the desk of his own, much more modest, office. In a polo shirt and khakis, anticipating the weekend. Just done slogging through the Lunar Gateway project's most recent monthly report. (Over budget. Behind schedule. Chasing the latest nuisance-level air leak. Nuances aside, this could have been the summary from any of the past several months. Or, as likely, any of the *next* several. Until the gateway could refuel spacecraft using lunar resources, that collection of tin cans would remain a budget-eating solution in search of a problem. Like the International Space Station before it, the lunar orbiter had come to exist primarily to maintain and operate itself, more toll booth than gateway. M&O continued to consume its ever-ballooning budget.) Just starting a new slog, this time of tardy, lunar-oriented upgrades to the Deep Space Network. (At least these snags offered some technical interest, and he scribbled copious notes for recommendations.) Swigging coffee to defy this contractor's opaque admissions and tortuous excuses. Letting calls roll over to voicemail, despite the lure of distraction. His door closed. If anything urgent arose, here should be the first place anyone would look for him. Before calling it a week, he *would* finish reviewing his damned stack of reports.

Five minutes later, radiating impatience, Van Dijk stormed in. From head to toe, Central Casting's notion of a senator. Handsome. Silver-haired. Tall. Broad-shouldered. Five minutes after that, Xander was changing into a borrowed blue dress shirt, navy blazer, and preppie necktie—the high-priced consultant's concession to casual Fridays. Two minutes further on, both men were on their way here.

Van Dijk wearing an impeccably tailored suit.

That short ride had been … awkward. True, they'd met before. Xander had been at meetings, as one face among many, with Van Dijk. But the recently confirmed administrator had yet to invest much of his time administering. Instead, there'd been: a grand tour of NASA centers. The boondoggle to Paris, where ESA had its headquarters, and then a half dozen other ESA facilities across Europe. Lots of interviews with friendly journalists. Redecorating his new office. Nor, it seemed, did the former senator from Boeing-Mitsubishi ever miss a launch.

The worst part? Rather than an engineer or scientist, the man was an MBA.

Compared to that tense, monosyllabic car trip, the process of getting admitted as far as this room had been a joy. Even though, as with Mordor, one doesn't just simply walk into the Oval Office.

The president signed something with a flourish, slapped its leather folder shut, set that on a stack of similar folders, and looked up. The aide who'd admitted the men to the inner sanctum had, at some signal or gesture too subtle for Xander, loitered nearby. She swept up the piled folders and scurried off. As she bustled from the room, another man entered.

The newcomer was gaunt almost to the point of cadaverous, his close-cropped hair steel-gray, his expression world-weary, his teeth clamped on an unlit cigar. He seemed familiar, maybe from the Sunday morning talk shows. This was the … DNI. Director of National Intelligence!

What was going on? Xander wondered. How in the worlds could it involve *him*?

The president stepped out from behind the desk. In person, Carla DeMille appeared even tinier—shorter, more petite of frame, more delicately boned—than on television. But no matter how detractors described her as *birdlike*, they'd missed the mark. With that piercing gaze? The chiseled nose? That aura of determination? Far from fragility, the woman shared but one trait with *any* avian: the predatory focus of a hungry hawk.

Her snide, inside-the-Beltway nickname, Cruella, might have had more going for it than misogyny and the coincidence in consonants.

The president nodded at Van Dijk before raising an interrogatory eyebrow. "Who's this, Matt? The head of our manned space program can't afford a suit?"

"Alexander Hopkins," Van Dijk offered. "My human-exploration lead is out sick today. Hopkins here is her IT guy. He has her delegation."

Her IT guy? Jesus! Not a bad man, Xander told himself. Merely a bad fit. A *terrible* fit.

What had the president been thinking?

"It's an honor to meet you," Xander managed. The words came out in a mumble.

She gave no sign she'd even heard. "Well, *shit*, Matt. You brought me an IT guy. I guess you imagined I called over to you to fix my Twitter feed. Apologies to the woman's sniffles, but get her ass over here."

"Well, why *did* you call me?"

DeMille pointed at one of the room's two facing sofas. The head spook, by then, stood to her side. (Xander had even retrieved the man's name: Arthur Schmidt.) "Sit."

Sit. Then what? Fetch? Roll over? Enough was … enough. Xander cleared his throat. Loudly. "My boss, Doctor Nguyen, the Associate Administrator for Human Exploration and Operations, remains in

35

post-op following surgery late last night for a burst appendix." Because more than Xander's boss, damn it, Rebecca was his friend. His very good friend. He was godfather to her oldest son.

"That's enough, Hopkins," Van Dijk cautioned.

As Xander's grandma used to say, as well hung for a sheep as for a lamb. "I'm the directorate's senior engineer for systems integration. And, by the way, it's Doctor Hopkins."

Van Dijk glowered. "Now, look *here*, Hopkins—"

"However, Madam President, if you're having issues with your Twitter account, I can have a look."

"Okay, so you're not a potted plant." The president flashed a grin. "Now, if you're over your snit, maybe one of you can explain"—her eyes narrowed, her tone turned sharp, sort of like someone who *would* make a fur coat out of puppies—"how the *fuck* it is the Chinese expect to beat your lot at getting people to fucking *Mars?*"

Xander's mind raced.

NASA and its commercial partners were consumed by the Lunar Gateway and the occasional foray from there to the lunar surface. Exploration of its south-polar Aitken Basin with its precious ice reserves had only begun. Sure, a few aerospace companies *talked* big about Mars—but their actions said otherwise. Their investments, aside from flights undertaken on NASA's dime, focused on micro-gee resorts in Earth orbit and gearing up for lunar tourism.

"Sit," the president repeated.

She and the DNI sat on one of the facing sofas. Xander hardly noticed Van Dijk settling onto the other, from where he tugged Xander's sleeve.

Xander dropped onto the sofa. Assuming what he'd heard was true—and given the source, it would be—the news was incredible.

"How do we know?" Van Dijk asked.

Schmidt shrugged. "I can't tell you that."

"I've held a Top-Secret clearance for years," Van Dijk said.

As must many senators, Xander supposed, especially those serving on defense, homeland security, or intelligence committees. "But I don't." Or any clearance, for that matter.

"Wouldn't matter," Schmidt said.

"He was approved on an hour's notice to come into my fucking office," said the president. "His file can't show anything more serious than juvenile jaywalking. Till I hear a reason otherwise, he has a provisional TS clearance. See to the details once we finish here."

"Doesn't matter," Schmidt said again.

"Fine," she snapped. "Provisional SCI clearance." Whatever that meant. "Make it happen."

"*What* do we know?" Xander asked. Unless they'd share that, he might as well leave.

"Arthur?" prompted the president.

Schmidt pursed his lips. "Sunday evening, Beijing time, Wu Lingyun will be giving a national address. We've … just this morning gotten a preview."

President Wu. General Secretary of the Chinese Communist Party Wu. Boss (with yet another impressive title, this one slipping Xander's mind if ever he'd even known it) of the Chinese military. Paramount leader of the People's Republic.

Not someone apt to preview his speeches with the US.

Up from Xander's subconscious bubbled a phrase from spy novels: sources and methods. *Very* need-to-know stuff—and he didn't. Still, it didn't take a genius to connect the dots. Either there was a mole highly placed in the Chinese government, or the NSA had hacked that government's most secret communications.

He leaned forward. "What's Wu going to say about Mars?"

Schmidt said, "We don't have a lot of details, but what little we know shocked us."

"Which is?"

"JFK gave this country nine years to get astronauts to the Moon. Wu will claim he'll have his people on Mars within two."

The president glowered at Van Dijk. "While we do what? Circle the Moon some more? Send another robot go-kart to Mars?"

Van Dijk squared his shoulders. "Well, hell, Madam President. These things are a matter of priorities and funding. Say the word, and all NASA's efforts will focus on Mars. American ingenuity can beat *anything* those commies try. They say less than two years. Fine. Then NASA will do it in one."

Demonstrating, once again, that MBA stood for Master of the Bullshitting Arts.

"Nineteen months or so," Xander said. "*That's* when they propose to arrive on Mars."

Schmidt blinked. "How can you know that?"

From basic orbital mechanics, which politicians had no reason to understand. It'd have been nice if the NASA administrator did, but Van Dijk was also a pol. "We can launch missions to the Moon pretty much whenever we want. Travel between planets is different. For trips from Earth to Mars, there's a practical launch opportunity around every twenty-six months, a period that lasts only a couple of weeks. We're midway between such opportunities. Any other time, given the performance limits of chemical rockets, the fuel that's needed for the flight is prohibitive. Even then, fuel-efficient trips to Mars last about six months."

That summation glossed over its own share of details. The optimal launch periods and transfer times between the worlds both varied over a fifteen-year cycle. The fuel requirement and flight duration, even with optimized timing, changed substantially over that cycle. And between the optimal windows, marginally practical windows did sometimes open. For this audience, at least for an initial conversation, he deemed the generalities good enough.

They were still mulling as Xander continued. "Oh, after reaching Mars, you're stuck till a *return* launch window rolls around." Not that there'd ever been a return flight. "That makes for a stay of sixteen or more months."

Nor was that last statement quite accurate. You *could* slingshot around Mars and get back to Earth about two years after waving at the Red Planet. A launch opportunity *did* open to head home from Mars after a mere one-month stay—followed by a fourteen-month return flight involving a gravitational-slingshot maneuver around Venus. To venture so close to the sun would require shipboard refrigeration equipment of no use *except* to survive the Venus flyby, carted along at the expense of payload useful while on Mars. Except as an exercise in orbital mechanics, who could care for either of those options?

The president nodded pensively. "So, absent some super-duper rocket we know nothing about, China expects to launch when the next opportunity presents itself. Thirteen months from now, then six months for the flight. That's your nineteen months, Doctor." She flashed another grin, this one almost subliminally brief. "Or may I call you Alex?"

38

Sure thing, Carla.

Sanity kicked in before those words slipped out. What was *wrong* with him? Apart from the rich stew of wonderment, bewilderment, insecurity, curiosity, and how many other emotions this wasn't the time to catalogue? All raging. One or more of them flooding his bloodstream with adrenaline.

"Of course." Never mind that he hadn't gone by *Alex* since middle school.

"Meaning, anyone not ready in thirteen months has to wait another twenty-six to follow."

"Right. As for better rockets, propulsion superior to chemical rockets *is* possible in theory"—nuclear-thermal propulsion being the leading candidate—"but I don't believe the Chinese have it." Because testing any booster, scaling up the technology for bigger and bigger payloads, and using the full-scale system on at least one long-range *un*manned mission would have been a humongous undertaking. "We'd know."

Schmidt nodded. "SBIRS wouldn't have missed any test launches."

Something something infrared satellites. Xander could parse that much of the acronym. Or, perhaps, infrared system. Either way, early-warning tech for missile launches.

A system for spotting intercontinental ballistic missiles couldn't miss the launch from Earth of anything even close to interplanetary-capable and large enough to carry people. No matter how advanced a rocket engine, its exhaust would be *hot*.

But scant seconds after asserting certainty, stomach churning, Xander had second thoughts. Assembling systems in orbit wasn't anything the military or intel communities did.

Yet.

That he knew.

But NASA did routinely. So, in recent years, did CMSA—the Chinese Manned Space Agency. Hell, privately owned Space Vegas had been constructed in orbit. What if an advanced-propulsion test hadn't launched from Earth? Frantically working through the possibilities, he managed to swallow a reflexive, "Umm, hold on."

Because: *Put brain in gear before engaging mouth.*

Space Fence—the military-run, space-junk-tracking radar system on which NASA also relied—would have revealed anything of any size being assembled in orbit from payloads lofted aboard conventional rockets. If Space Fence and SBIRS both, somehow, had missed a Chinese interplanetary test? Some infrared astronomer, somewhere, interested in whatever, would have screamed bloody murder at a super-rocket test ruining his undoubtedly long-planned observation campaign.

As best as Xander could tell, no one had noticed his transient waffling.

At his side, Van Dijk was nodding. "Could be worse, then. We have the same basic tech, the same launch constraints. It means we all get there at the same time."

Schmidt coughed. "Bringing us back to the president's point. Why haven't we been planning for this?"

"Why do you think?" snapped Van Dijk. "Money. It always comes down to money. We can do only so much with what we have, and"—he turned back to address the president directly—"your predecessor's priority was a Moon base."

She said, "It's that simple, is it?"

"If Wu's going out on a limb, publicly? Yeah, it must be that simple. It just takes the commitment. So, say the word."

Simple?

"To put people on Mars that soon?" Xander blurted out. "It's a … one-way trip."

What he *really* thought was: It's a suicide mission.

The president and DNI exchanged a sharp look.

"Bingo," Schmidt said. "They're going to call it a settlement mission."

"Alex, you're two for two. You know pretty much what we know." The president glanced at a Rolex far too big for her tiny wrist. She stood, and the rest followed. "Meanwhile, the speaker is cooling her jets outside, and I can't afford having her too pissed off at me.

"So, here's the deal. Someone brings me options for what *I* can announce. That'll be you, Alex. You've proven it should be you. But know this: Conceding the Mars race to China is *not* an option. I'm old enough to remember how Russian prestige cratered when they abandoned the Moon race."

Cratered. A lunar pun? Not the most urgent question. "When?"

Inexplicably, Van Dijk was *beaming*. "A must-win space race this close to the election? With launch a scant few months after Inauguration Day? With every friendly pundit shouting to the rooftops that we don't dare change presidential horses in midstream? Could be a lot worse."

The president smiled right back at him. "No shit, and I'm okay with a silver lining."

"When?" Xander asked her again.

"Be here with options for me tomorrow evening at eight. That's short notice, but it's also only twelve or so hours before Wu speaks in Beijing."

"We'll be here," Van Dijk asserted.

"No need, Matt. Your sidekick has this."

"But I *should* be here."

The president waved a hand dismissively. "You, Matt, *should* be schmoozing with our former colleagues." Congress critters. "Reminding them that whatever the destination, NASA does its spending on Earth. That much of any increase in its budget—they can think for now you'll be ramping up your lunar programs—will find its way to the constituencies of ardent supporters. Because it sure as hell looks like NASA will need buckets more money."

Huh. Maybe the man did serve a purpose.

"Riiight." Van Dijk nodded at Xander. "Okay. Between us, we've got it covered."

As if. It was noon, give or take. Thirty-two *hours* to sketch out a crewed Mars program? Xander managed not to chew on his lip. He felt … numb. "A mission you'll announce ahead of Wu's address?"

The president shook her head. "With due respect to Arthur, the intel could be wrong. After *losing* a Mars race, the last thing I'm willing to do is start one. But we *will* be ready to counter whatever Wu has to say."

"How much can I tell the people who'll be assisting—"

"Nada," the president said. "There can't be any last-minute interest shown in getting to Mars. NASA must have decades of Mars-related studies and white papers. Work from those."

"And let *me* be clear." Schmidt began shepherding the other men to the door. "Not a *word* of this gets out. You don't discuss it with anyone but the president and myself. Even with us, only in a face-to-face or over the secure devices I'll give you. Because, well, never mind."

Connecting those obvious dots again. Revealing a leak from the highest level of the Chinese government wouldn't go over well. "Understood," Xander said.

As the door closed behind Xander, the president's parting shot came: "You'll be prompt tomorrow, Alex, and you *won't* disappoint me."

Inbound to the Oval Office, the least among the security precautions had been relieving Xander of his folded datasheet. Outbound, Arthur Schmidt seemed in no hurry to have it returned. First came formalizing Xander's new tippy-top security clearance, its associated paperwork turgid even by NASA standards. (Except for the part about his legal jeopardy for any disclosure, however inadvertent, of classified information. With a mental shrug, he'd signed. Declining hadn't felt like an option.) Then came signing for a secure phone and instructions on its use. (How difficult could that be? The phone came with *one* contact loaded: Schmidt himself. Besides, didn't a senior-level position at NASA make him an honorary rocket scientist?) Exchanged his temporary pass, after much jumping through of hoops, for a permanent White House ID badge. (As ominous a portent as that was of recurrent command appearances, he didn't ask. The sooner Schmidt let him go, the sooner he could get to the actual task.) Followed by a counterproductive lecture on the urgency of the situation.

Well before all that wrapped up, Van Dijk and the NASA motor-pool car were long gone.

By the time Xander had recovered his datasheet and gotten an Uber, he had eight texts queued up. Every one from Rebecca. They began with curiosity at how things fared in her absence from the office, proceeded to mild annoyance at his lack of response, and had progressed to: WTF'S UP? WHAT'S THIS OUTSIDE MEETING VAN DIJK DRAGGED YOU TO?

Someone must have taken her call or text.

He texted back (his hands shaking; go figure): YOU JUST HAD SURGERY, BECKS. IT CAN WAIT TILL YOU'RE BACK. Which wouldn't be before Monday, surely. In another era. In a post-speech, or -speeches, era. If the need for secrecy remained, *her* boss could make excuses.

Almost faster than he could glance up to glower at the traffic, his datasheet chimed. Another text from Rebecca. NOT BECKS. YOUR *BOSS.* TRY AGAIN.

ASK MATT. A bit of self-indulgence that made Xander smile. In the office, for even the privileged few not required to go with the administrator title, it was *Matthias*. Presidents have prerogatives.

I'M ASKING *YOU*

ASK MATT, he repeated. NOT SAYING ANY MORE.

Don't like that answer? Don't give me your delegation.

Because the problem that had been tossed into his lap? It seemed ... impossible.

No payload yet landed on Mars had massed more than about a ton. A mission transporting people, their consumables, and the equipment to make their presence useful? A hundred tons, at least. He'd guess more.

Delivering that much mass to the surface would be a nightmare. Mars, in some ways, was the worst of all possible destinations. Its atmosphere wasn't even one percent as dense as Earth's. That was enough air to make entry blazingly hot, yet not enough for wings to do any good. Aerobraking and parachutes had yet to be used on Mars missions for anything bigger than a rover. The president's crack about go-karts? Not altogether unfair. Meanwhile, the planet had enough gravity—more than a third that of Earth; twice that of the Moon—that a powered landing on rocket engines would require prodigious quantities of fuel.

Even supposing aerobraking and parachutes could slow a much bigger ship on its way *down*, they'd do nothing to help it get back *up*.

Someone nearby honked. Xander tuned into his surroundings enough for a traffic snarl and his location to register. In fifteen minutes, they'd gone about a half mile. "Pull over here, please, and ring me up," he told the cab. The AI took any disappointment it may have felt in silence. "I'll walk the rest of the way."

Two miles at a brisk pace was more than long enough to brood upon other challenges. What happened after you landed? You couldn't breathe the air, too thin and too toxic. You couldn't spend much time outdoors. With neither a magnetic field nor an ozone layer, with almost no atmosphere, the intensity of solar and cosmic radiation reaching the Martian surface was brutal. The planet offered nothing to eat, nor—a once-popular novel and its movie notwithstanding—could you readily grow crops there. Toxic perchlorates and peroxides permeated the local dirt.

Lost in thought, he got himself back to the office—nearly run over twice. He emerged from distraction long enough to collect a couple of burgers from a food truck. Those, Snickers from the emergency stash in his desk, and breakroom coffee would have to do for a while. If about little else, the president was correct about one thing. NASA had a ton of studies on file pondering how best to reach and survive on Mars.

Behind a closed office door, his first cardboard-quality burger in hand, Xander started to search agency servers.

March 13, 2032

Saturday's heel-cooling outside the Oval Office somehow felt less intimidating than Friday's. Maybe it was the almost painless entry a permanent ID badge gave him into the White House. Or, this time, having on a suit. Xander did own one, if only because funerals happen. Or, after a night without sleep, he lacked the energy for worry—certain presidential rage notwithstanding. Or maybe it was by comparison with Dale Bennigan, the tall, dark, and incongruously blond woman seated beside him, nervously spinning her wedding band. (As might he, if he'd still had reason to wear one.) She wore the frozen expression of a deer caught in headlights.

He'd be willing to bet she had just learned what was on her boss's mind.

Bringing Dale into the loop made perfect sense. Her interactions with NASA favored flight surgeons over techies like Xander, but he understood that. She was a medical doctor and research microbiologist—popular qualifications since the COVID pandemic for any presidential science adviser. However dissimilar their backgrounds, she was objective, detail-oriented, and almost scary-smart. He'd welcome whatever contributions she'd have to offer.

As for Arthur Schmidt, also waiting, he seemed as unflappable as ever.

"This sure is *something*." Dale's Jamaican accent, even in a whisper, was charming.

Schmidt glowered at her. For good measure, he glowered at Xander. After that, they sat in silence till an intercom buzzed, and the receptionist directed them inside.

As they settled in, science types on one sofa, the president and DNI on the facing sofa, a steward bustled into the Oval Office with coffee service. Not mismatched mugs bearing random vendor names, à la NASA, but fine china. (Wedgwood, if Xander were any judge. Which, he'd have ventured to guess, Charlene would have declared he wasn't. As though to be fancy-china impaired was one of those irreconcilable differences. In the end, pretty much anything he did or didn't do, knew or didn't know, aggravated her. He couldn't help but wonder what fault she'd have found with his newfound role as a presidential confidant.)

Not now! Xander chided himself. He burned his tongue swigging an entire, ridiculously tiny, demitasse of coffee, then poured himself another.

"Okay," the president said. "While you caffeinate, Alex, we'll start easy. Last time, you predicted the Chinese were planning a one-way mission. How'd you know?"

Dale startled a bit at that *Alex*. She knew better.

Xander sipped. Gathering his thoughts. Mentally simplifying. "It takes lots of oxygen and fuel to launch off the Martian surface. I can't imagine CMSA landing that much mass, together with everything *else* a mission to the surface would require, to accomplish a return flight." Leaving out that they might park some of the return fuel in Mars orbit, from which an *Apollo*-style smaller lander would descend and to which it would return. Even then, lugging adequate fuel from Earth remained intractable.

He took another stalling sip.

"What about …?" Dale began. "No, never mind."

"Go on," the president said.

"Well, can't fuel be produced onsite? Didn't the old *Perseverance* rover prove that?"

"Yes and no," Xander began. "What little atmosphere Mars has is mainly carbon dioxide. The *Perseverance* rover could extract a few grams of oxygen in an hour by splitting cee-oh-two." Which it did by heating the carbon dioxide to 800 °C. The demonstration had required idling the rover's instruments to free up power to generate that much heat. "It'll take literal tons of oxygen to loft a crewed vehicle off Mars.

"So, you *could* generate oxygen onsite and chill it down to a liquid for storage. That'd take production-scale equipment plus a serious power source. You'd need different equipment, employing another chemical process to generate fuel, likely liquid hydrogen, from local resources. You'd have to—"

"We get it," Arthur interrupted. "That's the *no* part. It's impractical. Let's move on."

"In fact," Xander said, "this relates directly to the president's question. Producing oxygen onsite to breathe could be practical. Ditto, producing oxygen and fuel for a return flight. We can't *know* without trying. Among the ideas NASA has considered is landing a robotic oxygen and fuel station. If the trial facility stays up and running in a hostile environment, if it successfully produces, refrigerates, and stores the necessary tons and tons of oxygen and fuel, *then* we would dispatch a crew at the next launch period. Along with a *spare* factory flying shotgun. The second factory ship then serves as a failsafe or prepares for the next crewed mission."

"Ah," the president said. "If the Chinese send a mission at the upcoming window, they haven't sent ahead a fuel-and-oxygen factory. At best, a factory might accompany the people. You called it a one-way trip because they couldn't know otherwise."

Or even if they'll have oxygen to breathe long-term. "Correct."

"It's plain *reckless*," Dale said. "We can't allow it."

The president frowned. "Not that we get a say in their space program, but what's your problem?"

Dale frowned right back. "As your science adviser, I *must* emphasize that among the most profound scientific questions is this: Are we alone? Is life unique to Earth, or did it also arise elsewhere? Did life even originate here, or did it hitchhike to a then-sterile young Earth within a meteorite?

"Forget how inhospitable Mars appears today. It once had a proper atmosphere, oceans, and—for all we know—*life*. It might be home to life even now, if not on the surface, then a few meters below. Or in aquifers visitors would want to tap for water. Or within the polar ice caps. We haven't begun to work out how a mission to Mars can avoid contaminating—"

"Gimme a break," Arthur growled. "We've sent robots there for— what?—fifty or sixty years already. We've never found life. If we were going to contaminate the planet, it's already happened."

47

An all but irresistible urge came over Xander. To sigh. No, to scream. No, to resign, to dissociate himself from this madness. It'd be *so* much simpler to … do what? Go grow trees and lobsters in Maine. Or, even better, sit and stare while they grew themselves.

Instead, he took a deep breath, gathering his thoughts on how to politely present yet another *yes, but.* The findings of past missions were inconclusive. The bit of that planet so far explored was minuscule. As for the robots—Russian, Chinese, and American—those had been, as best as possible, sterilized before their sendoff. You couldn't do that with astronauts! He'd forgotten how many bacteria lived in the average human body, beyond that those numbered in the trillions.

"The thing is …" he began tentatively.

"*Enough*," said the president. "If China goes, we go. Period. So, *how* do we go?"

"The science is how to stop them going!" Dale said desperately. "We emphasize what will be jeopardized if they proceed. Call them out as irresponsible."

"*Enough*," the president repeated. "'We don't want you to go'"— delivered in a put-on, petulant whine—"would make America look weak and pathetic. Would seem an admission that we can't do it. I won't allow that—and don't anyone even *think* of making me ask again. How, on the same timetable as China, do *we* send people to Mars?"

All eyes turned to Xander.

Dale shivered. This was *insane.*

Any American mission on that timetable should be considered one-way for the same reasons the Chinese mission would be. While the president had brushed aside Dale's concerns, plenty of scientific organizations and environmental groups might share them. No, they would and *should* share them.

Moreover, planetary protection went both ways. Concerns would inevitably arise at the prospect of astronauts returning to Earth with possible Martian pathogens. Even the ever-unfunded proposals for a *robotic* sample-return mission from Mars had come to envision strict quarantine. If this mission got the go-ahead, the requisite, first-of-its-kind, sample-return facility would have to happen. She guessed it wouldn't be cheap.

To judge by the bags under Xander's eyes—not to mention the out-of-character, wary expression, the slumped shoulders, and the tremor in his hands—he'd also sought answers that weren't there.

"You *did* bring me options?" the president prompted. Demanded.

Xander straightened. "Can it be done? In theory. Given how little time we have to prepare, it'll have to be done with existing spacecraft. The ships we use for lunar missions, if refueled in Earth orbit, can make it to Mars. They won't have the fuel capacity to land with any useful payload aboard and take off again, but with parachutes and heat shields retrofitted, I believe they can land. We'll need at least two such ships to bring a reasonable level of supplies. You'll also remember that producing fuel on-site is untested technology. Best case: Anyone who goes is there for a long stay."

"Good, good." The president nodded along. "I can promise you volunteers, even on the assumption that the trip is one-way."

Uh-huh, Dale thought. Some people would be that crazy, though she had her suspicions *volunteer* should have come with air quotes. The radiation, lack of oxygen, the isolation ….

But that was the gut reaction of her physician side. As a science adviser, she should also consider the discoveries to be made in geology, planetology, and climatology. Because Mars *had* once been a very different world. With a real atmosphere. Deep oceans. A protective magnetic field. But for the last several billion years … not.

"Worst case," Xander persisted, "the trip *is* one way. The payload will need to include everything the crew would need to live off the land. To generate oxygen. If they can, to generate fuel. To drill down to aquifers or mine underground ice. To construct long-term, radiation-proof shelter. To prospect for ores and minerals and be mobile enough *to* prospect. To grow hydroponic crops because Martian dirt is toxic. Seeds. A major, dependable power source. A—"

"Years' worth of vitamins and trace nutrients," Dale contributed. "Medicines. Some sort of infirmary. Food to last till the first crops—"

"It's doable," the president said, glowering, "or Wu won't be making the claim. Alex, you've said it's doable." (Xander had. So much for that qualifier, *in theory*.) "If they go, we go. Full stop."

"With respect, *why*?" Dale demanded. "Is scoring points against China reason to condemn a few 'volunteers' to a desperate existence in a deadly environment? Or in our haste, risk"—recklessly!—"ever knowing if Mars at any time bore its own life? To my knowledge, no solution has been found to avoiding contamination, much less safely doing a sample return."

"If the Chinese are there anyway, what risk would *we* add?" Arthur asked.

Certain her objections would change nothing, Dale said, "Two missions. Twice the contamination hazard."

"We *go*," the president repeated. "If NASA can't figure out a way, the Space Force will." (So much for volunteers, Dale thought, or any serious prospect of new knowledge from the enterprise.) "If Wu gives the speech we expect, I'll announce our own—"

Dale stood. "Then you have my resignation, ma'am. I cannot be a party to this."

"I don't accept your resignation," said the president. "Now, park it."

Reluctantly, she sat.

"What if …?" Brow furrowed, Xander ground to a halt. "Maybe this circle *can* be squared. Suppose we could have it both ways."

"Meaning?" demanded Arthur.

Xander leaned forward. "Meaning, we put our astronauts on the scene, where they do responsible science *without* contaminating the planet. We make what we expect the Chinese to propose look rash."

The president leaned forward. "I'm listening."

It boiled down, Xander felt, to simple physics.

"We go to Mars, and on the same timetable. But we don't land on it. Instead—"

"A flyby?" the president scoffed. "The Chinese land, and we do a fucking *flyby*? No."

"Not a flyby." Xander shook his head for emphasis. "We land people … on Phobos. That's the inner Martian moon. It orbits a scant few thousand miles above the planet's surface."

"How's that better?" Arthur gnawed on his unlit cigar. "Or even useful?"

"First, it's more practical," Xander began. "Landing on and return-ing from Phobos takes less fuel than landing on and returning from the Moon." Drawing blank looks because Phobos was also *a* moon. "I should've said, than Earth's moon. Than Luna. A lunar landing and return must contend with that world's considerable gravity. Landing on and returning from Mars means contending with its even stronger gravity. Phobos, on the other hand, is mere miles across. Its gravity is negligible. So, it takes less fuel to go to and from Phobos than to and from our moon—and we know how to do *that*."

For a robotic mission, that summary was a simple fact. But when the payload included crew? Adding food, water, and the like for the round trip and long stay? It'd take weeks, at least, to compile a proper cargo manifest, then determine the extra fuel required to cart along *that*. Even so, a Phobos rendezvous had to be a lower hurdle than a Mars landing.

"To do nothing is easier still," Arthur scoffed. "How is going to Phobos *useful?*"

"Rovers," Xander said. "A *lot* of rovers. They'd be dispatched from Phobos, distributed around the planet, and controlled from Phobos." The latest puzzled stares registered. "We direct rovers by radio. When Mars and Earth are at their closest, a radio signal takes more than four minutes to cross. Each way. At their farthest, we're talking more than twenty minutes, again each way. If we tried to control a rover from Earth, by the time operators noticed a hazard in its path, it'd already be too late to order a halt. Instead, our rovers use customized command files, uploaded for each short segment of travel, to cross short distances we *know* are obstacle-free.

"The signal delay between Mars and *Phobos* is negligible, a small part of a second. With rovers controlled from Phobos, we can accom-plish more, and do it much faster, than all the missions that have set down on Mars over the past half-century."

For the first time, Dale smiled. "Plus, rovers, unlike people, *can* be decontaminated before they're dispatched. This way, we can explore safely for Martian life or its remains."

Xander nodded. "Any promising or puzzling samples—those would weigh almost nothing—can be boosted to Phobos for in-person assessment."

The president's expression also changed. Maybe she intended it as a smile, but it came across more as a smirk. "So, our folks are on the scene, doing the science, and we have the moral high ground."

"Also, our folks can expect to come home," Xander reminded.

"Arthur," said the president. "You look skeptical."

No, Xander thought, he looks like his dog has died.

The DNI shifted uneasily, straightened his tie, and stroked his chin. "Alex's way being easy is the problem. The Chinese will mock us for stopping—what did you say, Alex?—a few thousand miles short."

Who said it would be *easy?* He'd called it *more practical.* "I beg to differ. The general public will no more grasp the comparative challenges of the two mission concepts than …."

"Than we ignorant pols?" Arthur completed.

Yeah, than you two. *Not* helpful to say. "Than any physics-intensive topic."

Dale added, "Whereas anyone can understand we'd be being responsible while they'd be being reckless. The contrast might even shame CMSA into changing their plans."

"Well, whaddaya know," the president said. "We have a plan. *You,* Alex, are the man. You'll be my eyes and ears. All the way."

Leading the development of NASA's first crewed Mars mission? "It's … an honor, Madam President. I'm honored." And more than a little overwhelmed. Also, at a loss for words other than *honor.* "But respectfully, I'm a techie. I'm not a manager."

"Lead it?" She laughed. Arthur almost managed a fleeting smile. "Hardly. But you're forty-two. By my standards, that's almost a kid. You're healthy. Anyway, you were at your most recent physical. You just went through a nasty divorce. You're not seeing anyone new. So why the fuck not?"

As the implication registered, Xander tamped down the rush of anger at her prying into his private life. "You don't mean …?"

"Of *course,* I mean. *You,* Alexander Hopkins, take off for Phobos in thirteen months."

March 16, 2032

W ang Kai stared blankly into space. Not in a literal way, with which he had so much experience. Not in a relaxed, tuning-out way. In the hopeless, can't-bear-the-pain-of-reality way.

He perched, hunched over, at the end of a lumpy, narrow bed that was little more than a cot. In a tiny bedroom. In a humble apartment. In a depressing, age-worn, hivelike building complex. In a character-less residential district outside the nondescript city of Fuyang. Where, in self-imposed penance, he had been staying.

Where dear Li had grown up.

Kai and Li had repeatedly tried to relocate her parents to a bigger place. They could well afford, and had promised to take care of, any increase in rent. Kai had even lined up an apartment for them in Beijing, such that they and Li could visit far more often.

Every overture rejected.

"We do not wish to take advantage," her father had responded again and again.

Kai had always taken that as criticism. As disapproval of his chosen career. Disapproval, at the least, of how, for months on end, that work kept Kai away from home. Disapproval of the failure—which they assigned to him—to provide them with grandchildren. In every way, disapproval of the man whom their precious daughter—an only child, like almost everyone of Kai and Li's generation—had married against their wishes. *He* wasn't in the least traditional—few in the taikonaut corps were—but the Zhous were as old-fashioned as the Great Wall. That they had always treated him as an outsider, not as one of their family? It stung.

Every day they remained in this backwater was another silent rebuke. Kai buried his face in his hands. Perhaps they were right.

Had he not been endlessly circling Earth aboard the Tiangong space station, wouldn't he have noticed Li growing pale? Losing weight? Becoming frail? Wouldn't he, having witnessed any of that, have urged her to see a doctor? Gotten her an earlier diagnosis? Had her into treatment far sooner?

Yes. Of course. Or so he couldn't help but believe. As though beliefs, his or anyone's, made any difference. As though cancer cared what anyone thought.

Birdsong drifted through the open window. The breeze ruffled his hair and rustled the curtains. In the next room, his in-laws and the latest visitors murmured.

Blaming him? Why not? He blamed himself.

Li was—had been—modern enough to have gone to university, where they had met and fallen in love. Modern enough to earn her own prestigious position, as a senior programmer, at CMSA. For all that, she'd been conventional enough to be conflicted over her "defiance" and to crave her parents' approval.

Such yearning made her "failure" to deliver even a single grandchild, in an era when the State permitted three, all the more distressing—especially given the reason. Her father was prone to depression, a condition widespread in his family. Li had not fallen prey to such dark moods, but she'd endured *his* melancholy often. She had seen that despondency wear down her mother. Li refused to risk passing the trait to her own children, or theirs, or anyone down the line.

So, Kai, respecting her wishes even in death, kept the truth to himself. Let Father and Mother Zhou blame the absence of grandchildren on his long absences or even on some physical inability on his part. Better those, as Li had insisted, than even to hint at any disrespect to her father or his revered ancestors.

Marrying Kai had been the one true act of independence in Li's too-short life. He told himself it had been enough. He told himself many things.

With hopes of making peace with her family, he had acceded to their desire that she be buried in this backwater, in the Zhou ancestral plot. Not that Father Zhou had made the concession easy: "You're seldom on this world, anyway," he had said. "Why would you care?"

Kai scarcely registered the comings and goings elsewhere in the apartment. Family friends? Relatives he'd met at the wedding and not seen since? Neighbors? He was in no frame of mind to interact with any of them. Was his absence even noticed? If so, what was one more disappointment in her father's tally?

His parents, after a token appearance at the morning's funeral ceremony, had already left. For pressing business in Beijing, they said. Unsaid: that they had disapproved of this match from the start. That they had never quite accepted Li. Because his family was modern. Successful. Connected. The Zhous were … none of those things.

Alone in Li's childhood room, solitary in his grief, Kai let the murmurs of condolence beyond the closed door wash over him—

Until the brusque, sharp knock, unlike any that had come before. The loud gasps that followed this squeak of front-door hinges. The obsequious, mumbled greeting of his father-in-law. The curt summons: "I am here for Major Wang."

With a sigh, Kai got to his feet. Straightened and buttoned his suit jacket. Opened the bedroom door.

The apartment's tiny, usually tidy, living room overflowed with wreaths of white and yellow chrysanthemums. The more permanent decorations—in the main, tasteful nature photos Li herself had taken and framed—were all but obscured. Some dozen strangers, most elderly, shared the room with Li's parents. Just beyond, at the open exterior door—rigidly erect, eyes narrowed, brow furrowed, in a crisp, pine-green uniform—stood a PLA general. His name patch read LAO.

Kai was in mourning clothes. A somber, modern-cut suit, such as most men of his generation—those from Beijing, anyway—would have worn. Not the traditional changshan robe, doubtless one more disappointment to his father-in-law.

Out of uniform, was Kai expected to salute? He'd forgotten the rule. More, he didn't care about the rule. Not now. Not here. Anyway, what did a Hero Taikonaut, the recipient of a presidential medal of Space Flight Achievement, need to prove to a provincial ground-pounder?

"You are Wang?"

Kai nodded.

"Come," Lao growled. "You are expected at once in Beijing."

"Can you be more specific?"

Throughout the crowded living room, eyes widened at Kai's temerity.

"The Aerospace Control Center." Mission Control for human spaceflight and planetary exploration programs. The beating heart of the nation's space agency. "A plane is being held for you at Fuyang Xiguan." The local airport.

This general had displeased someone important. To send him to retrieve a mere major—and from another service branch, at that— made the fact indisputable. The subtext for Kai was as transparent: No arguments. No delay.

It was too much. Behind a stoic facade, Kai seethed. At the cruelty of cancer. At the love of his life for leaving him. At her parents for their slights over the years. At himself for the lack of emotional discipline. Not least, he silently raged at the State's intrusion, with Li not one day buried.

Let the ground-pounder bear the brunt of Kai's rage—while reminding the Zhous, and everyone they may have misled about Kai, that *he* was a person of some importance. That their daughter had wed honorably.

"Wait outside," Kai said, "while I change into my uniform." The blue uniform of the Strategic Support Force. His ... rudeness? insubordination? ... triggered gasps.

That no explanation for this abrupt recall had been offered? None was needed. Not after President Wu's speech the evening before.

Father Zhou, it seemed, was in one matter correct. Kai *wouldn't* be on this world much longer.

March 22, 2032

Among the lessons drummed into Teri Rodriguez as an Army brat was: "To be merely on time is to be late."

Traffic in downtown San Francisco having again been the horror that it so often was—an observation an imagined presence rejected as mere excuse—she had arrived for this morning's meeting with fewer than ten minutes to spare. Evoking another of Sergeant Mom's mantras. "Failing to plan is planning to fail." How many times had she endured *it*?

Never mind that no one could plan for this city's traffic short of spending the night before within walking distance of their destination. Which, in this instance, would have required flying into town the day before. Which, given how erratic Left Coast weather had become in recent years, that morning proving no exception, in hindsight might've been the wise choice.

Damn Mom's standards anyway. Who felt the need to be punctual to their own hanging?

It seemed *she* did.

For as long as Teri had worked here, the big boss had been habitually late. Because he could? Early in his career, working for other people, Blake Wagner might have been different. Odds were, he'd have to have been. Maybe even a while longer, on the bumpy road to his first billion. Scrounging for investors, especially after a few startup failures, you didn't get to keep people waiting. But now? The owner of Interplanetary Enterprises marched to his own drummer.

Leaving Teri to cool her heels.

She'd spent the past half hour in contemplation of—at *best*—an epic chewing-out. More likely, Blake had "asked" her here to savor the firing up close and personal. In either event, fairly? No. But memories were fleeting. Or, per another indelible Mom-ism, "One aw shit obliterates a thousand attaboys."

The anteroom where Teri fretted was as over-the-top as the company's owner. A good twenty-five feet square. Richly hued carpet, its deep pile as thick as, well, she didn't know what. Eight wingchairs and a twelve-foot sectional sofa upholstered in butter-soft, beige leather. A glass wall offering panoramic views of the harbor far below. Huge displays on the three remaining walls, every screen but one cycling among dramatic images: company rockets launching, on orbit, and landing; the company space station; the solar powersat under construction; selfies shot by company lunar rovers.

Not even the bolt-upright back of Teri's chair could stop her from drooping. A day on Earth didn't begin to suffice for acclimating to this gravity. Not after six months off-world.

A SEAT OPENED UP ON THE NEXT FLIGHT DOWN, Blake had texted two nights before. WHY DON'T YOU POP IN FOR SOME R&R?

As though the trip were an option. A perk. As though some discreet inquiries hadn't revealed a last-minute, IPE-funded, grant renewal to the astrophysicist who would've been filling that seat. Had she had any question about the nature of the "suggestion," Blake's next text, hours after her landing, erased any doubt. CAN YOU SWING BY TOMORROW AT 11:00?

Surprise: A seat had also freed up on the normally packed company shuttle between the New Mexico spaceport and SFO. A flight which, in the event, had departed more than two hours late and bounced her around as much as any atmospheric reentry—but for much longer.

Thank you, climate change.

On the lone wall display not dedicated to air-blasting the company horn, cable news streamed. The topic of the day, as it had been for a week already, was Mars. Chinese plans. American plans. Contamination risks. Geopolitical implications. Dangers. Opportunities. The glory, or folly, or both of such extravagance. Most of the chatter, had anyone asked her opinion, naïve and uninformed. The interleaved sound bites replayed from the recent presidential addresses were little better.

"… great moment for the Communist Party of China and the Chinese people. As a nation of long history and great ambition, we aspire with confidence to our new, shared goal …"

A screen crawl offered, WU CHANNELS FAMOUS ADDRESS OF FORMER PRESIDENT XI JIN-PING. Which address? Delivered to whom? Unstated.

The sweeping generalities of Wu's oration might at least be attributable to the voiceover translation. Her president, in a yet-again repeated snippet, had no such excuse.

"… and so we invite America's partners around the world to join us on humankind's next great adventure. NASA welcomes your participation in the coming expedition to Phobos. Did our neighbor planet once host life? Does it still? Together, with prudence, we will find out."

In a long-ago high-school class, Teri had seen a recording of JFK's 1961 Moon speech. Even knowing the Moon had been abandoned after a few Apollo missions, she'd found the words inspirational. Kennedy, not that anyone had asked her opinion, had these modern pols beat.

As for finding hypothetical Martian life or its ancient traces? In two words: fat chance. The planet having long ago lost its oceans, it and Earth had similar land areas. How long—whether by a few Chinese taikonauts or a few American rovers—must even a token surface survey take? How long did one search, and how deep belowground or into the ice caps must one delve, until the lack of evidence could be deemed conclusive?

But *prudent*? Talk about stretching a word to its breaking point. Space stations required near-constant maintenance, plus supplies delivered from Earth or, in recent years, at least of such basic commodities as water and oh-two, from the Moon. If anyone ought to know, she would. So how safe would a six-month or longer flight without any possibility of resupply be? How safe would even a "mere" sixteen-or-so-months stay on Phobos be, much less a potential *lifetime* on Mars?

NASA, of course, had planned to test living-off-the-land tech on the Moon before venturing any further from the home world. Which she, *likewise*, ought to understand as well as anyone. Bringing matters back—in her brooding, anyway—to whatever punishment hung over her like the lightsaber of Damocles.

She scarcely noted the segue to yet another "expert" panel critiquing and handicapping the Mars competition. However riveting Blake's latest earnest-faced assistant found this uninformed bickering, in the week since the latest Space Race was initiated, every possible opinion had been expressed. It's a waste of resources. No, it isn't. The attempt will end badly for whichever country a particular pundit disfavored. It's far too early to send people to Mars. No, it's not. The people sent to Mars will die there. (Duh. What else might "one-way trip" mean?) And the most repeated of all: prestige demands we go—and that we get there first.

Stupid, macho chest-beating.

Eventually, one of the company's cycling propaganda displays grabbed Teri's attention with a closeup of IPE's orbital station. The outpost's central mass—an orb sixty meters across—transparent except for the small, ever-shifting area opaqued against the unfiltered sun. The twin docking ports extending from the sphere's poles. The concentric fat doughnuts—tori, to geometric purists—lazily spinning around the sphere. Spin decoupled, beyond the outer, ever-turning, gravity-simulating rings, a vast array of sun-tracking photovoltaic panels. The utility-shack/fuel-depot/shuttle-garage support facility tethered nearby, where it wouldn't obstruct the jaw-dropping vistas of Earth.

Taking all that in, Teri felt a surge of pride. Blake's deep pockets aside, *she*, more than anyone, had made the station possible. Not by herself building a stick of it, but by overseeing the whole damn thing. In its planning phase, here, dirtside. In its next phase, managing every cargo manifest and launch. As construction got underway, supervising onsite. Even honchoing Space Vegas's wildly successful debut as *the* destination vacation for the filthy rich.

Project managers made things happen. Her pride was well deserved. It wasn't for nothing she'd been tagged as PM for the company's newest ambitious endeavor: a Moon base for the next exotic vacation destination.

One aw shit obliterates a thousand attaboys.

Get out of my head, Mom.

She'd mentally rehearsed a defense through the entire flight from New Mexico. Nothing had changed, but she reviewed her argument

60

anyway. Mooncrete casting on anything but the most trivial scale was unproven tech. Might everything scale up perfectly? Work on the first try on the undeveloped frontier that was the Moon? Offer no surprises? Sure. It might.

But how likely was that?

It would be better to discover closer to home what didn't work. With plenty of engineers already on hand. With replacement equipment hours, not days, away. Better, in other words, to experiment *before* a skeleton construction crew deployed to the Moon.

So, yes, she'd taken it upon herself to alter the launch schedule from the station. She'd offloaded and held onto a batch of mooncrete-casting gear. Sent on the unburdened lunar lander to retrieve tons of lunar regolith. Slowed the station's outermost ring to simulate mere lunar gravity. Reconfigured one sector of that ring for vacuum and Moon-mimicking temperature swings. All on the basis of *Don't ask the question if you might not want to hear the answer.* Because if even one potential snag were discovered early—

"Ms. Rodriguez?" Earnest Young Man interrupted her brooding. "Mr. Wagner is ready now. But he asked that I hold onto your datasheet."

This from a man infamous for his short temper and near-apoplectic rages. Whom she did not much like. Had never liked. But she loved her job. To remain hers, she anticipated, for the length of an epic harangue which—not that, until that moment, she'd had any intention—would go unrecorded.

Jaws clenched, Teri handed over her device and went in.

The inner sanctum was windowless, paneled in some dark wood, unornamented. A desk and chair, three visitor chairs, and a credenza/liquor cabinet were the only furniture. The single screen belonged to a darkened tablet. The desktop was otherwise bare except for a single manila folder. The anteroom was meant to impress. This room was for serious business.

Blake himself—his dark mop of hair characteristically tousled, uncharacteristically in suit and tie, amber-colored decanter in one hand—stood by the liquor cabinet. Something about his eyes always brought Shakespeare to mind: *Yond Cassius has a lean and hungry look; He thinks too much: such men are dangerous.* "You want one?"

She didn't smoke. So, Scotch as a surrogate for the condemned woman's last smoke? "Sure."

Anyway: Why not? Here in San Francisco, it was after one in the afternoon. Past two in Truth or Consequences, where, without having slept, she'd begun her morning. (Truth or Consequences. Named after a game show. She'd always thought the label weird. But, weird or not, it was the single town of any size near Spaceport America. Today, rather than weird, the name felt … sinister.) Her body clock, still operating on station time, considered it eight in the evening. Like NASA's station, Space Vegas ran on Greenwich Mean Time. Tiangong, the Chinese orbital station, was on China Standard Time. Marching to *their* own drummer. That last bit of arcane lore about to become irrelevant to her.

He poured two generous dollops, held out the fuller of the two tumblers. Thick, leaded glass: Had she been accustomed to the gravity, the libation would still have been heavy. He made no move toward a chair, so neither did she. "You look like you could use a picker-upper."

Sympathy? *Not* the vibe she was expecting.

He sipped. "So, how's the husband?"

Off, in some way she had yet to parse. Preoccupied. Curiously uncurious about this summons. Bored. Well, that last she understood and could maybe do something about. With the shit about to hit the fan, getting *Jake* some new responsibility and maybe a salary bump could be helpful.

"Honestly? Underutilized. He's too skillful a pilot to be chasing old satellites to refuel and random junk to deorbit." Never mind how much those mundane services contributed to the station's operations budget.

"I see." Inexplicably, Blake smiled.

Teri was too tired, too tense, for small talk. She downed a healthy swig of … wow. A *very* smooth Scotch. "Look, about the regolith experiments I initiated on the station. If I was a bit too independent in my—"

His unencumbered hand waved dismissively. "Under different circumstances, we might be having that conversation. Today, we'll chalk it up to a sensible demonstration of initiative."

"I'm confused."

He took another sip and gestured for her to do the same. "If we've managed things right, there's no way you wouldn't be."

"We?"

"Yes, we." He drained his tumbler, set it on the desk, took a few quick steps, and rested a hand on the back wall. Her eyes drawn to a specific wall panel, Teri noticed dark hinges and a recessed latch. "The rest of that merry band is eager to meet you."

The windowless room behind Blake's office was empty, unfurnished but for its many wall displays. But on screen after screen ....

Teri's mind reeled.

These men and women—the several, anyway, whom she recognized—were among the wealthiest in the world. Multibillionaires, larger-than-life titans of industry, most self-made, from around the world. Others, from names shown on the displays, she knew only by reputation: also moguls, some notoriously reclusive. The remainder? Of like kind, she presumed.

Her gut reaction at spotting several of Blake's aerospace arch-rivals was some manner of collusion. Price-fixing? Bid-rigging? Market allocation? A scheme she was too naïve to imagine? Only how would any of that involve the owner of an agribusiness, or a semiconductor foundry, or any of several other random-seeming enterprises?

The collective wealth of just the people she recognized exceeded the GDP of most countries—and that was only their declared assets. The commercial entities, empires, most of them controlled were privately held, free from public disclosure and most regulatory scrutiny. Unlike countries, these tycoons had no obligation to support aging populations, national debts, or military establishments.

The poorest among them, at least among the names she knew, might lay claim to only a few billions. Computer and network security weren't as lucrative as the other industries represented. But the ability to keep sessions like this private? That, Teri suspected, contributed significant value on its own.

Under different circumstances. Blake's words echoed in her mind.

What was she expected to overlook or enable, that her sins be forgiven? No advantage less than colossal could matter to this assemblage. How confident of her acquiescence these conspirators must be to reveal to her their ... conspiracy.

Even as she noticed a screen featuring herself in closeup, looking shell-shocked, Blake said, "Everyone, I'd like you to meet Maria Theresa Rodriguez. You've seen Teri's file. To recap, she's a world-class industrial engineer. No, *worlds*-class. The project manager for the construction of my orbital station. For those of you who've enjoyed its hospitality, that's Space Vegas. She stayed up there to manage routine operations. She's done double duty of late, creatively laying the groundwork for IPE's lunar initiatives." That last attribution came with a wink. "No serious accidents on her watch. Schedule-driven. Of the many contenders we've reviewed these past few days, a significant majority of us have agreed. Teri is our best candidate to lead the New Earth Partners effort."

The *partners* aspect was clear enough. But *New Earth*? Well, she was already involved in Blake's lunar ambitions and, it would appear, not to be fired for—how had he put it?—her creativity. "Respectfully, what's this about? Some jointly funded enterprise on the Moon?"

"Nothing so mundane." Blake grinned. On every side, legions grinned back. "The project you've been chosen to lead—an undertaking which, for as long as this can be accomplished, is to be organized in secret—involves a different world. One also to resolve your husband's desire for challenge.

"And let me be clear, Teri. The NEP team, your team, will arrive on Mars *first*."

"Know yourself, know your enemy, and you will not lose in one hundred battles."

—Sun Tzu, The Art of War

"The greatest deception men suffer is from their own opinions."

—Leonardo da Vinci

"Only the Paranoid Survive"

—Book title by Andrew S. Grove, founder (and former CEO) of Intel Corporation

MISDIRECTIONS

March 25, 2032

Head down, towing a roll-aboard, newly off a crack-of-dawn flight from Houston, Xander trudged down a hallway at NASA headquarters. Blinking, he came to a halt. Voices—indistinct but the tones unhappy—penetrated the closed door of an office that should have been unoccupied. He sidled up to the sidelight. His boss, face drawn and cheeks pale, was behind her desk. Two men, backs to the door, sat facing her.

Becky, spotting Xander, gestured him inside. He shook his head, not wanting to interrupt. The men, curious, turned. He knew both: the heads of NASA procurement and legal. She gestured again.

Now Xander was curious. He went in.

"We're about finished here, right?" She even sounded weary.

"Well …" began Legal.

"Yeah, we are," Procurement said, standing. "Griping aside."

That was a sufficient hint for Legal to get up and moving.

Becky said, "Close the door on the way out, guys." As soon as one did, she slumped in her chair. "I'm glad you're back. We have things to discuss."

Such as why she wasn't still at home. "No offense, Becks, but you look like something the cat dragged in." No better than when he'd stopped by her house ahead of the Houston trip.

A wince terminated her laugh. "More like something the cat coughed up. But if you haven't heard, there's a Mars mission to plan. Oh, wait …." She eyed him expectantly.

"My interviews and the long-duration flight physical? They went fine. As of yesterday, I'm an ASCAN." Agency-speak for astronaut candidate, a status that at once exhilarated and terrified him. Remaining earthbound seemed so much simpler, both in personal terms and hoping for any bandwidth with which to help shape the mission. The months ahead of grueling training? Also daunting. "That makes *one* of us the vision of health. As for you, my friend, it's only been two weeks since surgery."

"So? Patients often get back to their routine in as little as a week after an appendectomy."

Going to Mars would be nothing like a mission in low Earth orbit or even on the Moon. Mars would mean years away from any hospital. Body parts he didn't need that might go wrong? Out those would go before launch. Wisdom teeth. Tonsils, too. Foremost, his appendix, possible problems with which the med staff had expounded upon in gory detail.

"Yeah, Becks, you're right. For a laparoscopic appendectomy"— such as it seemed he'd be getting—"one to three weeks to resume normal activities. But with cleanup after a *ruptured* appendix? Maybe six."

"I see you met one of our chatty flight surgeons." She managed a wan smile. "Okay, granted. I'm pushing it. But did you really suppose I'd stay home for six freaking weeks? Even without Van Dijk texting twice an hour to check on my progress and name-drop the prez?"

In her shoes, he'd have felt the same even without the pressure from on high. He parked himself in the guest chair Legal had vacated. "From what griping did I rescue you?"

She took a long sip of water. "You know Blake Wagner?"

"Of the Planet of the IPEs?"

She snorted. "Working on new material, I see."

Fair enough. He usually rendered the Interplanetary Enterprises acronym as *Yippee*. "What about our favorite billionaire?"

"Well …."

"To bring Doom and Gloom here, something must have gone wrong."

"Yeah." She began fidgeting with a pen. "Van Dijk contacted Wagner right after the president's big speech. Said we wanted three new Moonships, with priority on their delivery."

Which, of course, Xander knew. Repurposing the proven tech NASA already bought and used for its Moon missions had been his idea. He'd made the pitch for, among the big-ticket items, three ships. Wondering as he did how long Congress would take to provide any Mars budget at all. Wondering if, after the inevitable pushback, "We have problems to solve first here on Earth," he'd get even the *two* ships he considered the bare minimum.

Except maybe Van Dijk did have the Midas touch at lobbying his erstwhile colleagues. Or the prez had pulled out the stops to get an emergency supplemental appropriation. Xander's own guess was that no special effort had been necessary. In the current climate, even a bickering Congress could agree on not losing face with China.

Since, by all accounts, NASA would be getting the money, that left … what? "In a seller's market, IPE is jacking up the price?"

"You'd think, wouldn't you? But no. IPE won't take our money." She stopped clicking and started twirling the pen. "Which *isn't* the company making a patriotic contribution."

"Bringing Doom and Gloom to deliver the bad news in person."

"Who is which? No, don't tell me." With a rueful glance at her hand, she dropped the pen. "Bart"—the chief procurement officer—"was the bearer of bad tidings. Ernest"—the agency's general counsel—"came to brainstorm options."

Bart and Ernie. *So* close. "Options?"

She pinched the bridge of her nose and began rubbing. (Fair enough. He was developing a headache, too.) "Well, option—singular. The Defense Production Act. It requires companies to accept contracts and prioritize deliveries for things necessary to the national defense, and it prohibits hoarding and price gouging."

Legal stuff. Pretty much any engineer's least favorite topic. In any event, Xander's least favorite. "Defense, you say. Racing CMSA to Mars wouldn't seem to fit."

"You'd think. But for practical purposes, Ernest claims, 'defense' is whatever we say it is. The government invoked the act during the COVID pandemic to prioritize delivery of ventilators and vaccines."

Explaining his vague familiarity with the law. "Let's back up. *Why* doesn't IPE want our order? I mean, three Moonships, from their biggest customer?" As best Xander knew, IPE's *only* customer for that tech, apart from its announced, ground-yet-to-be-broken, lunar tourist facility. "Together worth the better part of a billion bucks."

She grimaced. "Has other plans for them. That's all he'd say."

"I can't imagine Cru"—and caught himself—"the president wouldn't go for using the DPA to grab the next units off the production line. What's the problem?"

"IPE's already been threatened with that. I take it the prospect of a DPA order usually suffices to get cooperation. Forcing the government to invoke the act smacks of disloyalty. Major bad press."

"And?"

"And Wagner said he'd see us in court. Up to the Supremes, if need be."

Taking … months? … they couldn't afford. Not with the mission clock ticking.

Never mind the inevitable shitstorm of presidential rage, the sad, competitive truth of the matter was: At this point, Xander didn't want to admit defeat. Make that, he *wouldn't*.

"Well, then, I say *screw* IPE. NASA owns four Moonships. We reconfigure two for the Phobos mission while we sue Blake Wagner's sorry ass. Yeah, that'll disrupt the lunar programs, but they can absorb the hit till we get our replacement ships."

"Whoa." For the first time since Rebecca had collapsed in pain in this office, he saw her smile. "I think I like astronaut you."

May 20, 2032

"Is beautiful, no?" a voice asked from behind Kai in pidgin, Slavic-accented English. Unmistakably, Ivan Vasiliev. The man's scattered bits of Mandarin were even worse.

"That it is," Kai agreed, using proper English. Beautiful, he presumed, referred to the world down upon which he had been found gazing. The world they so hastened to abandon in frantic preparations that consumed most of their waking hours.

Indeed, Earth was lovely. Seen from aboard Tiangong, at that moment almost 400 kilometers above a sunlit ocean, sparkling blue water and glistening white cloud predominated.

And yet.

By the calendar, the North Atlantic hurricane season had not even started, but much of that cloud cover came in the form of three named tropical storms. Equally unseasonable smoke, transported by jet stream from raging California wildfires, had hardly dissipated when the space station's orbit had carried it over North America's *eastern* coast. On the last daylight pass over China, where untimely torrential rains had sent the lower Yangtze far outside its banks, the view had been even more disheartening. Thousands there had drowned. Millions were homeless.

Storms, fires, or floods: It didn't matter which. Nor, though not naked-eye visible from this altitude, droughts and the corresponding likelihood of famine. Historical disaster seasons no

71

longer represented meaningful bounds. Climate change was all too real and only getting worse.

"A very fragile beauty," Kai added.

"If you have a moment?"

A gentle nudge against the nearest bulkhead set Kai slowly spinning, anticipating another urgent assignment from Mission Control—never mind that he was scant minutes into one of his rare, unscheduled waking hours. Dragging the same hand against the opposite bulkhead brought his rotation to a halt facing his visitor.

Ivan, at least by cosmonaut standards, was a great bear of a man. He was pleasantly homely, with a broad forehead and a thatch of black hair almost as dense as fur. His eyebrows, bushy and all but merged, evoked nothing as much as two woolly-bear caterpillars kissing. The man was boisterous and gregarious, implausibly likable, with a dark sense of humor. At least Kai hoped the relentless cynicism was Russian humor.

"Is everything okay, Ivan?"

"Is better than okay. Is best money can buy. Is yet better, day by day, as we toil." Ivan gestured at the window. "If only we had a few thousand more days to complete the work."

Making the topic, rather than planetary scenery, the ship visible at the closest docking port. Three of its four seats—and with those, piloting privileges, naming rights, and discretion over part of its cargo manifest—had been acquired for more rubles than anyone had publicly disclosed. Billions, no doubt.

However loath Kai was to express it, he shared the Russian's concern for their onrushing launch date. What sane person wouldn't?

It would have been unfair to say that President Wu had committed the nation without seeking technical guidance. Also (what was that quaint American expression?) career-limiting. But had the input to that bold speech been *sufficient*? Not even close.

No one in the active taikonaut corps—anyone who might have been expected to bring Wu's bold commitment to fruition—had had a part in the big announcement. At least among the colleagues Kai had cautiously asked, none admitted to having been consulted or to knowing anyone who had. Because they'd been deemed too much in the public eye to involve without raising speculations before the president's speech? Or too apt to let something slip?

Resulting in: three of CMSA's never-even-made-it-down-to-the-Moon, transfer-and-landing ships being reconfigured in orbit for the much more ambitious Mars mission. It didn't take a feng-shui master to question the propriety of such repurposing. Equally ambitious improvisations that proceeded in parallel, transforming this research station into the equally mission-critical orbital shipyard, machine shop, supply house, and fuel depot. Design details for both projects changing again and again as individual alterations succeeded or failed.

All the while, and unavoidably, short-staffed. Tiangong was crammed beyond design capacity to accommodate "just" the Mars mission's eight assigned crew. The lunar ships being retrofitted occupied two of the station's three docking ports. Their only in-person assistance came from three-person rotating teams of taikonaut engineers, living aboard a Shenzou orbital craft docked at the station's remaining port.

Only months hence—with most preparations complete, with the much-reconfigured *Yuri Gagarin* and *Zheng He* once more reliably providing life support—could on-orbit staff increase by a few. Even then, one of the station's docking ports would be occupied while they finished adapting the still unnamed third ship, strictly for cargo, to accompany the Mars crews.

The long, post-launch, coasting voyage to Mars would be restful by comparison.

Kai and his crewmates should have been on the ground, training—but traditional mission preparation relied upon an understanding, in excruciating detail, of the spacecraft's every quirk and characteristic. That wouldn't, couldn't, come about till the reconfigurations were complete. Their hands-on experience must suffice. As for the customary drills to prepare them for everything that might go wrong—because something always did and at the worst possible moment. There'd be time enough during the long flight to run simulations. After, based upon the ultimate ship re-re-redesigns, suitable simulations could be finalized. Kai could hope.

But while the pending dash to Mars was audacious in the extreme, in at least one way President Wu's cloistered planners *had* shown a decent element of caution. The ships' cargo-mass budget and, from that, the fuel margins. Which was damned fortunate. Alighting in unfamiliar terrain—*not* that Kai was a pilot—seemed certain to be tricky. If they managed not to burn through that reserve while hovering, seeking out a practical landing spot, they'd retain some flexibility later to hop the ships about to explore. Because the mass allocation budgeted for their ground vehicle, yet another mission-critical component in the work-in-progress category, looked skimpy for a dune buggy, much less a long-range, life-supporting, passenger vehicle ….

Ivan cleared his throat.

"How may I be of assistance?" Kai asked.

"No assistance. Not today, anyway. Do not tell Kolya, but I have interesting information." Ivan winked. "Also, not to tell Colonel I refer to him so familiarly."

Russia might have moved on from communism, but Col. Nikolai Antonov, the senior Russian officer, was as doctrinaire and formal as any commissar in the PLA. If Kai understood such people, the last thing Antonov would want to share was information. But the day's schedule had Antonov, among others, laboring outside on station upgrades.

"What sort of information?"

Ivan extracted a folded and wrinkled sheaf of papers from a pants pocket. "Read fast."

Kai found pages of detail about the American mission, starting with the target departure, less than a year off: April 17, 2033. That date was neither public information nor unexpected. CMSA had announced that same date, likely for the same reason. It was optimal in terms of fuel efficiency and so, to maximize cargo capacity.

Besides, a great race *deserved* a single starting pistol.

He continued skimming. NASA would be adapting its lunar-transfer craft—one of the few mission parameters already disclosed. What *wasn't* public was how little modification to those vessels NASA envisioned. This, too, Kai understood. A Phobos landing involved neither aerobraking nor parachutes.

For lunar missions, the American ships accommodated a crew of eight. Reconfigured for the longer-duration Mars mission, each would carry only three. Much of the deck area vacated of acceleration chairs and crew berths would go to exercise machines like those Tiangong carried. Workout gear made sense: microgravity en route would sap muscle strength and leach bone mass. Tiny Phobos would offer no meaningful improvement. Absent hours of daily resistive exercise, the NASA team would become enfeebled.

CMSA's mission plan required no such equipment. Outbound, strong cable would link each transfer module with its spent booster. Slow rotation about the pair's center of mass would simulate gravity until their final approach. After landing, they'd have Mars's significant gravity.

But if onsite fuel production proved practical? If, someday, they were able and permitted to launch for home? Lacking counterweight and exercise equipment, they'd reenter Earth orbit as feeble as newborn kittens. Not that Kai *expected* to return, but still ....

His composed facade must have slipped.

"What?" Ivan demanded.

Kai wasn't about to reveal misgivings. Leaving ... what? "There's no cable in the NASA manifest like we'll use for artificial gravity. Just the exercise gear."

"So?"

"It's yet another upgrade to vessels designed for Moon missions that we must make, and they don't."

Ivan sighed. "What is one more?"

Kai flipped through more pages. Ten robot landers to deploy many dozen smaller, robotic rovers. A pair of general-purpose, humanoid robots. (*His* mission lacked the mass budget for *any* robots; he foresaw years of manual labor ahead.) Two chemical plants to produce fuel from buried ice. Mining gear to extract that ice. A generous fuel allocation for the robots, doubling as a reserve for the crews' planned return flight to Earth orbit if in-situ fuel production should fail its trial. Conservative food supplies, as well. 3-D printers with a variety of feedstocks. Parts for a solar farm. Spools of power cable. Well-stocked, miniaturized biology and geology labs. Other inflatable structures. Vast quantities of consumables. Most of these specifics as yet unannounced by NASA.

Inwardly, Kai shrugged. Russians spying on the Americans came as no surprise. Ivan offering a peek at their findings? That did. As did the few minor cargo items the MSS, Ministry of State Security, hadn't already identified on its own. Suggesting—was this Ivan's cynicism rubbing off on him?—the Russians knew what Kai's people knew, and this unsolicited "sharing" was a ploy to engender misplaced trust.

Did the covert activities go beyond information-gathering? Would Russia's agents, or those of the MSS, try somehow to impede America's mission? Might his Russian crewmates—and at this speculation, Kai couldn't suppress a shiver—sabotage *Zheng He* and so claim a Mars-race victory for themselves?

Or was he imagining things?

Ivan's wristband beeped, and he reclaimed the papers. "Kolya will be back inside soon. What do you think of other side's plans?"

That the NASA-led expedition would be safer and better equipped than theirs. That the superpowers working *together* could accomplish so much more than either alone in this pointless competition. That, without Li, he found it hard to care who reached Mars first.

And yet, he was here. Anything less than outward enthusiasm would have dishonored his parents. Besides, what but the mission did he have to live for?

"I think," Kai said, "they're also in for an adventure."

"Not to worry, my friend. Mars will be just like Siberia." Ivan chuckled. "Except without the air."

CryptexNomicon hacked for £500M

Trading platform CryptexNomicon disclosed that hackers have plundered the exchange of Bitcoin and other cryptocurrencies valued at more than a half billion pounds. This is only the latest, if the largest, recent theft of virtual assets.

CryptexNomicon shares plummeted with the announce-ment of losses far in excess of the company's capitalization. Traders anticipate a speedy bankruptcy filing, with the com-pany's thousands of accountholders recovering, at best, a few pence on the pound for the erstwhile value of their holdings.

—The Economist

Dozens Killed, Hundreds Injured, in Market Explosion

A backpack bomb detonated inside City Mall St. John brought slaughter and massive damage to the popular Yangon (Rangoon) shopping center. Seventeen fatalities have been reported. With hundreds sent to area hospitals, the death toll is expected to rise.

As yet, there has been no claim of responsibility ....

—Myanmar Times

June 29, 2032

It wasn't as though Dale never dealt with the press. She interacted often with all kinds of media: semi-knowledgeable reporters for popular-science websites. On panels at every venue imaginable, alongside academic and industry experts. With local broadcasters, ever delighted to interview anyone from Washington.

But as the star attraction of a press conference in the fricking White House Briefing Room? Fielding questions from dozens of members of the national press corps? Not so much.

Dale knew she was overthinking things. The tier upon tier of track lights shining on the podium area weren't, in fact, super-bright. Neither, and she tamped down a smile at the synapse misfire, were most reporters. The questioning wasn't even entirely chaotic. Besides, Xander (on a break from training) and Cat Mancini (on a break from instructing) had netted in from the ISS for topics outside Dale's wheelhouse. Lance Kawasaki, the diminutive White House press secretary with the incongruously booming voice, stood by her side to deflect as necessary.

Yet none of that introspection made the lectern Dale sheltered behind feel any less insubstantial. None made her any the less self-conscious of her once-crisp suit and blouse. Both had gone limp, despite raincoat and umbrella, in the few windblown, soggy steps between her Uber and the White House entrance. The *dregs* of Hurricane Hanna

78

amounted to a thousand-year rain event—making it DC's second such in three years. With the Atlantic hurricane season yet young ....

Matters had begun benignly, with softball questions for the astronauts. In every instance, the only possible answer was some form of *yes*.

To Xander: Was he enjoying his time in orbit? (Are you kidding? Rich folk spent millions for a day or two in space. He was getting weeks of it on the government's dime.) Would he have sufficient time to prepare? (Yes, and in spades. Till they reached Phobos, he was along for the ride. He'd spend much of the long flight in further study and training simulations.) When would that be? (Barring surprises, on October 26, 2033. Forgoing the nits and grits of launch windows, fuel efficiency, and optimized payload, he went for a laugh: in time to get ready for trick-or-treaters.)

To Cat: Was she certain the crews would get sufficient training? (Hell, yeah. Sure, some mission specialists were newbies. *She* wasn't, and she'd whip everyone else into shape. Plus, what Xander had said about in-flight sims.

Left unmentioned: everyone on the mission would spend years in a high-rad environment. Excepting pilots, for whom hands-on experience was surely vital, there was much to recommend crew *without* prior years in space.) Did she agree with the president ceding four of the mission's six seats to people as yet unselected by the EU, Canada, and Japan? (Well, duh. The deeper the talent pool, the better.) Could any undertaking so complex come together on such a tight schedule and still be safe? (Piece of cake, folks.)

But before long, the questioning went hardball. About: Hanna. Europe's killer heat wave the week before. The twice-Manhattan-sized ice floe calved that morning from a Greenland glacier. The latest expensive fiasco of a large-scale carbon-capture demonstration. All of *that* came straight at Dale. None of which she had expected or was prepared to discuss. None of which was made any easier by terse notes a White House intern kept texting to the lectern's display. Apart from naming reporters and their outlets for her, the pop-ups did nothing but distract.

She somehow found the bandwidth to wonder which West Wing genius had come up with an impromptu Mars presser—much less with her as the star attraction—to change the subject from a failing Supreme Court nomination. Because how lame an excuse for this presser was, "The administration is pleased to announce a contest for American students to name our Mars mission?" Because how long was *that* going to divert a pack of national reporters? (Answer: less than ten minutes.) Because how often could she say of NASA's fluid—to euphemize the chaos—mission plans, "That's still being worked out," before the press corps smelled blood in the water? It wasn't as though any presidential science adviser often came into this room.

Hindsight might be 20/20, but 20/200 foresight should've seen this was a bad idea.

"Dale, I've got a follow-up." The lectern's display identified the speaker as Lyle Donovan from the *Chicago Tribune*. "Given our climate woes, is this the best time for a Mars boondoggle? The Apollo program, in constant dollars, ran to about $200 billion. We're still struggling to do much with the Moon, and the price tag for that keeps creeping up. How much will this regatta we have going with China end up costing taxpayers?"

"I ... I'm ..." she stammered. "The thing of it is—"

"The thing of it is," Lance Kawasaki interjected smoothly, "Doctor Bennigan isn't from OMB." The Office of Management and Budget. "C'mon, folks. My guests today have been more than accommodating, but let's stay on topic. That's not the climate, or economics, but *Mars*. If any among you has a heart"—drawing a laugh—"something about the mission's medicine or biology aspects would be kind."

"Here's one," someone called from the back of the room. The name Ira Coleman, unfamiliar, popped up on the lectern. The accompanying media logo, beyond its New Age-y feel, also meant nothing to Dale. When someone gestured for her attention from the last row, she didn't recognize the face, either. He had horn-rimmed glasses and the neat, not-quite-a-beard, all-over stubble that took daily effort to maintain. He looked ... intense. "I've been talking with people." He stopped, staring at her, as though expecting a reaction.

"People. That's rather nonspecific." Earning Dale a few chuckles.

And one disdainful scowl. "The Planetary Protection Legions. PPL. People. NASA's sending a team to Mars in hopes of finding life there. How do we know a returning Mars mission won't put us at risk?"

Not so long ago, Dale had been the one preaching caution, but she'd convinced herself the risks could be managed. "Mainly, NASA seeks evidence there once was Martian life. Robots dispatched to the surface will first have been thoroughly sterilized to avoid contamination."

"Rightly so, Doctor, because People"—this time, there was no mistaking the capitalization—"*do* worry about contamination of another world. But that doesn't address *my* question. The Chinese mission, we're told, expects to stay on Mars. The contamination they'll cause goes only one way. Not so, NASA's mission. Anything interesting NASA rovers may encounter are to be returned to Phobos for hands-on analysis. The astronauts will, at the next return window, come home from Phobos."

"I wouldn't call it 'hands-on.' A robot will transfer any retrieved samples to a compact but well-equipped biolab"—still being prototyped, like so much else for the mission—"capable of reproducing various Martian environments. That could mean mimicking surface or subsurface conditions, or ice, or Martian aquifers. Samples in that containment can *only* be handled with mechanical manipulators or inside a glove box. The lab itself will be distinct from the habitat module. A trained mission specialist"—who for *damn* sure would have a Ph.D. in microbiology plus years of lab experience—"will perform the examinations. The detailed protocols"—like everything but the launch date!—"remain a work in progress, but they'll take into account—"

Coleman chuckled dismissively. "As if any Martian microbe or virus—adapted to the harsh radiation, the near vacuum, the desiccation—won't *also* survive on the outside of a sample container and on every robot and glove on Phobos that handles that container. As if those transplanted microbes won't thrive in the dust of Phobos through which your team will daily tromp. The dust they'll track into the habitat airlock, and then *inside* the habitat."

Out of the corner of an eye, she saw Lance wince.

Dale clenched the edge of the lectern to subdue trembling hands. "If there are Martian microbes or viruses—and I mean *today*, not ages ago, when there was an atmosphere and surface water—that would be a wondrous discovery. Even granting the possibility, such microorganisms or viruses must be quite different from life on Earth that we needn't worry about—"

"The same way coronaviruses couldn't jump from bats to humans?"

"Fix this," Lance hissed sotto voce.

Xander, bless his heart, ventured from the ISS, "I'm not expecting a lot of Martian bats."

Coleman ignored the dig and the ripple of laughter. "*I'm* referring to the possibility that neighboring planets might have related life forms. Something colliding with either planet can blast out debris that reaches the other as a meteor. Thirty-six years ago, President Clinton stood on the South Lawn to discuss possible fossils seen in a Martian meteorite.

"Can you say life on Earth didn't originate with some bacterium hitchhiking on a meteorite from Mars? Or that life on Mars didn't start with a meteorite from Earth? Or that life on both worlds didn't originate at some third place? Because if *any* of those were so—"

"I'll take your last scenario first." That was panspermia, the theoretical speculation that the seeds of life drift about the cosmos, here and there taking root. "True, a few simple organic molecules have been detected in interstellar nebulae. That's a far cry from *life* existing in …."

Text strobing on the lectern caught her eye. IF YOU'RE EXPLAINING, YOU'RE LOSING.

In the hyper-partisan environs of DC, those five pithy words were practically every pol's mantra. But she was a scientist, damn it! She was trying to talk about the science. (Uh-huh. Standing at a lectern in the White House, with *presidential* as the first word of her job title.)

"We have a winner," Lance boomed, in tones more stentorian even than usual. "Who in the betting pool had the lunar green-cheese theory of interplanetary contagion?"

She took offense at that triviality—but also the hint. "Apologies, folks, for dragging you down into the weeds. Suffice it to say that we're planning"—and I'll continue to do so—"to properly handle any traces that might be found of ancient Martian life, or even actual microbes that survived to the present day. Of course, we think the latter is improbable."

"Ancient doesn't mean *harmless*," Coleman rebutted. "Back in 2000, or so I've been told, dormant bacteria were recovered from deep underground." (Told by whom? Dale wondered. She didn't ask.) "Near Carlsbad, New Mexico. Crystallized in salt deposits. The thing of it was—"

"Follow-ups are one to the customer," Lance interjected, "and our astronauts need to get back to work. The good doctor here, likewise. We'll take one last question. I'll say … Glenn."

Glenn turned out to be Glenn Nielsen of the *Miami Herald*, and few things were as popular in Florida as the heaps of government cash spent every year on the state's so-called Space Coast. Hence Dale got to end on an upbeat note, agreeing that the Mars program *would* be good for the economy.

"Thanks, everyone," Lance said. "That's it for today. Do remember to get out the word about the mission-naming contest. If only my daughter submits, our Mars venture will end up called Milky Way."

Amid chuckles, she hoped unnoticed, Dale slipped out through the press room's staff door. She couldn't help brooding how matters would have gone had Coleman been allowed to continue. The Carlsbad-area bacteria—recovered from 1800-plus feet beneath the surface, dated to 250 million years ago—had been successfully revived.

Lance might have kept the Carlsbad anecdote off that day's evening news. Dale didn't doubt that, soon enough, the persistent Ira Coleman would get out his message. Never mind that—speaking in round numbers—Mars had lost its atmosphere four *billion* years ago. An innumerate pundit class that seldom looked beyond the next election cycle couldn't be expected to distinguish between four and a "mere" quarter billion years.

July 7, 2032

Teri had always considered Interplanetary Enterprises headquarters in San Francisco the epitome of posh. No more. Compared to the private suite to which she had been directed, IPE's executive offices were modest, verging on shabby.

The understated brass plaque beside the suite's primary entrance read NIELSON EDMUND PARETO. If not even Google knew anyone by that name? Soon enough, the world would come to know the monogram.

Teri still struggled to wrap her head around the knowledge that, by New Earth Partners standards, her boss was a parvenu. Fortunately for Blake, his associates needed spacecraft far more than money. As for *why* these moguls cared about winning the Mars race? In establishing a private presence on Mars? That was need-to-know, and apparently she didn't.

Once inside the partnership's as-yet undeclared headquarters, past the reception/security desk, she ambled about, exploring the sumptuous environs. The sprawling, high-ceilinged, open floor plan. The Persian carpet with a larger footprint than her *house*. Potted plants—rhododendrons, ficuses, cacti, the shortest of those a foot taller than she—scattered about. Two sectional sofas and four conversation pits. Huge wall displays, at that moment inactive, on the sound-baffling partitions that separated these pits. A collection of oils—Renoirs and Monets on two walls; Pollocks and (she guessed) Mondrians on a third—to shame many national galleries. As for the long, curving fourth wall, it was floor-to-ceiling glass, with a view ....

She caught herself gawking.

Compared to the Burj Khalifa, the world's sky-scrapingest sky-scraper, Blake's fifty-story pride and joy was a toy. On level 150, not quite at the tippy-top of this tower, she could see almost forever. The Strait of Hormuz, far below, sparkled a lovely turquoise.

For what might be the hundredth time, Teri wondered: How was she even considering leaving this beautiful world? Minimally, for years?

Except *considering* rather understated the state of affairs. She was neck-deep in making her departure possible. Also bone-weary from the effort. Now, after Blake's inexplicable insistence that she shift the final vetting of her latest pilot candidate, she found herself in, of all places, *Dubai*.

Video calls to orbit weren't cheap, but tough. She had five minutes until the interview. Jake should be rising soon for another day training those of the crew already selected. NEP's suite had world-class comm gear, and the tycoons would never miss the money.

On the sixth ring, Jake picked up.

The first glimpse of that handsome face set Teri beaming. The hairy chest emerging from the sheet had some of her other parts aflutter. She missed him, missed even the tiny, spartan, closet-sized personal quarters in which he floated. Emails and quickie calls aside, it'd been *months*.

"Hi, hon." How original.

He raised an eyebrow. "Well, this is unexpected."

The wife calling? "Good unexpected, I trust."

"Of course." He flashed the so-familiar toothy grin. "Dubai today, right? How is it?"

She leaned aside to reveal her sumptuous surroundings. "Observe how the thousandth of a percent lives. Jake, you wouldn't believe the view from here. This suite is like a third of a mile up. I'm pretty sure the haze I can see in the distance is the coast of Iran."

"Well, *I'm* three hundred miles up. I'm quite certain I can see Iran." He brushed sleep-tousled hair off his forehead. "Or I could, once I'm dressed and out of my cubbyhole. Oh, and when the station's come around to that side of the planet."

His cubby, not *theirs*. She let it slide. "How fare the new recruits?"

"Fine."

"Are you sure? I heard some hesitation." Which concerned her. Two of the mission specialists selected early and sent to Space Vegas for training had been space-flight virgins. "Even our *wunderkind*?" She being Paula Kelly, M.D. and microbiology Ph.D. Among the youngest winners ever of a MacArthur genius grant. The youngest so far selected for the crew. A mere thirty-five years old.

"All in your head. She'll be ready." This time, unambiguously, hesitation. "Promise."

"Let me know ASAP if we have a potential problem. We have alternates for a reason."

"Right. Anyway, thanks for the call, but this isn't a good time. I need to get up and out. No rest for the wicked and all that."

They'd been talking for maybe a whole minute. Thanks for the eff-ing call?

Was this petty retribution for their months apart? As though the mad dash to Mars had been her idea. As though *he* wasn't gung-ho on making the trip himself. As though running around the globe—and herself ragged—was by choice. As though expediting supply shipments and their launches to orbit, finalizing crew slots, keeping the consortium's partners sold on the billions of theirs she'd been spending and the billions more she *would* spend, all the while keeping the preparations secret, were some kind of lark for her. Not to mention how richly she and Jake would be rewarded if—no, *when*—they succeeded.

As though, come April, she and Jake wouldn't have as much togetherness as two people *could*, in yet cozier quarters aboard ship.

She shook it off. "Got it. Work calls. Here, too, anon. Love you."

"Me, too." He hung up.

She was still chewing on his tepid response when the building concierge called out to report that her afternoon appointment was on his way up.

Reuven Ben-Ami was tall by astronaut standards, desert-tanned. Wavy black hair and a thin mustache gave him a Rhett Butler air. His eyes, a pale blue, twinkled. If Dubai, metropolis of the United Arab Emirates, made him uncomfortable, the Israeli hid it well.

From the security station at the suite entrance, Teri led him to the conversation pit offering the most spectacular view of the city and toward the Gulf. "Take a moment to enjoy the scenery."

He gazed outward for a few seconds, nodded, then sat with his *back* to the glass. Because he, too, wouldn't admit to any vantage below orbital being noteworthy? Pilots!

"So, Reuven—"

"Reuben, please. Or Rob if you're in a hurry." He spoke English like an upper-crust Brit, which wasn't surprising for an Oxford grad. "Unless you speak Hebrew."

As close as she came was the occasional bagel. With, however heretical, grape jelly. "Reuben, then. Thanks for coming."

"Sure."

His credentials were impeccable, or he wouldn't have gotten this far. Aeronautical engineer with a minor in mechanical engineering. Had flown F-35s for the Israeli Defense Forces, followed by design work at the state-owned Israel Aerospace Industries. Currently flew orbital tourists for Space Ventures. Recommended to pilot the mission's second ship by, among many, Blake Wagner.

New Earth Partners made strange bedfellows.

The main thing on which the billionaires agreed was diversity. Across: their commercial empires. Countries and continents. Ethnicities. Picking a crew for the first trip to Mars *and* keeping the prima donnas happy? It was a nightmare. Without an AIde's assistance sifting the partners' many nominees, assembling candidate crews within those constraints would have defeated her. It might yet.

"Before we continue, let me remind you of your NDA." Nondisclosure agreement.

Reuben had the standard cocky, pilot grin. "Oh, the one where I'd forfeit my right arm and first-born child if I blab? Yes, that rings a bell."

She set a pen and another copy in front of him. "Then you won't mind signing it again."

"Fine." For all she could tell, his quick scrawl was Hebrew. "So, what'll I be flying to Mars, and how much does the gig pay?"

No lack of confidence here. "We'll be using IPE Moonships. You've never flown one."

"Doesn't matter. For one, I have flown spacecraft. We wouldn't be talking otherwise. For another, a trained monkey could launch from

Earth orbit to a Mars transfer orbit. The tricky part will be setting down on Mars, and *no one* has ever done that. You can call it a Moonship, but by the time the necessary retrofits are made, it'll be quite something else." He favored her with another of those devil-may-care grins. "Whoever you pick will spend much of the outbound flight doing rendezvous and landing sims. It might as well be me."

True enough, and doubtless Reuben was qualified to pilot the mission's second ship. Unquestionably, several partners would be happy for him to fill the seat.

Leaving the biggest, squishiest criterion: Would he fit in? The mission needed a *team*. She was selecting for competence *and* compatibility, for skills *and* savoir faire—under circumstances without precedent. However long an orbital or even Moon mission lasted, help and resupply were always, at least in principle, hours to a few days away. So how useful were the psych profiles and HR packets submitted along with resumes?

"Tell me a little about …"

Reuben's gaze had shifted to the side. She glanced over her shoulder—

At *Blake*. Striding toward them from some secluded interior area of the suite. Looking relaxed in khakis and an untucked tee.

Her detour to Dubai had begun to make sense.

"Reuven, right?" Blake said. "I'm going to borrow Ms. Rodriguez for a little while. While she and I chat, our chef will take excellent care of you."

As Reuben went off, Blake plopped into a seat. "How's he look?"

"Too soon to know." Hint.

"It's quite the cosmopolitan bunch you're assembling. Presuming Ben-Ami"—which, damn it, *was* presumptuous—"throw in a penguin, and you'll have all the bases covered."

"I know bosses have prerogatives, but I'm kind of busy. Why are we here, Blake?"

"Penguin. Antarctica." He shrugged. "Tough room."

"Right now, it's looking like four Americans and one each from Brazil, New Zealand, and Liberia. Plus the to-be-filled second pilot slot."

"About half and half." Blake rubbed his chin. "Same as the NASA and CMSA ventures."

"Uh-huh." It would've been hard *not* to be diverse, given the candidate lists the partners had submitted. Not that she had any cause for complaint: They'd all been qualified. Whatever else the partners had in mind, they took success seriously. "May I ask *why* you showed up here?" Why it required interrupting a critical interview?

"Do you get to see your family often?"

"Not much of late." Maybe because he had her running hither and yon around the world. Also … huh? Conversational whiplash.

"You should. I mean, you'll be gone a long while."

Right. In her copious spare time. "True enough."

"Your parents live … where?"

"Mom is in Madison, Wisconsin. My father left"—abandoned us—"ages ago. I have few memories of him."

"People should know their roots. You should reach out before you leave."

Uh-huh, and *you* should mind your own business. "I don't see it happening, not least because he went back to Mexico."

"But you were born in the US."

It wasn't even a question, as though he'd been checking up on her. She managed a fractional nod.

"Well, how many Rodriguezes can there be in Mexico? Anyway …." He trailed off as his datasheet rang. (Except *rang* fell short as a description. The ominous organ passage sent a chill down her spine. Or a touch of pique did. Rules, such as who could keep their devices with them, were for the little people.) "Sorry, Teri. I need to take this."

For perhaps thirty seconds, he listened in silence. "Well, it was inevitable. Frankly, I'm surprised we went this long. Thanks for the heads-up."

There was a TV remote in the drawer of an end table. He woke the nearest wall display. Beneath talking heads, a bold banner proclaimed: A CNN EXCLUSIVE!

"… the full composition of which is not yet known. To recap, if you are just joining us, CNN has learned that some number of the world's richest privately held companies have banded together to launch their own expedition to Mars. New Earth Partners claims their mission will arrive before the American or Chinese teams. Like NASA, this latest entrant to the Mars race plans to use, with modifications, Moonships made by Interplanetary Enterprises. We have reached out to IPE for comment. As yet, we have not heard—"

"In good time," Blake told the TV, even as he hit MUTE.

Teri's mind raced. Would public scrutiny make her job harder? Would an end to toiling in secret make it easier? For sure, it'd be *different*. "How do you suppose they found out?"

He moseyed to the glass wall and peered down at the city below. With a nod—to himself, to his own thoughts—he turned back to face her. "Best guess? A rejected crew candidate or supplier violating their NDA. Could be a subcontractor or two figured it out. It hardly matters. In a few weeks, when the DPA case goes to trial, it'd come out anyway."

She needed a moment to parse his second acronym: Defense Production Act. Having had nothing to contribute, she'd long since put the federal suit out of her mind. If Blake lost, game over. "What's the trial have to do with this?"

"Given the launch window, NASA's engineers need to be modifying their Moonships now." He turned back toward her, smugly grinning. "As we're doing now. We control the only ships NASA doesn't, so they've been suing under DPA to get ours."

"Still not following. What's the outing of NEP have to do with it?"

The grin got smarmier than ever. "To paraphrase a former president, it depends on what the meaning of the word 'we' is. Having sued IPE and me, the feds are about to learn the ships we control aren't ours. They're *owned* by NEP." His datasheet sounded again, this ringtone far less ominous. He swiped that call to voice mail. "Fewer than half the partners are American, so good luck suing NEP for the ships."

"What about Space Vegas? The utility shack where the upgrades are being done? If your company still owns those ...."

"Mission critical, and still mine." He winked. "All partners are equal, but some partners are more equal than others."

"Then the ships NASA wants remain under your authority. NEP or not, can't the feds still sue *you*?"

"Suppose they do, and they win. What's next? Sending the Marines to Space Vegas?"

Sure, she wanted to go to Mars. Of course, she wanted to be first. But these shenanigans? The scheming around the government. Her government. His, too. It felt *wrong*. "Aren't you worried they'll come after you personally? For contempt or something? Toss you in jail?"

He turned back to the glass. "Beautiful city. Also, as it happens, the emirates don't have an extradition treaty with the U.S."

An emotional dam … burst. Questions she'd only dared hint at, and that Blake had always deflected, came pouring out. "Why, Blake? Why is being first worth going to such extremes? Why not do the patriotic thing? Why not sell NASA the ships they want? You'd make a pretty penny, I'm sure."

"Some guy sold Columbus the *Santa Maria*. I suppose he got a few pesos, too." Blake turned to face her. "But what vast estates in the New World did that guy end up with? How much of the gold? Does anyone even remember who sold Columbus his ships?

"I'm not making that mistake. My friends won't, either. If you want to end up on the winning side, neither will you."

August 20, 2032

Mars Now

After national space programs first put men in Earth orbit, sixty years passed before private citizens followed. Once NASA put men on the Moon, it was again about sixty years until private industry did the same.

New Earth Partners see no benefit in repeating that pattern of dithering and delay. Let there be no misunderstanding. NEP will be the first to reach Mars, and we will see to it that humanity benefits.

—New Earth Partners press release

Vast seas of frozen lava. Range after range of towering mountains. Deep rilles snaking for hundreds, even thousands, of kilometers. Craters large and small, piled one upon another. If you knew where to look, the scattered, modest signs of human visitation.

None of these features were new to Xander. He was, like many a NASA employee, an astronomy buff. He owned a decent hobbyist telescope, though seldom—since Wu's speech, never—the opportunity to enjoy it. But streaking over this much-tortured moonscape? Taking it in with his naked eyes, a scant 3000 kilometers below? It was … mind-blowing.

With a sigh, he looked away. He had bigger fish to fry. Much bigger.

Xander was aboard the Moonship—recently renamed, after one of America's greatest explorers—*Meriwether Lewis*. Following the comparatively minor retrofits required for a Phobos rendezvous mission, *Lewis* had docked on its shakedown voyage at the Lunar Gateway station. If all went well, a second Moonship—renamed *William Clark*, of course—would receive the same upgrades. His presence aboard amounted to his own shakedown cruise.

Two months of immersive, sixteen-hours-a-day training aboard the ISS and the lunar-transfer vessel docked to it had left his brain near to bursting. Presidential endorsement notwithstanding, everyone on the as-yet-untitled Phobos mission had to pull their own weight. The generic-but-prospectively-life-saving drills in micro-gee maneuver, cabin-leak response, spacesuits, and EVAs were just the beginning. As the IT mission specialist, he was expected to understand—and, as necessary, to repair—every embedded microprocessor and computer aboard *Lewis*. It involved him in damned near every subsystem aboard the ship! Once he'd somehow mastered all that, the cargo manifest stabilized, and designs for the Mars landers and rovers got locked down, he'd have even more embedded computers to master.

All that, somehow, was the easy part of his job.

He half sat, half floated, loosely belted into *Lewis's* pilot's seat, where the arc of the flight console semi-surrounded him. Some LEDs blinked; others glowed steadily. Text scrolled on display panels. Things beeped, chirped, and chimed. While he monitored the various diagnostic programs—his contribution to preflight checkout for the scheduled return to Earth orbit—his crewmates, aboard the marginally more spacious gateway, schmoozed with astronaut buddies they hadn't seen in months.

Leaving Xander with a long-range comm capability—and a biometrically secured flash drive—to himself.

One morning in the blur that was the week before Xander left for Cape Canaveral and a flight to the ISS, Arthur Schmidt had summoned him.

From outside, the headquarters for the Office of the Director of National Intelligence, like the adjacent National Counterterrorism

Center overseen by the ODNI, might have been any nondescript metro-DC office building. Inside was another story. Passing through layer upon layer of security with a tight-lipped escort leading the way, Xander was deposited in the director's spacious office.

Schmidt stubbed out his cigar and emerged from behind his desk. Unlike at the White House, the DNI had shed his suit coat and loosened his tie. There might have been a soft grunt by way of pleasantries. "You know what a onetime pad is, Hopkins?"

Xander had read his share of spy novels. "Pre-shared, random, single-use codes for secret-key encryption. Messages encrypted with those can't be cracked if the keys remain secret."

"One more detail. For complete security, a message can't exceed the length of the key used to encrypt it." Schmidt took what looked like a flash drive from a pants pocket. "This is your copy. I have its mate. They share the same thousand very long keys. Those should be enough."

A *thousand?* Xander could hope the number was pure overkill—why *not* fill up the flash drive?—rather than an estimate for the number of hush-hush communications they'd be exchanging. "To communicate ... what, now?"

"That's the thing. We don't know what we don't know. What I *do* know is that something will come up. Something will go wrong. Something, don't ask me what, won't feel right. Something you'll need to communicate in private. Or something I will." He grimaced. "Which is why I'll also guarantee the other guys will fly with their own onetime pads.

"Meanwhile, my friend, you'll be in the thick of things. The president, for some reason, places a lot of stock in you. So, eyes and ears open. This"—finally, he handed over the flash drive—"assures that when that time comes, there'll be no delay, and no leak, getting your news bulletin to me. Through me, as needed, to *her.*"

After a review of the device's ultra-secure text/email/audiovisual app, setup of its biometric authentication measures, a test call, and several gratuitous admonitions to keep the drive secure, Schmidt sent Xander on his way.

NASA had provided the *Lewis* crew with new datasheets certified safe for netting with the spacecraft's comms console and, through that, with NASA's Deep Space Network. The same could not be said of the classified flash drive Xander carried everywhere. The app on it was supposed to work with (tunnel through? preempt? bypass? Arthur Schmidt refused to discuss the tech) every DSN-approved comm protocol.

With a shrug, Xander plugged the hush-hush flash drive into his datasheet. If the NSA's software had flaws, there was no hope for any type of secrecy.

On Xander's third try, the integrated fingerprint and pressure sensor recognized the authentication pattern of squeezes. While the drive's onboard app synchronized through the datasheet with the comm console, he sent an innocuous-but-crucial text: WE NEED TO TALK NOW. However invested Cruella was in winning the Mars race, her DNI had to have many other irons in the fire. Schmidt wouldn't be plugged in round the clock to *this* backchannel.

Two minutes later, the green LED on Xander's flash drive began flashing—his device and the DNI's had synched. The comm console awakened with a soft beep.

"Aren't you off gallivanting?" Schmidt asked. (Audio only, and with lossy compression: the less bandwidth they expended conversing, the fewer of their onetime encryption keys they'd need—and render thereafter useless.) "Never mind. What's going on?"

"Short version? I need you to pull strings and get our stay here extended by two days."

"Well, get on with—" Schmidt paused abruptly. Knowing where Xander was hadn't extended to remembering the light-speed comm lag. "Sorry. Continue."

A *red* LED blinked once on the flash drive. That marked one key gone forever, their secured conversation advancing automatically to the next. Maybe a thousand entries in the onetime pad *wasn't* overkill. A scary thought for another day.

Xander said, "You'll have seen the latest NEP broadside. It got me thinking." Worried. Anyway, *more* worried. "Their declared flight profile mirrors ours and CMSA's. Break Earth orbit April 17, the optimal departure date. Take the most fuel-efficient, six-month-ish transfer orbit to Mars, arriving October 26, thereby maximizing the payload and reserves they can carry. So, how are they so confident they'll arrive first?"

Maybe three seconds later, Schmidt laughed humorlessly. "You're just now imagining the possibility of sabotage?"

Jeez! Until that moment, the worst complication he'd considered was a lack of cooperation. After the fact, it had become obvious enough why IPE hadn't sold NASA any Moonships. Why the company continued to fight the government's invoking of the Defense Production Act. Why Blake Wagner had holed up in a nonextradition country. But sabotage? That could *kill* people.

"What are you thinking?" Schmidt prompted.

"Here's the thing. *Lewis* and *Clark* will need full tanks when they break Earth orbit. The *only* facilities capable of doing that are the IPE utility shack co-orbiting with Space Vegas and, once the Chinese finish their upgrade, Tiangong. I got to thinking, what if IPE finds a reason not to cooperate?"

Distinctive laughter penetrated *Lewis*'s closed hatch. Like his corny sense of humor, David Berghoff's guffaw was unique. The ESA pilot had flown shotgun to the Moon. He and Cat would trade seats on the flight back.

Xander could have used a good laugh.

Schmidt said, "At the risk of repeating myself, you're just *now* imagining that possibility? Remind me, who was it who discouraged upgrading the ISS as a fuel depot?"

"Do you remember my job before the president dragooned me? Who I worked for? What I did? The simple fact is the ISS was designed to last fifteen years, while we've used it more than twice that long. It's creaky. *Ancient*. Keeping it safe for habitation has been a challenge. Adding big cryogenic fuel tanks, and the infrastructure to support them, could damn well break it, and never mind"—another red flash—"the challenge of getting such retrofits completed on time. There's a reason why, a few years back, NASA supported IPE's plan for an orbital refueling capability."

"Didn't *Lewis* top off its tanks at Space Vegas a few days ago?"

Yes, and that proved nothing. If Wagner's company meant to throw a monkey wrench into the works, it'd come as a burst hose or broken valve at the last minute ("Oh, no! So sorry!") when the *real* flight was prepping to launch. Why tip their hand early?

But, just maybe, Xander had a workaround.

96

Another red flash. Was that the fifth? Sixth? Even with most of the keys left, the flashes made Xander feel rushed. Perhaps the LED blinked for that very reason.

"Here's the thing, Arthur. The Lunar Gateway is meant to become a fuel depot. Once the infrastructure is deployed aboard the gateway and below, it'll be way easier to refuel from lunar resources"—from primeval ice, trapped for eons in sunless craters near the poles—"than from Earth. Leaving from lunar orbit will burn less fuel than departing from near-Earth orbit." Next to the real benefit—having a trusted depot when they needed one—that smidgeon of efficiency was almost in the noise category. Still, for whatever reason, Schmidt fixated on every detail of the cargo, down to each ship's planned loading sequence. If a tad more payload capacity might seal the deal, all the better. "We could revisit the scaled-up biolab Dale's been pushing.

"I'm *almost* certain it can be pulled off in time for Mars launch. Not on the cheap, though, and NASA doesn't have the upgrade in its budget, nor even in the administration's Mars supplemental. Anyway, that's why I need a couple more days here. To confirm feasibility."

"Reaching Mars first? Embarrassing Wu? That's a national priority. We'll take what's needed from one black budget or another." Noise like the drumming of fingers. "I'll need to decide who deserves the hit for giving the president so little warning. I'm thinking CIA." More humming and *another* red flash. "I'll get you a few more days up there. But answer me this. Why do you trust the gateway's contractor any more than you trust IPE?"

"Trust has nothing to do with it. The gateway is a NASA facility, although Boeing-Mitsubishi operates it for us. We can keep an agency quality-insurance inspector aboard from now till launch." An assignment for which Xander already had three candidates in mind to propose to Rebecca. Each one with obsessive attention to detail.

"Moreover, every company behind NEP is said to be private. The few who have admitted to being in the partnership *are*. Blake Wagner and his ilk don't need to disclose what they spend and the risks they're taking. I don't see how a big publicly traded company"—and they didn't come any larger than B-M—"could get away with hiding a role in NEP."

Schmidt seemed to be chewing that over. Maybe literally chewing, given the ever-present cigar butt. "Legally, of course, they couldn't hide it. As a practical matter, I agree it would be difficult. That said—and if you quote me, I'll deny it—the SEC and IRS can be convinced B-M is due for audits of proctological thoroughness. But Xander …?"

"Yeah?"

"While you're poking about, give some thought to how best to detect freelance hanky-panky. The NEP types have more than enough money to hire themselves a saboteur there, too. Then, in your spare time, give some thought to how NEP plans to beat out the *other* team. The Chinese aren't dependent on IPE's fuel depot."

"It all looked so easy when you did it on paper—where valves never froze, gyros never drifted, and rocket motors did not blow up in your face."

—*Milton W. Rosen, rocket engineer*

"Anything that can go wrong will go wrong."

—*Murphy's First Law*

DEPARTURE

April 17, 2033

Impossible as it seemed, the day had arrived.

Teri floated in Space Vegas's grand micro-gee "ballroom," that transparent sphere bright with earthlight and crescent moonlight. Off the planet, at last. Removed, if only symbolically, from Blake's micromanagement. Literally and figuratively, a great weight had been lifted from her. Today, she told herself, we leave for *Mars*.

Both crews, *her* crews, floated around her. Ready to board their ships. Ready to make history. Suited-up per safety protocol, apart from helmets and gloves stashed in the nearby debarkation tunnel. As for the hotel's guests, they'd been banished to the station's gravity rings until after launch. They would still have a ringside seat for the launch.

"This is the last time we'll be together until Mars. Each of you is exceptionally qualified for our unique mission. Each of you is a trailblazer." A poke she hadn't been able to resist taking. The ceremonies were being broadcast, of course. The *Lewis* and *Clark* bunch would catch her reference, if not appreciate the humor. "I couldn't be more proud of, more confident in, every one of you."

Their voyage would be epic. This moment was ... extraordinary. Teri struggled not to grin like an idiot. Several of the team didn't even try. That Jake and Reuben were more somber, more composed? She could appreciate seriousness in her pilots. Julio Silva, their construction engineer, was wide-eyed in the realization: It *was* happening. As for Paula Kelly's obvious nerves, Teri chalked those up to a noob's pre-flight jitters.

"It's been a slog to get this far, yet our job isn't nearly done. It's only entering a new phase. You've taken your leave, for years, from family and friends. From all of humanity. And why? For the adventure, I expect. But more than that, to open an entire new world *to* humanity."

She kept from the vast earthly audience the crews' final motivation. They were being very well rewarded. If they didn't return, their families would be.

For a wonder, she was the one giving the pep talk. Blake had wanted—so much he could taste it—to be here, aboard his premier property, delivering the sendoff speech. But while her boss often seemed first among equals—without *his* spacecraft, this wouldn't be happening—his partners had insisted. Till the day all were willing to reveal themselves, the disclosed partners weren't permitted such grandstanding. Not that Blake was exactly suffering. Live-streamed from the Space Vegas ballroom, this video had to be the greatest free media ever.

Never mind that Teri still didn't understand how the NEP folks expected to recover, much less make a profit on, their massive investment. Martian tourism? Sherpa-ing scientists? She didn't see it. Then again, *Blake* was a self-made billionaire. *She* was a wage slave.

Teri gestured grandly toward the beautiful globe, blue ocean sparkling, white clouds gleaming, spread out beneath their boots. "The next time we get to enjoy this view, we'll be on our way to a hero's welcome and a ticker-tape parade.

"This is a quite different moment"—that line cueing a countdown clock to dramatically appear over the video feed—"momentous in very different ways. It's a time to take pride in how far we've come. To humbly acknowledge the challenges yet before us. To appreciate the gallant and forward-thinking actions of the New Earth Partners."

Her entire short speech had been previewed and argued over and wordsmithed by the partners and their media minions. But *gallant*, for chrissake? That bit of self-congratulatory hype had just popped up on the teleprompter. She hoped no more surprises had been slipped in.

"Above all, now is the time to make our way to *Bradbury* and *Burroughs*. May these illustrious names"—chosen for their lack of any national theme, never mind that both authors happened to have been

American—"honoring literary giants whose vivid imaginings of Mars have inspired whole generations, ever inspire *us*."

Translucent cables crisscrossed the ballroom. With a practiced nudge against the nearest cable, Teri launched herself toward the tunnel to the Space Vegas docking ports. One by one, with (again, scripted) cheers, the team followed her up the tube.

Cycling, two by two, through the ships' airlocks lacked drama; for a precious few minutes they were in a place free of cameras. As the countdown clock between docking ports dropped below three hours until launch, she and Jake were alone. Cocooned in bulky, less than huggable spacesuits, but alone.

Finally. Good lord, but the man was handsome. "Our last privacy for quite a while."

"About that. Change of plans, Ter."

Huh? "Tell me on *Bradbury*."

"That's the change. I'm taking *Burroughs*."

"I ... I ... don't understand."

"Reuben's agreed to switch with me. So Paula and I can stay together."

Had there been gravity, Teri's knees would have buckled, and the blood would have drained from her face. How? When? Most painful of all, *why*? She couldn't bring herself to ask any of those. "The plan is the plan, Jake. You can't switch ships. I won't allow it."

"What are you going to do, Ter? Ground me?" He ... *laughed*. At *her*. "Who do you suppose is mission-critical with the clock ticking down? The pilot or the passenger?"

She wanted to cry, or scream, or slap his smug face. Blake *would* insist the mission go forward. Which required two pilots *now*. Project management when they got to Mars? The long flight would offer plenty of time for someone else to study up on that. So, anyway, Blake and cronies would conclude. Which was why Jake had waited until the last instant to spring this on her. Unless she intended to get *herself* kicked off the mission and then doubtless fired; to alienate and enrage many of the richest people on the planet; to have her humiliation shared with the billions breathlessly watching, not just with the crew whose respect she must already have lost, that damned cheap skank among them ....

"I see you understand." Jake rapped on *Burroughs's* outer airlock hatch. "Ready, bro."

Reuben, when he emerged, had the decency to look embarrassed. Without a word, he headed up the short tunnel branch toward *Bradbury*. Numb, she followed.

People of Earth! Two great nations and their allies aspire this day to criminal negligence of existential proportions. An international consortium, a cabal of the world's greediest, undertakes to do the same.

What is their crime? Endangering whatever life may reside on our nearest planetary neighbor. Endangering, in turn, life on our own world. Endangering all of us. Endangering *you*.

Since soon after the missions to Mars were announced, we have made the case against this existential risk. Logic, alas, has had no effect. Nor prudence. Nor even warnings.

So let us speak yet more plainly. Humans must never set boot on Mars. Samples from Mars must never return to Earth. Admonition having failed, we will have recourse in *action*.

—*Communiqué of the Planetary Protection Legions*

Craning to his left and slouching in his acceleration couch, Kai peered through an open hatch onto *Zheng He*'s claustrophobic bridge and—whenever Zhao Jin's head, bobbing about as the pilot checked one readout after another, didn't block Kai's view—out the canopy at stars. Soon enough, and for months, there'd be nothing to see but stars. Contorting even more, Kai could glimpse the merest sliver of Tiangong, alongside which *Zheng He* remained docked.

Neither view merited the discomfort or the effort.

Chen Xiuying, seated beside him in the passenger cabin, was streaming the station's panoramic Earth view to her datasheet. In her place, he supposed he would have done the same. A mere month ago, Xiuying had yet to go to space. But if they dare not attempt the mission without a doctor and biologist, neither dare they bring someone who panicked—as Yang Yan *had* outside the station during what should have been a routine training exercise. For better or (in Kai's opinion) worse, medical qualifications had overshadowed space experience in selecting a replacement.

Xiuying was short and stocky. Widely spaced eyes gave her an expression of perpetual surprise. He might never have met anyone this intense—or humorless, as some of his colleagues put it in private. As if any of *them*, with scant weeks to prepare for any mission, much less *this* one, would have obsessed less over the masses of detail to be mastered. That Xiuying permitted herself a respite from studying mission materials? It went to show she was human.

Kai *didn't* take this opportunity to gaze digitally at Earth. As lovely as the home world could be from this altitude, no camera's view had ever done it justice. Anyway, his computer held many such images.

Instead, he sampled the latest worldwide media coverage of the Mars race, scrolling past yet more pretentious bluster from PPL. Puzzled in parallel with his web surfing at Colonel Zhao's recently having taken him aside. ("Always remember, Major. Should anything happen to me, you become the mission's senior PLA officer." True, because he would then be the *only* PLA officer. Duty-bound, Kai had to assume, to then hold to account whatever Martian hordes had assailed the colonel.) Replayed President Wu's proud proclamation, naming this mission Chìdì One. (After Chìdì, the traditional Red Deity. Translated for Western audiences, from the god's animal form, as Red Dragon. That Chìdì *also* translated as Red Emperor? Few at home would miss Wu's subtle self-congratulation.) Skimmed last-minute, emailed good wishes from his parents and colleagues in the taikonaut corps. Permitted himself a moment's annoyance at Li's parents' silence. When that palled, he began cycling among the station's views, *not* of Earth, capturing the final, pre-launch flurry of activity.

Throughout, the calm bridge patter reassured him that everything proceeded per plan.

From Day One, it had seemed impossible to be ready for this launch window. But within two hours, they *would* launch. Because, like some celestial ballet, the myriad steps of the hastily designed project—together with more improvisations than he cared to remember—had come together. Because necessity *was* the mother of invention.

Large external tanks for water, and for the liquid oxygen and liquid hydrogen to be produced from the water, lofted from Earth and integrated with the station. Electrolysis and cryogenic plumbing, ditto. *Everything* mission critical, the water for fuel production included, ferried up from Earth. Refitting of the ships. The quick loop around the Moon and back to Tiangong as a final checkout—the week before Xiuying's arrival. The final, exhausting loading of late cargo ….

That last, labor-intensive, contortionist task, Kai had no problem believing. He had the sore muscles still to remind him.

"It's unfortunate, don't you think?" Xiuying said abruptly.

"What?"

"Named after a failure." She gestured at his datasheet. The latest image to appear there showed a vessel nearby, juxtaposed against the Moon, backing away from the station with gentle puffs of its attitude jets. "It would have been better, surely, to honor success, as we and our Russian colleagues did."

India's giga-rupee investment had bought, besides a berth aboard *Gagarin*, the naming rights to the mission's cargo craft. ISRO had chosen to honor Kalpana Chawla, the first woman Indian astronaut—killed in NASA's 1986 *Columbia* shuttle disaster. Perhaps Indian culture had no equivalent to feng shui. Dear Li would have known. Antiquarian beliefs had fascinated her.

"It's just a name," Kai said. "I wouldn't worry about that."

Not with so many better reasons to worry. By their nature, space missions were complex—this one more so than most. No, more so than *any*. *Chawla*'s retreat from Tiangong was but the latest act in an elaborate choreography. Because hydrogen molecules were *tiny*. Because, no matter how advanced the composition of fuel-tank linings, traces of liquid hydrogen always escaped. Because geometry. Only the station's original pair of docking ports were within hose reach of the refueling module.

His datasheet switched views again. This camera saw *Gagarin* gliding toward the port *Chawla* had vacated. They watched *Gagarin* dock, watched spacesuited station crew attach to it the long, insulated hose from the station's liquid-hydrogen tank. In the background, *Chawla* came to a halt perhaps a hundred meters distant.

The point of view shifted once more, revealing *Gagarin* and *Zheng He* docked side by side. They watched yet another spacesuited figure jet alongside the latter, releasing the power umbilical and opening the cover over the refueling inlet. However minuscule the gain from topping off last, from tapping the station's electrical resources till the last practical moment, that benefit would accrue to the flagship.

"Tiangong, *Zheng He* is ready for final fueling," Zhao Jin announced.

From the bridge's other seat, Wu Mingmei added, "*Gagarin* reports their fuel adjustment is complete."

Kai powered down and folded his datasheet before stowing it in a nearby latching bin. (Xiuying furtively searched for a similar bin on her side of the cabin before doing the same. He pretended not to notice.) "But what *is* auspicious"—as though their discussion of ill-named ships hadn't been a good while earlier—"is Tiangong itself."

Because, by a fluke of nature, the optimal moment of departure from Tiangong came first. A good half hour before the NASA mission would leave their Lunar Gateway. More than two hours before the New Earth Partners mission would leave Space Vegas. No one could argue with orbital mechanics.

For a wonder, Xiuying smiled. "Every good omen is welcome."

"Topping off begins ... now," Zhao Jin called.

The faintest of vibrations transmitted through the hull told Kai the same. A few minutes of this, then decoupling, and they'd edge away to join *Chawla*. Minutes after, *Gagarin* would follow. Thereafter, a short while in formation, loitering until the ideal moment.

Whump.

The ship ... twitched. Outside the bridge canopy, the heavy refueling hose writhed like some giant, tormented snake. That spewing hydrogen was colorless, invisible, making the scene that much more surreal. All too real, between thumps as the thrashing hose bashed the hull, was the sudden faint hiss of what could only be hydrogen spewing from a damaged shipboard tank.

So much for leaving today for Mars.

As an alarm wailed, Kai couldn't help but brood. If *Gagarin* would launch for Mars without them. If the Russians had, somehow, caused this disaster. If there weren't something, anything, useful *he* could do while the station crew struggled to capture the hose and address whatever fault had set it loose. If the president regretted identifying himself so personally with this mission—and who would take the blame.

But mainly, Kai couldn't stop remembering PPL's latest pronouncement. It no longer seemed like bluster ....

❖ ❖ ❖

Strapped into the lone seat in *Lewis*'s main cabin, with nothing to contribute before launch but keeping quiet and out of the way, Xander ... surfed. When radio squawked on the bridge, or Cat responded to Mission Control, he made do with the closed captions.

"... been a slog to get this far, and yet our job isn't near to done. It's only entering a new phase. You've taken your leave, for years, from family and friends. From all of humanity. And why? For the adventure, I expect. But more than that, to open an entire new world *to* humanity."

He didn't quite hate Teri Rodriguez. Thought her priorities were screwed up. (Thought—no, knew—her hiding-from-extradition boss's were.) Thought it a damned shame the exploration of Mars had devolved to such an accident-prone rush, the first disaster having already occurred. Knew, logic, judgment, and any sense of self-preservation aside, that he envied her a little. Also, viewing her pep talk a second time, taking note of the smile dimples and the pert nose, seeing how the sky blue of her vacuum gear brought out the blue of her eyes, had to admit she was cute.

That last was a rather odd observation, given, well, lots of things. He resented her choices. She was married. They were, and would remain, literal worlds apart. But if his odd reaction suggested he was finally moving past Charlene, he'd consider it a positive data point.

Also, an immaterial one.

Cat and Sonny were discreet, but secrets were near impossible to keep in the cozy confines of the Gateway. Their mutual attraction was clear enough.

Anyway, the data to which he *should* be attentive were numerals on the bulkhead separating this cabin from the bridge. Twenty-seven minutes and change. Steadily decrementing as *Lewis* and *Clark* coasted to their departure point from lunar orbit.

"Ares One, this is Mission Control. Over."

Ares. As though what had grown into an international contest had been needed to come up with *that* name for a Mars mission. But with both ships named for American explorers, with ESA having, after NASA, the most skin in the game, major ruffled-feather smoothing had been in order. The Euro-mythological reference to Ares had done the trick.

"*Clark* actual, over," David Berghoff acknowledged.

"*Lewis* actual, over," Cat drawled. "Wishing us bon voyage, Mission Control?"

The long pause was … ominous. "We have a situation. Ares, RTB. Repeat, RTB. Over."

"Situation," Xander muttered under his breath. Understated NASA-speak could drive a person to distraction. A return-to-base order, *now*? This was serious shit.

On the bridge, Cat's voice went cold. "Say again?"

"I say again, RTB. Houston just sent the word. Half or more of your food could be tainted. Aboard both ships. Over."

"*Could* be? Well, *that* sure sounds definitive. We're supposed to RTB because, oh, I don't know, some PPL jackass made a crank call to NASA?"

Xander twitched. Longstanding NASA practice—subtext: we're a peaceful, civilian program—kept comms in the clear for the world to hear. As, doubtless, much of the world *was* listening. CMSA, NEP moguls, and Arthur Schmidt's spooks included.

"Well, Cat, how do you feel about salmonella? Because that's what's maybe hitching a ride with you. So says the FDA, not People." CAP-COM's voice took on an edge. "RTB, *over*."

Salmonella. It suddenly felt plausible. Some food-processing plant in Iowa or wherever would've been a *whole* lot easier to compromise than anything at the Lunar Gateway. And Tiangong's late-breaking mishap was scary enough ….

"What's the plan? Over," David said.

"Ares, this is Flight," a new voice cut in. (Clipped. Moreover, pissed. Bypassing CAPCOM? That happened, oh, once every decade or two.) "The plan? Offload everything from the suspect production lots. For good measure, lots for a few days on either side of those. Replace it all from Gateway food reserves—if the furious review Houston is or-ganizing doesn't declare those for any reason suspect. Get everything done before the launch window slams shut. Now, RTB. *Over*."

"Wilco, Flight." Cat said. "*Clark*, RTB. *Lewis* will follow in five minutes. Over."

"RTB, Wilco," David agreed, sounding, if possible, more stoic than Cat.

As *Lewis* was on its final, ignominious approach to the gateway, Xander couldn't help but wonder how this snag would go over in Washington. Beyond certainty that someone's head would roll ….

❖ ❖ ❖

After all the prep, after all the buildup, to actually set out from Space Vegas for Mars was … anticlimactic. Over with sooner than a launch to Earth orbit, while pulling fewer gees. The proverbial piece of cake.

Not the distraction Teri needed.

Nor, moments after the main engines cut off, no matter how welcome the confirmation, was Reuben's observation, "We're in the pipe, five by five." Cocky pilot-speak only evoked … cocky pilots. In both meanings of the word.

For all that, she couldn't help but cheer as her crewmates did. Seconds later, over their low-power comm link with *Burroughs*, others joined in. Two voices among them she did her best to tune out.

"Transferring a priority message back to you, boss," Reuben called over his shoulder.

Because, never mind the shotgun seat she'd long ago assigned herself, Teri couldn't bear to sit cheek-by-jowl with Reuben. He had chosen friendship with Jake over loyalty to her and to the mission. At her gesture upon boarding, Julio had scurried forward to occupy the window seat, empathetic enough to switch places without comment.

The message, other than identifying Mission Control in its header, didn't open. With a sigh, she plugged a flash drive with its onetime pad into her datasheet.

It was from Blake. Who else? FLAWLESS. WELL DONE. YOU MUST BE FEELING GREAT.

If he only knew. THANKS.

WHAT YOU MIGHT'VE BEEN TOO BUSY TO KNOW? There followed gloating over CMSA and NASA glitches.

BLAKE, REALLY, I GOTTA GO. THINGS TO DO HERE.

Rendezvous with *Burroughs*. Tether the ships to spin up for gravity. Get her head on straight. Get her game face on. People were depending on her. *Lives* depended on her. Even if two of them were a cheating bastard and a skank. The mission couldn't work without everyone.

LESS THAN YOU THOUGHT. WAIT A WHILE BEFORE TETHERING. MAYBE A FEW DAYS.

Huh? She tapped in, WHY?

INSURANCE.

Teri twitched. She saw only one reason to delay: another engine burn. A burn that would get them to Mars a bit earlier—but at a cost. WE HAVE A FUEL RESERVE FOR *EMERGENCIES.*

110

THE OTHER GUYS HAVE DECLARED RESERVES, TOO—
ASSUMING THEY LAUNCH. THEM MAYBE CATCHING UP?
I'D CALL THAT AN EMERGENCY.

She wanted to scream. At Jake, foremost, but that wasn't an option.
Blake was next best. Because this directive hadn't come on a whim.
She couldn't fly a spacecraft herself, but she'd been married to a pilot long enough (For how much longer? She tamped that question
way down) to know orbital mechanics was complicated. Someone had
been running the numbers to see what the fuel reserves on hand could
manage. Leaving *her*, supposedly in charge, in the fucking *dark*.

THIS IS THE *LAST* SURPRISE, she typed. BECAUSE IF
THERE'S ANOTHER, THE WORLD'S GOING TO LEARN WHO
ALL THE NEP PARTNERS ARE.

For a wonder, the response was … no response. Until finally—
UNDERSTOOD.

"Reuben," she called forward. "We're deferring rendezvous for now.
Call over to *Burroughs* and advise them.

"Copy that."

As anger simmered, Teri kept telling herself that first woman to set
foot on Mars remained a prize worth striving for.

April 19, 2033

A Time for Action

People of Earth! For more than a year, urgently and often, we have addressed you on the dangers inherent to Martian adventurism. Many have listened, have added their voices to the chorus demanding a halt to all such recklessness.

And still, governments and plutocrats proceeded in haste with their irresponsible plans.

Until, admonitions having failed, we warned.

Those warnings, too often, also fell upon deaf ears.

Two of the three missions have already failed. Think about that.

—*Communiqué of the Planetary Protection Legions*

Kai tapped Wu Mingmei on the shoulder of her spacesuit.

Even that gentle touch set her drifting. With practiced nudges against *Zheng He*'s hull, she arrested her motion, then turned.

He briefly tilted his head and closed his eyes, miming sleep, before raising two gloved fingers. *Give me a couple minutes.*

Winded, and looking wearier even than he felt, she nodded agreement. Human limitations aside, no one dared be overheard discussing any respite. Not with the eyes and ears of the nation, and more, of the *world*, upon them.

Kai chinned a release lever in his helmet, dispensing another Modafinil lozenge. His third? Pretty soon, not even stims would keep him going. Then again, if the repairs weren't finished soon, it wouldn't matter.

For all his exhaustion (or, perhaps, because of it), their situation felt unreal. Catastrophic bursting of the station's liquid-hydrogen pump, and cascading failures, were certain enough. If, in the moment, he couldn't have envisioned such a disaster, imagination was no longer required. At the end of his short tether, the blowout of *Tiangong's* recently completed refueling depot was unmistakable. The consequent damage to *Zheng He*, as well, its hull looking as if it had stopped a shotgun blast.

But *how*? Faulty material, perhaps. A faulty component from any of the numerous parts vendors. Faulty assembly of components by the pump manufacturer. The merest instant of inattention while packaging, launching to orbit, or installing the pump. Because at every step along the way, here and on the world below, the demands to Get It Done had been relentless. To shortchange one's usual tests because any problem would be detected by someone responsible for testing at a later stage? The temptation must have been irresistible.

Or some ill-timed, unfortunately aimed speck of meteoroid or manmade space junk could have done the deed. Or simple bad luck.

Or, of course, sabotage.

China Daily had already "speculated" at treachery. A near-accusation like that, posted by a propaganda organ of the Party itself, must have been approved at the highest of levels. If Kai had had to guess, by the president himself.

Realistically, the incident's cause might never be known. The pump fragments necessary to establish the truth of the matter could well have blown into space amid the cloud of debris and the gushing, evaporating fuel. Which hadn't stopped *China Daily* from railing about "Western extremists and the hegemonic power that permits them to run rampant."

How was that theory supposed to reconcile with the West's own mission problems? Kai knew better than to ask.

Whether from wishful thinking or the stim, he began to feel more alert. He pointed at a dimpled and punctured hull panel. Again, his shipmate nodded. As they removed the panel to inspect the damage beneath, he knew he could have done worse than having Mingmei out here with him. Beyond her years of taikonaut experience, she was a mechanical engineer. He hadn't expected that expertise to be useful until Mars. Well, it wasn't the first mistake he'd ever made. It wouldn't be the last.

Still, given the choice, he'd have preferred Nikolai Antonov. The dour Russian pilot was likewise an old hand and an engineer. And if not the colonel, Kolya was at least brawny. It was hard to imagine Mingmei, no matter how indomitable her spirit, continuing much longer.

"Let's get this damned thing off," Mingmei radioed.

"Roger," Kai agreed.

Many small, recessed bolts secured each panel. Removing those was the least of the task. Positioning and stabilizing oneself was the more onerous chore. But bolt by bolt, through a thick protective glove, he felt the whirring motor of his recoilless power wrench.

Mingmei, still uncomplaining, looked ready to pass out.

What was that expression of his mother's father? Right. Distant water does not put out a nearby fire. The Russians, watching through the canopy of *Gagarin*, weren't physically remote, but they might as well have been. Since the mission abort, stubbornly, they had remained aboard their vessel. As though their compatriots might otherwise have made off with their ship.

Not that Kai knew Beijing wouldn't have ordered that. Or that the Russians wouldn't have departed on schedule had not Tiangong's quick-thinking commander locked the docking port's mechanical latch to *Gagarin*.

Leaving no one to chase after the NEP ships.

Meanwhile, as the transfer window began to close, the fuel requirement—if they even *could* refuel—crept up. Meanwhile, President Wu himself insisted that China's mission *would* launch. That they *would* yet be the first to the Red Planet.

Returning ignominiously to Earth after the transfer window slammed shut wasn't an option. Leaving the desperate expedient that mission planners in Beijing had somehow concocted.

Which was why he and Mingmei, well into their third change of oxygen tanks, were still out here. Why their crewmates, with some of Tiangong's crew, were as busy improvising a way to refuel and scavenge parts from *Chawla*.

April 20, 2033

Next question, please. Next question. *Next damned question!*

Dale, her heart pounding, sat bolt-upright in the dark. She had a vague sense or memory of … shaking.

Bed. Bedroom. Her nightstand clock read 2:08.

"Hon! Are you okay?"

She looked down at her husband. The concerned expression clashed with adorable, sleep-mussed hair. What he had left of it. "Fine. Go back to sleep, Patrick."

"I will if you *can*."

"That's the plan." Without admitting to a lack of high hopes. She'd had too much practice of late at dissembling. "Just a bad dream, hon."

"Uh-huh. What about? To which I expect, if I may quote someone, the answer will be, 'Next question.'"

"You got me." She willed hands to stop kneading a wadded edge of blanket. "Pressers at the White House. Not my favorite thing."

"Nor anything you signed up for." He propped himself up on an elbow. "So maybe let someone else do them. Maybe, I don't know, I'm spitballing here … the press secretary?"

"As though Lance could discuss the dangers of salmonella, especially among people sharing a smaller space than our master bath. Or the uncertainties of how symptoms might present in micro-gee, or

Martian gravity. Or the limitations of the primitive, onboard cooking facilities to handle contaminated food."

"Uh-huh. How many of today's questions involved medical minutiae?"

"You never know what will come up," she deadpanned. Salmonella humor.

"Allow me to repeat, why *you*? Why not the person the media *really* wanted to hear from?"

Which was the president. Who had had no interest in being grilled. Who could claim, and *had* claimed, being too busy for comment beyond a (platitudinous) written statement: that the mission had been delayed out of an abundance of caution. All hands were on deck. Every effort was being made to resolve the problem—if, in the final analysis, there was a problem. Every effort would be made to ensure mission success.

"Short answer, sweetie? Bosses have prerogatives." And Cruella wasn't shy about exercising hers. Or about anything, for that matter.

Leaving Dale the stuckee to dodge endless speculations. Given PPL's recent threats, could *they* have been behind the problems? (I have no reason to believe that.) What about NEP? (Same.) China or Russia. (Ditto.) *Can* NASA get its mission out the door on time? (As though she would contradict the president.) Question after question she was the wrong person to field—but planted behind the lectern, she suspected, precisely for her sincere ignorance.

But the most cutting of questions were those Dale could have been expected to answer. What, *exactly*, does the government know about a salmonella threat? *How* do they know? The answers to which she'd struggled to obtain before the inquisition began.

Rebecca Nguyen, in charge of NASA's manned missions, could only cite an anxious outreach from the FDA. Aaron Tanaka, administrator of the FDA, referred Dale to his agency's inspector general. The IG played her a recorded snippet from an anonymous tip line: of a self-described railroad worker reporting a refrigerator car, designated for expedited transit through to Cape Canaveral, standing for hours in the rail yard while displaying a high-temperature alarm. That, and only that, as best she could ascertain, had led to the last-minute mission delay.

It didn't take a medical degree to know traces of salmonella and E. coli were nigh unto ubiquitous, sanitation processes notwithstanding, and that with a loss of refrigeration, such pathogens would prosper.

Nor did it take a medical degree to place a crank call.

Anxious, if determinedly uninformed on the latest legalities governing domestic surveillance, she'd contacted Arthur Schmidt. Scant minutes before the presser was due to start, the DNI had called back.

In circumlocutions slicker than anything Dale ever hoped to achieve, Arthur alluded to analysts associating the metadata for the anonymous call with a South Carolina diner's landline. He'd confirmed some Ares One mission food shipments *had* passed through a nearby rail yard. (Feverishly multitasking as they spoke, she'd confirmed daily highs temps in the nineties—thanks, global warming?—throughout the area the entire mid-March week in question. Those temperatures, loss of refrigeration, *and* sunlight beating down on a metal railroad car? Not good.) Then, with the glibbest indirection of all, he'd validated her suspicions about the questionability of even having an answer for her.

Leaving her cursed with inventing new ways to attribute matters to "credible sources." Silently questioning her use of the plural. Wondering how credible was her standard for *credible*. All while deflecting efforts to pin the blame, without evidence, on assorted foreign, plutocratic, or planetary-protection-extremist villains.

But if the lengthiest fraction of her ordeal had boiled down to, "How certain were you of a danger to the crew, and why?" it was another question, the presser's closing question, that haunted her. That had—screaming, apparently—jolted her awake.

"Maybe the planetary-protection folks have a point," NBC's White House correspondent had said. "It seems we can't guarantee even the safety of food prepared on Earth. How can NASA, or anyone, claim they can shield humanity from a possible Martian pathogen?"

Xander "swam" back and forth across the Lunar Gateway's habitation module. It was about as satisfactory by way of exercise as would have been running laps in a closet. The mindless activity proved equally as ineffective at clearing his mind.

Both ships uselessly docked at the gateway bore the names of early heroes, but it was a yet earlier American icon whose most famous aphorism—"Guests, like fish, begin to smell after three days"—the

117

station's crew seemed to have internalized. Or maybe the locals worried about the Ares mission's bad luck tainting their food. Which, grumbling suggested, was also suspect.

Whatever the reason, Xander's offers to help unload and survey the Gateway's pantry had been politely rebuffed. This latest work shift, not even politely. Given the double shifts and worse these guys had often pulled the past three months to be ready—futilely, as it turned out—to serve as a fuel depot, Xander couldn't fault their misplaced anger. In the case of him personally, not even misplaced.

Sun Ying semi-emerged, gopher-like, in the open airlock of the docking port where *Lewis* remained berthed. "May I join you? I'm persona non grata, too."

CSA's representative—physician, biologist, and nutritionist to the Ares mission—rivaled Xander in the frustration department. Not that she wasn't eminently qualified, but (Becks had let it slip) the tiebreaker on the Canadian's selection—Sonny's parents both being Hong Kong expats—had been the figurative poke in China's eye. Maybe Sonny suspected as much. Whatever the reason, she'd taken personally the RTB order without a chance for any of them to comment.

"Of course." Coasting to the end of a lap, Xander grabbed a hand-hold. For sure, *two* people ought not to bounce around the module at the same time. "Now, what's bugging our hosts?"

"An excess of candor?" She smiled sadly. "I opined that a shipload of new, space-ready food can't be prepped, transported to Cape Canaveral, sent here, and transferred to *Lewis* and *Clark* in time to do any good."

"Yet we haven't been recalled."

Cat and *Clark*'s three crew were on that ship, killing time with a movie on someone's datasheet. The soundtrack had long since identified their selection as *Casablanca*. That made the sudden laughter … confounding.

"Right," Sonny said. "My prediction? So that the prep and invest-ment isn't a *total* loss, we'll be sent off to do something else. On the Moon, maybe. If we're lucky, it'll be a near-Earth asteroid excursion."

"Could be." The sad truth of it? Not that long ago, participating in either of those undertakings would've seemed a grand adventure. Now? It would be only a poor consolation prize. "At least, that'd ex-plain Houston's ongoing advice that we be patient."

"Which you're *so* good at."

He would've agreed, would've laughed at himself, but more cackling preempted it. Puzzled, Xander launched himself toward the open hatchway to *Clark*. Definitely *Casablanca*. Definitely *not* a comedy—

Until the scene changed to show Rick and Ilsa. Who, rather than Bogie and Ingrid Bergman, were … Jim Carrey and Lucille Ball. Speaking in those voices, too. The most egregious recasting of all? Capt. Renault, when *he* entered the scene, was a cigar-chomping Groucho Marx.

David Berghoff—given his hobbies, the likely architect of this travesty—had much to answer for.

With a sigh and a gentle shove, Xander backed away. Digitally remaking movies had to be the most perverse waste of computing power since NFTs.

"So," Sonny said. "What's your bet? Moon, asteroid, or slinking home with nothing to show for our efforts?"

Xander shrugged. Wondering, for the umpteenth time, what the hell Arthur Schmidt had meant by his last secret, cryptic text: KEEP YOUR POWDER DRY.

While fretting, again courtesy of Ben Franklin, that *lost time is never found again.*

Even as acceleration squeezed Kai, he experienced a rush of feelings. He was pleased. Proud. Exhausted. More than a little amazed. In every instance, with good cause. Because against all odds, *Zheng He*, alongside *Gagarin*, had launched before their goal receded beyond reach.

Just before.

And so, another part of that roiling stew of emotions: anxiety. This had ceased to be a mission to which anyone had signed up.

Chawla, stripped of vital parts, drained of its fuel, had been left behind. The fuel pump the now-crippled cargo vessel would have employed on Mars, and the load of fuel meant to propel it there, might yet save the day.

Tools and supplies of every sort had been offloaded, slashing cargo mass and fuel requirements. They would, Mission Control blithely asserted, learn to do more with less. (Removing caged lab rodents and years' worth of their food pellets? *That* Kai had accepted without objection.)

119

Even that was not nearly enough.

Absent *Chawla*'s fuel-producing module as a backup, a lengthy sojourn on Mars morphed from geopolitical posturing to a high probability of being stranded. That harsh reality suggested a new "opportunity." If they couldn't get crops to grow on Mars within a year, the odds were they never would. Why, then, prolong the inevitable? So, half their food had been offloaded.

Nor were even those economies sufficient, so already minimal personal-effects allowances were cut to squeeze a few more kilograms from their departure mass.

That *still* hadn't been enough.

Sometime before they arrived, a new landing zone would be chosen for them. Its lower elevation—wherever that turned out to be—would offer a slightly thicker atmosphere, making their parachutes slightly more effective. Because every gram of fuel savings helped.

Fuel *reserves* were that much more unproductive mass to lug around. Better to use them. And so, in scant minutes—once the ships attained the suboptimal Mars transfer orbit still available to them, once their engines cut off—fuel reserves would be down to almost nothing.

Still, if nothing else went wrong, *Zheng He* and *Gagarin* would land on Mars two full days before the NEP vessels. That prospect added gratification to Kai's emotional stew.

But what were the odds nothing else would go wrong?

April 21, 2033

Tap, tap.

Had Teri been able to sleep, she might not have heard that gentle knocking on the flimsy, pull-down door of her coffin-like personal compartment. But suspense, waiting for Blake's other shoe to drop, had rendered sleep a foreign concept.

At least that worry distracted her from picturing Jake and Paula together in another cozy compartment.

Tap, tap.

"Yes?"

"I'm so sorry," came the soft, lilting response. Islah, of course. Until they were properly on their way, someone would man the bridge around the clock. Most recently, it was the Liberian chemical engineer's turn on third watch. "Dirtside wants you. Said to check your messages."

With a groan, Teri woke her folded datasheet. Its clock read 3:37—ship's time. Greenwich Mean Time. In Dubai, it'd be four hours later, and who but Blake would be bugging her now? He bragged about needing only four hours of sleep a night and refused to understand that most people needed more.

Well, shit. In point of fact, she hadn't been sleeping.

"Thanks, Islah."

She found an OTP-encrypted message. So, yes, from Blake. Received all of fifteen minutes before. Her onetime-pad app unlocked it. CMSA LAUNCHED A FEW HOURS AGO. SANS CARGO SHIP.

A DAY LATE AND A DOLLAR SHORT. Metaphorically, anyway. Really, more like four days. Hitting SEND, Teri told herself to be patient, the comm delay to/from Earth already approaching a half minute. By the time they caught up to Mars, the light-speed roundtrip would be more like twenty-two minutes. Any interaction but texting was impractical.

YOU WISH. THEY'RE ON A TRANSFER ORBIT TO HAVE THEM ARRIVE OCTOBER 24.

The fuel-efficient, cargo-maximizing course her ships were on—that all three missions had claimed they'd use, would get them to Mars on October 26th. But the 24th? Between the late departure and the earlier arrival, the Chinese had to have cut payload and safety margins alike to the bone. Maybe to the marrow.

If only to postpone the obvious, she answered neutrally: OKAY, THANKS FOR THE UPDATE.

YOUR TURN, TERI. LEAPFROG THEM. MY ANALYSTS SAY HALF YOUR RESERVES WILL DO IT.

THEN WHAT? THEY BOOST AGAIN, AND THEN WE DO? UNTIL MAYBE NO ONE HAS THE FUEL FOR A SAFE LANDING?

Did she have the balls to refuse Blake? If she did, would it matter? He could go over her head to the pilots. Maybe only she shared a one-time pad with him, but there was no way anyone could intercept comms from Earth *to* their ships. Somehow, she didn't see Jake or Reuben denying the request as long as they could retain *some* fuel reserve.

Threaten to play her trump card? What if Blake called her bluff? Was it a bluff? If not, what was her encore? She'd not reached a conclusion on any of those questions when another text arrived. NOT TO WORRY. THEY'VE SPUN UP.

That changed things.

If the past few years had kept her immersed in program management, staffing, and even running a hotel, she was, damn it, still an engineer. She'd have understood even if Space Vegas hadn't had spinning rings to provide the hotel's long-term staff—and the occasional customer who couldn't adapt to micro-gee—with artificial gravity.

Her modified Moonships—and NASA's, had they gotten out of the starting gate—were single-stage. One piece. For simulated gravity during the long flight, *Bradbury* and *Burroughs* would tether nose to nose, then use attitude jets to slowly uncoil the tether and begin the tandem rotating. It'd involve a brief spacewalk. Big deal.

CMSA's approach was closer to the old Apollo program. To and from lunar orbit, Apollo had flown a crew portion mated to an un-pressurized service module. They jettisoned the service module before reentry into Earth's atmosphere. Each Red Dragon vessel like-wise had two sections: an integrated command/landing crew module and a disposable booster. *Their* spin gravity relied on a tether between the module and booster. On final approach to Mars, explosive bolts would sever the tethers, flinging away the boosters. The crew mod-ules would then land.

For CMSA's mission to reboost *now*? First, each crew module would have to re-mate with its booster. Did they even have a docking mechanism? To launch from Tiangong and then separate, all they'd needed were simple, low-mass, explosive bolts.

If, somehow, the module/booster pair *could* dock, there remained the issue of the deployed tether. A crew module could readily enough *un*wind a long tether: use its attitude jets to ease away from the booster with a simple, free-spinning reel. Rewinding tether for redeployment would seem to require a more massive, motorized reel. Why would they have had such a thing?

Even granting the necessary equipment, the reboost scenario struck Teri as an accident waiting to happen. CMSA couldn't be *that* crazy. Could they? Or nuts enough to jettison tethers, forging artificial gravity to gain a few days? *That* expedient would deliver their crews to Mars effectively crippled.

So, yes. This news changed things.

Teri wrote, *HALF* OUR RESERVE? YOU'RE SURE? AND IT'S CERTAIN *THEY'VE* SPUN UP?

YES TO ALL. THAT LAST IS PER OUR SOURCES WITHIN ROSCOSMOS AND ISRO.

She didn't doubt NEP could afford a few bribes for the inside scoop. FINE. SEND ME THE NEW NAV PARAMETERS.

Because to be merely on time is to be late.

April 28, 2033

Untainted supplies from Earth. Finally.

Also, too damned late. The Mars transfer window was closed. Glued solid. Nailed shut for good measure. Why bother sending replacement food *now*? If for some new destination, the Ares crews remained in the dark.

The craft on final approach to the Gateway was the repurposed topmost stage of a heavy-lift expendable launch vehicle. Normally, the Space Force used its ELVs to loft big, classified payloads into low Earth orbit. It couldn't carry more than a few tons to *lunar* orbit. A single such delivery? Xander saw no way it could make any meaningful difference.

Day after day, he'd run mission sims. What else had he had to do? As of days ago, draining the ships' tanks bone-dry—forget holding back any reserve—would no longer have sufficed. Next, he'd modeled reducing their payload by abandoning some Mars landers and their rovers. Never mind losing the damned Mars race. Halving the mission payload could no longer get *Lewis* and *Clark* to Phobos and home again, much less accomplish any useful science.

Yet even that morning, Arthur's daily secure text had amounted to *it'll be okay.*

Clark had backed away from the Gateway an hour earlier, freeing a docking port for unloading the ELV. This wasn't a first for *Clark*. It had briefly undocked two days before, making way for a robotic water tanker from NASA's ice-mining base near the lunar south pole. Producing the liquid hydrogen and oxygen still uselessly aboard the Ares vessels had depleted the Gateway's water reservoir.

"I've assumed control of our inbound," Barney Gomez, the station commander, announced. "Should be within arm's reach in five."

Five minutes, that meant. *Arm* was the station's giant robotic limb, aka Canadarm, used to snag any incoming vessel incapable of docking itself. In this case, use of the arm reflected that neither NASA nor the military cared to attempt first-time automated docking with a new spacecraft type.

"Copy that," Cat drawled from *Lewis's* bridge. "We'll get into position."

Sonny and Xander had been waiting, idly afloat, inside the ship's main cabin. They exited to the station, Sonny stopping in the hab module, Xander continuing the few meters to the docking port vacated by *Clark*. Cat, meanwhile, would have taken up a position in *Lewis's* open airlock.

"Okay, the bucket brigade's in place," Cat called.

Forget a brigade. The three of them didn't amount to a half-assed bucket *squad*. Xander had lost interest, part way through Mission Control's gobbledygook excuses, why the station contractor wouldn't assist. Something about nonunion workers having loaded the cargo, or cargo arriving aboard a non-NASA spacecraft, or unplanned overtime. Maybe it was the lot of those.

From Gomez on down, the station contractors denied understanding—not that they minded a pass on schlepping the few tons of groceries. They'd been spacers quite long enough to experience the difference between weight, or lack thereof, and inertia.

"Three minutes out," Gomez updated. "In the pipe."

Impending stevedore duty did nothing to alleviate Xander's frustrations. Maybe nothing could. He'd racked his brain for a way out of this fiasco. Becky and all the NASA resources at her disposal had, too. The nuttiest idea had to have been transferring most of the mission cargo to a water carrier like the one on its final approach. Only it, aside from propulsion and guidance, was nothing but a big water tank, heating elements to keep the water from refreezing, and plumbing. Retrofitting a hatch and enough decking and lockers for the mission's bulky cargo? Yet again, an impossibility before Mars receded out of reach.

A possibility that might yet work was commandeering NASA's final two Moonships and splitting the mission's payload over *four* vessels. Given how the Defense Production Act case against IPE was crawling through the courts, as Blake Wagner's people did everything possible to run out the clock, that would mean abandoning the Moon and, with it, NASA's many international commitments. Even the president was unwilling to do that.

Leaving … squat. So, what the *hell* was this piddling delivery expected to accomplish?

"Got it," Gomez called. "I'll have your groceries docked and latched right about … *now.*"

The merest of vibrations signaled the cargo ship's arrival. A status lamp turned green to show secure docking. As Xander opened both the docking port's airlock hatches, frigid air spilled out.

"Xander, what do you see?" Cat called out.

"Bags and boxes." Wedged in every which way, everything in opaque shrink wrap. "Behind those, I assume, more bags and boxes. Unloading will take a while."

With the first several boxes he touched, inertia confirmed the bad news on the labels. To replace some of the mission's shelf-stable, more or less edible (when not tainted) provisions, this was freeze-dried crap as if from the Stone Age of space travel. Maybe it *was* from that Stone Age. Sure, the swap would eliminate some water mass—replaceable from the ice they expected to mine on Phobos—but again, too little reduction to get them there and back.

Then, in the bowels of the cargo hold, Xander encountered a stack marked ASSORTED FREEZE-DRIED VEGETABLES—its massive inertia proving the label to be a blatant lie. He found three more disguised items behind the first.

Someone had gone to a lot of trouble to get these, whatever *these* were, to the mission. Camouflaged. Aboard a Space Force craft. Off-limits to the Gateway contractors.

Even before the folded datasheet in Xander's pocket emitted the distinctive trill he'd assigned to incoming secure messages, he felt certain he knew which wily old bastard had been behind this. Well, if Arthur hadn't trusted CMSA and NEP to stick to their announced mission timelines, he'd only been right.

Xander just wished that sneaking these … things onto the Gateway, and clearing mass budget for them aboard *Lewis*, hadn't entailed the sacrifice of so much doubtless *un*tainted food.

May 3, 2033

This is insane, Xander thought. Followed by, I'm going to freaking *Mars!*

The semi-cryptic, pilot-to-base chatter somehow made the final minutes before launch crawl. Alone in *Lewis's* main cabin, Xander distracted himself as best he could. First, securing his helmet nearby before settling into the cabin's lone acceleration couch. Then with *Lewis's* external cameras, offering views in every direction. Of the Lunar Gateway: still impressive, even a good half-klick astern. Of *Clark*: likewise glittering in sunlight, a mere fifty meters to starboard. Below, as the ships swept along their orbit: a brief glimpse of perhaps the Moon's youngest crater. Where bright rays of fresh ejecta converged, whatever classified technology the expendable Space Force spacecraft once carried had been obliterated. And forward—

Xander *really* didn't much like his view forward.

He tried orbital mechanics. Done in his head, even approximating furiously, the math wasn't an exercise for the faint of heart. Worse, it only reconfirmed what he already knew. Unaided, Mars had receded out of reach.

As for that aid ….

Reluctantly, his gaze returned to the view straight ahead. To the fueled-up lunar water tanker about to give *Lewis* and *Clark* a quick tow. To the long tethers—having attached one himself—loosely stretching from the tanker to both Ares-mission ships.

The tanker, its water reservoir pumped dry, could provide quite the boost. If the long tethers delivered by the ELV didn't snap. If tension along the tethers, even with the most gradual of accelerations, didn't tear open one ship or another. (At *that* thought, he reassured himself his helmet was within easy reach.) If the improvised trailer hitches on both ends stayed put. If explosive bolts worked at the proper moment to sever the tethers. If the faceless orbital analysts in Space Force were as smart as Arthur had counted on them being.

Even as Xander imagined the myriad ways matters could go wrong, the bridge chatter segued to a final countdown. The countdown gave way to single digits, "… seven … six …"

At five, *Lewis*'s starboard-side attitude thrusters came online. *Clark* would be doing the same, only on its port side. The sideway thrusts, all but imperceptible, would prevent tethers about to go taut from crashing the towed ships together.

"Two … one …"

"Let's blow this popsicle stand," Sonny cheered from the bridge's shotgun seat.

Did he feel the slightest of pressures against his back? An instant later, the sensation wasn't so slight. An instant after that, there was no question: They were accelerating. A bit more. And more ….

"Approaching separation," Cat soon warned. "In ten … nine … eight …"

At *two* began a flurry of activities almost too close together to register individually. His sensation of acceleration shifted ever so subtly: *Lewis* creeping ahead on stern thrusters, relieving a bit of the tension on the tether. The flash (glimpsed through the open bridge hatch and out the canopy) of an explosive bolt firing: releasing the tether's near end. Stern thrusters cutting off, and the abrupt halt to even any faint notion of acceleration. The tether (in another glimpse out the canopy), freed of the great mass it had been towing, whipping out of sight.

At *one*, the distant flash of an explosive bolt marked the release of the tether's far end. The water tanker, starboard thrusters suddenly firing, veering away from the recoiling tether, beginning its long, arcing course back to the Gateway for recovery and refueling.

At *zero*, a firm hand pressed Xander deep into his acceleration seat.

Son of a gun. He was on his way to freaking *Mars*.

❖ ❖ ❖

"Boss," Reuben called out. "Broadcast from home base. Looks like your president held a press conference."

Teri had been idly reading and sipping coffee at the fold-down table in *Bradbury*'s main cabin. Mars-standard spin gravity still felt luxurious. En route to Mars, did she need to stay up to date with political blather? Not really. Besides, whatever NEP sent them got recorded. "I'll catch it later."

"Based on the screen crawl, you'll *want* to see this. Trust me."

Julio and Islah, playing chess with a magnetic set, perked up.

"Okay." Teri put her datasheet to sleep. "Start it over on the display back here."

"I have a short statement," Carla DeMille began. She looked ... smug. "After the statement, I'll take a few questions. Earlier today, having resolved the issues that had made a brief delay prudent, the Ares mission departed the Lunar Gateway for Mars. No one should be surprised." (Maybe not, but Teri sure in hell was. Also, to be fair, proud. NASA still had some of the right stuff. Even with Blake denying them new ships.) "America and our friends have done what we set out to do. We always have. We always will. The Ares mission will land on Phobos, as planned, by October 26. Meanwhile, both crews will be—"

Okay, pride and *relief*. Not that Teri understood how even October 26 was achievable, she'd happily take it. She expected to beat that date by close to three weeks.

Julio began, "How in God's name did—?"

"Patience." Not that Teri had any idea how NASA could pull off a Mars mission at this late date. Shedding scads of cargo had to be a big part of the answer.

They didn't wait long for an answer. The video cut away from the White House to a telephoto view from the Lunar Gateway of three ships in a steeply acute triangle. (Huh? Where'd the third ship come from?) The view changed again to a familiar view out the canopy of a Moonship. A tether disappeared into the distance toward the mysterious front vessel. Audio that began with a snippet of triumphant orchestral music segued to a countdown and—

The show lasted about a minute. They were returned to the Briefing Room and a gloating president.

"*Brilliant!*" Islah proclaimed.

More than that: ballsy. "Let me hear, please," Teri said.

"… with full confidence the mission will achieve its every objective. Now if there are any questions?"

A clamor demonstrated there were plenty of those. The president relinquished the podium to her science adviser.

It appeared Dale Bennigan had come prepared. About: how the trick had been done. Any tainted food had been replaced. With the boost from the lunar water tanker, *Lewis* and *Clark* hadn't had to off-load any significant amount of cargo. Both crews were in fine spirits. It went swimmingly—

Until Bennigan's nemesis spoke up. "Ira Coleman, the *Eco Herald*." He cleared his throat ostentatiously. "The secrecy and obvious improvisation aren't reassuring with regard to protecting Martian life from Earth's, or vice versa."

"Was there a question?"

"I considered it implied," Coleman said snippily. "After this Hail Mary pass to salvage the mission, shouldn't we be more worried than ever about cross-contamination?"

Teri almost enjoyed the hapless waffling that ensued. There was little danger that anything on Mars was alive. If anything on Mars ever were alive. If anything was, or had been, alive there, humanity must have more in common with moths and millipedes than with Martians, being one more reason not to fear cross-contamination. Still, extensive precautions were being planned, just in case any samples *were* eventually returned.

After stumbling through those contradictions, the president's glower ever darker, there came an abrupt reversal. Of course, they *hoped* to discover something alive, or at least its extinct traces. Because no one, and certainly not the president's own science adviser, dare admit the true reason for this three-ring circus: sparing Cruella embarrassment.

Amid that faltering performance, Teri was distracted by the arrival of a secure text. Blake, of course. In Crimea, of all places, a radar telescope had confirmed *Lewis* and *Clark* were on the transfer orbit announced by NASA. The tidbit arrived encrypted, suggesting this news wasn't public, and she wondered how much the near-immediate corroboration had cost NEP.

Meanwhile, she'd missed a segue. She thought she recognized the chief White House correspondent of *The New York Times*.

"... long missions. The three teams, I suspect not coincidentally, have equal numbers of men and women. Further, CMSA suggested from the beginning that their team might remain permanently. Given that mission's delayed departure, and without fancy tow trucks"—drawing chuckles—"that seems more than likely. What I'd like to know is, will American ingenuity give us the first baby born on Mars?"

If anything, this question made the good doctor *more* uncomfortable. After the obligatory shout-out to the professionalism of the crews, Bennigan rambled about the medical uncertainties of embryo and fetal development in anything less than standard gravity, about plans not yet underway to experiment with breeding mice on the Moon—which, as she must damn well know, might prove nothing. Mars had more than twice the gravity of the Moon.

Some of NEP's members, for whatever strange reason, had exhibited similar curiosity. (Spinning down Space Vegas's Earth-gravity ring to Mars normal for the experiment? Somehow, not the same. "Besides, my sources"—Teri had known better by then than to ask Blake for specifics—"say the CMSA bunch will have test animals. We can't let them have all the limelight.")

Cute little lab mice lived maybe two years. Mice would have been well into middle age before ever reaching Mars. That left the New Earth mission carting along long-tailed chinchillas. Those were good for ten years or longer.

Some people found chinchillas adorable. Not Teri. The damned rodents were like some bizarre cross between a squirrel and a giant rat. Males each weighed a pound, females almost twice that—and daily, they ate up to five percent of their body weight. There were so many better uses for their limited payload than hay and other rodent chow. Human chow, for one. Which was why she expected CMSA's post-mishap improvisations had included jettisoning of *their* rumored menagerie.

The four chinchillas, critters that pooped a couple of hundred times a day, were aboard *Burroughs*. Picturing Jake and Paula cleaning it up was ever so satisfying. Teri could hope the ship had already begun smelling like a cat litter box. No, like a *barnyard*.

Followed by guilt without the pleasure at the thought of that ship's *other* crew.

But Jake, the cheating bastard, had *chosen* to be there.

131

As Teri's attention returned to the present, the press conference was wrapping up. She'd watch it again later and see what, in her wool-gathering, she'd missed. Also, to revel a bit in the certainty that *her* team would reach Mars *first*.

Aboard *Zheng He* (and, Kai had to believe, *Gagarin*) the crew were all smiles. The American-led team, notwithstanding their undoubted cleverness, would arrive a distant third. Even then, they wouldn't be setting boot on Mars.

May 10, 2033

At the West Wing security station, stifling a yawn, Dale encountered Rebecca Nguyen. Awakened at *five* that morning by a call from the White House, Dale had barely made it in time for her eight o'clock summons. Damned Washington rush-hour traffic.

For what? The president required Dale at a meeting. That was everything the switchboard operator knew or had cared to divulge. The motor-pool car dispatched for her knew no better.

"Here to see Her Nibs, I assume," Dale whispered to Rebecca.

"Yeah. I got the call at oh-dark hundred."

"Same. Do you know why we're here?"

Drawing an apprehensive shrug.

On her ride in, Dale had imagined a few possibilities. A reaming about *Lewis* and *Clark* being Tail End Charlies. Some absurd demand in denial of orbital mechanics. (Not that Dale did orbital mechanics, but she trusted NASA's folks who did. Rebecca ran a smart shop.) The hole blown in NASA's budget by the delay for resupply and Space Force's bat-shit crazy workaround, never mind that the "tow truck" ruse had worked. Or perhaps the budget-buster Dale continued to push: construction of a level-four bio-containment facility on the Moon. Then there was her less-than-stellar performance the week before at the president's latest press conference ....

But when they were ushered into the sanctum sanctorum, the woman emerged from behind the *Resolute* desk … smiling. She gestured at the coffee service, steam rising from the carafe, waiting on the low table between facing sofas. "Help yourselves."

"Madam President," Dale mumbled. The friendliness confounded her. "About my rambling on at last week's presser …."

The president gestured dismissively. "Water under the bridge. Dale, Rebecca, for a change, there's *good* news. Take a seat."

They sat. Rebecca poured three coffees.

"First off," the president said, "main Justice reached a settlement with IPE. We'll withdraw the DPA suit and the threat of nationalizing the company once the paperwork's signed. NASA gets the next three Moonships off their production line. Thereafter, for five years, NASA has right of first refusal for every second Moonship off the line." There followed a fleeting scowl. "At a fifty-percent markup from what the agency's been paying. Gonefs."

Rebecca, who'd been nodding along, looking pleased, frowned.

"Thieves," Dale offered sotto voce. You couldn't grow up in Brooklyn without acquiring some Yiddish.

"Supply and demand," the president continued. "Supposedly, that higher price is what NEP will pay. With IPE returning a fat rebate under the table, I don't doubt. Rebecca, I expect your procurement folks to find another supplier, stat. See to it we don't get ripped off."

"They can't hope to recoup their investment by gouging NASA," Dale said. "Can they?"

"I don't see how. Or any other way, for that matter. My economic advisers, who can't agree on a pizza, agree on this much: They also don't see a way. Maybe it's a colossal ego trip."

"Three new ships NASA can rely on? That's encouraging," Rebecca said cautiously. "Depending on the delivery dates, my people can begin planning another Mars mission for two years out *and* reinvigoration of our lunar efforts. In parallel, we'll start a new procurement. But, respectfully, is that why we're here?"

Dale had wondered the same thing. Contract minutiae weren't Cruella's thing. *Smiling* wasn't her thing, unless kicking puppies were involved. Why, then, the twinkling eyes?

"Busted. It was an excuse for putting you both on my calendar. Damned public-records act. You're here for, well, let's call it a reward for jobs well done."

"I don't understand," Dale said.

"No way you could. I've arranged a private field trip for you. You leave from here"—there had been a gentle knock on the door—"now." The president raised her voice. "They'll be right out."

Dale said, "But what's this—"

"Go," the president said. "And … enjoy."

From the open external hatch of *Lewis*'s cargo hold, Earth looked pea-sized. Certainly, much smaller than the Moon as seen from Earth. Still, helmet-visor magnification showed most of the Western Hemisphere clearly enough. Not much of the Gulf of Mexico, though, beneath the latest, enormous, preseason hurricane.

Xander tried to banish from his thoughts any speculation about where the storm might make landfall. About how wind and torrential rain would pound that region. About how freaking long a plunge to that distant world would last. How flimsy his safety tethers seemed.

Not that he *could* fall to distant Earth. Momentum being what it was, he could only coast the other way. Then again, the direction wouldn't matter. Were he somehow cast adrift, he'd die within hours when his battery pack ran out.

With a shiver, he rechecked the tethers.

At his side, Sonny tapped his sleeve. In a bulky spacesuit, she looked more diminutive even than usual. Her expression somber, she radioed, "Our last look at home for a while."

"Too true."

"Indeed," Cat contributed on the common band. Her role in the pending festivities kept her on the bridge. "More relevant is what you don't see."

"And what can't see us," Xander agreed. That being any of the radar telescopes in Russia and China or, for that matter, anywhere on their side of the planet.

"Can't see us *now*," Cat said. "But the world's gonna keep on turning."

"Yes, sir," Sonny said.

Xander grunted in acknowledgment.

Seconds later, he *and* Sonny were grunting. Two Space Force drones, so deviously sneaked to the mission, were massive and as tall as him. He booted up the first drone, and together he and Sonny eased the autonomous craft out of the hatch. The device coasted to a halt at the end of its own long tether.

"Alpha deployed," Sonny reported.

"Copy that," Cat said. Seconds later, she added, "Local link established. Deploying its solar panel … now." Its simple, motorized hinge operated as expected. "Long-range antenna … now." A fat spar telescoped from the tip of the drone. More dramatically, a comm dish unfurled, as from a beach umbrella. "Acquiring Earth … now."

Step by step, Cat did a final checkout of everything Xander had preconfigured and tested aboard *Lewis*. It still worked. Sonny, with two safety tethers, went EVA and released the drone from its tether. They repeated the process with Beta, their second drone. This time, Xander took the leap. Once he was back aboard, Cat put both drones through a few simple maneuvers.

Only then, more than three hours into the procedure, did Cat compose a short text: BASE, THIS IS MARY ACTUAL. RADIO CHECK. (Mary meaning Meri. Signifying Meriwether Lewis. Not the subtlest of codes.)

She didn't direct the text to Mission Control. Nor even to Earth, exactly.

Instead, her message went toward Venus, to NASA's orbiting *Veritas* probe. Its latest software upload, surreptitiously altered by another of Arthur Schmidt's machinations, repeated her short message within a digitized radar image and then uploaded the altered image to Earth. (Xander could hope that touch of image degradation would, someday, get reversed by subtracting the overlaid message. This wasn't the day or even the month.) One of the DNI's minions, somewhere within NASA's Deep Space Network, would recover Cat's message and pass it along. *If* everything worked.

Minutes passed. And then—

ROGER, MARY. OVER.

A flurry of messages followed. At low power, across the few klicks separating *Lewis* and *Clark*. To and from Venus a second time, now with *Clark* (identifying as Kal-El, that being an aspect of Clark Kent's

136

secret identity). Then with Mission Control in Houston, relayed through the drones.

"Okay, y'all," Cat drawled. "Time to boogie. Get yourselves buckled in."

"Shotgun," Xander called back.

"Damn," Sonny muttered.

As acceleration thrust Xander into his seat on the bridge (with a view this time of, well, nothing but stars), he told himself the other guys had tried pulling a fast one first.

Dale wondered, for the umpteenth time, what was going on. The black SUV's young driver, unfailingly polite, was the personification of mum. Never mind his civvies; posture, mannerisms, crew cut, everything about him screamed *military*. Under orders, it seemed, not to spoil the surprise. Arthur's orders, she surmised, because she knew no one else with such a penchant for secrecy. As for that surprise, Dale had almost ceased trying to guess. This day only got weirder and weirder. Just having a human driver was weird.

As giant dish antennas peeked over the horizon, Rebecca began nodding. The gesture segued to a headshake at Dale's interrogatory eyebrow raise. "I have a guess. We'll know soon enough."

"It's several hours past soon enough," Dale grumbled.

It had already been quite a day. The black SUV from the White House to Joint Base Andrews in Maryland. (Relieved for the trip of datasheets and, to Dale's embarrassment, her quaint, 5G cell. As though anyone would want to track *them*. The paranoia was another reason to sense Arthur's hand in this.) Drop-off at the foot of the stairway onto a waiting small jet. If not Air Force One, then nice enough: a spanking-new Gulfstream from the small Air Force fleet tricked out for government VIPs.

The long flight west—the sun in the sky and the terrain beneath being their only source for even that information. After a couple of hours, Rebecca, who'd been dozing in one of the overstuffed leather seats, glanced out her window and said, "Good. We're past Leavenworth. That's encouraging," and went back to sleep. Dale envied her.

Landing at another government airfield. The desert and the duration of the flight suggested Nevada or southern California. Met on the tarmac by another government-issue black SUV. Driven, more or less east this time, for an hour now.

As more big dishes made their appearance, Rebecca said, "Okay, I think we landed at Edwards AFB. If so, we're coming into Goldstone. Part of the Deep Space Network."

"Why drag us out here?" They had the credentials to access DSN from anywhere. In the week since the Ares launch, Dale had often done it herself, exchanging texts with Xander and Cat Mancini. "Why the skullduggery?"

Rebecca shrugged.

Their SUV stopped beside a beat-up old Volkswagen minibus. ("Diesel," Rebecca remarked. "Electrics and even the sparkplugs in old gas engines emit too much RF noise for anywhere close to the big dishes.") Under a cloudless sky, the midday heat was brutal. Her White House-appropriate business attire didn't help.

The VW's driver-side window rolled down. Arthur, all right. He waved them over to the van. Ignoring questions, he drove a short distance to a dish a good seventy meters across. It might have been slowly tracking something. They parked beside the old, weathered trailer near the antenna's massive pedestal. Three dusty mountain bikes leaned against the trailer.

The trailer's interior was dim and blessedly cool. As sun-faded as the exterior was, everything inside looked brand-new. One man and two women sat at terminals. Tees, jeans, and sneakers notwithstanding, they came across as military.

Was that ... a radar screen?

Arthur distributed bottles of chilled water from a mini refrigerator. "Figured it out yet?"

"This is Goldstone," Rebecca said, "which, aside from its comm functions, offers the only serious radar-astronomy capability in this hemisphere. I'd bet we're standing beneath the lone radar-equipped dish. I'm also guessing that, in the main control room, they've been told the radar system needs maintenance, or an upgrade, or some such, so your folks—Space Force?—can camp out here with the local controls."

"So far, so good," Arthur said. "Do you know why?"

"*I* sure don't," Dale said.

"Soon." Arthur leaned down, reading over an operator's shoulder. The screen looked empty. "Are we tracking them, son?"

"We're receiving telemetry, sir," the man said.

Rebecca sidled over to read the dish's coordinate settings. "From Ares. Right?"

"Let's find out." Arthur tapped the other man's shoulder. "Light them up, Lieutenant. One ping."

The wait was interminable. "How long …" Dale began.

"Not long," Rebecca said. "Still under a minute round trip. *If* I'm right."

To which surmise, Arthur smiled enigmatically. "And … now."

Two blips popped onto the display. Dale had just opened her mouth to ask the point of this when—another two blips appeared. As best she could tell, identical blips.

"What the *fuck*?" Rebecca blurted out.

"You didn't seriously believe," Arthur said calmly, "the Space Force resupply to the Gateway was all snacks and tether reels. Did you?"

Of course, Dale had. That's what she'd been *told*, damn it. "Some type of radar decoys?"

"Autonomous drones with active spoofing, and that's classified tech. If we could've retrofit *Lewis* and *Clark* for stealth, we'd have done it. That, alas, was a Golden Gate Bridge too far. The farther pair of blips are our ships. They boosted this morning, burning some of their fuel reserves, onto a slightly different, somewhat faster transfer orbit. Pretty soon, they won't be where anyone would think to look. Wu's folk and their Russian partners included."

Rebecca's eyes narrowed to slits. Her voice got husky. "How in God's name do our folks out there and Houston keep in touch?"

"Same as usual. The drones operate as comm relays, too." Arthur downed a long swig of water. "We're already annoyingly distant for talking in real time. It's going to be texts and recordings, anyway. What's it matter if those come and go a little slower?"

"Incoming text, sir," another operator said. MARY ACTUAL. WAS THAT YOUR PING?

Arthur laughed. "Tell Cat, yes."

First, the hours of mystery. Now, things coming at Dale too fast—including the revelation that had popped into her mind. "There never was a food problem for Ares, was there? The retrofits to the ships, the whole towing scheme? That was planned well ahead of time. We lied—you set *me* up to lie—to the world."

"Yeah, sorry about that." Arthur shrugged. "After the president, on this world you're the mission's public face. She was willing to dissemble with that '*by* October 26' assertion, but that's where she drew the line. You, meanwhile, don't have a poker face."

"Why lie at all?"

"Given our best intel on the other guys' fuel margins and payloads, none of our analysts quite believed their published flight plans. So, shocker: *Everyone* intends their mission to reach Mars first, our boss among them. If no one suspects we've taken the lead? It won't occur to them to tap into any remaining fuel reserves to leapfrog us."

"What about the fears raised about the safety of everyone's food supply? The hit to my reputation, my credibility, when this comes out? Or to NASA's credibility? You had no right—"

"Yeah, and I'm pissed, too," Rebecca said. "Too pissed, in fact, to deal with the betrayal. So, for now, I'll go with a more basic question. How much sooner will Ares get there?"

Arthur looked … pained. As though sharing the information hurt him. Just maybe it did. But the president, after all, had invited them here. "Lieutenant?" he eventually prompted.

For the first time since they'd entered the trailer, the young man glanced up from his display. "Three weeks earlier than NASA's announced plan and before the drones. A few minutes before midnight, Zulu time, on October fifth."

"Putting it another way," Arthur smirked, "Ahead of anyone else."

"'You might die, it's going to be uncomfortable and probably won't have good food,' Musk said, adding that it will be an 'arduous and dangerous journey where you may not come back alive.'

"'Honestly, a bunch of people will probably die in the beginning,' he added, but insisted it would also be 'a glorious adventure and it will be an amazing experience.'

"'It's not for everyone,' he said. 'Volunteers only!'"

—Elon Musk, CEO of SpaceX, interview about Mars for the X Prize Foundation (April 25, 2021)

"Insanity is doing the same thing over and over and expecting different results."

—Albert Einstein

"I have considered whether a landing on Mars could be done by the private sector. It conflicts with my very strong idea, concept, conviction, that the first human beings to land on Mars should not come back to Earth. They should be the beginning of a build-up of a colony/settlement, I call it a 'permanence.'"

—Buzz Aldrin, second man to walk on the Moon, Reddit interview (July 8, 2014)

D I G G I N G I N

October 20, 2033

Phobos had begun to feel, if not like home, at least less like primeval wilderness.

It certainly wasn't that Xander found the new accommodations luxurious. Still, compared to *Lewis*, the inflated habitat was roomy. The view inside sucked—or, rather, buried under "sand" bags to block solar and cosmic radiation, there *was* no view—but any venture outside more than compensated. Mars, ever overhead, seemingly close enough to touch, never got old.

Alas, gawking got no work done.

With Sonny still gazing skyward, Xander felt a tad less guilty. His smile hidden behind the reflective sun visor, he knelt to clip two safety tethers to one of the guide wires radiating outward from beneath the igloo-habitat's airlock. Tiny though this world was, a misstep likely wouldn't launch him into space—escape velocity was about forty klicks per hour—but carelessness *could* leave him hanging aloft for a mockably long time.

While Sonny continued to admire the celestial view, he surveyed the local attractions. Dwarfed by the vastness of Stickney Crater, at the bottom of which much of the mission's gear lay scattered, the sights, from left to right, were:

— their partially deployed solar farm;

— a dish antenna, at that moment tracking Earth;

— their most recent drilling site, giving hints of ice in minable quantities (and so, likely also where they'd end up deploying electrolysis and hydrogen/oxygen liquefaction equipment);

— the "landing" field where *Lewis* and *Clark* would remain tethered for many months;

— the tarp beneath which Mars landers were garaged pending dispatch, where David and Hideo were performing final checkout of a pending flight's batch of rovers.

— the miniaturized biohazard lab, folded up on itself like some giant origami, he and Sonny had off-loaded the day before— and were *supposed* to be setting up.

Not bad for two weeks' effort. And yet, only a start ....

"Ready when you are," Sonny announced on the private radio channel they'd share on their errand.

"Huh. You *are* awake." Xander glided hand over hand a few meters along his chosen guide wire.

She snorted, his caffeine consumption being a longstanding bone of contention. Well, she wasn't the first doctor to take him task over that. She *was*, however, the most bored.

"You'd think," she had often groused on the long flight, "*someone* would have the decency to break a bone." Or pull a muscle. Crack a tooth. Cut a hand while slicing a bagel. Develop an ingrown toenail. Choke on the nasty, reconstituted food. The litany of misfortunes neither he nor Cat had had the decency to suffer had been near-endless. Barring a medical emergency, there was little to occupy their doctor and biologist here, either, unless and until one of the rovers found something interesting for her to examine.

"Cheer up," he had told her a few days earlier, "the damned dust"— absurd amounts of which they'd already tracked into their igloo—"has given me a major case of itchy eyes." Which wasn't a surprise. Lunar visitors, back to the Apollo missions, often had such allergic reactions. The space-weathering processes that had produced lunar regolith also operated on Phobos.

She'd dispensed an antihistamine, muttering, "Now my day is complete."

Once Sonny had double-tethered herself, Xander resumed his hand-over-hand journey along the wire, pausing every ten or so meters with a gentle squeeze to transfer first one carabiner, then the other, across an anchoring piton. The maneuver had become second nature. "You know the terrain out where we're headed? I've been pondering how best to situate and secure the biolab—"

"Because waiting a minute longer till we reach the site, till we can see the terrain, bothers you?" She sighed. You hardly ever heard sighs, helmet to helmet. "You and your damned caffeine."

And she was off. Hadn't he ever wondered why plants made caffeine? (Not till she'd brought it up. Why would he?) Why unrelated plant species around the world, sources of coffee and tea, colas and chocolate, had independently evolved biochemical pathways to produce the drug? (How could he not *now*, as often as she nagged about it?) Did he not consider it significant that caffeine production discouraged bees from pollinating nearby, competitor plants?

What if humanity's most popular psychoactive compound *had* evolved to repel herbivores? He was no damned herbivore, no matter the paucity of meat in his recent diet. Didn't *she* know it'd take fifty ordinary cups—even twice that, depending on the type of bean and method of preparation—for caffeine intake to reach toxic levels? Daily! Of course, she knew.

He limited his rebuttal to, "Not that I'm a bee, I don't have much opportunity these days to do any pollinating."

Nor had he in the final, frigid months leading up to the divorce. That he couldn't remember last thinking about Charlene? Becks had assured him the sadness would fade, and it seemed she'd been right. Optimistic about the timing, but right.

Smothering a snort, Sonny allowed, "Touché."

They glided over a skinny crevasse, up a shallow slope, toward the worksite, Sonny venting all the while. Xander kept further snark to himself because friends humored one another.

To his right, Marslight glinted off an octopoid robot inching its way up to the rim of Stickney Crater. The bot (always gripping the ground with at least three tungsten-carbide-tipped claws) was anchoring a zigzag of pitons, through which another guide wire would be threaded. *That* guide wire would be the first to exit Stickney Crater.

However apt their location for dispatching, controlling, and retrieving Mars bots, this deep basin could be nothing like primordial Phobos. A *big* rock had excavated this nine-klick-across crater, as another had blasted the two-klick-across pit within. Those impacts must have utterly stirred/tainted/melted the local geology. Samples collected here, however interesting in their own right, would never resolve longstanding arguments about how or where Phobos (and its sidekick, Deimos) first formed, and how they came to be in their current orbits.

As curious as Earthbound specialists were, no one could be more eager for Giselle Delacroix to leave this impact zone and start collecting relevant samples than … Giselle. However underutilized Sonny had felt aboard *Lewis*, the mission's geologist, aboard *Clark*, had had *nothing* to do. Once landers began returning from the planet with samples? Giselle might be the busiest of them all.

As for poor Sonny, activities out and about on Phobos, handling massive but deceptively weightless equipment, could only increase the odds one of them *would* break something. She could (but denied doing so) hope.

"You aren't even listening to me," Sonny complained.

"Nonsense. If I may paraphrase: Caffeine bad. Drink less."

"You are the most irritating man—"

"We each have our special skills."

"Humph."

A gentle hand squeeze on the guide wire brought Xander to a halt by the folded, shrink-wrapped, to-be-inflated biolab. With nearby outcroppings as handholds, remaining tethered, he edged aside to let Sonny approach. "Okay, Doc. Let's get your toy shop open for business."

Sonny pointed to a nearby flattish region about six meters square. "There. Agreed?"

Within easy reach even without extending the guide wire. With only minor slope, well within the module's self-leveling capability once anchored. In fact, the spot he'd had in mind since reviewing the terrain map. "Agreed."

They lugged the lab into position. Oriented it with its main airlock convenient to the guide wire and the robot-accessible side toward the landing zone. Exchanged radioed pleasantries with Giselle, in the LZ, then connecting LOX and LH2 hoses to *Clark* to fuel a lander. Pounded in tent stakes around the lab module. Unwound the lab module's tethers and secured them to the stakes. Radioed Cat, luxuriating back in their igloo, requesting she start an octobot dragging power cable to them from the solar farm. Waved at Hideo, their mining engineer, busy at the drilling site. Cracked open the lab's built-in compressed-nitrogen tank to begin its slow inflation. Watched David, having altogether too much fun chucking microsats, if not at fastball speeds, into space. (Thrusters would nudge the tiny craft from basically co-orbital with Phobos to lower orbits better suited to close-up planetary observation. Muscle power plus low-mass ion thrusters were efficient—however clunky.) Watched the biolab glacially rise.

As Phobos—with its frenetic, seven-hour, thirty-nine-minute orbit—prepared to plunge again into Mars's shadow, Sonny flicked on helmet headlamps. "Hanging around while this inflates is as productive as watching paint dry. I say we're done till we have power out here for work lamps, or daylight, or, at the least, more than crescent Marslight."

True enough. Phobos was among the darkest bodies in the Solar System. When it got dark here, it was *dark*. He said, "I could get used to a three-hour workday."

"Me, too, until I get something to study." Pause. "If there is anything for me to study."

Because Mars might turn out to be as dead, to always have *been* as dead, as a bowling ball. Which, however disappointing, wouldn't surprise many people. But it sure as hell would make Sonny's stay here tedious.

"Enough of that," she continued. "Don't you wonder what progress they're making below?"

Below. Where there was sufficient gravity to be *useful*. With twenty-four hours, and not quite a spare forty minutes, to the local day. With eight people per team, rather than six. But, to be fair, though it hadn't yet been an issue, also the prospect of global dust storms. "Indeed, I do wonder."

Being all the more curious ever since authorities on Earth—three sets of them—had discouraged radioed fraternizing.

October 26, 2033

Were it not so cliché (and had there been heavy crockery at hand, and were not projectiles of any sort in an inflatable shelter surrounded by near-vacuum a Bad Idea), Teri might well have tried to bean Jake. She was that furious.

"We're on Mars for a *reason*," her husband said with a smile. (Her cheating—and so, estranged—husband. Also, curse him, still the poster child for bad-boyish charm. The man whom, try as she might, she hadn't stopped loving. Feeling betrayed? Remaining pissed? Those newer sentiments she had down pat.) "We're here to *do*, not loiter till a return window opens."

As for intentions to loiter, he mustn't have intended his visit to take long. Apart from the helmet, he remained in vacuum gear: a head-to-toe, in-her-face reminder that he chose to live—with that woman—in the other shelter.

Leaving it to the troops to christen this base and their shelters? That ought to have been harmless. Fun, even. In fact, the lighthearted debate *had* been fun—till the *Burroughs* four united to carry the day. Until this base became Barsoom and their two shelters Helium and Zodanga.

How could Jake have allowed that? Did he not know how hurtful that was? That for a thousand years, those two great Martian cities of the Edgar Rice Burroughs canon were bitter enemies? Or could he be that oblivious?

"Yo, Teri. Are you with me?"

Sure. As much as you're with me. "I just remembered something. Continue."

At least, before reopening this debate, he'd waited for an opportunity to speak in private. Did that reflect some residual respect, at least for her role as mission commander? She wanted to think so. Was this about a sincere difference of opinion over priorities? She'd wanted to believe that, too.

She failed, especially on the second wish.

"*You* may be ready to explore, but my first duty is to everyone's safety. That means we focus first, among other things, on assuring our ability to get home."

Jake gestured dismissively, making her long yet again for crockery. "Whether our refueling stations demonstrate full-scale ops tomorrow or a year from tomorrow won't make a difference. Not to mention it's *stations*. Plural. We brought a spare. But if we find something our patrons deem useful? That will pay off for us big time."

If they got back to Earth. Money did them no good here.

She jammed fists in her pants pockets. It beat wringing her hands. "Discovering your unnamed *something* can wait six months. Whereas, if assembly and checkout of the refueling plants fight back, or the plants fail to hold up under steady usage, or enough ice for return-fuel production is hard to come by, or solar-panels efficiency degrades faster than we expect, or—"

"We won't find a big ice deposit by hunkering down here," Jake said. Smirked.

Damn! In any debate, your case is only as strong as the weakest argument put forward. She *knew* that. Why did she let him rattle her?

Except she knew why. "Would you be as quick to gallivant if I were the one riding shotgun?"

"Our first venture out exploring," he mansplained in a smarmy, *I'm the soul of reason*, tone, "is where an accident is most apt to happen. Isn't our doctor the appropriate person to join me?"

Well, bucko, it needn't be *you* in the driver's seat—except that, by far, Jake had the highest ratings of any of them on the Mars SUV simulator.

If he hadn't cheated on that, too.

Teri took a deep breath. Gathered her wits. Took another deep breath. Opened a datasheet across the shelter's tiny, fold-down table.

149

Linked it to the camera that endlessly pivoted atop a nearby mast. The view swept downhill, over the dirt piles marking the all-but-dry holes from their first ice excavations, toward the nearby rim of Tithonium Chasma. The chasm's depths went unseen from this angle, but the far rim—thirty klicks away—more than hinted at the canyon's vastness.

He smiled that crooked, endearing smile of his. "I see a world waiting to be explored."

Did he imagine she didn't? After five years together, could he understand her so little?

The nearby abyss that put the Grand Canyon to shame? It was itself but a minor side branch of Valles Marineris. *That* ran for 4000 klicks—a quarter of the way around the planet. Was in spots up to 200 klicks wide and 7 deep. Of *course,* she was eager to explore it. And Mons Olympus, towering to well over twice Everest's height, with a footprint the area of freaking *Italy*. And the inconceivably vast impact basin that was Utopia Planitia. That was not only the largest such feature on Mars but in the entire freaking Solar System. (Also where the Chinese had set up camp, but in an expanse 3300 klicks across: the distance, as the crow flew, from New York City to Albuquerque! It wasn't as if a visit would have the two groups bumping elbows.) All these exceptional sights, all the unique experiences that NEP had, with supreme confidence, already pitched to the bored billionaires become too good for Space Vegas, and Moon walks, and any other exotic destination recently affordable to mere hundred-millionaire riffraff.

"Wait for it," she said.

If not as soon as Teri would have wished, the camera's sweep surveyed the little settlement. The snugger-than-snug, sandbag-covered igloos. (Helium and Zodanga, damn it.) Their solar farm. In the distance, the heat-of-entry scorched, fifty-meter-tall, silvery obelisks that were *Bradbury* and *Burroughs*. So far, causes for pride. But then: the first refueling station, yet to be started up. The brick kiln, ditto. The smelter and foundry station, aka Little Pittsburgh, beginning to turn rust-rich Martian regolith into iron bars, struts, panels, and other structural elements to frame permanent accommodations—if only, limited by the available power, at a snail's pace. The miniature, automated factory yet to produce batteries from that same iron oxide, to give them more than a day or two's backup power from the solar farm. The hydroponics dome, the first of what would be many. Of course, the dome itself was the simple part of setting up a farm. They needed water and assorted ironwork—pipes, trays, an airlock frame and hatches—before crop experiments could begin. At least they *didn't* have to manufacture pumps and a control module for that airlock; those components were lightweight enough to have brought a decent supply.

The camera completed its 360° circuit, and she continued. "I see critical work yet to be tackled here."

"When won't there be work to be done here?"

"It hasn't even been a month, Jake."

"When?" he repeated.

When, for a longer while, we've gotten to see each other daily. When, just maybe, you've seen the error of your ways—or (more likely, if I'm being honest with myself) I've accepted the futility of that hope. None of which was appropriate, or constructive, or she had any intention of expressing. "When we're not living on the ragged edge."

"Uh-huh. When?"

Damned stubborn bastard. "Months. That's the best I can give you."

Stony-faced, Jake turned away and retrieved his helmet.

"Touchdown. And the crowd goes wild."

Hooting and hollering, most of Xander's colleagues did just that.

More crash than touch, he thought of Cat's pronouncement. The call ought not even be considered close, given their bird's-eye view of the event from Phobos. Yes, one of the mission's erstwhile decoys *had* struck. Drilled a pinprick into the ginormous, southern-hemisphere impact crater that was Hellas Basin. Lofted a big dust plume, however briefly, into the thin atmosphere. But their other decoy had sped straight past Mars, on an elongated solar orbit that would carry it deep into the Asteroid Belt before turning back sunward.

"Also, one incomplete pass," Xander muttered.

"What's that?" Cat asked.

"Nothing." Let her interpret that however she wished.

November 3, 2033

In spacesuits—the Martian atmosphere, for most purposes, being essentially a vacuum—nothing ever went quickly.

Mingmei and Kai had settled into Day Two of erecting ribs for the semi-cylindrical tent of a future aeroponics farm when the fireworks erupted. Colonel Zhao shouting? Not unusual. But over the mission's common radio channel? *That* was.

Soon enough, Kai began to grasp Zhao coming down so hard and so publicly on poor Oorvi. Her assignment for the day was an expanded survey around the current drilling site. Where ground-penetrating radar—and, five days earlier, their young Indian geologist—had suggested a buried ice deposit, meters of drilling had encountered only a layer of clay. Ice meant water, oxygen, and fuel. Clay provided none of that, however useful the material would be in the longer term for brick manufacture.

There had been some brief delay in starting the day's outdoor work—Oorvi being a bit too slow after breakfast to emerge from the Winter Palace, as the *Gagarin* group had grandiloquently dubbed their shelter. (Did Antonov fancy himself the czar of Mars? Not that the name Zhao decreed for the Chinese shelter had been any more subtle. Zijincheng: the Imperial City. Though should the Russians choose, Western-style, to interpret that name as the Forbidden City and stay away? Kai would have no problem with that.)

It appeared Oorvi had spent several minutes handling some last-minute request of Colonel Antonov's. However minor the hold-up, Zhao had not authorized it. Therein was the message of Zhao's rage, and Antonov its true target. Time would tell if the Russian had received it. Should a verbal reaming also reinforce with Oorvi that her months aboard *Gagarin* didn't make the pompous Russian the boss of her *here*? It could only be a plus.

Risking reprimands of their own, Kai and Mingmei went to see what was going on. Soon enough, everyone converged in the small, open area amid the nascent community's few structures. Tiananmen Square. From the color drained from the young Indian geologist's face, Kai knew Zhao's tirade had hit at least one mark.

With Oorvi reduced to stunned silence, studying her boots, Antonov jumped in to defend, *not* her, but the utter reasonableness of the trivial task he had asked of her. The appropriateness, no, his right, to have made it. The unfairness of Zhao taking umbrage.

Interleaved in those protestations were Zhao's rebuttals, rejections, and, finally, mockery. It ended with Zhao's derisive reminder of whose nation had built *Gagarin*. Whose had had to pay for the privilege of naming it. Whose alone could accomplish resupply. And because divided command was never wise ....

Once the shouting ended and the feuding colonels had slogged off in their separate directions (a sliding shuffle being as close as anyone on Mars could come to stomping), Kai waggled a gloved hand, a finger raised. *Private channel one.* Oorvi nodded.

"Don't take it personally," Kai advised. "It wasn't about you."

Though his protectiveness, which he hoped didn't show, might have been personal. Oorvi was tiny, with delicate features—just as Li had been. By reflex, the resemblance had him aching to defend her.

She shook her head. "It felt personal."

"Kill a chicken to scare the monkeys."

With a furrowed brow, she studied his face. "Confucius? Mao?"

"My father's brother." Doubtless not original to Uncle Hu, but Kai had never asked. Such a question could only have brought on a tedious, rambling story.

"With me the chicken of this scenario, and Nikolai the monkey."

"You have to understand, Colonel Zhao is ...." Kai trailed off. Because criticizing the mission commander felt wrong? Because "private" radio channels were private only by convention and, for all Kai knew, his colonel, or both colonels, sometimes listened in. For that matter, what were the chances that software didn't record everything? Add some basic keyword recognition or a simple AI, and monitoring everything spoken outside would be simple enough.

"… is under a great deal of pressure," Kai completed, hoping the awkward pause might go by unnoticed. Automated monitoring, as soon as it had occurred to him, seemed inevitable. "He bears a great deal of responsibility."

"You and I don't?" She managed a sad smile. "Before I earn another reprimand, I'd best get back to work."

Hadn't we all? Kai thought.

The NBACC (en-back to its denizens) was one weird structure. From some angles, it might have been any boxy office building anywhere—and then, there was the edifice's longest side. It, for mysterious reasons, bowed out with a graceful curve. From that side, more than anything, the NBACC resembled a cruise ship. Its roof even extruded seven pipes that (with a touch of imagination) could pass for smokestacks. Apart from the niggling detail that cruise ships didn't come an hour west of Baltimore or berth in the middle of landlocked Fort Detrick.

Then again, anything as exotic as the National Biodefense Analysis and Countermeasures Center merited a distinctive appearance.

"Shall we go in?" Dale's guide asked.

Dr. Jonah Plotkin was a big guy, radiating competence and confidence. The virologist had met her in the parking lot at the fort's visitor entrance; shouldered them a path (like the college fullback he'd once been) through the raucous demonstration; waved off the news crews with their cameras; sped her through the security checkpoint. If the tumult fazed him, he hid it well.

Protesters in their hundreds had rattled *her* more than she would have cared to admit. Any crowd this size would. But beyond their sheer numbers, more than their palpable anger, the forest of waving placards had struck close to home. PPL FOR THE PEOPLE. PPL, NOT PANDEMIC. SAY NO TO BIOWARFARE. And on scattered signs, lest Dale somehow delude herself this encounter was the result of unfortunate timing: her face (rendered in Wicked Witch of the West green) under the universal circle-and-slash symbol for NO.

So much for coming alone, keeping a low profile. If she ever discovered who'd leaked word of her plans? That'd be one West Wing blabbermouth kicked to the curb.

"Doctor Bennigan? You ready?"

Not really. "Call me Dale. Yes, let's do it."

"Jonah, then." Inside, walking backward down a hallway to a bank of elevators, he launched into practiced-sounding patter. "The National Biodefense Analysis and Countermeasures Center is, without doubt, a one-of-a-kind facility. This is a jewel in the crown of Homeland Security research facilities. Our mission is defending the nation against biological hazards of any kind." He grinned. "Even the imaginary ones."

"From your lips to PPL's ears," she said. Never mind that *improbable* and *imaginary* were different things.

They got an elevator to themselves, and on their short ride Jonah continued his spiel. "The NBTCC, the National Biological Threat Characterization Center, is uniquely qualified to identify and prioritize new biological risks. Their work, in a sense, complements that of our other half. That's the National Bioforensic Analysis Center, NBFAC. *It* specializes in identifying specific pathogens from specific incidents." The elevator doors opened and, again walking backward, not missing a beat, he continued. "With that as background, Dale, we're ready for a look at one of our BSL-4 labs. We're one of fewer than a dozen BSL-4 sites in the country."

Biosafety Level Four. Ground Zero for investigating airborne and suspected life-threatening pathogens, in particular those without vaccines or treatments. Nasty, *nasty* bugs. Ebola. Yellow fever. Marburg virus. Other scary things. NBACC was the *closest* such facility to DC, and so the most convenient for her to familiarize herself. Too bad it hadn't occurred to her that the lunatic fringe would catch word of her visit. Fort Detrick was convenient for them, too.

They stopped at a window overlooking a "hot" side. The lab within was idle at the moment. Jonah described the biocontainment capabilities she'd come to see firsthand: access controls. Airlocks and air-handling equipment. Sealed "moon" suits and their air hoses. Glove boxes. Sensors to detect leaks and their alarms. Multistage decontamination measures. Instrumentation suites. Waste disposal. Backups for … everything.

She'd seen such setups before—in movies. Her lab work as a molecular biologist, back in the day, had never required such things.

"Sorry," Jonah concluded apologetically, "I can't bring you inside. No one's allowed in without extensive training."

"I understand." Not to mention relieved, no matter how impressive the safety protocols. Accidents happened.

"Any questions?"

She had several, none more important than the one she ended with. "Are you familiar with the facility standards for a sample return from a restricted body?"

"Restricted body. Mars, I presume."

"Right."

"You'll want BSL-4 precautions, naturally."

Unless someone could imagine more stringent measures. "Right. As it happens, that's among the lesser-known provisions of the Outer Space Treaty. Article Nine."

"I'd guess you'd need to do everything, storage included, under Martian conditions. The low atmospheric pressure and the cold."

"Underground conditions, too, including aquifers. Also, glacial conditions." Mars's polar ice caps, she'd come to know, being a mix of water ice and frozen carbon dioxide. "We can't know where our folks might find interesting samples."

"Hmm. Okay, I can see that."

"Beyond protecting investigators from the samples, we'll also need to isolate the samples from any terrestrial contamination. The samples must remain pristine."

"That's a lot to consider. I use these facilities, but that doesn't make me an expert on their construction. I do know that building one runs well north of $100 million, generally taking years to construct and certify. Oh, and ongoing maintenance is a big deal." He scratched his head. "Sixty people? Seventy? You may want to check with the bean counters about support staff."

To create a sample-return facility from scratch? Dale had seen studies predicting that an SRF would take seven or more years to build. The Ares mission would be returning in more like two. She managed a smile, however insincere. "The lone resource the Ares team has in near endless supply? Money."

"Are you thinking of an upgrade to accommodate Mars samples *here*?"

She expected to star on the evening's news just for having been spotted entering. She'd stream for months to come on conspiracy sites. It no longer mattered how comfortable she became with BSL-4 safeguards (and never mind how ecstatic she'd be if even ancient microfossils were found on Mars). She wouldn't recommend an SRF anywhere in the populous East Coast, much less so near the District. If she did, surely the president would veto it.

"No, not here," Dale said. He looked relieved. Because projects here wouldn't get disrupted? Or from nagging doubts whether precautions designed around terrestrial pathogens could be trusted with unearthly microbes? (Or even to recognize them?)

"Then are we finished, Dale?"

"Indeed." She was done *here*.

But in the bigger picture, not even close. The more she studied the challenges, the more she pondered the uncertainties, the more she felt the ideal solution—and for PPL-deluded masses, perhaps the one saleable solution—would be constructing a sample-return facility on the lifeless Moon.

Even hard-ass project managers need the occasional bit of downtime. Teri was sipping a (bad) coffee, scanning the latest news upload from Earth, when an alert popped up on her datasheet. PHOBOS ON THE LINE. PUT IT THROUGH? KJ.

KJ was Keshaun Johnson: solid, stolid electrical engineer. The electronics igloo was the closest the base so far had to a nerve center. When he wasn't outside wiring or troubleshooting equipment, the shack was convenient for keeping an eye on things. For monitoring comms, too.

Rather than answer with a text, she called.

Keshaun looked tired. (No surprise there. They all were.) Sooty, clothes splotched with the damned, ubiquitous regolith. (Ditto.) Worried.

That last attribute worried *her*.

"What's Copperhead want? She have some new notion for gloating?" Teri didn't actually have any issues with Cat Mancini or her mission. That the NASA-led effort had been sneaky and less than forthcoming? There'd been enough of that to go around. If anything, with Teri's company hat set aside for the nonce, NASA's success was a source of pride. The two missions weren't even, in any objective sense, competitors. But some healthy rivalry boosted morale and helped get work done.

Keshaun shook his head. Rubbed the scraggly mustache he'd started once they'd arrived. Clicked a pen open and closed a few times.

"Out with it, please."

"No, not her. The NASA *guy*. Xander Hopkins."

"Okay. What'd he want?"

"To pass along a weather report." Click-click. "Dust storm brewing in the southern hemisphere." (Where they weren't, but he knew that.) "He says NASA's weather model predicts it'll go global within a week or so. Thought we and the CMSA folks would want to know."

"Inconvenient, sure, but we're safely down. In any event, with the air so thin, what harm can it do?"

"Not the point, boss." Click-click. "The nice solar panels generating most of our power? They won't output diddly in a dust storm. If we're lucky, and if we can keep them clear of dust, maybe at a quarter capacity. The wind won't hurt them, you're correct there. Abrasion's another story." Click. "The worst part? The NASA model says the storm could last for a few months."

"Shit." Then, once more, with real feeling, "*Shit!*"

"Uh-huh." Click-click. "Dust storms killed a couple NASA rovers over the years. Batteries run down, and heating goes off. Electronics can't take the nighttime cold here."

A hundred degrees below was no picnic for people, either. They could shelter aboard the ships if worse came to worst, but would any of their hard work of the past weeks survive?

She said, "Power's your bailiwick. Suggestions?"

"Bury our power lines." (Those cables swooped from post to post, whether from the solar farm or the ships' onboard nukes, to everywhere power was needed. Turning some of Mars's rusty dirt into iron posts had been a simple, early test of their smelting and foundry capabilities, and aboveground power distribution had been quicker and seemed easier than trenching for hundreds of meters. As though, in the long run, *quicker* ever turned out to be *easier*. Another misjudged judgment call.) "I have to believe weeks of dust storm can't be good for them."

"Anything else?"

"For the extra half kilowatt it'll give us, I'll arrange to tap into the RTG"—radioisotope thermoelectric generator—"of the Mars SUV."

"Anything else?

Keshaun looked grim. "Yeah, and you won't like it. Drop everything else we're doing to produce batteries. Whatever power we can store, whether from solar, the shipboard nukes, or the SUV? We're going to want it."

November 14, 2033

One among the many shoehorned around a shelter's fold-down table, Kai studied the series of recent satellite images.

They told a very dark tale.

A mere two weeks before, the distant dust storm had seemed not only inconsequential but irrelevant. And yet, scant days later, its growth and persistence had triggered alerts in a CMSA weather algorithm.

Nor only in CMSA's algorithm. The Phobos mission, applying observations from NASA's Mars orbiters, had radioed a matching—and unsolicited—advisory to Fire Star City. (Kai assumed NASA had also alerted the other Mars base. As he assumed that whatever handful of huts China's planetary rivals had erected had its own pretentious name. Billionaires City?)

Information wasn't flowing the other way, though. Both colonels, in a rare act of comity, had agreed—to say nothing. The military mindset wasn't about to disclose an independent forecasting model that might provide an advantage. Someday, somehow. Mere major that Kai was, the title honorary, at that, he knew better than to question the decision. Aloud, anyway.

Three days earlier, the disturbance had all but swallowed the southern hemisphere. That had still seemed distant, but now the storm had oozed into the northern. Soon enough, the plutocrats' camp would disappear from satellite view.

Colonel Zhao cleared his throat. He stood apart from the rest, as best this igloo allowed. With eight of them crammed into the one shelter, that wasn't far, nor would life support accommodate everyone together for long. "Two weather models, ours and that of the Americans, give similar forecasts. Perhaps within a week, and certainly within ten days, the storm will reach us even here." At almost fifty degrees *north* latitude. "Available power will be impacted."

"Precipitously," Maria Petrova presumed to add.

To Kai's right, Mingmei blinked. On his other side, Xiuying stiffened. Kai himself didn't react (he hoped!) while waiting for the sky to fall. Zhao, more than the mission commander, was, by virtue of cross-training, the closest they had to a power engineer. An implied criticism, however oblique, from one of the Russians? From the *botanist*?

Oorvi coughed into her hand. (Counterintuitively, she had become *more* assertive since her public chewing out. Not even close to forceful, but willing to speak her mind. Kai approved.) "I, for one, do not relish the prospect of weeks huddling in a shelter, or back on one of the ships, while accomplishing nothing. So, never mind whether *our* weather forecasts ought to be state secrets." Suggesting, clearly, that she felt otherwise. "I wish to revisit the offer from Phobos."

A portion of the weather-alert message the colonels had dismissed out of hand.

Maria nodded.

"Not as much an *offer*," snapped Antonov, with a glower, "as an *insult*."

"But as you say, in part an offer," Kai said. Injudicious? Maybe. But if it could be avoided, he, too, would rather not spend weeks, or longer, cooped up. "We could make use of the power they offered. If, that is, the Colonel finds their proposal practical."

If it remained practical, given the week they might have spent preparing but hadn't. Kai wasn't about to be that forward.

No matter how close-mouthed CMSA remained (and at the agency's insistence, also its junior partners), NASA and *its* partners publicized countless details about developments on Phobos. CMSA forwarded everything so generously—foolishly, Zhao and Antonov would have it—volunteered. And so, they knew the Phobos team had deployed a solar farm comparable in size to the one on Utopia Planitia. But exploiting unadulterated sunlight, not the weak version, and soon to be much weaker, that penetrated to the planet's surface. Supporting two fewer people. Banking any unused power in an array of batteries which Kai could only envy.

Receiving excess power from Phobos would be the tricky part. But not impossible. The Americans were offering up to 200 kilowatts throughout the emergency, to be beamed as microwaves at times Phobos was overhead and their base in sunlight. Though airborne dust scattered most radiation, not just visible light, a judicious choice of microwave frequency would keep beam-power losses to a minimum. But transmitting that power would be pointless without a receiving station on the ground ....

"It's *not* practical," Zhao barked. "We'd spend the next week or more at nothing but making preparations. Fabricating and deploying an array of dipole antennas, diverting our available power to do so. Running cables from those antennas to the main power distribution frame. Scavenging the electronics we'd need to convert and condition the power. Then, after that? After our scavenging for chips has disabled much of our other equipment? It will have been for *nothing*. At the last moment, the Americans will 'discover' a reason why they can't downlink power after all."

Antonov grunted his agreement. "Even the NEP group, half American, their leader included, knows better than to trust this offer."

The other settlement *had* declined. (This was an inference, Zhao as loath to speak with NEP's people as with NASA's, but Kai trusted the conclusion. Were Phobos expecting to share their excess power across settlements, they'd have offered less beaming time to Fire Star City.) But had the people at Tithonium Chasma declined for technical reasons? Or were they captive to the same stubborn pride he felt was the colonel's true issue?

Kai limited his dissent. "This is speculative."

"If we accepted the offer and it was sincere?" Zhao laughed humorlessly. "Back on Earth, Americans would laugh at our dependency. Our countrymen would be shamed by our lack of self-reliance. I will not bring such disgrace on our mission, on our country."

Stubborn pride: confirmed. Likewise, misguided. There must be as much disgrace in weeks—at best—of do-nothing survival. Except these were also thoughts Kai knew better than to express.

❖ ❖ ❖

Bored, bored, bored—and if this dust storm was typical, it had at least weeks to go.

Leaders don't pace, Teri told herself. *I* don't pace. I don't fidget, or chit-chat, or play solitaire. Leaving ... not a lot.

She'd already uploaded her report for the day: STORM CONTINUES. WE'RE SAFE BUT IDLE. Read and dismissed Blake's latest nag that she somehow resume their work. Taken an out-of-turn shift outside, meeting Maia near Zodanga's dome to clear dust *again* from their solar panels.

At the igloo's table, Reuben worked yet another crossword puzzle. Across the shelter, Islah watched the reboot of a twenties sitcom that had been vapid in the original. She wore earbuds, but a faint laugh track still intruded. Julio, the lucky bastard, pored over rocks and core samples taken before the storm. (At least, semi-lucky. His left foot was propped on a blowup pillow, the lower leg in a fiberglass cast to the knee. He'd tripped over, well, he didn't know what, on *his* last dust-clearing excursion till the cast came off. This once, Teri couldn't resent Paula playing doctor.) As fascinating as Julio found his collection, none yet was of practical use nor gave the slightest intimation of past or present Martian microbes.

Teri dashed off short, news-less notes to her mother and friends back home. Reviewed project plans long ago committed to memory and on hold until the storm passed. Helped herself to cookies she didn't need. Surveyed the neighborhood (as best she could, given the endless, billowing dust) through exterior cameras. Checked on Zodanga to inquire how their power reserve was holding up—to be embarrassed by Keshaun's carefully bland expression reminding her she'd already asked today. Peeked over Keshaun's shoulder as Maia passed food scraps into a chinchilla cage. Saw no evidence of Jake and Paula beyond a closed sleeping compartment. Heaved a mental sigh of relief as the comm console blinked to announce an incoming signal.

"I'll get it," Teri announced.

A face popped up on the display. Facial rec annotated it XANDER HOPKINS. He had a long face, gray eyes, and something of a wistful expression. He could have used a haircut, but so could any of her bunch. "You guys okay down there?"

Yeah. Hunky-dory. "On the idle side, but yes. Why do you ... ask?" That had almost slipped out as: *Why do you* care?

"Moral support. I wish we could help."

She hoped there was no more to his question than that. "You offered. There wasn't any way we could get an antenna field ready before the storm hit."

He grimaced. "It's just so damned *frustrating*. We have rolls of lightweight photovoltaics to spare that we could've sent down on a lander, but the storm would've shredded those in no time."

Teri had seen the specs and agreed. "Did our neighbors to the north accept your offer?"

"They gave us a 'Thanks, but no thanks.' Sonny thinks we offended their honor." His expression brightened. "New topic. I hear congratulations are in order."

Had this become a social call? "How so?"

"ESA tells us your chinchillas are expecting."

Yeah, sexed-up rodents seemed like something Blake would boast about. Did the man not know how many ways pregnancies could go wrong, even on terra firma? *She'd* have kept the news in-house until they'd seen a healthy litter. "True story. Wish them luck."

"I will. First pregnant mammals on another world is awesome."

Teri *hoped* the chinchillas were the first. Paula damned well better be doctor enough to take precautions.

"… you know?"

For circumstances Teri told herself not to obsess about, that she could do nothing about, she sure let those two distract her. "Sorry, what was that?"

"How far along are the pregnancies?"

"We separated the Xs and Ys"—among the four-footed rodents—"till we landed. So, they're a month along, give or take. I understand typical gestation is more like four months."

"Well, give my best to the happy couples. If you don't mind, let me know how it goes."

Did she mind? "I can do that."

"Well, we're about to drop below your horizon, so I'll wrap this up."

"Okay. I appreciate you checking on us." The surprising thing was, she meant it.

November 20, 2033

Dale found the sprawling Lyon campus of INSERM (France's National Institute of Health and Medical Research) delightfully familiar, rapid-fire French aside, much like the CDC in Atlanta. Until she and Pierre Dubois, her bilingual guide, approached the local BSL-4 facility. At once, the flashbacks to Fort Detrick began.

"You will understand," Pierre said suavely (or perhaps the accent made his every utterance sound suave), "the most dangerous and contagious of pathogens require the most serious of precautions."

"Of course." She stifled a yawn. Some people could sleep on long flights. Not her. "Lead on, Pierre."

Nothing on the tour surprised Dale, nor should it have. The CDC had defined the four biosafety levels and set the standards for each. A Fort Detrick visit had shown her all she'd needed to see—but it had also been a PR disaster. Never mind that she could ill-afford the time, the Powers That Be wanted her seen at a non-American, non-military biolab. Truth be told, jet lag aside, the view through the thick glass as researchers studied the latest super-strain of Ebola was (in the whistle-past-the-graveyard sense) fascinating.

Dale told herself dinner in France before her return flight wasn't the worst thing. Reminded herself, as she emerged into blinding, late-afternoon sunlight, that the news crews waiting outside the lab building were expected, that being observed here was the purpose of her visit. But rather than the anticipated photo op, hungry expressions on the mic-clutching reporters suggested *ambush*.

Maybe French authorities also had a domestic audience to placate. "Doctor Bennigan! Doctor Bennigan!"

Knowing none of them, she could only choose at random and point. "Oui. You, monsieur"—her French thus all but depleted—"in the front."

"Can samples returned from Mars be safe on Earth? How about astronauts?"

She relaxed, if only a bit. This was a softball question, whether or not anyone on this side of the pond played softball. "Of course. Samples will be handled with the utmost caution, the chief concern being their protection from contamination. Out of an abundance of caution, returning astronauts will undergo a period of quarantine."

"Yet here you are," another reporter interjected.

Dale managed a smile. "Yes, I'm here even though every indication is that for billions of years, conditions on Mars have been beyond life-hostile. For a lack of air and surface water, and from intense radiation." There were outlier estimates of transient surface water as recently as a mere 700 million or so years ago. Emphasis on *outlier* and *transient*. Those were no reason to muddle her message. "We think it possible to find ancient traces, not life itself. Even so, we will be cautious. I'm here to review best practices in isolating even the most dangerous pathogens. Should any live samples be found, which would be quite the surprise, we will be prepared."

She indicated another reporter, this time a woman.

"Is it not true that life survives in Chile's Atacama Desert, a place which can go decades without rain?"

"Yes, although without anything like the cold of Mars."

The woman rebutted, "Then what of bacteria found in Antarctica's frigid McMurdo Dry Valleys? There, temperatures drop—for months of polar winter—as low as nighttime temperatures at equatorial Mars. Due to the ozone hole yet to reseal over that continent, those valleys, like Mars, are drenched in ultraviolet radiation."

"Well, yes, but Antarctica has an atmosphere."

"Then what about—"

"Let's give someone else a turn. You, in the back, in an orange blazer."

"Then what about the streptococcus germs found on the camera of the *Surveyor 3* lunar lander, retrieved more than two years later by the *Apollo 12* crew?"

Dale began to feel tag-teamed. The problem was that her team was … *her*. At home, only Ira Coleman hassled her this much. Or perhaps Lance Kawasaki was the missing ingredient, with his gift for defusing situations with a quip.

She took a deep breath. "It's believed that camera was contaminated on Earth, sterile-handling procedures of that era not meeting modern standards."

Orange Blazer retorted, "Won't 'modern' standards also come to seem insufficient?"

Suddenly sensitive to the clicking of cameras, of Pierre having backed away, arms folded across his chest, Dale resorted, in desperation, to a standard DC evasion. "I don't comment on hypotheticals." She chose another face from the crowd. "You, monsieur, with the orange-and-blue striped tie."

"What about Conan the Bacterium, retrieved in 2020 from a pallet of bacteria mounted outside the ISS for three years? Were standards also different this recently?"

"Three years and three billion? Not quite the same." Had she managed to channel Lance? "You, green blouse in the third row back."

"Why return *anything*? Why not study materials there? Or transmit images and test data? Either alternative must be safer."

"No mission could bring along every sort of lab equipment that might prove useful. No one or two biologists can be expert in every subspecialty that will prove relevant." Anymore, damn it, than *she* could. Worse, the second part of Green Blouse's challenge required a deep dive into the prodigious quantities of data that might be collected. Into interplanetary signal-to-noise ratios and the limitations of NASA's Deep Space Network. Into lossiness of any significant image compression. While silently yelling at the reminder scrolling across her mind's eye ("IF YOU'RE EXPLAINING, YOU'RE LOSING") to *just shut up*.

With French press loudly on the record against accepting Mars samples, Pierre *finally* brought the inquisition to a close, "So that zee madame docteur can catch her flight to Paris." His accent by then had long since lost any charm.

Dale flagged down a cruising autocab and collapsed in the backseat. "Saint-Exupéry International."

"Bien sur," the car answered. Recognizing her accent, it translated, "Of course."

Four in the afternoon here meant not ten in the morning in DC. She'd be everywhere on the evening news back home. She might already be the star of the day's 24-hour news cycle.

To be followed, doubtless, by a presidential chewing-out.

Xander's primary assignment, unless and until something computerized went haywire, was prelaunch configuration and checkout of the Mars landers and rovers. On the rare occasions when some equipment *did* go wonky, only the nastiest glitches merited his attention. Like regular maintenance, he'd left straightforward troubleshooting to David. Xander's sysadmin understudy wouldn't retain his IT skills without regular and extensive hands-on. As for Xander's tertiary duties, robot *pilot*, those had also become routine. Chalk one up to regular practice on the lander and rover simulators throughout the interminable outbound flight.

Meaning—with Mars landings paused and, as the dust encroached even to high latitudes, point-to-point hops to redeploy rovers also on hiatus—Xander had *no* work. Landers and rovers below alike were in their safe modes, conserving battery power to (hopefully!) ride out the storm. As for a sample return to Phobos, he wouldn't hold his breath for many—and those, only to independently confirm bot findings—even once the literal dust settled. No Ares bot had yet encountered anything earlier generations of robotic missions hadn't already seen.

After the hectic early weeks here, he'd found himself with a lot of downtime. At first, he'd felt okay with that. In weeks, or (worst case) months, he'd be busy again. Once the storm abated. Once landers could again land, rovers rove, and drilling resume. Once some rover found *something* surprising. If, in the interim, their own prolonged tedium didn't cure Cat and David of disparaging remote piloting as a video game best left to the IT guy.

No, he wasn't past Cruella's casual slight.

Stop it! Xander chided himself. Quit feeling sorry for yourself. Sure, you're bored, but unlike *some* people, the Phobians (as no one but he called them) weren't shivering with thermostats cranked almost down to freezing, helpless as abrasion degraded their equipment.

Giselle and Hideo, at least, stayed happy collecting samples of the nearby rocks and regolith. Gone out on yet another scavenger hunt, they'd signed up to also top off the habitat's reservoirs with more of the locally produced water and oh-two.

It seemed everyone craved diversion as much as Xander. Sonny looked for it in the study of … sludge. (Not history-making Martian organisms, alas. Just the most recent extrusion from a 3-D printer, a brew of locally sourced carbonaceous materials, ammonia, water, and—Giselle having yet to find any phosphorus compounds on this little moon—a soupçon of phosphates from their cargo. In theory, her experimental concoctions were edible. In practice, no multicellular Earthling had as much as considered putting the notion to the test. Even sacrificial dabs of microbes, a standard lab strain of the common gut bacterium E. coli, had so far showed little enthusiasm for it. This latest goo combined the visual appeal of soap scum with the delicate bouquet of a boys' locker room.) While Sonny puttered, David and Cat indulged themselves in the black humor of Dale Bennigan's media mugging in France.

Trying not to breathe through his nose, tuning out the vid, Xander remained at loose ends. Dale was his *friend*, and that vid had been painful on first viewing. With the reporters recast as the Big Bad Wolf from an ancient Disney toon? With Dale morphed into some wide-eyed anime naïf? Nope. Not amused.

His back turned to the tittering twosome, Xander texted Dale. I SAW HOW YOU WERE AMBUSHED. FWIW, GISELLE APOLO-GIZES FOR FRANCE.

Well, that had occupied maybe half a minute.

What Xander didn't know about biology, much less, astrobiology, much less if or how distinct biospheres might interact, had to be most everything there was to know. He'd had no need to know. Unsympa-thetic though he was to the undisclosed (and, he presumed, rapacious) goals of the New Earth Partners, he viewed Mars as a source of vast, untapped resources for humanity. Whatever had once lived on this world, if anything ever had, must be long extinct. Mars had had no surface water for eons.

Dale's serial mugging, one *but what about?* after another, had been cherry-picked biological oddities. Multiply those individual (im)probabilities, and any Martian hazard—again, supposing anything had ever lived there—had to be vanishingly ... well, improbable.

He had nothing but confidence in Dale. And Sonny. And in colleagues he'd met at NASA's Astrobiology Institute long before Wu, and then Cruella, had swept him up in this madcap escapade. None had foreseen any danger to Earth from Mars samples, only a reverse risk that careless handling might contaminate such samples.

Still, wouldn't it be nice to base his certainty on more than trust?

He shot a quick text to the director of the Astrobiology Institute. SLOW GOING HERE TILL THE DUST STORM PASSES. CAN YOU UPLOAD SOME READING FOR ME ABOUT MODERN BIOLOGY?

Or, in IT-speak: When all else fails, read the manual.

Mass Protest Against Mars Missions

(Lyon) A tour of INSERM's Jean Mérieux Laboratory by Dr. Dale Bennigan, science adviser to American president Carla DeMille, ended this afternoon in a contentious televised press conference and public outcry. Bennigan, a leader of the international Ares mission, came to INSERM's laboratory to "review best practices" in the handling of unfamiliar biological materials. Her interest in the subject comes as the Ares team collects such samples for eventual study on Earth.

Within an hour of the press conference ending, demonstrators converged on presidential residences in the United States, Canada, Japan, and across Europe. President Laurent was not in residence at Élysée Palace, where five hundred or more protesters remain gathered this evening. Minutes ago, Laurent issued a statement. "No plans exist to bring Martian samples into France. No such materials will be allowed anywhere within the nation absent an independent review of safety protocols by Académie des Sciences and a resolution of approval by both houses of Parliament. I will advocate for similar policies across the EU."

A spokesperson for PPL (the English acronym of Légions de Protection Planétaire) declared after the contentious event, "We once again see that the Mars missions are ill-considered and, in particular, that the American-led Ares mission is not ready to deal with suspected biological materials. These hastily-planned ventures are a danger to us all."

At her press conference, Bennigan seemed unprepared or unwilling to address several hypothetical risks. These topics included ....

—Agence France-Presse

Wu Challenges Other Mars Programs

(Beijing) President Wu reconfirms that China's trailblazing Red Dragon mission has no return component. He challenges the other Mars missions to do the same ....

—Xinhua News Agency

November 24, 2033

It might have been easy to hate Paula if she were drop-dead gorgeous. (Which she wasn't. The good doctor was, being charitable, pleasant-looking, with mousy brown hair, features somewhat askew, and a nose too large for her face. Never mind that judging another woman by her appearance made Teri feel catty and troglodytic.) If Teri herself hadn't selected Paula for the expedition, highly qualified as both doctor and astronaut. If the woman hadn't, soon after landing, found an opportunity to take Teri aside, eyes downcast, and murmured apologetically, "I never meant for anything to happen with Jake. But, well, it did."

What if it wasn't easy? Teri managed. Whenever they had to interact. As was about to happen again.

Maia and Keshaun had entered first. Even as Maia was shedding vacuum gear, Keshaun—still in his suit except for the helmet—had launched into explaining American traditions to Teri's Brazilian, Israeli, and Liberian roomies. He was going on about how *his* mamma did a ham for Thanksgiving, not a turkey, when the inner hatch finished cycling. The lusting couple stepped out, Paula with a sealed satchel in hand.

Teri forced a smile. "Happy Thanksgiving. Welcome to the party."

"Thanks," Paula mumbled. "I think I'll go check on my patient." She put as much distance as possible (which wasn't much) between

172

herself and Teri before setting down her medical bag and starting to wriggle out of her vacuum gear.

"Julio is in good hands," Jake said.

You would know, Teri thought. "Ready for turkey?"

"Wasn't I always?"

"Uh-huh." And another batch of once-happy memories turned to ash. "Well, I should mingle. Big day."

"I can hope we're not still trapped inside by Christmas." With that, Jake retreated to shed his own vacuum gear.

Before the *Burroughs* four had arrived, Teri had queued up the latest update. Mission Control had promised a special holiday edition. They worked on GMT, delaying highlights of the day's big games. But all wasn't lost: The frozen opening frame on the igloo's big wall display showed the Macy's Thanksgiving Day Parade.

Wondering what else special was in store, she hit PLAY. As traditional floats and balloons glided past, some of the tension drained out of her. "Reuben, will you do the honors?"

"My pleasure." He proceeded to uncork one of the few bottles of wine Teri had brought for special occasions. Their first big holiday on Mars—for half of them, anyway—qualified. He was handing Teri the last glass when the comm console chimed.

She paused the parade and took the call. Both NASA types on Phobos. Their habitat and clothes were as dust-stained as hers. Regolith was a nuisance everywhere.

Cat had a half-filled drink bulb in her hand, the half being beer-colored. "Happy Thanksgiving."

"I trust you guys brought along turkey," Xander Hopkins said.

"Thanks, and we did," Teri said. In a manner of speaking. Basic frozen dinners, but still turkey and fixings. "Why'd you call?"

"The holiday *is* why we called," Xander said. "Only two of us here celebrating it."

"That's gracious of you!" Jake called out. "But if you know anything about the Bears and Cowboys game, keep it to yourself."

Cat laughed. "No time travelers here. Damned GMT. Way to ruin Thanksgiving."

So much for "no fraternizing." Well, Teri also found the guidance silly, not to mention unenforceable. Which wasn't to deny this conversation was a tad forced and awkward. Cat soon excused herself.

But Xander … lingered.

Teri delegated heating their dinners, transferred the vid connection to her datasheet, and restarted the parade for her team. The igloo didn't have corners, but she retreated to an unoccupied short stretch of wall. "Are you all right?"

"Yeah. Okay, not really. It's my first Thanksgiving since the divorce was final." Xander grimaced. "Sure, we'd be apart today no matter what, but it's still hard. You're lucky to be with your husband."

Yeah, real lucky. "You've got Cat to celebrate with."

"Uh-huh. In the absence of football, her notion of Thanksgiving entertainment is *Trains, Planes, and Automobiles.*"

At sudden whistling and clapping, Teri looked up at the parade. On the heels (literally) of a Spider-Man balloon came … an IPE Moonship balloon labeled *Bradbury.* It trailed a streamer reading FIRST ON MARS. Blake Wagner at work. Arranged from Dubai if she had to guess. She gave her team a thumbs up.

"What's going on?" Xander asked.

As she turned her datasheet for him to see, the *Bradbury* balloon exited the camera's view and a *Burroughs* balloon slid onto the wall display. "Free enterprise at work."

"It would appear so. Anyway, again, happy Thanksgiving. I should let you get back to your party."

Perhaps he should. Clearly, he didn't wish to. "What would you prefer to be watching?"

"We always had my sister and her family over. The kiddos and I would stream *A Charlie Brown Thanksgiving.*" He sighed. "The girls are twins, ten. By the time we're home, they'll be too old and 'mature' for such things."

The *Burroughs* balloon marked, if not the end of the parade, at least the end of that segment of NEP's update. A still image of the White House came next, captioned THE PRESIDENT'S THANKSGIVING DAY ADDRESS TO THE NATION.

Dullsville, Teri thought, surprised this had made it into the upload. Jake and Keshaun seemed interested, so she tuned out the expected pro forma blather and kept chatting. Until the screen crawl offered PRESIDENTIAL SHOUT-OUT TO THE AMERICANS ON PHOBOS AND MARS.

"Gotta go, Xander. Have some pie. I find that always helps."

She backed up the vid about a minute and restarted.

"… are so fortunate to live in a second Age of Discovery," the president pontificated. "While we appreciate and support the international nature of the current explorations of the latest New World, America has special reasons to be proud. The NASA-coordinated mission operating from Phobos includes two American astronauts, with the team ably led by our own Cat Mancini. And a private consortium is also investigating Mars itself, its team half American and led by our own Teri Rodriguez. Both teams, I'll add, reached those other worlds aboard American-built spacecraft. To these brave countrymen and-women, today so far from home, I thank you for your dedication and sacrifice.

"Of course, many other Americans, here at home and overseas, keep us safe. To the women and men in service, I say …"

Teri nodded along as the president spoke. NEP and NASA had both used IPE vessels built in America. As for the mission rosters, the numbers were what they were. Blake's certain apoplexy aside, Teri felt only pride.

"Talk about chutzpah," Reuben muttered.

Mid-sentence, the president was cut off. Blake Wagner, of all people, appeared next in the upload. Behind a podium bearing an NEP seal (the first Teri knew the partnership *had* a seal). Wearing (how unlike him) a suit and tie. "I've been asked by my colleagues at New Earth Partners to correct the record regarding an implication left earlier today by President DeMille in her holiday comments. While it can be said of our eight intrepid explorers, that four were born in America, it's also true that Teri Rodriguez, our expedition leader, is half Mexican and a dual citizen. NEP rejects the notion that any nation can assert sovereign jurisdiction over our private partnership's development of Martian resources or …."

Teri's mind … reeled. Dual citizen?

Across the shelter, Jake studied her, his expression confused. Of course, he was puzzled! He knew damned well how she felt about the man who had abandoned her and her mother, who had been out of her life since she was *two*.

From seeming ages ago, an odd interaction in Dubai came rushing back: Blake inquiring about her family. Those questions, like partner thumbs on the scales of her crew selection, had been calculated. Deliberate. Cold-blooded. Planning ahead lest America, on any basis, try to claim jurisdiction over this mission.

175

But dual citizenship? Vaguely, Teri understood that one Mexican parent qualified her under Mexican law. She'd never looked into the process, much less applied.

Not that she supposed NEP would mind greasing a bureaucrat palm or two.

Even as Teri struggled to put her rage into words, the inevitable email arrived from her mother. Abrupt. Anguished. Angry.

MARIA THERESA, WTF?

Indeed, three letters had it covered. If ever her hands quit trembling, she'd be sending that question herself.

Blake, what the actual *fuck*?

January 4, 2034

With the once-global Martian dust storm abating, the Ares mission has successfully delivered its first rock-core samples for study on Phobos.

—@NASA

Proposed Lunar Biolab

In response to widespread and growing apprehensions as to the theoretical threat of Martian pathogens, US president Carla DeMille today announced a study on the feasibility of constructing a quarantine facility and state-of-the-art biology lab on the Moon. The president invited NASA's partners, CSA, ESA, and JAXA, to take part.

Speaking for the UK, the prime minister expressed both interest and concerns ....

—*BBC World News*

ZAPnet zapped

Demanding a $100M payoff in Bitcoin, the GrimReaper ransomware group has shut down ZAPnet, a major regional network of high-speed charging stations for electric vehicles. Wait times have tripled at alternate networks across much of the Midwest. Central States Power Cooperative, owner/operator of ZAPnet, released a statement deploring the irresponsible act, refusing to pay ransom, and predicting the restoration of normal operations "in the coming days."

As impatient commuters across the region gambled on reaching home without recharging, tens of thousands of stalled vehicles clogged major traffic arteries. The National Guard has been activated in major metropolitan areas of Michigan, Wisconsin, Illinois, and Indiana to clear highways and help direct traffic ....

—Detroit Free Press

Quarantine camp on the Moon? It seems like an expensive way to keep Dale Bennigan off the evening news.

—The Late Late Show with Deena Patel

Terminated?

A California state judge today declared a hung jury in the latest high-profile, digital-appropriation case. Retired actor and former governor Arnold Schwarzenegger had brought the suit alleging unauthorized digital appropriation of his persona in a fitness-center ad campaign.

Schwarzenegger vows to fight on. Or, as he promised reporters outside the Los Angeles courthouse, "I'll be back."

—Entertainment Weekly

PPL Rejects Fake Solution to Sample Return

Some might believe vetting Martian samples on the Moon will protect us on Earth. As if we won't then be told better-equipped labs on Earth are needed for further study. As if there won't be advocacy for repatriating astronauts long steeped in unknown pathogens.

We are not so naive. No returns will be permitted from Mars.

—Communiqué of the Planetary Protection Legions

February 12, 2034

Out of This World Adventure

Have you been to the summit of Mount Everest? (View pans slowly over piles of refuse left behind by past climbers.) Admired the Grand Canyon? (View of tourist hordes in T-shirts, cut-offs, and flip-flops, mugging for their selfies along the canyon rim.) Checked out Antarctica? (View of a many-decked cruise ship, hundreds of passengers lining the railing, gawking at a glacier a good half mile distant.) Popped above the atmosphere for a few minutes out of gravity? (Close-up of a floating space tourist, seeming on the verge of vomiting.)

Perhaps the better question is, who *hasn't*? (Quick shots cycling among scenes of urban centers indistinguishable apart from scattered differences in clothing.)

For those of you ready for true adventure, exclusive adventure, the experience of a lifetime, look no further ... than Mars. (Panoramic images taken from low Mars orbit.) Because, with Out of the World Experiences, you can scale Mons Olympus, the tallest mountain in the Solar System. Hike Valles Marineris, a rift system to put the Grand Canyon to shame. Explore the twists and turns of Noctis Labyrinthus, the fabulous Labyrinth of Night. Scale the ice cliffs of the planet's southern polar cap, more than two miles thick. And so much more ….

For the discerning traveler. Round-trip packages beginning at $500 million per person. Taking reservations now for departures estimated to begin in 2035. Deposit only $10 million.

—Personalized ad during Super Bowl LXXVIII for Out of this World Experiences (A New Earth Partners company), exclusively streamed to individuals on the Forbes "2033 World's Billionaires List"

February 15, 2034

Teri couldn't help but grin. Without a doubt, this was a Big Day.

Six tiny chinchillas scurried about the cardboard carton lined with paper scraps. The litter was not quite an hour old. Had she not *seen* these kits up and about so quickly, she wouldn't have believed it. Nor did Martian gravity explain their neonate agility. On Earth, too, chinchillas were mobile almost from birth. The way everyone crowded around the box, Teri wasn't alone in her fascination. Islah, with a huge smile on her face, filmed their antics.

Damn, but the little critters were cute. The ears they would need time to grow into. The fuzzy gray fur. The tiny forepaws. The babies looked … perfect. Other than exhausted, Momma also looked fine.

Which made what must follow all the harder.

"These two," Paula decided. Scooping up both even as she spoke, allowing no one an opportunity to object. Because what she euphemized as *harvesting* was, by Teri's standards, *killing and dissecting*.

Climate Change Threatens Cherry Festival

In Kyoto today, cherry blossoms reached full bloom on the earliest date ever recorded. Traditional accounts back to the year 815 CE show full bloom in mid-April. Even as recently as 2021, climate change had accelerated full bloom only to late March.

—*All Nippon News*

Boredom, Xander had concluded, wasn't the worst of their situation. The endless futility was. Eight round-trip lander missions to date, with up to eight rovers deployed per mission, and often dozens of samples, from multiple sites, collected per rover. A half dozen distinct terrain types inspected.

Hints of Martian life, past or present? Zero.

Big planet, Xander kept repeating to himself, big planet, big planet, big planet, until the syllables faded into a mantra. In area, the arid surface of Mars rivaled the entire land surface of that water world, Earth. A wall map (with past landing sites denoted by tiny circles drawn in green grease pen, with rover paths radiating from the circles marked in blue) showed more than enough Mars incognita to keep them busy until their return window opened.

Keep *Sonny* busy, anyway.

Standing shoulder-by-jowl with her in the Phobos biolab, not exactly hoping she'd need IT support, he marveled at her cheerfulness. In his more cynical moments, he wondered if her spirits were as feigned as *his* public optimism. In support of this theory, the once nonstop, animated expositions as she'd gone about her work grew ever more sporadic.

After the short hand-over-hand glide from the habitat, they had remained in their vacuum gear. He'd have defied Houdini himself to wriggle out of a counterpressure suit in this confined space. In a terrestrial biosafety lab, they'd have been wearing the euphemistically named moon suits for protection. Actual Mars suits (custom-made for their mission, with antibacterial polymers blended into the plastics and woven into the fibers) served double duty.

Sonny slipped new disposable gloves over her spacesuit hands— her filthy, bulky, outdoor work gloves already set aside—then slid her arms into the sturdy, elbow-length rubber gauntlets that protruded into the lab's Martian-climate-controlled side. The drill core from lander return-flight eight, site two, rover three, awaited her attention, deposited there by a bot dedicated to handling returns from the planet. "Umpteenth time is the charm."

"If not," as he expected, "then the umpteenth and first." Big planet. Big planet. Big goddamn, taunting, teasing planet.

"From your lips to Mars's ears."

His mantra having again failed him, Xander switched to mentally lecturing himself. That by any normal person's standards, this was the adventure of a lifetime. That for the opportunity to stand on Phobos—with the grandeur of Mars overhead, seeming close enough to touch—many people would trade their right arm and a kidney. That between studies and osmosis, he was picking up a lot about biology. That any day now, he might witness the greatest scientific discovery since, well ... maybe *ever*.

Yeah, right.

He hadn't begun this way. Negative. Cynical. Depressed?

For a long while, he'd been too busy to notice his mood. There'd been challenge after challenge in prepping their mission. The daily struggles, the workarounds for one unanticipated complication after another. The compressed schedule, and the training, and the world's fascination with every step along the way. Even command performances for the president and the DNI—along with at least a touch of vanity at being a confidant (or so he flattered himself) to some of the most powerful people on Earth. All that had absorbed and, yes, exhilarated Xander like nothing he could have imagined. When, somehow, all *that* was over, even the long, cooped-up flight had offered the suspense of the (pointless) race.

But since arrival and initial deployment, months of dull routine, and the prospect of months more, to be succeeded by *another* long, dreary flight, had drained his last atom of enthusiasm. As for his private connection to Washington's elite, what revelations remained to share? That another location on Mars had rocks?

Introspection wasn't working any better than a mantra. He needed ... he didn't know what he needed. Other than serious change.

Sonny hummed to herself as she worked. Painstakingly wielding her microtome, shaving the thinnest of sample sections from the latest drill core. (This latest batch appeared to Xander's untrained eye to be dense, ice-free rock. Yet again.) Studying section after section beneath an optical microscope and, less often, when some feature caught her eye, with an electron microscope. Transferring random dollops of pulverized rock to petri dishes half-filled with a glucose solution to join the hundreds such already incubating—all so far unresponsive to warmth, moisture, and possible nourishment. Laser-ionizing traces of other random sample sections for analysis by mass spectrometer.

Lab supplies, incubators, and all her fancy instruments resided behind clear plastic on the lab's pseudo-Martian side—as much of that gear, anyway, as had survived the trip. Breakage had run the gamut from simple glassware to a centrifuge, a gas chromatograph, a cell sorter, a pH meter, and—the source of much grumbling—*both* gene sequencers. Blame might rest with careless packaging, but Xander's bet was on the clumsy, rushed, and improvised cargo shuffle performed at the Lunar Gateway. Not that, as far as he could tell, the subterfuge with the drones and "winning" the race had mattered.

Then again, neither did the unusable equipment seem to matter. Sonny had found no cells to sort, much less any genome to sequence—as though there was any reason to suppose Martian cells would be terrestrial-like enough to be sequenced. Forget DNA or its hypothetical Martian equivalent. *No* Martian hydrocarbon even moderately complex had made an appearance, while the little that had been encountered was mainly methane, CH_4. Thirty years of robotic observation had yet to suggest that anything but geological processes was needed to explain the wisps of that simplest of hydrocarbons in the thin Martian atmosphere.

Sonny finally looked away from the most recent core sample. "Nothing noteworthy here." If negative results yet again disappointed her, she hid the frustration well. "Let's archive these sections and move on. I've tagged everything from this delivery."

With a blue grease pen, alongside the green circle within Candor Chasma, Xander X-ed off the end of a trail. X did *not* mark the spot. Yet again. And yet again, he wondered if the famous Edison quote was apocryphal: "I have not failed 700 times. I've succeeded in proving 700 ways how not to build a light bulb." As he wondered when the purple grease pen reserved for promising sites would dry out from disuse.

Xander glanced at a wall display to confirm which sample came next. "Channel three. Handler One"—one of their humanoid bots, biding its time outside the lab—"archive the current test sections, deliver the remainder of the current sample to the Mars-conditions side of the geolab, then bring in the payload case from rover four."

The bot radio-clicked once: acknowledgment.

At least the geology often varied among samples retrieved from sites scattered across the planet. Giselle and Hideo's lab had its own microscopes and a mass spec, plus instruments unlike anything here. They also worked behind a partition, following biosafety protocols—as much as they groused about that—lest something biological had eluded Sonny's random sampling.

Yeah, right.

As Handler One entered from the biolab's Martian-side airlock, Sonny extracted her arms from the elbow-length gauntlets. She peeled off and discarded disposable gloves and disappeared into the lab's claustrophobic chemical shower for a rinse. Once she reemerged, he followed for his own precautionary rinse. By then, she wore new disposable gloves, had removed her helmet, and was knuckle-rubbing a cheek. "Been needing that for a good half hour."

He popped his own helmet. "You have only to ask."

If she heard any double meaning in the offer, she pretended otherwise. "As Handy will be ten minutes at least at its task, I'm up for a bite. What'd you bring?"

Most days accompanying Sonny, the peak of his contribution was snack provisioning. But vacuum was dangerous, no matter how brief the excursion, so someone had to come along when she ventured from habitat to lab. "We've got Snickers, Cheetos, and sandwiches of, shudder, reconstituted cheese. Also, bulbs of hot coffee, hot tea, and ice water."

"Cheetos and water, please."

He handed those over, then helped himself to a Snickers and coffee.

She tore open the foil pouch. "The thing about this search? If we never find signs of life here, the significance is every bit as profound as if we do."

In principle, Xander got it. Young Mars had had an atmosphere and oceans. If biology were something that developed naturally under congenial circumstances, this world *should* have brought forth life. If Mars never had, the knowledge would make Earth, somehow, special. Would make life, somehow, more precious. "*Profound* and *interesting* turn out to be different."

Sonny laughed. "Ye of little faith. We've hardly scratched the surface here."

"That's just it! Scratching the surface is all we ever do. Our rovers can't collect cores from more than two meters down." Which, while three times the depth managed by the NASA's *Perseverance* rover in the Twenties, remained … a pinprick. Trivial. "Life could be teeming deeper in the rock, where it's warmer, or in a deep aquifer, and we'll never know."

She somehow pulled off looking meditative while crunching corn puffs. Already her new right glove had acquired an orange sheen. "It'd be nice to drill deeper, but you know the tradeoff. Lots of small rovers or a few more massive ones. We could as easily strike out by searching in too few places as from sampling too shallowly."

"Uh-huh," he grumped.

More Cheetos disappeared, washed down by a long swig. "Anyway, you make it too cut and dried. Water supposedly does sometimes break through to the surface."

Emphasis on *supposedly*. Over the years, during the Martian spring, NASA's higher-resolution orbiters had often imaged "recurring slope lineae." Pure water couldn't be liquid anywhere near the Martian surface, but salty enough water might.

If wishes were horses, then beggars could ride. Not one RSL site probed so far had confirmed an eruption of water. Sand spills, to be sure. Also, sulfates and non-hydrated salts that had interacted to cause landslides. So, yes, something sometimes broke through to the surface to run downhill in narrow lines. But most often, a rover's closeup look just showed how often remote-sensed data of these tiny features were false positives.

Regardless: no reason to drag *her* down. "That's fair. Point taken."

"Not by you, I gather." She whacked his arm, leaving a faint orange handprint. "Never play poker. Not with that face. Look, I admit we haven't yet found life signs, but circumstances haven't cooperated. Right?"

"Right." Because RSLs were in the main springtime and near-equatorial phenomena. The Ares team had arrived at Phobos during southern-hemisphere spring—in time for the dust storm to begin there. Many candidate RSL sites were only now reemerging as the global dust storm receded.

"Our next sample might hit the mother lode." Sonny finished her snack, crumpled the foil bag, and tucked it into a refuse bin. She picked up her helmet, ready once again to brave imported dirt. "Or one of the teams below will. Then we'll know where to focus our attention."

For sure, that hadn't happened yet. NEP or the Chinese government would have been crowing—and rubbing the president's face in the Ares mission's failure. "One small problem with that hope, Sonny. They have other priorities."

"Unless you have a better idea, let's just carry on."

Did he? Randomly firing synapses, perhaps. Nothing that rose to the level of half-baked, much less an actual idea. At best, possibilities to further ponder on his own time. "Okay, my friend. You carry on, and I'll see whether I can imagine a better alternative."

March 18, 2034

Dale stepped out of the neighborhood dry cleaner, one hand tucking her garment receipt into a jeans pocket, the other occupied with preventing the shop's door from slamming. It was not quite ten in the morning, but the day was already sweltering.

"Dr. Bennigan?"

The voice sounded familiar, but Dale couldn't place it. Neither, glancing that way, did she recognize the man in shorts and a faded E Street Band T-shirt who expectantly studied her. Was this some random guy who recognized her from one or another damned press conference? Or a person she should know, her weary brain refusing to make the connection? Something about those horn-rimmed glasses ...?

The penny dropped.

"Mr. Coleman," she said coldly.

"Guilty as charged, and I'm neither stalking nor planning to harass you." He gestured past her. "I was headed to Starbucks when you emerged. Care to join me?"

Care to? *Hell*, no. Would humoring him buy her some goodwill or set her up for an ambush?

"It's not a trick question. I save those for while I'm working. You might even find that, off the clock, I'm a genuine human being."

"The conversation to be all off the record?"

He raised a hand. "Scout's honor."

"Well, maybe a quick cup." And I'll buy my own.

They ordered, collected their cups (and, for him, a bear claw larger than her hand), and found a table. "So, Mr. Coleman," she began, "are you from around here?"

"Off the clock, it's Ira. For about a year." He named a nearby apartment complex. "You?"

"Dale. About a mile or so." As if Google wouldn't reveal her address in an instant.

He smiled. "*Not* stalking you. Remember?"

Dale took a cautious sip. The coffee was too hot, as usual. She set down the cup to let its contents cool. "I assume there's something on your mind."

"Always. But off the record, I promise. Convergent evolution. Ever heard of it?"

"Let's see. I'm a doctor and biologist. Have I heard of evolution?"

He took a chomp from his pastry, chewed, swallowed. "Evolution, sure. I asked about *convergent* evolution."

"Why?"

"Some people I know think it's a big deal. I don't understand the topic enough to have an opinion."

She managed not to sigh. "People? Or PPL?"

He bit off another chunk of his pastry. "It started with the latter. I've moved on to the former. Maybe I understood enough to qualify as confused."

"Convergent evolution." Absently, she drummed fingers against the tabletop, thinking back. Tested her coffee again. It had cooled just enough for a decent swig. "Like fish, porpoises, and ichthyosaurs independently having fins and streamlined bodies."

He chewed and swallowed. "Yeah, like that. As I understand it, because common problems, in common environments, may have a few, or maybe only one, good solution."

"One-of-a-kind forms *also* happen. Like giraffes. I don't imagine tall trees are unique to Africa. Then there's *us*. Humans." Across the dining area, a pair of teenage boys laughed raucously at something, and she lost her train of thought. In time, it found its way back. "What do PPL care about this? They expecting our guys to bring home fish and porpoises from Mars?"

"Yeah, I didn't get their concern, either. It might just be me, though. I'm not all that sure I get evolution." He waved off a rejoinder before Dale could comment. "Don't get me wrong. I believe evolution happens, but I'm fuzzy on the details."

Had she nothing better to do with her Saturday morning than recap Biology 101? If it might avert press-room ignorance someday, maybe not. "It boils down to variation and natural selection.

"Random events change genes. The occasional transcription error can alter a gene when a cell reproduces. Or the number of instances of a gene on a chromosome changes spontaneously. Sometimes, cosmic or solar radiation directly alters DNA. Whatever the cause, if the genetic change does fatal damage, that's the end of the story. All that's the variation part.

"Okay, on to natural selection. Suppose some variation, some mutation, leads to any sort of advantage. Plants or animals with that difference are likelier than those without to live longer and reproduce." She had in mind Darwin's famous Galapagos Island finches and (as vaguely as she recalled the specifics) island-by-island variations in beak characteristics, the better to exploit local seed types. "Other times, a genetic change might be both harmless and useless. Unless some environmental shift later turns that mutation relevant—a drought, say, that now favors a plant's latent ability to lose less water to evaporation—such mutations, starting out rare, will peter out."

"That it?"

The last time she'd had cause to think about this stuff was in genetics class. That was in first-year med school. Evolution hadn't been a factor in practicing medicine or while researching (how long ago *this* seemed!) the ways polypeptide chains folded up to form proteins. Much less trying to understand why such chains on occasion *mis*folded, with nasty consequences.

Still, she dredged up one last memory. "I'd emphasize the unpredictability of the process. Everything from stray cosmic rays to a dinosaur-obliterating asteroid strike affects it, plus every sort of chance occurrence in between. Whether a mutation even occurs? Whether it helps or hinders an organism's prospects for survival? Those are iffy things."

"The butterfly effect, then."

That was the speculation that the flapping of an insect's wings might, days or weeks after the fact, through some unforeseeable cascade of events, cause a hurricane far away. So, literally, very different things. But metaphorically? "Sort of."

"Then convergence, when it happens, is a fluke?" He took a folded datasheet from a pocket and began tapping and swiping. He set it on the table facing her, a column of animal images on display.

"What's this?" she asked.

"You tell me."

"Top to bottom, a mole, a flying squirrel, a … groundhog, I think that is, a cat, and a wolf."

"Placental mammals, all of them."

"Well, yeah."

"Zero for five. They're a marsupial mole, sugar glider, wombat, quoll, and thylacine. All marsupials, from Australia." He reached across the table to tap the datasheet, bringing a second column of animals into view. "*These* are the critters you named."

"That's a lot of convergence."

He nodded. "Yeah, so PPL tells me. Also, that there are many more examples."

"You don't know why they're interested?"

He shrugged.

"Well, I don't see it, either. However"—she slid back her chair—"I've got things to do."

Taking the hint, he stood. "Nice chatting with you." With a smile, he was off.

Leaving her to wonder, from errand to errand, about evolutionary coincidences and PPL's curious interest in them.

March 20, 2034

"That," Giselle allowed, "was excellent," and murmurs of agreement rose around her.

Xander could only concur. Once each day's dinner and (busy)work ended, the six of them often stayed for a movie in the habitat's common area. They took turns choosing, and that evening Cat had done the honors: for its special effects, the 2030 remake of *The Terminator*, with the leads digitally recast as Schwarzenegger, Hamilton, and Biehn from the original. If the mash-up wasn't, in Xander's opinion, as good as the 1984 version, it still had more than merited the raid on their dwindling supply of popcorn. Even Hideo, whose tastes ran to samurai epics and spaghetti westerns, nodded in approval.

Now's my shot, Xander thought. While everyone's feeling mellow. "Guys? I've got a work suggestion."

"Way to spoil the mood," Cat said. With a smile. The comment meant nothing.

David started a circuit of the room, sticky slippers *thp-thpping* as he went, collecting empty popcorn bowls. "First to circumnavigate Phobos might be some kind of record. I don't think it counts as work. Or sane."

"A reasonable guess, David, but no. Not that."

Because Xander *had* pitched such a project, with helmet cameras recording the voyage as he went: Around the World in Eighty Minutes. Take *that* Phileas Fogg!

A steady twenty-five miles or so per hour would do the trick: a rate, coincidentally, approaching escape velocity. The only possibility of reaching and sustaining such speed in a hand-over-hand glide along a guide wire was tether-free—sans pauses to shift carabiners past piton after piton. Still, questioning his sanity felt … harsh. *If* he managed to hurl himself off-world and into orbit around Mars, a lander could tow him back.

But fun, games, a prospective mention in Ripley's, and debatable recklessness aside, such an expedition had a purpose. Five months in, they needed a *challenge*. Stickney Crater and its surrounding territory had been thoroughly explored. Their small chemical plants were long since up and running, turning the local ice into water, oh-two, and more fuel for the landers. In the hydroponics dome, a second batch of salad veggies was almost ready for harvest. Their 3-D printers (however unpalatable the experimental, so-called food they synthed) excelled at knitting super-strong cables from locally produced carbon nanotubes.

Leaving, with almost fourteen months until their return window opened … what? More poking, likely futile, at Mars's surface. More down-and-up lander jaunts to configure (for Xander, too, become a tedious video game) to support that idle scratching and scraping. At least extending the Phobos guide-wire network would give Giselle and Hideo, geologist and mining engineer, different samples and a change of scenery.

Never mind Edison; Einstein had had it right. Insanity was doing the same thing over and over again and expecting different results.

"No," Xander said, "not the Phobos trip. Something more ambitious."

David took the empty bowl from Xander's hands. The few un-popped kernels rattled at the bottom. "Then are you finally aboard with sending a lander or three to study Deimos?"

A robotic visit to Deimos being David's latest hobbyhorse, having supplanted simulations of landing *Lewis* or *Clark* on Mars. Sans massive heat shields for aerobraking. Sans parachutes. The ships had neither, their descent to Mars itself never intended. The simulations considered a slow, controlled flight all the way down, with engines blazing, of a ship refueled on Phobos.

The planet-landing simulations had themselves replaced digital recasting of news bulletins and classic movies. Xander didn't miss the dramacide. *Night of the Living Dead*, with the six of them transformed into zombie extras? Creepy. On the other hand, he had to admit Giselle made a fine Arwen when David had had the temerity to fiddle with *Lord of the Rings*. But David as Aragorn? In his dreams. Where, if Xander had to guess, Giselle made appearances.

It was marvelous how David could entertain himself—when he kept it to himself.

From Phobos, a mission to the other moon would be far easier than landing on the planet. The better question was *why*? By every indication, both moons were quite similar. Given that David found one rock as uninteresting as the next—and still griped on occasion that Cat had landed *Lewis* first—Xander would've given good odds that David's interest was in being first to land on Mars's other moon. Even if that encounter would happen by remote piloting and not in person.

"No," Xander said. "Not Deimos, either."

"Fine. What *is* on your mind?"

"Drilling way deeper. I propose that—"

"As if we don't all want that." Giselle exhaled sharply, exasperatedly, through her nose. "As if, as much as anyone, I don't." Any ancient fossils would fall squarely in her domain—and would be found, if anywhere, in long-buried Martian strata. "This is only a useless wish."

As Cat and Sonny exchanged disappointed frowns, Hideo took his turn. "I follow your guidance on computing matters, Xander. I trust you'll pay heed to my experience. We're unequipped to take cores from deeper than two meters. To get even a little deeper, we'd need longer, stronger drill barrels. Those are—"

As though everyone here hadn't taken turns prepping rovers. "Little more than simple metal pipes. One end with sharp edges. The other end threaded to screw onto the drill shaft."

"Right. Sorry. To go deeper, we'd also need a mechanism to insert the drill, barrel and all, to the bottom of the shaft. Were those difficulties addressed, the drill and barrel would need to be raised from the ground after every few meters dug, and the latest core extracted from the barrel. Accomplish all that, and we'd still be in trouble. Drilling into Martian bedrock would soon ruin, would grind to dullness, the cutting edges of those drill barrels we have. If even those obstacles were somehow overcome, we'd still need a heavier-duty drill, a bigger battery to power the bigger motor, and more onsite dexterity than our rovers can provide.

"We lack such equipment by choice. We lack landers with the payload capacity for them by choice. Given the cargo limitations of *Lewis* and *Clark*, such a strategy would have meant fewer landers, fewer rovers, fewer sites explored. Our agencies collectively decided against gambling on such a limited number of sample sites. You *know* this."

Abruptly, as though embarrassed by his outburst, Hideo fell silent.

David piled on from the habitat's tiny galley. "Which part of follow the mission plan don't you get?"

Which part of we're millions of miles from home don't *you* get? Or that the purpose of having people on the scene, not just robots, was to adapt? Xander said, "If everyone's done, I'll explain why I think this is doable."

Cat shrugged. "Fine. Give it your best shot."

Xander took a deep breath. "Assume for the moment we have the new drill barrels and higher-capacity batteries we'll need."

David returned from the galley. "No small assumption."

Maybe not. Xander had an answer, but that was where the real controversy would be. "Let's start with the upgraded drill. That's easy. We have reels of spare copper wire. If you're hesitant to dip into that, then we scavenge wire from a few rovers. We can easily"—because you don't depart Earth for years without some type of machine shop—"wind stator and rotor coils for a more powerful BLDC." Brushless DC motor.

"Okay ..." Cat allowed. "Go on."

"As Hideo pointed out, we'll need periodically to raise the drill to process successive core segments. That means removing the barrel, extracting the core, wrapping it, labeling it, and stowing it aboard the rover or lander. Then remount the barrel, lower it into the shaft, and repeat. These simple tasks call for hands and hand tools on site—so we send down a Handler. Folded up on itself as it was in our cargo hold, a Handler will fit aboard a lander. The arm of a rover sent down first can pull the folded Handler down a lander's deployment ramp, after which the Handler can unfold itself."

"You *have* been thinking about this," Cat said.

"Wait a minute," Sonny interrupted. "The handler bots are essential to maintaining quarantine of samples."

Xander countered, "One Handler is. I see no better use for our spare than maybe getting you samples *worth* quarantining."

"What if the Handler left on Phobos breaks?" Sonny asked.

"Then the unit below folds itself up, a rover pushes it back up the ramp into a lander, and that lander returns the spare." Glancing about the room, Xander saw plenty of skepticism but perhaps less of the aggravated impatience with which this dialogue had begun. Did they start to believe? "As for the hard part, one word. Iron."

"Consider expending a few more words," Cat said.

His mouth gone dry, Xander took several long swallows from his coffee bulb. "Iron pipe. Iron-oxygen batteries. Iron dipole antennas."

"Batteries and antennas?" Sonny echoed.

Xander nodded. "Every item on a rover, drill included, runs off its batteries. The few square feet of solar panel the rover can carry barely dribble out power. To go deep, much less at any decent pace, we'll need lots more power below. So, we beam our excess solar power. It'll take an array of dipole antennas at the drill site to receive the beam and rectifying electronics to convert the power to DC to charge the batteries. *Then* we do serious drilling."

"Okay, iron," Cat summarized.

David glowered. "That'd be great if we *had* a great deal of iron. Which we don't. Or if Phobos had iron ore. Which it doesn't. If we had either, we don't have smelting or foundry equipment, or any notion of how to work metal in negligible gravity. If none of that were the case, how many lander flights do you see this scheme consuming? No, this is impractical."

"*We* don't have that much metal," Xander agreed. "But I know a place whose surface is paved with iron oxide." He pointed at the roof—

And through that, toward the Red Planet. Given its distinctive russet color by the ubiquitous rust ....

March 22, 2034

Mocking rather than cheery, morning sunlight streamed through the open blinds of Rebecca Nguyen's NASA office. Or maybe, Dale told herself, *you're in a foul mood.*

As if there were any *maybe* about it.

"Have a seat." Rebecca closed the office door and took a seat. The small conference table was cleared apart from a communal jar of jelly-beans. "I appreciate your coming, especially since I'll have to keep this quick. In a half hour, I'm off to the Hill. Congress critters to placate."

About the latest lunar BSL-4 cost estimates? Dale didn't want to ask. She took another chair at the table, her back to the window. "Been there. Done that."

Though not recently. Her position had been on life support since the fiasco in France, and everyone knew it. Just waiting for Cruella to pull the plug. Waiting for the day her "resignation" might distract from something more embarrassing to the administration. Struggling, even before the axe fell, to gain access to assistants to assistants to anyone important at the White House.

Rebecca took a deep breath. "Xander's personal email to us. What do you think?"

I think it's effing brilliant. *Buy* what they need. "Could work."

Because both missions on Mars's surface were already producing structural elements and batteries from Martian iron. Cranking out

198

iron drill barrels would be simple enough. CMSA and NEP were also making LOX and LH2 from buried ice—even if the former bunch was close-mouthed about their production rate. Either group could fly drill barrels and iron-oxygen batteries to wherever the Ares bunch would want them. In a pinch, Phobos could dispatch empty landers to take delivery. That would delay deeper drilling, but not for all that long.

"You don't find it odd that his proposal is off the record?"

Dale shrugged. "Yes and no. You're friends. I like to think he and I are, too."

"Oh, I imagine Xander's counting on that." A pigeon fluttered by the window, and Rebecca's eyes briefly followed. "That was the 'no' part. What did surprise you?"

"It isn't surprise, exactly, but I wonder about him going around Cat Mancini."

"Knowing them both well, I read the situation differently. I'd wager Cat agrees with Xander. But she can also read the tea leaves. She's not willing to stick her neck out." (What tea leaves? Dale didn't get it.) Rebecca rapped the table. "Okay, that's enough speculation. Let's deal with the substance. You said, 'could work.' That implies reservations."

"Well, I'd want to work out protocols for the handover of the drill barrels. Decontamination procedures. Ideally, all handling of the drill barrels done by robot." Dale rubbed her chin. "But do I think those details can be worked out? Sure."

"I don't doubt it could work. But do you believe it will fly?"

Dale was less than fluent in Politic. She needed a moment to translate. "You mean, do I think the administrator will go along?"

Rebecca glanced over her shoulder as though reassuring herself her office door remained shut. "My boss is a weather vane."

"And my boss"—who's freezing me out—"is the wind?"

Rebecca winked. "Your words, not mine."

Dale helped herself to a few jellybeans. She ate them one by one, chewing slowly, stalling. The best evidence suggested she was the worst possible person to judge the president's preferences. "Cruella championed the mission. Why wouldn't she want it to be successful?"

"You don't get it," Rebecca said. "As far as she's concerned, the mission *is* a success. We got there first ... in a manner of speaking. I doubt she ever cared whether Mars has, or had, life, only that seeming to care covered for our inability to go straight to the surface.

"Which explains Van Dijk now pushing—meaning, the president demanding—Mars landings via the next outbound launch window. Ceding an entire planet to China and friends? Not popular. Hesitating to put American boots on the ground after the Fat Cat Consortium began advertising for tourists? I'd say that's a draw-and-quartering offense."

Which also explained, Dale thought, the foot-dragging she encountered every day in committing to a lunar BSL-4 lab. Maybe also that opaque tea-leaves reference.

Rebecca continued, "Whatever you, or I, or the astrobiology team here thinks, there's little appetite at either end of Pennsylvania Avenue for searching harder for Martian life. Trading with, so to speak, the enemy to do so? Not. Gonna. Happen. If you want my advice, do *not* bring this up with the president."

As if I could get on her schedule. "Uh-huh."

"My advice to Xander will be that he not use his almost-direct line to her, either. Because …?"

"Not gonna happen."

"Right," Rebecca said.

Dale grabbed another few jellybeans. "So, *can* you put people on Mars launched in the next window?"

"The short answer? Yes. With IPE delivering Moonships again, however reluctantly, it seems so. Not the scary-as-shit, straight-to-the-planet, skipping-stone-and-parachute approach the others have used, either. We're looking at a refueling stop on Phobos, followed by a much more controlled, powered descent. By then, we may even have a second ship supplier." Rebecca glanced at a wall clock, then stood. "Sorry. A couple minutes, and I have to be out the door."

"I should quit." The frustration just burst out. "Salvage whatever dignity I can."

"Or I can wait a few more." Rebecca sat back down. "C'mon. Don't do this. Forget the Ares mission. There's more than that in your portfolio. Isn't there?"

"Well, yeah." If nothing as important as what Ares was doing. What, anyway, that bunch *should* be doing.

"Then do that," Rebecca said. "Get out of town. Far outside the Beltway, where no one follows this political crap. Where no one knows you're on the outs. Find a few worthy endeavors that are under the radar. Help those along."

"While I can."

"If you must be fatalistic, then fine. Help while you can. What's wrong with that?"

"Nothing." Dale stood. "I needed that pep talk, not least of all because you're right. There are things, important things, I can look into. Things I *should* look into. So, thanks. Anyhow, don't let me make you any later."

Pondering a web article she'd skimmed days before about the latest antimicrobial-resistant variant in the staphylococcus genus, she trailed Rebecca from NASA headquarters.

"There are costs and risks to a program of action, but they are far less than the long range risks and costs of comfortable inaction."

—John F. Kennedy, President of the United States

"In a world that is changing really quickly, the only strategy that is guaranteed to fail is not taking risks."

—Mark Zuckerberg, Founder and CEO of Facebook

"Take calculated risks. That is quite different from being rash."

—Gen. George S. Patton

"If you want a guarantee, buy a toaster."

—Clint Eastwood

DEFIANCE

April 10, 2034

Sun shining brightly. Temperature a full five degrees centigrade above freezing. Winds mild and intermittent, with only a few high, scudding clouds. That the air was unbreathable and so thin that, with the imminent sunset, the temperature would plummet to seventy or so degrees *below*? For Mars, this was a balmy spring day.

Teri stood in sunlight, two paces from the hydroponics dome and its row upon row, tier upon tier, of lovely, lush, entirely *un*-Martian, greenery. Popping her helmet and breathing the fresh garden scents would have made the day perfect. With a smile, she dismissed the fantasy. That dome's miniaturized airlock—crops planted, tended, and soon enough harvested by little, specialized bots—was one of the countless tradeoffs made prelaunch. In what seemed another era, she'd been all about reducing payload mass in any way practical. But here? Now? Denying the crew access felt plain wrong.

Still, she told herself, things are coming along.

With the passing of the dust storm, they were all outside, productive, every day. Storm or no storm, a day without wind was a rarity; today was Reuben and Keshaun's turn to brush the latest patina of dust from the solar panels. Maia and Paula supervised bots assembling shelves and tray racks in what would be their second hydroponics dome. Julio and Jake constructed a low wall with the latest trial run of bricks. Islah, having drawn the day's short straw, was burying the latest accumulation of human and chinchilla shit. Sterilized, of course, in hopes of holding down PPL yapping. Teri herself—other than prioritizing and coordinating, arbitrating competing demands for oversubscribed power and other resources—pitched in wherever an extra pair of hands would be most useful.

Looking around for where next to pitch in, she saw everyone at work as expected. Everyone except Jake. Where the hell was he?

She twitched, then whirled, at a sharp tap on the shoulder. Jake. Like everyone, his counterpressure suit was filthy. "Jeez, don't sneak up on me like that."

"What? You think the Martians are out to get you?" Spoken with that wry, impish, devil-may-care grin she no longer found charming.

"Then your radio *is* working," she countered.

"Yeah, well. Can we go private?"

Teri checked which radio bands were in use before raising a fist, thumb and two fingers extended. "Suit, switch me to channel three." Jake nodded. "Okay, Jake. What's up?"

"We need to talk."

She shivered at the four most ominous words in the English language. It wasn't enough that her father had abandoned her. That her husband had betrayed and humiliated her. Now Jake was going to make *his* abandonment official. She was about to preempt him, to save whatever shred of dignity might remain to her by bringing up a divorce first, when he surprised her.

"I didn't come to fucking Mars to homestead."

She couldn't help it—she blinked. "Why did you come?"

"To be the first pilot to land on another planet." A distinction she had denied him. "To *explore.* To make NEP gobs of money so that a small fortune would trickle down my way."

"What are you saying?"

His expression hardened. "One way or another, I *am* going out to explore. Soon. I won't lack for someone to ride along, either. And trust me, Blake and his pals will support me on this."

One way or another? Meaning with or without her permission. As for that *someone,* Teri had a damned good idea who that would be. The skank.

If he went out on his own, blatantly defiant, what pretense would remain she was leader of the expedition? None. It would be one *more* betrayal. It would obliterate whatever crumbs of self-respect and purpose she might have left.

She wouldn't, *couldn't*, abide that. "It'll happen, Jake. You know the dust storm set us back. Have some patience."

"The storm receded weeks ago."

"The priority has been catch-up. But we're getting there."

Turning, he pointed at the latest trial brick wall at which Julio still labored. "Yeah, if *there* entails playing with blocks."

As if sarcasm helped … anyone. "Give it a few weeks. Till we've accumulated a bigger fuel reserve. Till the second hydroponics dome is in operation, taking some of the pressure off the food supplies we brought. And yes, on the subject of bricks, till we find a dependable recipe." Because some blend of regolith, clay, and other local constituents, cooked for the right length of time, at the right heat, and under the right pressure, would yield a superior building material. So, anyway, chemical engineers on Earth had confidently asserted. "Until then, we can't scale up production, can't build proper structures, can't quit huddling in the inflatables like weekend campers. *Then* it'll be time to move out."

"Bricklaying doesn't take eight people, Ter. Let's get real."

"Meaning?"

"Meaning, I'm not twiddling my thumbs for indeterminate 'weeks.' Meaning, I'm going to take the SUV and make the bosses happy. To begin, by scouting the canyon rim for places where paying customers can descend into Valles Marineris. Then, with that under my belt, Olympus Mons awaits."

Those bosses, to her pleasant surprise, hadn't yet complained about the delay in exploring. Not that they didn't complain—just that, so far, they'd focused their grumblings instead on the pace of infrastructure deployment. As though she were putting up modular townhouses in the burbs and not pioneering on Mars.

Regardless, she couldn't risk Jake so openly defying her. She *couldn't*. At best, his insubordination would have everyone questioning her authority. At worst, with a mere text, Blake would demote, depose, oust her. Would put someone else in charge. Might well put Jake in charge, damn him.

What beside this job did she have going for her these days?

Teri said, "Say that you do go. There's preparation for that, too. The SUV hasn't gone more than a few meters from *Burroughs* since we arrived." For all its importance, their custom sport-ute, given its great size and mass, was one of their few pieces of unduplicated cargo. Its breakdown on the road would be a *major* problem. "The cable trailer"— and its motorized reel, wound with literal miles of the super-thin, super-strong cable required for a descent into Valles Marineris—"is still aboard *Bradbury*. We'll need to check out both, take a couple short excursions, before venturing far. Organize the supplies and equipment for the trip and pack them aboard the SUV. Plan a route. Maybe you'll find you need to tow a second trailer to bring more supplies. Meanwhile, I'll need to redo work schedules here."

"None of which," he insisted, "should take more than a week."

"I'd guess ten days." Not really, but this was a negotiation. "How's this? We work together on the plan: A supply manifest. The precise route. Weather forecasts. All with the goal of departing in ten days."

"If you commit here and to Earth that that's the plan? Then I could live with that."

"If *I* announce this as the plan."

"I can live with that, too."

Damn him, the arrogant bastard. But it could work. The others might buy that she was still calling the shots. They should at least buy the pretense. "Okay, deal. I'll announce it at dinner tonight."

"Tell you what. I'll go lay a few bricks." Looking smug, Jake turned and strode away.

April 18, 2034

Deep in his bones, Xander felt all he'd done for the past two years was eat, sleep, and breathe a Mars mission. Conceptualizing, refining, training, flying—each in its own way wearying—had taken their toll. Only for *boredom* to become his biggest challenge ....

Six months on Phobos hadn't been entirely futile. They'd extracted water, oxygen, and rocket fuel from local resources, and even (loosely speaking) food. In so doing, they'd proven that this little moon could support explorations not only of the nearby planet but far beyond. They'd examined more of Mars than all the spacefaring nations of Earth had accomplished in the preceding half-century. They (okay, Giselle) had ferreted out long-mysterious details of the local sulfur cycle. Onsite study of the moon, which looked more and more like a captured asteroid, was revealing as much about the primordial Solar System as anyone could have hoped for.

At least Giselle was happy. Back home, the planetary geologists were, too.

Xander had parked himself in the habitat's compact, communal space. Nursing a bulb of foul, freeze-dried coffee. Nursing a foul mode. Idly scanning, before these were transmitted, a random few of "his" AIde-generated responses to the stream of NASA-encouraged— and endlessly repetitive—space-junkie questions and fan mail. (Never mind that the mission AIdes had long ago mastered everyone's personal style well enough to render most spot checks pointless.) Plodding through, absorbing at most half of what he read, another chapter in the latest biology text Sonny had netted him. Knocking out overdue ("Still having a ball here," white-lie) replies to recent family emails. Wondering if even his parents or sister would notice if he also delegated these notes to the AIde, as Cat had done months ago for her family. Reviewing a week's worth of event-free system maintenance logs that David had already examined. Nursing more foul coffee. All done in total silence, although David, Sonny, and Hideo were also present, immersed in their separate datasheets after their own monotonous days. Cat and Giselle, meanwhile, had retreated to their separate personal spaces, their blackout curtains drawn. Giselle's curtain wasn't quite pulled shut, her cubby leaking enough flickering light and faint murmurs to suggest she was streaming a video.

Something in Xander ... snapped.

"We can't go on like this. Not for another *year*." Slightly more than a year, in fact, until their return window opened. "We'll go nuts. We need to change things."

Hideo glanced up from his datasheet. "Change, how?"

"You know how. Dig more. Dig deeper. Take being here seriously."

"We're doing plenty of digging," Hideo said. "Maybe it's just as well we've found no hints of Martian life. If we realize how special *Earth* is, maybe we'll take better care of it."

There was an old joke about a drunk searching for his misplaced car keys. Not where he'd last seen them, but by a streetlamp—because the light there was better. Scratching only the literal surface? "We can learn what's here"—if we stop looking only near the proverbial streetlamp—"*and* appreciate what's there."

Sonny sighed, folded her datasheet, and tucked it into her shirt pocket. "Maybe it's for the best I haven't found anything."

Et tu, Sonny? Xander was, well, not shocked exactly. Dismayed. "How so?"

"For all the fuss back home about a facility to receive samples, I haven't heard a lot of *progress*. Suppose we dock, whether at the ISS or the Lunar Gateway, with possible biological samples. What then? How will those be transferred to a fully equipped lab? How will those be protected from cross-contamination during transfer and within biocontainment? If anyone's ever combined a high-grade cleanroom with a BSL-4 lab, it's news to me."

Issues Xander knew Dale had raised, over and over, till it was evident no one in authority cared. Nor, as she'd vented in emails, did Dale expect that to change unless or until the Ares team had something to isolate and study. When, arguably, it was already too late.

"Chicken and egg," Xander said.

"Hold it down," Giselle called out. "Some of us are trying to watch a movie."

Then wear earbuds, Xander thought. "That's it? We throw up our hands? Bide our time till we can go home?"

David (who, to all appearances, had until then tuned out the discussion) slapped the table. "Do you all not understand? The entire point of our being here is that we got here. We're no different than *Apollo*, a rock-collection and a flags-and-footprints show. Accept it."

Thoughts roiling, disheartened, Xander swallowed the dregs from his coffee bulb. Better than most, having been there from the beginning, he knew the truth of that flags-and-footprints barb. That didn't preclude them from making something of the situation. Though this toxic stew of cynicism and defeatism pretty much guaranteed that they would.

"Cat, Giselle," Xander called, "we need to talk. All of us."

Giselle appeared first, looking annoyed.

Cat came last. She'd taken a few seconds, it seemed, to compose herself. Change into something unrumpled. Run a comb through her hair. Maybe compose her thoughts. Assume mission-commander mode. "This griping is counterproductive. You want to drill more, Xander? We're doing as much as we can. You have a better idea where to drill? Convince Giselle or Sonny, and I'll listen. You want to drill deeper? We can't with the equipment we have, and your trial balloon to obtain more has been shot down. Unless you have something *new* to propose, I expect you to stick with the program."

That trial balloon, Becks and Dale alike had made clear, would go no further. Arthur Schmidt, when Xander had screwed up his courage and reached out through their secure channel to the DNI, had limited *his* response to a laughing emoji. No one would broach with the president buying what they needed from either of the teams on the ground. Leaving ....

He took a deep breath. "Yeah, Cat, I do have a new proposal. None of us asked officially about a trade with the folks below. Hence, we were never told no officially. Who's to say we can't reach out on our own initiative?"

Except Xander knew who: Cat herself. She was in charge. But he could at least hope she remained as conflicted, as disappointed, as he. She had, after all, gone along with his off-the-record trial balloon. After it crashed and burned, she'd given him an I-told-you-so-smirk, but still. If the mission commander said no, that was the end of the matter.

Instead, Cat shrugged. "Let me think on it."

April 20, 2034

Trillions for the Taking

ESA today announced their discovery and preliminary orbital determination of a priceless, metal-rich asteroid. Observations from a constellation of orbital observatories indicate an object replete with gold, tantalum, palladium, platinum, rhenium, and osmium, plus at least a smattering of rare-earth elements. Apart from its size and orbital parameters, this newfound M-class (metallic) asteroid resembles the yet more remote 16 Psyche, visited by a NASA probe in 2026.

The Minor Planet Center, under the auspices of the International Astronomical Union, has given this unique object the provisional designation of (583188) 2034 FL. As for an official name, subject to approval by the IAU, the ESA investigators propose "Croesus."

On Earth, this mineral storehouse would have a value in the trillions—take your pick of pounds, euros, or dollars—at least, until such vast quantities of these precious materials were to reach the market. Unfortunately, the space agency concluded, Croesus lies well beyond our reach, orbiting as far beyond Mars as Mars does beyond Earth.

—*BBC World Service*

Teri led the gang, all eager, from their shelters. Their inaugural ground expedition was about to depart. The waiting Mars SUV (despite its name resembling, more than anything else, a bladeless bulldozer) faced east. A cargo trailer piled high with supplies was hitched behind it, and the cable-reel trailer behind that. Parallel shallow ruts encircled the camp, worn into the Martian terrain by the tracked vehicle on its thousand-lap, auto-piloted, shakedown cruise. To the south, at the chasm's edge, sat a half-meter-wide boulder: the test mass twice lowered and retrieved to check out the motorized cable reel.

Jake and Paula stood by the SUV, chomping at the bit to be gone. Teri and the rest gathered, facing them.

Jake may have been right, Teri conceded, if only to herself. True, a couple of construction tasks, neither urgent, *had* slid to the right on the schedule. But as for venturing from base camp, they seemed as ready as they'd ever be.

She hoped that was ready enough.

By local standards, the -50 °C chill notwithstanding, the spring morning was pleasant. There wasn't much wind, the occasional gust failing to spin the anemometer and scarcely raising bits of dust. The sky was clear, in a butterscotch sort of way, and only a few high clouds scudded overhead. That the sun seemed not half as large as viewed from Earth and was not even half as bright? Compared to the human eye's adaptability to varying light levels, those differences barely registered. Meanwhile, to the *west*, the sort-of-football-shaped lump of Phobos was rising.

Teri didn't much like Phobos, and no longer because its reappearance three times a day still evoked a second-place finish and Cat Mancini's taunts. Forget the Man on the Moon. Phobos, at about a third of the Moon's apparent size, had but one prominent feature: Stickney Crater. Julio had jokingly likened the overall effect to an eye. To which Reuben had quipped, and Teri now couldn't *not* see, "the unblinking eye of Sauron." Her knee-jerk reaction to *that* was stupid, really. If the NASA bunch were watching (and why would they bother?), a good dozen remote-sensing satellites whizzed about Mars in orbits much closer than that of Phobos.

Mind on your work, Teri scolded herself. "So, explorers, what thoughts do you care to share before heading out?"

214

Jake, in his fire-engine-red counterpressure suit, cleared his throat. "This will be one short drive for a man, one giant road trip for mankind."

Paula, in apricot orange, standing at his side, mumbled something.

"What was that?" Teri asked.

"Humankind," Paula said.

Whatever, Teri thought. "Who else?"

"Have room for a passenger?" Reuben asked, grinning.

"Sure," Jake said. "Hop on either trailer."

"Take your time," Islah said. She had a valise in hand. While the explorers were away, she'd be joining Maia and Keshaun in the otherwise half-empty Zodanga.

Moving in ought to be easy, Teri thought. Suddenly. Bitterly. It wasn't as though Jake and the skank used separate personal cubbies. At that moment, it struck Teri that the sky blue of her counterpressure suit was the farthest on the rainbow from Jake's red of anyone here. But his red and Paula's orange? Rainbow-cozy.

Why didn't she believe that had happened by coincidence?

Teri shook off the foul mood. Sad personal story aside, it was a proud moment. An epic moment. Those two would be driving east along the rim of Valles Marineris, the largest and deepest canyon on the planet, surveying for places where Blake's giga-buck tourists might best descend. But the distinction of being *first* into the valley? That would be Jake's. "Anyone else?"

"Don't do anything I wouldn't do," Keshaun said.

Jake grinned. "Which would be?"

"Bungee jumping into the canyon."

"Spoilsport."

"Samples," Julio offered. "Plenty of rock samples. Pictures of them first in situ."

"Keep an eye on your air," Maia said. She'd slept aboard the SUV for two nights, giving its onboard CO_2-to-O_2 recycler something of a test. For a third night, Islah had joined Maia to add load to the recycler. The system hadn't given even a hint of trouble, but Maia's caution remained warranted. Lugging along oxygen for a weeks-long expedition wasn't practical.

"One other thing," Julio said. "Don't die."

Jeez, who tempts fate like that? "Always good advice. Okay, guys. Have a good trip."

"Will do." Jake slapped the SUV's exterior hatch control. The hatch popped open and glacially slid back like the side door of the first SUV Teri and Jake had owned. The cabin was far too compact to accommodate an airlock. On the plus side, blasts of escaping air would expel most of the regolith that would be tracked aboard. "Let's do this."

"To the Batmobile," Paula said.

Jake laughed. "Making me Batman."

Paula said, "You wish."

At that moment, Teri could almost like the woman. Almost.

Magnificent Mile Ransacked

A masked, early-evening flash mob of an estimated 200 individuals rampaged across the North Michigan Avenue retail district, looting clothing boutiques, jewelry and electronics stores, and the Water Tower Place shopping mall. Security guards and police were overwhelmed ....

—*Chicago Tribune*

Quintillions Claimed

On the heels of the European Space Agency's discovery of the invaluable metal asteroid nicknamed Croesus, the New Earth Partners consortium made their own announcement.

"New Earth Partners intends to tap the incalculable wealth of Croesus," partner Blake Wagner declared at a hastily called press conference. "Timid national space agencies may consider this invaluable object beyond their reach, but we feel otherwise. Given our base on Mars, and the refueling station we anticipate building on that planet's outer moon, Deimos, the exploitation of Croesus will be eminently practical."

Long-term precious-metals futures plunged ten percent or more on the announcement ....

—*Reuters News Service*

April 22, 2034

Heart pounding, muscles straining, sweat not pouring only because Phobos didn't offer enough gravity to make anything flow, Xander marveled, and not for the first time, at the purported existence of endorphin rushes from exercise. Or of runner's highs. Or that any-one, anywhere, ever found working out to be anything but a chore. A necessary chore, to be sure, if he didn't plan on returning to Earth as a limp-noodle basket case, but a chore, nonetheless. A daily, hours-at-a-time, odious chore.

The implement of torture just then, in a manner of speaking, was a weight machine. Of course, he'd have needed literal tons of mass here to offer any meaningful weight—and the inertia of so much mass wouldn't have been manageable anyway. Instead, he used (complete with the NASA-standard pretentious name) an Advanced Resistive Exercise Device. The ARED's vacuum pumps and flywheel cables mimicked actual weight.

Not an arm's length away, Cat jogged on the treadmill, safety harness and bungee cords keeping her down, indifferent to his bare, sweat-slicked torso. Whereas he was all too aware of her sweat-sodden, clingy tank top. Or, rather, what that tank top barely restrained. Oh, *so* perky in this all-but-nonexistent gravity ….

Huh. Though he still brooded about Charlene more often than he'd have chosen to admit, about how their marriage had gone south, it

217

seemed neither was he dead. Not that Cat would care; she and Sonny appeared happier than ever. David and Giselle, meanwhile, had settled into some sort of frenemies-with-benefits relationship, skulking about as if the benefits were a secret. Maybe they believed that.

Xander had to wonder how long *this* diversion would hold David's interest.

"Something on your mind, sport?" Cat asked.

Two things, those best left unmentioned. "Insanity is doing the same thing over and over …."

"Like drilling the same shallow holes all over?"

"You said it."

"Tell me again *why* going deeper is the answer?"

What he didn't know about geology was—just ask Giselle—pretty much all there was to know about geology. Of areology, the *Martian* planetary science, even less. Still, after tapping the mission's not inconsiderable digital library, and long-distance recourse to Wikipedia and Google, and consulting—some would say, pestering—Giselle, he'd learned a few things.

Time to see how persuasive those were.

"Can I show you something, Cat?"

She glanced at the treadmill control panel. "I'm a captive audience for another ten minutes."

Xander set down the faux barbell and extracted himself from the infernal device. He got the datasheet from his gym-shorts pocket and swiped through to the file he wanted. He started the video, holding the datasheet so they both could watch. "This is from the lander descent into Juventae Chasma. What do you see?"

"A hole."

"So, it is." In the sense the Pacific Ocean was damp. "A hole about 250 klicks by 100. Also five freaking klicks deep. What else do you see?"

"It's layered. Like the Grand Canyon, carved by the Colorado River. Been there, rafted that. You're going to tell me this canyon is also old, was once carved by water, and those are sedimentary layers." She slowed the treadmill to a cool-down pace. "But don't take my knowledge of geology for granite."

"Duly noted."

For years, NASA's mantra for Mars had been *follow the water*. Life on Earth depended as much on water as on carbon. Of *course*, Juventae

Chasma was on their priority target list. Like every other landing zone, the rovers delivered there had found nothing noteworthy.

"Those layers upon layers, kilometers of them, are the point. Not only in the chasma, but everywhere. Giselle says that by the best evidence, Mars lost its oceans about four billion years ago. How deep do you suppose are the traces of extinct life from so long ago?"

"Assuming there are any to be found." Cat grabbed a towel looped around a treadmill rail and blotted her face and neck. "Other than *very*, I have no clue. But that's a generalization. Back home, people find fossils all the time. I speak with authority, having been to Dinosaur National Park and seen a few fossils sticking out of the ground."

If Xander didn't know a ton about geology, he did know dinosaurs. For years, although not anymore, those had been his nieces' obsession, and he'd refreshed his childhood memories the better to bond with them. The recollection brought pangs of guilt. Kids grew up so damned fast, and beyond him not being there, it had been at least two weeks since he'd as much as sent a note to the munchkins—or to his sister, for that matter. He took a mental note to do so after this conversation.

First things first. "Even the earliest of dinos go back only a quarter billion years, and *their* remains are, shall we say, *large*. No one expects anything like that here. Sonny's hunting for microfossils. Like, 100 microns and smaller."

"I am aware."

Flimsy pocket curtains suspended from a flimsier rod divided the exercise space from most of the habitat's common area. In theory, those curtains directed air flow to activated-carbon filters without stinking up the rest of the living area. Like the utility of scratching at the Martian surface, this was a theory that hadn't panned out. Still, in a triumph of hope over experience, the curtains were drawn. Behind those, when he'd ducked into the exercise "room," Hideo, David, and Sonny had been watching some projected movie, the audio track streaming to earbuds. To judge from the snippets that escaped those air buds, something with ample explosions and car chases.

Giselle, however, had been parked at the fold-down dining table, back to the vid, tapping away at a datasheet. She might have been working, might have been doing personal correspondence. Either way, Xander hoped she hadn't retreated for the night to her personal cubby with its semi-effective sound baffling and noise cancellation.

"Giselle," he called out. "Are you there?"

"Yes. What is it?"

"Would you mind coming here?"

"Give me a minute." In about twice that, she parted the curtains and edged into the exercise area. Her nose crinkled at the locker-room stench. Maybe the curtains did help a little. "What's up?"

Questions whose answers Xander believed he knew. Answers that would have more credibility coming from her. "On Earth, what are the oldest signs of life?"

"This couldn't have waited till you sponged off? Very well. Suspected microfossils have been found up to three billion years old. Bubbles of methane gas found trapped in ancient stone and other possible chemical biomarkers suggest life for perhaps another half billion years."

"All single cellular?" Xander prompted.

"The oldest examples? Yes, of course. Apart from traces of microbial mats, primitive sponges, and few other simple forms, nothing multicellular appears in the geological record till about 600 million years ago."

"Life on land is younger still?"

"Yes. By most estimates, that began on the order of 430 million years ago. Some people think perhaps a little earlier."

Cat brought the treadmill to a stop. "Back up. *Suspected* microfossils. *Possible* biomarkers. Explain."

Giselle said, "For the oldest examples, about all we can go by are hints. Tiny patterns found in ancient limestone resembling the calcium-carbonate shells some contemporary bacteria grow. Those methane bubbles I mentioned because, on Earth, most methane is biogenic. Sedimentary rocks exhibiting atypical carbon-isotope ratios, commonly interpreted as a life sign because biochemistry favors C_{12} over the also stable isotope C_{13}. From these and other inferential methods, the preponderance of evidence is compelling as to the life's ancient roots. As for whether any particular ancient rock sample holds biological or evolutionary significance, people argue endlessly."

"Okay …" Cat allowed.

"Now, how precise is the dating of those ancient traces?" Xander asked.

Giselle brushed wispy bangs off her forehead. "Stratigraphy has become comparatively well-established. That's the time-sequencing of geological layers, in most cases determined from patterns of paleomagnetism and the sort of fossils found in the rock. It's been a necessary area of study because, in so many areas, the original layering was disrupted. By earthquakes, for example.

"Estimating absolute dates is another matter, reliant on radiometric methods. To date ancient layers, we look at the ratio of the decay products present from radioisotopes with very long half-lives, such as U_{238}. That presumes finding those decay products, and in a context to suggest those traces aren't contamination washed down from more recent strata. Mainly, this involves finding bits of uranium locked in tiny zircon crystals. It's complicated."

What isn't? Xander thought. "Regardless, we're talking billions of years ago for the earliest life signs."

Giselle nodded.

"One more question, Giselle." One last domino to set. "How many regions on Earth expose rocks as old as those earliest life stages?"

"That's another thing geologists argue about. A literal handful, no more. The two most productive places for paleobiology are in the Barberton Mountain Land, in South Africa, and the Pilbara Hills in the Australian Outback."

"Mountain Land. Hills," Xander repeated. "Because these are ancient sea bottoms raised over eons by plate tectonics, the younger strata over them then eroded over yet more eons. Plate tectonics being a process active on Earth and long stopped, if ever it functioned, on Mars."

"Well, yes," Giselle said. "To all of that. Which I know you knew, as we've discussed this before. Since you dragged me here to make some point, perhaps you'll get to it."

Guilty as charged. "I'll connect the dots. On Earth, life took billions of years to leave the oceans. When Mars lost its oceans, the planet wasn't yet one billion years old. Meaning to look for life, we need to concentrate on onetime ocean. Even on Earth, where plate tectonics can raise ancient seabeds, it's rare to find rocks as ancient as our search for life *here* requires."

Leaving connection to the final dot—hence, we need to drill *way* deeper—as an exercise for the mission commander.

Cat frowned. "I admit some of this detail is new to me, but I'm a rocket jockey. Plenty of smart people in our agencies should have known this."

"*Did* know this," Xander said, even as Giselle murmured agreement. Just as the experts doubted any microbe could survive present-day, near-surface conditions on Mars, what with the near-vacuum, wild temperature swings, unending radiation, and so much peroxide and perchlorate lacing the soil—because no known earthly microbe could. "So, how'd we get here? Part practicality. Until Wu's big speech, NASA's budget for Mars struggled to accommodate plunking down a rover every so often. To sustain funds for even those took dangling the prospect of a spectacular discovery."

Even *that* was a charitable interpretation. More than a few of his NASA colleagues had indulged in magical thinking. *Field of Dreams* territory. Dale, to an extent, and look how much grief she'd incurred for it.

Or they were all like that proverbial drunk hunting for his lost car keys ….

"At ESA, too," Giselle said.

"Rewind," Cat said. "*Part* practicality. What else?"

"Flags and footprints, same as Apollo. Remember?" Had Xander not invented a doable Mars mission to counter Wu's, and a plausible way to spin it, would the president have exiled him to the NASA tracking station in Guam? Maybe. Hard to know. Nor, just then, did Guam seem like hardship duty. "If our being here was about anything other than, well, being here, and doing so *first*, there never would've been the charade about tainted food, and our fake-out delayed departure, and the sleight-of-radar with drones.

"The bottom line, Cat? If very important people understand the challenges to our finding life signs, they won't care." From things Becks had shared in confidence, they *didn't* care. "Us coming to Phobos let Cruella take rhetorical potshots at NEP and China, let her claim the moral high ground, while NASA preps to launch a landing mission during the *next* window."

Cat retrieved her overshirt from a nearby hook and slipped it on. "So, politics, with a healthy dollop of inside-the-Beltway budgetary gaming. Knowing all this, why are you here?"

For the adventure and glamour. Those had once seemed important. Also, more than he cared to admit, for an opportunity to stick it to his ex. *See who could've been the wife of a famous explorer.* None of that anything he would speak aloud.

With Cat's hard stare unrelenting, Xander shrugged. "Saying no to the prez ain't easy." However dissembling and incomplete that answer, at least it was true.

"Yeah, I get that," Cat said. "Not seeming worth it anymore?"

Worth, by the time they got home, close to four years of his life? To take part in an elaborate PR stunt? "Not so much."

Giselle smiled sadly. "I'd be delighted to discover any artifacts of ancient Martian life. Do I expect to? No. Did I ever? No. But for the hands-on, well, gloves-on, opportunity to explore the geology of Mars and of this moon, feigned enthusiasm was a modest price to pay."

Conversation sprang up behind the curtains. The movie must have ended.

"Still …" Xander said.

"What?" Cat demanded. "Your cynicism is past its expiration date? You want to start looking where something might be found?"

"Kinda like that. So, I—"

Giselle raised a hand. "Matters are as they are. I see nothing to be gained by bemoaning the facts. You two argue if you wish. I'm going for a snack before bed." She brushed aside part of the curtains and stepped out. Moments later, the microwave oven started up.

"So," Xander resumed, "about getting the drill barrels and other things we'd need to make this a serious search."

Cat sighed. "Yeah, I did say I'd think about it."

He recovered his T-shirt and slipped it on. "And?"

"And I haven't made up my mind. Who below would you ask?"

"The NEP folks. Teri, their boss, strikes me as a reasonable person."

Cat snorted. "Two days after the fat cats mocked NASA and every other space agency, practically claiming Croesus for themselves? You *do* like to live dangerously."

Yeah, the president wouldn't appreciate that. Contacting NEP for help might well tick off Becks, too. But what were they going to do about it? Dock his pay? "The Chinese bunch, then."

"Your funeral."

"You know what? I think Giselle was on target with the bedtime snack idea." And you know what *else*, Cat? I'm okay with taking "your funeral" as a go-ahead.

April 24, 2034

Water, water everywhere / nor any drop to drink.

Kai kept the couplet to himself. Colonel Zhao had little enough use for any literary matter. Nineteenth-century English epic poetry? At best, any recitation would have brought Kai a condescending lecture about Anglo-Saxon decadence.

With or without Coleridge, the mission's failure to obtain water beyond the occasional small ice pocket was more than a little ironic. Utopia Planitia qualified as a plain, true, but by no definition did it qualify as utopian. (Hmm. Now his idling subconscious had dredged up a *sixteenth*-century English literary work.)

Meanwhile, this misnamed arid expanse was but an offshoot of the vast, circumpolar basin where once an entire ocean had been. Oceanus Borealis, the planetary scientists had named it. Northern Ocean, assuming his Latin-translating app was correct. All that remained where water had once stood kilometers deep was the basin. Vastitas Borealis. Northern Desolation.

At least *that* name wasn't a cruel hoax.

Where had all the water gone? Long-since lost to space, much of it. Maybe most of it. More locked up in the polar ice caps. Traces scattered in shallow, buried ice pockets; those they sometimes—but all too seldom—managed to find. But lots more must have made its way deep underground. Somewhere.

Coleridge required an update, Kai decided. Water, water had been here / Nor any drop in sight. He thought Li would have approved.

His wife had so enjoyed matters literary and cross-cultural. That being the case, so had Kai. It remained far more pleasant to ponder those, to play with language, than to deal with the colonel and his dreary, utilitarian mindset.

Literary interests notwithstanding, Li had had a traditional side. He pictured her now, her expression sad, offering the ancient wisdom that to die is to stop living but to stop living is something entirely different from dying. That she wanted better for him than either of those outcomes. That while his mind played games, while he visited with ghosts, matters of life and death were at hand. Matters of water, which, on this bleak world, *was* life.

Indifferent to Kai's presence, scant steps away in the little shelter, Zhao and Antonov debated strategy about water. Where next to drill. What further measures might be added to their recycling regimen. How much stricter the rationing of water could go without endangering everyone's health. Whether to recombine any liquid oxygen and liquid hydrogen back into the precious water from which it had been split. Whether to undertake an arduous trek to the northern ice cap, where water *would* be found.

The datasheet draped across a table showed a local map. The yellow circle at the center represented their camp. Two large, flanking, ashen blobs denoted bountiful subsurface water reservoirs—which had not held water at all. Where reflections sensed by satellite-based, ground-penetrating radars had promised briny, underground lakes, and so determined the mission's landing zone, one test bore after another had encountered only clay. Boundary reflections, the "experts" in Beijing now admitted, could be tricky to interpret.

Nursing his morning water ration, Kai could only hope heads there had rolled.

The map's few small, pale green dots, scattered among many more small, ashen ones, indicated the few areas successfully mined for their scraps of ice. Dark green dots, farther from camp, showed other places where ground-penetrating radar suggested buried ice might be found.

Or, as likely, not.

The more one colonel, then the other, tapped, slapped, or fist-pounded the map, and the more intense their voices became, the more difficult Kai found it to concentrate. On any aspect of work. On not craving a tall glass of ice water. On not listening to the dispute, or, as tuning it out proved impossible, trying to fade further into the background.

He wished he were anywhere else. Kilometers away, with Ivan and Masha, at the current drill site. Nearby but still outside, with Xiuying and Mingmei, sweeping the previous night's dust accumulation from the solar panels. With Oorvi in the Winter Palace, at that moment standing vacant—rather than the two of them stuck *here*.

The geology app a former colleague at Hansraj University in Delhi had sent Oorvi wasn't playing nicely with her CMSA-approved datasheet. Rather than tote his extensive suite of hardware and software tools to her, Kai had thought it easier to ask her to his shelter. Indeed, it had been, for perhaps fifteen minutes. Until Antonov's arrival. Until long-simmering differences of opinion over how best to handle the looming water crisis boiled over ….

Kai whispered to Oorvi, "What do you think they'll decide?"

The Indian geologist hesitated. She'd had her say before the arguing had flared—only to be ignored. "I know only what I would try next."

Implying one colonel or the other had rejected her advice. The loud, posturing Antonov, Kai supposed. The Russian had pushed to explore the ice cap almost since they had landed.

"Where do you recommend?" Kai followed up.

"The candidate drill site about thirty kilometers northeast of us. The terrain there is—"

A shrill warble interrupted. Colonel Zhao glanced at the comm console and waved dismissively. "Wang Kai, see what they want."

They?

With the altercation rejoined, as heated as ever, and the incoming-signal warble repeating, Kai read from the console what Zhao must have noticed. An unencrypted digital channel relayed by one of NASA's satellites. Audio *and* video. The Phobos group?

Kai drew a "room" dividing curtain, slipped on a headset, and opened the connection. He recognized the man on the display: an American. "Fire Star City here."

"Fire Star City, this is Asaph Hall base on Phobos. May I speak with Colonel Zhao?"

"He is unavailable." Also, not inclined to speak with your bunch.

"Perhaps you can help me. My name is Hopkins. Xander Hopkins."

"Carter." Like many Chinese for generations, Kai had taken a Western professional name. (Or, as Chairman Mao had put it, *When in a village, sing that village's songs.*) It wasn't just Jackie Chan and Bruce Lee. "What's on your mind, Mr. Hopkins?"

"Xander. A trade. Informal. You scratch my back, and I'll scratch yours. We—"

Scratch his back? Coleridge wasn't this obscure. "Sorry?"

The American smiled. "My bad. It's an expression. You must know we have robots sampling Martian geology. It'd speed up our work to have more iron pipe as extenders to our drill barrels. Likewise, more iron-oxy batteries. Phobos doesn't have iron, but the stuff's all around you."

"A trade, you said. Trading what? For that matter, *how?*"

Hopkins rubbed a stubbly chin. "To be negotiated. Perhaps some of our excess power, beamed as microwaves to wherever you deploy a rectenna array. Deliverable while Phobos has a line of sight."

Given more power, could they drill faster for ice? Probably. Or tap into an aquifer? Perhaps. "What else, Hopkins?"

"Xander, please. Phobos has plentiful carbonaceous material if that'd be useful as feedstock for your printers. We could land a hundred kilos or so at a time."

"Understood." Kai wanted to ask about *water*, but Zhao would never approve of revealing their need. Nor would Antonov, for that matter. Still, he could fantasize. "Anything else?"

"Tell me what you could use. We've got spare in several categories of supplies. Medical inventory, for example. So far, we've managed not to hurt ourselves."

Of *course*, that team had a surplus. Stuck on their little moon, they hadn't brought a ground vehicle massing *tonnes*—which brought to Kai's mind a different aspect of transacting. "How do you envision collecting pipes and batteries? Us loading them onto your landers?"

The American glanced off-camera, shook his head about something, and turned back. "Sorry about that. Yes, we could take delivery with our landers. I expect my boss would prefer that one of our robots do the loading under our supervision. The problem is, taking delivery in that manner is apt to require multiple flights. For drill sites within your driving range, I'd hope you can deliver the goods."

The *boss* might prefer. Did Xander speak for anyone but himself? "Thank you for this offer. I will bring your inquiry to my mission commander."

"I'll be here when you or he are ready. Xander ... out."

The screen went blank.

Zhao flung back the curtain. Clearly, he had been eavesdropping. "What did the *laowai* want?"

Kai recapped the conversation, ending with, "Is this matter worth pursuing?" Having no doubt in his mind that it was.

"Of course not," Zhao said, while Antonov shook his head once. If on nothing else, it appeared the colonels could agree on Kai's naiveté or American guile.

Kai took a deep breath. "Respectfully, I do not understand. China's factories sell across the world and to Americans more than to most. Our factories run on fossil fuels"—ignoring the shortsightedness of that—"imported from around the world, even from America. How would trading here be different?"

Zhao said, "At best, the American mission is failing. It is not in our interest to help them. At worst, this is some ploy on their part."

"A ploy, Colonel?" Kai repeated. "What possible kind of—"

Glowering, Antonov interrupted. "Do you not understand? *We* need all the drilling apparatus we can produce. We have no reason to believe Hopkins even speaks for his mission commander. As for preempting our buggy as their delivery truck: No. Just, no. Unless we locate an ample supply of water nearby in the next few weeks, that vehicle is spoken for."

It seemed the colonels' argument had ended in a compromise. Find water close-by, and soon, or change tactics. But was a polar expedition the next thing to try? Had they no course of action less extreme to attempt first? "The NASA team must intend to drill within driving range of us. If *they* find water or ice, *we* can then use it."

With the lift of an eyebrow, Zhao signaled his disappointment. "You misread the situation. The American mission wishes us to fail. Let them drill deep near us, find water there, and they'll shout to the world that they have found traces of life. That we, and their commercial rivals, must abandon Mars."

"They can drill near us regardless," Oorvi protested.

228

"Not deep, it would appear," Antonov said. "Not to make plausible claims of discovering biological traces in deep aquifers, in the water that, in the long run, *we* need. Not unless we are so gullible as to provide them lots of pipe."

"You can't be sure of that," Kai insisted.

"Nor do you know otherwise," Antonov snapped.

With eyes narrowed, Zhao declared, "This discussion is over."

Leaving Kai, all too parched, all too aware how little of his morning's water ration remained in his cup, to wonder if—for all their simian chest-thumping—the colonels might not be right.

If their situation truly *was* that desperate ....

"The life of the dead is placed in the memory of the living."

—*Marcus Tullius Cicero*

"Live how we can, yet die we must."

William Shakespeare

"Better pass boldly into that other world, in the full glory of some passion, than fade and wither dismally with age."

—*James Joyce*

DESPERATION

April 26, 2034

THERE'S BEEN AN INCIDENT.

The alert manifested as text on Teri's heads-up display—and yet, Reuben's voice came to her mind's ear with the emotionless, laconic delivery pilots reserved for disasters. In *Houston, we have a problem* calm.

Four of the team were outside with Teri, all within eyesight. Reuben, sidelined for a few days by a sprained ankle, was indoors, texting cryptically. That left Jake and Paula: at their most recent check-in parked at yet another scenic overlook of Valles Marineris. A good 200 klicks away as the hypothetical Martian crow flew. By Batmobile, detouring around craters and ravines, the drive had been at least twice that long.

That the "incident" must, somehow, involve their two travelers? It would explain Reuben reaching out by text and not over the common radio channel everyone tuned to. Suggesting no one here could contribute, so why upset them? Further suggesting that the "incident" *was* upsetting.

Teri wasn't one of the people who took to helmet texting—picking letters off a HUD's virtual keyboard with mere eye flicks and blinks—like ducks to water. More like a duck to a bicycle. She fat-fingered a brief reply through her forearm keypad: CHSNNL 9. That'd be close enough.

A few more taps switched her helmet comms to sending and receiving on that channel. "On my way, Reuben." Because the summons had been implicit. "Do you want anyone else?"

"Keshaun, maybe."

Among several skills, their IT guy. A comms problem with the others? The tightness in Teri's chest eased. "We'll join you in a few."

"Maybe skip the rinse cycle," Reuben added.

Tracking in noxious perchlorates and peroxides, doubtless killing the air handler's current filters within hours (and still causing eye and skin irritation) but getting them through the airlock minutes sooner. The tension in her chest returned, worse than before. "Copy that."

Keshaun was running a power cable from their solar farm to the newest hydroponics dome. Her wave caught his eye. She did a come-here finger crook, then pointed to Helium. He nodded and headed that way. Without comment or question on the radio. Smart man.

She returned transmission to the common channel. "Hey, guys, Keshaun and I are going inside for now. Keep doing what you're doing." Which, if they did, would occupy Maia, Islah, and Julio for hours. "I'll explain later." Once *she* knew the nature—and ideally, the resolution—of the situation.

Teri met Keshaun by the airlock. Waiting for it to cycle, she mouthed, "Channel Nine."

"What's up?" he asked on that band.

"Reuben wants us. That's all I know." Whatever else I surmise.

When, at last, the airlock cycle completed, they popped their helmets. She followed Keshaun inside, squeezing past the inner hatch even before that finished its sideward slide.

"Okay, Reuben," Teri said. "You have our attention."

"Maybe just a comms failure. I thought you'd want to know."

More unflappable pilot attitude. But how was that any different from the imperturbable mission-commander certainty she ever had to project? No matter how badly her guts roiled. "Specifics?"

He slid aside his chair and stood, revealing the shelter console's biomonitor. Wear vacuum gear, and the system wirelessly monitored your vitals. Icons for Maia, Islah, and Julio shone a steady green: all healthy. Icons for Reuben, Teri, and Keshaun were grayed out: Reuben wasn't in vacuum gear, while she and Keshaun, still in counterpressure suits, had properly disconnected. Leaving—in scary, pulsing red—icons for Jake and Paula.

Reuben said, "Those alarmed within seconds of one another. Jake's first, I think. Right away, I radioed on the emergency band." The radio channel that you heard no matter how helmet and SUV receivers were configured. "No response from either. I texted you, Teri, then tried them again. Still nothing. As you guys were cycling through the airlock, I tried looking through the Batmobile's cameras. No luck there, either. It's offline."

Could be anything, Teri told herself. Comms glitch. Or bad software. Let it be some type of technical malf. Any kind. "What else?"

"Not much," Reuben said. "I confirmed there are comsats overhead. NASA and ISRO."

Teri said, "Since dropping below our horizon, their helmet comms go straight to and from an available comsat, right? Not relayed through the SUV?" Which would require, if comms were the problem, near-concurrent faults striking two independent satellites. Or *three* near-concurrent faults: in both helmets *and* the damned Batmobile.

"Uh-huh," Keshaun grunted. "Give me a sec." Not waiting for an answer, he plunked himself at the console and began typing. "Both birds return test messages." He kept typing, frowned, then typed some more. "There. Good. I've reestablished contact with the SUV and initiated its self-diagnostics. Something's put its computer into safe mode."

"Fifteen minutes, then, till we have access?" Teri hoped she had misremembered the timing.

"Yes and no." Keshaun swiveled his chair. "Yes, if all tests pass. That is, if the problem was transient. If something's broken, and the comp needs to reconfigure around the fault using its redundant gear? Add fifteen additional minutes for each diagnostic cycle."

Meaning at least fifteen minutes until its onboard computer might accept nonemergency commands. Such as *upload video buffer* and *pan camera*. Such as, *tell us whatever the* fuck *is going on*. "Shit."

Keshaun nodded. "Well put."

Teri couldn't imagine anything except software knocking helmet comms *and* the SUV offline. But what software did suit electronics and the vehicle's computer have in common? The underlying operating system, if nothing else. Could that OS have been hacked? Infected with malware? If so, why hadn't anyone here experienced the same problem?

Facts first, she told herself. Only, what other facts could she get until the SUV began to respond? *If* it would respond. "There are satellites overhead. Anything with a hi-res camera?"

Reuben shook his head. "I checked, boss. None for an hour and a bit. A Chinese satellite. Even then, we're talking about resolution of about a half-meter per pixel."

Which would show, with little detail, the SUV and its trailers. People would appear, at best, as a handful of pixels. "I guess we wait. Unless someone has a better idea."

No one did. While the men speculated in hushed whispers, Teri did her best to keep an open mind—and her fears at bay.

After thirty minutes that stretched like geologic time and repeated, unsuccessful attempts to reach Jake and Paula by text and radio, the shelter's console chimed.

"The Batmobile is back online. All tests passed." Keshaun looked up at Teri. "You want the chair?"

Only clasping her hands behind her back kept them from shaking. "Stay put. Why'd the SUV go into safe mode?"

As Keshaun finger-swiped through a downloaded log file, Reuben whistled.

Teri turned toward him. "You see something?"

"Yes, though I don't understand it. The SUV's accelerometers registered several jolts, seconds apart."

Keshaun poked some more at the console. "Based on the timing, those shocks are what put the onboard computer into safe mode. My guess is they jarred some circuit boards loose from their sockets. We're lucky no two boards of the same type got dislodged."

Because duplication was the extent of the redundancy in the Batmobile's electronics.

Teri sidled closer, puzzled, peering at the console display. "Isn't Mars geologically inactive? I mean, for eons now?" Islah would know, but Teri wasn't ready to involve—and worry—anyone else just yet. "Either way, wouldn't a seismic event shaking the SUV that much have registered on sensors here? I mean, we're not that far apart."

"A small, nearby meteor strike?" Reuben guessed.

"Forget I asked that," Teri said. "*How* isn't the immediate problem. Our people are. Keshaun, are the SUV's cameras back online?"

Tappety tap tap. "Here's the dash cam."

An image opened, its view along the jagged rim of the nearby chasm. No one in sight. Nothing moved but a distant dust devil. Their perspective, and hence, the SUV, seemed level. That didn't disprove Marsquake or meteor strike, nor did it support either theory.

"Fast reverse," Teri said, "back to when … things went wrong."

Except they couldn't look back that far because the cameras buffered just the most recent fifteen minutes, overwriting anything older, expecting the ground vehicle's main computer to download and archive every five minutes. Which required a computer that was still running.

She tried again. "Okay, let's see recent video in the archive." Which should come near to—ideally, up to the moment of—whatever had knocked the SUV into its safe mode. "Show *that* in reverse."

And … madness.

The SUV tipped left. No sooner had it started to settle back than something shook it again. Then down, seemingly as far as shock absorbers would compress, and bouncing up. Jolt after jolt. In seconds, it—whatever *it* had been—was over. Or rather, as they were watching in reverse, had yet to begin.

A *quick* disaster, then.

Teri said, "Now forward, Keshaun. Quarter speed, please."

Aside from writhing flickers (shadows of unseen dust devils? These seemed too wispy for that explanation, so likelier a trick of the light), she spotted nothing new. Not even stepping through the vid frame by frame revealed what, again and again, had set the vehicle rocking.

She remembered the discussion—in another life, on another world—that capturing more than a few frames per second was wasteful overkill. It wasn't as though Martian scenery would be going anywhere. But whatever this was? It wasn't the scenery.

Oh, how she wished *kill* hadn't popped into her mind. No matter how dark the scenarios already roiling there ….

Think now. Brood later.

"Okay, now show me the archived view from the rear camera. Same minute, at quarter speed." This provided a closeup of the supply trailer, its cargo secured beneath a bungee-cord-secured dust tarp. Again, the flickering hints of … what?

The tarp parted as if ripped by a giant claw. A roiling white cloud (water from a burst canister vaporizing at the negligible atmospheric pressure?) soon obscured the view.

"Rewind. Then walk us through frame by frame."

Which Keshaun did until—

A slender arc, ash gray, popped into view. Her blood ran cold. "That's descent cable."

Cable woven from whisker-thin diamond fibers. Elastic as hell, unlike typical diamond. Stronger by far than the most tensile steel wire. Stronger even than cable woven from carbon nanotubes. Only the coating applied for ease and safety of handling made diamond-fiber cable as thick as twine. The motorized reel of the cable had lowered and raised their test mass repeatedly before Jake and Paula set out. Two days ago, reel and cable had staged supplies to the floor of Valles Marineris for their exploratory hikes. The day before, the same gear had lowered the travelers, one at a time, to look around, then raised them to spend the evening in the comparative comfort of the SUV's cabin.

Super strong ... to begin. But what about abrasion and recurrent stresses? What about bending fatigue as the cable had been repeatedly unwound and rewound? What if, through recurrent use, individual fibers within the bundle had torqued, cracked, unwoven?

What if that cable was no longer strong *enough*?

Today's schedule had Jake and Paula descending again into the canyon, hiking in a new direction to scout out a candidate trail for Blake's damn tourists. What if the cable snapped? Under the tension of supporting a man or woman in full vacuum gear, plus (depending on how much cable was deployed at that point) perhaps miles of the cable itself? It would writhe and thrash and recoil like .... God, she didn't want to imagine what it had been like.

Get a grip, woman! "Real-time, SUV-top view. Angled down"—she tried to picture the width of the SUV and the height of the camera mast—"thirty degrees from vertical. Slow pan."

Cable snarl surrounded the sport-ute and its trailers. The camera on its mast couldn't view the vehicles themselves nor the ground nearest them, but she feared the worst. As for Jake and Paula, boot prints were the only evidence.

"That's a *lot* of cable," Reuben said. "Maybe they're in the canyon, somewhere without a line of sight to satellite."

Could it be so? Jake had planned to have them out of the canyon by this point in the day. Resting from their exertions, if needed, otherwise prepping to drive on. If he and Paula had run late for whatever reason, had hiked farther than anticipated, they *might* still be safe in the canyon.

But both? Teri found it hard to believe. The cable was likeliest to snap while bearing a load beyond its own weight. Still, it could be that the cable broke as the first of them ascended, close enough to the canyon floor to survive the fall. God, she hoped so! "In which case, they'll be okay while their power lasts." Because once the power ran out, their suits would cease recycling carbon dioxide back to oxygen.

Reuben started across the shelter, limping.

"Stop. Where are you going?" she asked.

"To suit up. To prep a ship for a rescue."

"Hold on." Keshaun did something at the console. "There's been line of sight from at least one comsat to most of the nearby canyon floor through much of the past hour. I've had an automated 'check in ASAP' text going out every minute the entire time. Unless they've hunkered down smack against the canyon wall, line of sight isn't the problem."

"They'd know better," Teri said. Yes, *they*. Never mind that both being alive seemed implausible. "Once the cable"—their only way out of the abyss—"snapped, they'd reach out first thing."

"Enough speculation," Reuben said. "We have to assume they're okay, awaiting rescue. Seeing as I'm the only pilot here—"

"You can't take unnecessary chances," Teri interrupted. "An unplanned flight, without prior training sims, when you've not touched the controls for six months? No one wants to save them more than me, but I'm responsible for *everyone*."

Reuben kicked off his slippers. Wincing, he began working the foot with the injured ankle, bulky in its elastic bandage, into his counterpressure suit. "Ask the others what they think. If *they're* willing to do nothing. While you dither, I'm going to prep *Bradbury*."

"Hold on," Keshaun said. "I've brought the SUV's drone online. It's got a full charge. Diagnostics say it's undamaged. I can fly it from here."

The drone! Days ago, in a more innocent era, it had had its own nickname. But Batplane, like Batmobile, had become too frivolous to speak. "Good idea," Teri said.

"You do that," Reuben forced out through gritted teeth, still maneuvering the injured leg into a counterpressure-suit leg. "You know where I'll be. Call if you learn anything."

Faster than Reuben could suit up, the quadruple-rotored drone had launched. It streamed video via satellite: of the SUV from the front, wound in bands of cable. From the SUV's left, where loops of cable had snagged between track plates of the tread loop. Farther back, to yet more cable snarl, between the supply trailer's wire-mesh wheels and possibly around the axles. Farther back still, to a rat's nest ensnaring the cable trailer. Soaring *behind* the cable trailer—

To reveal orange chunks in dried pools of arterial red. Many pinned to the undercarriage. More, strewn across the ground. As if a blood orange had fallen into a food processor.

Paula, minced by the flailing, recoiling cable.

Flying an outward-spiral search pattern, the drone encountered Paula's head and helmet. No longer together. Neither intact.

Fighting a shudder, Teri asked, "Can the drone recover anything from the helmet comp?" Camera feed, perhaps. Last words still in a comms buffer. *Anything* to shed light on what had happened.

"Not a chance," Keshaun said. "Not from here, anyway. The battery pack is … elsewhere. Even if I had the helmet in front of me, I don't know. It looks pretty well shattered."

Reuben, meanwhile, expression grimmer than ever, his face gone pale, continued the struggle with his counterpressure suit.

She laid a hand on his shoulder. "Reuben, hold on."

He shrugged off the hand. "Jake's still in Valles Marineris. Gotta be. We wouldn't see this much cable unless it had been well extended before breaking."

Maybe they were seeing a kilometer of snarled cable. Hell, maybe even two. The canyon at that spot was a good seven klicks deep. In this pathetically thin atmosphere, once the cable snapped, it'd be like falling in a vacuum. Given the planet's low gravity, a fall accelerated slower than on Earth, but (quick mental calculation) from "only" a kilometer above the canyon floor, Jake would have reached 100 klicks per hour by the time he … arrived. Sixty damned miles per hour. Faster still if the cable had snapped with him farther from the ground.

Mouth and throat bitter with bile, Teri almost puked. Again. *Mission commanders do* not *puke*, she told herself. (Uh-huh. But wives do. Even rejected wives.) "Does the drone have the range to search the canyon floor?"

"Not sure." Keshaun pulled up a spec sheet. "I can take the drone down and search for, best guess, twenty minutes. After that, it'll need a full day's recharge to make it back up."

"Do it," she said. The possible loss of a drone was the least of her concerns. "Reuben, go ahead and see if either ship is up for the trip. Ample LH2 and LOX, redundant everything, clean bill of health from the diagnostics. The works. Let me know what you find. Channel nine. But do *not* launch without my authorization. There's no mission without confirmed life signs." Because I'm not going to lose you, too.

With a grimace and final tug, Reuben forced the injured leg all the way into the tight suit leg. "Got it."

The drone's descent was interminable, its relayed view a blur. With the quadcopter not yet halfway to the valley floor, Reuben, fully suited, went out the airlock. Maia radioed, asking why Reuben was outside. Why he wasn't responding on the common channel. Why he had waved her off when she approached, had boarded a ship.

Somehow, Teri found her confident, boss voice. "It's a drill, Maia, but time-sensitive, so please don't interrupt him." Or me.

In a meandering spiral, buffeted by random wind gusts, the drone descended. Until—

"I see something!" Keshaun called.

A red so vibrant to be foreign even to this world. It looked to her as if Jake had been spared the meat grinder of flailing cable. As if he might yet be alive!

With a destination in mind, spiraling ceased. The drone descended faster.

Gray haze she took to be a sprawling tangle of cable appeared at a distance from the bright red. Reuben was well into checkout of *Bradbury* when the expanding bit of crimson resolved into a human figure—

Limbs in unnatural, sickening positions.

"Bring it down." The words stuck in Teri's throat. The closer their view, the more her heart thudded, her head pounded, her breath caught in her chest. Jake was on his back, his faceplate … cracked. Suit torn. Sunk inches into the ground, or flattened, or both. She interpreted he'd landed face-first . And *bounced*.

Still, Teri couldn't not say, even while knowing it was hopeless, "Try reaching him again."

"He's gone," Keshaun whispered as the drone circled. "I'm so sorry."

Grieve later, she told herself. For now, do your damned job. Learn what happened. What went so catastrophically *wrong*. Stop Reuben before there's more needless, pointless death on your conscience.

She reached past Keshaun for the mic. Somehow, she held in the tears. For how long? She couldn't say. "Reuben, it's … certain. There's no chance. Stand down."

"We need to be sure. Let me—"

"We *are* sure. Repeat, stand down. Do you copy?"

"Copy." However grudging.

She tapped Keshaun on the shoulder. "Can you get a data dump from his helmet?"

"Unclear. Except for a stub, the helmet antenna's gone."

"Then get closer."

"Working on it." Raising a flurry of dust, the drone settled onto the regolith. Its camera faced sideways, a mere hand's-breadth from the helmet. "Good. The comps are talking. And …."

"And *what*?"

"There's video with a voice recording in the helmet buffer. Should I …?"

She'd have nightmares, she knew she would. But there was no choice, not really. "Go on. Play it."

"Well, this isn't good." Stated with that damned calm pilot bravado. "I don't seem to have comms at the moment, and it appears a moment is about what I have." Plainly true, ground features swelling with every word spoken. He had gone into a spin, every rotation giving glimpses of the canyon wall as he streaked past. Twice as they watched, he narrowly missed outcroppings.

Somehow, Jake managed to stabilize. A pilot to the end. "This recording will have to do.

"The cable snapped at some point well above my harness. You'll figure out how and where. The upper part whipped out of my sight so fast you wouldn't believe. The bottom length shot the other way. Even smacking my quick release, I'm damned lucky the recoil didn't get me. I suspect that's the extent of my luck today ….

242

"Never mind that I never envisioned anything like this as my final flight, I must admit"—and did, with all the brash self-assurance that had drawn her to Jake in the first place—"it's one hell of a view.

"So, last words. To *everyone* on the mission, it's been an honor to serve with you. I know you'll do fine without me. When it's time to go home and Reuben has to pilot one ship remotely, he's up for it.

"Teri, I apologize for hurting you. I did, I know that, but it was never my intent. Don't ever feel guilty about what's happening. Being here, now, is all on *me*.

"Paula, I'm sorrier than you can imagine to be leaving you, and"— self-deprecating chuckle—"on such short notice."

Details appeared: ravines, a sinuous ridge, a crater. Growing bigger. Bigger. Bigger yet.

That they were watching the onrushing ground? He'd chosen to go in *face first*! Why? Because that's how he always approached everything.

With seconds to spare, in that cocky, oh-so-very-Jake voice, with the chip-on-the-shoulder attitude she knew so well, and—admit it— loved so well *still*, came, "This is Jacob Walker, signing off."

Vid went dark. Audio simultaneously cut off, his last act: sparing them the final *crunch*.

Jake had wanted to be the first pilot to land on Mars. It hadn't happened, and in the moment Teri felt petty for having denied him that. But he would, forever and ever, have the distinction of being the first man to *die* on Mars.

April 27, 2034

Teri woke to the vague recollection of a nightmare—and the almost instant rush of memories that insisted the horrors were all too real.

With several deep, shuddering breaths, she got herself under control. The deaths? Those were too awful to think about. She forced herself to think *around* those.

Had she held it together long enough to call people inside and bring them up to date? As if seen through a gauze curtain, as if someone *else* had done it, she could picture the events. As if she'd been operating on autopilot.

Pilot. Just imagining that word set her trembling.

Before retreating to her cubby, had she ordered a general stand-down? Because they *all* needed to reflect on what had happened. They needed, before reacting, to ascertain more about how and why the accident had happened. They needed to understand the implications.

Yes, Teri decided. Some numbed part of her had done that as well. Had assigned Keshaun to prepare a status report for Mission Control—*not* to be transmitted until she reviewed it. Had tasked Reuben to investigate how the SUV might be cleared of cable tangle by remote control, and so driven back to camp—not believing this possible, but in hopes the analysis might keep Reuben from dashing off in *Bradbury*.

No one had raised the question how they might recover the bodies.

Soft voices penetrated the curtain of her cubby. Teri was used to being the first one up. Setting an example. Savoring a few minutes of quiet time alone with her morning coffee. Reviewing any overnight data feed from Earth. No alarm required; she just woke up.

Except today. Her datasheet read 9:32.

She shed wrinkled, tear-stained PJs and got into clean slacks and blouse. Tucked the datasheet into a pocket. Took a deep, cleansing breath. Threw aside the curtain. Stepped down. Reuben and Julio sat at the little table, empty plates before them. She presumed Islah, Maia, and Keshaun were in … the other shelter. "Gentlemen."

Julio stood. "Can I get you anything? Coffee?"

Uh-huh. That'll make everything better. She forced a smile. "Yes, please. Coffee. Black."

Reuben sighed. "Yesterday was horrible for us all. But for you? I can't imagine."

She accepted a plastic coffee mug, then sat. "It's … a lot to take in."

"For us all," Reuben repeated.

"What have you determined about the SUV?" she asked.

"Not much. Until the drone recharges and I can inspect the SUV and trailers, close up on all sides, I'd only be guessing. By late afternoon, I should know more."

Julio said, "You should eat something."

Coffee wasn't sitting well. She couldn't imagine food would. "Maybe later. The others?"

"Reached out before you got up. They're taking the morning to … process."

"Anything else, Julio?" she asked.

"Keshaun said he'd sent the draft report you wanted."

Not to her datasheet. She'd have heard a tone when the message arrived. She took her mug to the main console, found his message, started reading. The draft was short and to the point—if anything, too short. The last thing she wanted was a flurry of follow-up questions. She tweaked some sentences, added others, and appended a few frames culled from the less gruesome vid footage. She ended with IT'LL TAKE A FEW DAYS TO ANALYZE THE SITUATION AND DECIDE HOW TO PROCEED, then scheduled sending the message. An hour's delay was ample time for any second thoughts.

Reuben had followed, reading over her shoulder. "With luck, they'll take the hint. If I might presume, you should eat something and get some sleep. I'll get you if anything time-sensitive arises."

To sleep, perchance to dream. Ay, there's the rub. She shook her head. "There's something I need to do first."

But what message could she record for Jake's parents? For Paula's parents and brothers? Teri had no idea beyond that she had to reach out before NEP released the news to worldwide media.

April 28, 2034

Tragedy on Mars

New Earth Partners today announced the deaths of two astronauts on their Martian expedition. Jacob "Jake" Walker, one of the two mission pilots, and Paula Kelly, the mission's physician, died Wednesday in a freak accident while exploring Valles Marineris. Preliminary data implicate a defective cable as the cause of the accident.

Planning has begun for a short-range flight to the scene to investigate further, recover the bodies, and, if possible, salvage the expedition's only ground transportation ....

—*The Washington Post*

Statement on NEP Mission Disaster

NASA Administrator Matthias Van Dijk released a statement. "While we regret the recent loss of life on Mars, this incident, like the rumored water shortages of the CMSA team, underscores the haste with which Mars landings were planned ...."

247

Xander picked at his plate of insipid, reconstituted swill: chicken gristle with some mushy pasta, in a bland sauce. And thought: This was the best part of the day.

They had gathered as always for dinner. If holding this slop down took distraction (and yet again, silently, he cursed the pointless competition to which their more edible provisions had been sacrificed), well, they had such distraction. No, they *were* that distraction. The six of them on Phobos had grown as close as any family. As close as any friends he'd ever had. College buddies included. Becks included.

Every night, they'd share the latest personal news from Earth, whether to rejoice or commiserate. This night, there was: the latest installment of Sonny's family feud, once again concerning the wisdom of anyone being on or near Mars. Hideo's brother's MacArthur Foundation Genius Award for literature. Hideo was far too modest to mention it, so Sonny had. Vids of Xander's nieces at soccer. (They were awful. It was hysterical.) Cat's anguish at being stuck on Phobos when her mother had gotten a breast-cancer diagnosis.

That moment of vulnerability being out of character, Cat made a quick segue into a joke. "So, I'm at this restaurant in Boston. I ask the waiter, 'Have you got scrod?' He thinks about it for a moment and nods. 'You know, I've never been asked that question before in the pluperfect subjunctive.'"

With Cat and Sonny an item, with Giselle in her weird relationship with David, the dating pool for Xander was empty. It'd be a long time till *he* got scrod. "Thus ends another episode of The Young and the Tasteless." Drawing a chuckle from Cat. Drawing from the others, as many of his comments did, blank stares.

"You know what?" David said. He and Giselle had been quiet. "I think I'll take a load of laundry over to *Clark*." Of itself, doing laundry there wasn't unusual. Within the tiny, hermetically sealed habitat, the washer was a noisy, humidity-spewing nuisance. The announcement, however ….

Giselle stood. "You know, I think I will, too."

They'd no sooner suited up and left than Cat cracked, "Laundry. As if anyone who'd ever seen a sitcom couldn't break *that* code."

Sonny laughed. "Do you suppose one of them will hang a sock on the airlock hatch?

So, okay, a situation other than what passed here for food also required an occasional distraction. Xander opened his datasheet for the latest world-news download. Blaring headline and garish image jumped out at him. "Damn! Cat, did you know about this?"

"This what?"

He passed the datasheet across the table. Sonny and Hideo leaned in to see.

"Shit. No, I hadn't seen it." Cat skimmed, tapped through to a related article, then looked up. "Deaths aside, this won't be easy to recover from. Sure, the remaining six of them can hunker down in place. From what we've been told, they have enough nearby ice for consumables and fuel production. As for their bigger mission, my guess is that's pretty much kaput."

In a way, Xander had to agree. It'd be a sweltering day on Mars before billionaire tourists would risk a cable ride into Valles Marineris. "That said, I have to believe they'll recover their equipment. They're already talking about a flight there."

Cat returned the datasheet. "David and I trained for months for landing on Phobos, after a bunch of wonks put more months into developing the simulation. Doubtless, the NEP bunch did the same for their landings. And now? Their surviving pilot, I'm guessing, is being pushed, or is pushing *himself*, to fly within days.

"If the mission happens, you can be sure they'll also want to recover the bodies of their friends, and *that* means a descent into Valles Marineris. Doable? Yeah. But even if it goes off without a hitch, what are the chances they can land within a reasonable walking distance?"

Xander pocketed his datasheet. Stroking the scruffy beard that was more the product of indifference than intent, he pondered. Cat was almost certainly correct about two hops: first to the chasm's edge and then into its depths. Because even if they could unsnarl the cable trailer, and even if its reel retained sufficient cable to reach the valley floor, who'd trust it?

Even if they didn't also remember PPL's no longer veiled-seeming threats ....

Cat shoved back her plate. "Did you see Van Dijk's statement?" (He hadn't, and she related the gist.) "This is the first I've heard about our Chinese friends having a water shortage."

"Same here." If Xander had to guess, Arthur Schmidt and his spy cronies were behind the rumor. Whether or not it was true.

Hideo stood. "I'll leave the NASA gossip to you two."

"What he said." Sonny rose, too. She started stacking plates.

Xander bided his time until they left. "Cat. About the NEP folks …?"

"Yeah?"

"Maybe we can help them." He spelled out his idea.

"With Van Dijk taking potshots at both other missions, how do you suppose us helping will go across?"

"I don't propose to ask," Xander countered. "Look, forget who sent them. We're talking about *people*. Same as us. Far from home like us. They must be grieving. Beyond that, their mission lead's husband just died. Do you suppose she's thinking straight? Also, screw politics."

"Well, we can agree on the politics part. Even on the they're-people part."

"So, my idea. What do you think?"

"It could work." Cat sighed. "I shouldn't be the one to offer. Teri and I are like oil and, well, matches."

Whose fault was that? Who'd reveled during the big dust storm in sending HOW'S THE WEATHER texts? "I'll make the call."

April 30, 2034

Four days indoors, taking it in, pondering next steps. Four days of hushed sympathy. Four days with everyone around her walking on figurative eggshells. Four days of that was all Teri could bear. So, while she could've kept tabs on the recovery operation from the shelter, she was outside, taking a turn clearing the solar panels, video streaming to a corner of her HUD.

Beyond spectating, there was nothing she could *do*.

Minutes before, in a flurry of dust, a NASA lander had set down about fifty feet from the tangled ground vehicles. It was early morning, the shadows long. Xander Hopkins, muttering sotto voce, was going through some post-landing shutdown procedure. Until—

"Teri? If you're there, I'm ready to deploy rovers."

"I'm here. Proceed." She watched a lander panel, hinged along its lower edge, open to serve as a ramp. A pair of rovers on wire-mesh wheels crept to the ground. Each rover had a robotic arm: the leader bore wire cutters, the follower carried pliers. Clips on the rovers secured an assortment of other tools. "Thanks again for doing this."

"I hope it works."

Me, too. "We'll know soon."

"Bringing rover cameras online."

She'd been streaming the SUV's camera feed in the top quarter of her HUD. Shoehorning SUV and lander views into that small area was impractical. Alternating between SUV and lander views quickly proved disorienting. Adding rover feeds could only make matters worse. "Reuben, please launch our drone. Forward its feed to Phobos, too."

"Copy, boss.

The drone view came online, and she switched her streaming solely to that. She watched as, strand by strand, the first NASA bot snipped taut cable. Repeatedly, recoil ensnared that bot. The pliers-wielding bot, having stayed back a safe distance, would then roll in and tug loose the wire fragment. The rovers worked methodically (or their operators on Phobos did), the drone following along as those worked down the length of the SUV.

Within the hour, Teri had rendered the solar panels spotless. Not ready to go inside, she inspected the hydroponics domes. Dust never adhered to those like it did the flat solar panels, but she found enough streaks and smears to remove to continue feeling productive. Anyway, even through sun visor and dome plastic, the only greenery within thousands of miles was soothing.

By late in the robotic procedure's second hour, the sun now high in the sky, both track loops of the SUV seemed unencumbered. "Xander, can you pull back your bots? I'd like to uncouple the SUV remotely from the supply trailer, see if the former still works."

"Copy that."

"I heard you, boss," Reuben said. "Here goes."

Teri saw the coupler pop open. The SUV crept forward about two feet and began pulling to the side—toward the abyss! "Stop!" Which, sooner than she could get out the word, the SUV had. Pilot reflexes. "Thanks, Reuben."

Bots and drone in turn did close inspections of the SUV's track plates. None of those views showed an obstruction.

"Something impinging on the mechanism from underneath?" Xander mused. "I'll need a minute. Or ten."

In practice, it was a half hour before a rover—running newly downloaded software; dish antenna and robotic arm folded as low as they would go; flashlight socketed into the arm where wire cutters had been—crept into the shadow between the SUV tracks. The other rover had looped a cable scrap several times around the turret base of its mate. In a theory no one wanted to test, if the exploring robot got stuck, the other might haul it out.

The robot finally emerged into the narrow gap between the SUV and the decoupled supply trailer.

"I was afraid of that," Xander said. "Rover doesn't have a line of sight to any comsat at the moment. There isn't room for it to corner and get out from between vehicles. Hold on." The other rover dropped its towline and approached. "Okay, we have a relay through number two. Uploading inspection imagery … now. Transferring it to you guys."

They played back this vid three times before Islah, linked in from her shelter, called out, "Stop! Back, oh, five seconds. Then advance frame by frame."

There was the answer. The SUV, moving forward, must have snagged a cable scrap, some quirky recoil from the snipping-loose process, in its left-hand rear drive wheel. Mere inches of cable protruded. More had insinuated itself into the mechanism. It was a wonder they hadn't thrown the track from the drive sprocket.

Without extracting the wire, the SUV wasn't going anywhere.

"That's that," Reuben said. "We need to get onsite, lift the SUV, loosen the track, and dismount the sprocket."

As if she'd allow anyone beneath the massive vehicle teetering on an improvised jack. There'd been enough horrible deaths.

"Maybe …." Xander hummed to himself. "I'll need a minute."

This minute approached two hours, but Xander came back with an elaborate plan for short backward and forward rocking motions by the tracked vehicle, alternated with precise maneuvers by one of his rovers, to expose and extract the cable scrap inch by inch. At that, the solution remained conceptual. As during its slow surveillance crawl, the bot would be out of comm reach, directed by a program coded for the purpose. The elaborate choreography had to be coordinated between Xander and whoever here best understand the SUV's mechanics, then converted to code for the rover. Long before the software was complete, the drone and the rovers had drained their batteries. They'd need the rest of the day to recharge.

With luck, they'd try tomorrow.

May 2, 2034

"**Y**ou did good," Cat said. She stood behind Xander, a hand resting on his shoulder.

His hands shook. Maybe he could still code, though thankfully that phase of the effort was finally done. No way just then could he handle real-time control. Not of a rover, much less a lander. "Good would have been getting this done days ago."

"With you, every silver lining has a cloud."

He vacated his chair at the habitat's mission-command console. Its display offered four views of the work site: from the NEP drone, the lander, and both rovers. The salvaged, bulldozer-like SUV and its trailers, freed from the gruesome cable tangle and once more coupled, had retreated from the chasm's brink. "There's no silver lining here."

"No, I suppose not. But I'll say it again. You did good." Cat sat, then opened a radio channel to the ground. "Asaph Hall Base calling. We're ready on this end. Teri, are you there?"

"Yes, Cat. All of us are."

Teri sounded … sad. Why wouldn't she?

Xander took the mic. "We can handle this phase on our own." *Phase.* How antiseptic. "We'll call when it's done."

"Thanks for offering. For … everything. But please keep us in the loop. This is something we need."

As everyone *here* also felt. He stepped back several feet to stand with David and Giselle, with Sonny and Hideo, to observe as, under Cat's precise, economical movements, the rovers gathered … Paula. Chunk by chunk.

It felt like eons passed until the last remains were brought into the lander's rover bay, deposited inside a bag pre-positioned there. The NEP drone made a final slow circuit, confirmed only bloodstains remained behind. It settled to the ground, conserving battery for its next task.

The two rovers trundled up the ramp and secured themselves. The ramp/panel closed.

"Now we'll get Jake," Cat said softly.

"Copy that," Teri responded, softer still.

The six on Phobos and as many on the ground watched in silence as the lander's point of view descended into Valles Marineris. Watched from a rover point of view as the panel/ramp swung open. Watched as the lander's camera sought all around for a splotch of vivid red. Switched to the rovers again as those little bots trundled forward.

The NEP drone arrived, its aerial perspective capturing the rovers' progress. They saw the little bots pull a slick tarp, approach the body, secure the tarp's corners with rocks. With painful slowness, robotic limbs dug around the body. Only then could they drag Jake from the dent made by his impact. With the body not halfway onto the tarp, the drone, its battery discharged, settled to the ground.

Awkwardly, the rovers folded the body into the slippery tarp. They dragged/shoved the bundle into the lander and bungee-corded it in place. With the dregs of charge left in their batteries, they backed down the ramp and away from the lander.

Cat, looking dog-tired, slumped. Xander glanced at a clock. The operation had gone on for four hours. He whispered, "Are you up to this? We can deliver the remains tomorrow."

"Prolonging this for those guys? No. I'll cope." She took the mic. "Teri, Cat here. My apologies for this taking so long. We'll have the lander to you soon."

"Copy that, Cat. There's no reason to apologize. We'll … be ready."

Ready? That was a lot to ask, Xander thought.

May 5, 2034

Dale plopped into a chair, unrecognized (or, as satisfactory, not approached by anyone), the amphitheater-style classroom filling up around her. Her duties often had her attend major scientific conferences, but she hadn't sat in on an academic seminar in … well, she couldn't remember the last time.

Never mind how spur of the moment being here was.

She could have flown out of Reagan National this morning and made her afternoon appointment at the University of Texas at Austin with hours to spare. Instead, she'd flown into San Antonio last night. Dinner with an old college buddy had been terrific, and even more so the prospect of an entire night together—until Robyn said of her engineer husband, delayed by some last-minute office snag from joining the women at the restaurant, "Chuck's been excited for days about your visit. He has *so* many questions about the Mars missions and the accident."

Chuck and Patrick, *her* husband, were likewise the best of friends. If Patrick—somehow always able to channel Chuck's habitual boundless and often oblivious curiosity—had joined her this trip, Dale might have stuck it out. The four of them might have enjoyed an evening of contract bridge, like so many back during grad school. But Patrick, alas, had his own job to contend with. "The beans don't count themselves," he'd told her.

Leaving Dale alone to face those *so many questions*. Even before the accident and the pall those deaths had cast over all three expeditions, Dale had, for weeks now, done her best to steer clear of Mars. The last way she'd choose to spend an evening (speculation, perhaps, but—knowing Chuck well—*informed* speculation) was down some rabbit hole of how such an accident could have happened, who was at fault, what might be done better next time, etc.

So, she'd frozen. Improvised.

Hadn't she texted? There'd been a late change in plans, and now she had to be on the Austin campus bright and early. So sorry, but she couldn't spend the night after all. On the Uber from San Antonio, she'd booked a hotel room near campus for the night.

Not until this morning, scouting out the Johansson Life Sciences Center in advance of her (unchanged afternoon) appointment, had Dale encountered the bulletin board with a flyer for a seminar about primordial cellular biology. She hadn't considered evolution since med school. Effectively, since forever. Ira Coleman's crazy questions notwithstanding.

Attending the lecture made ditching Robyn and Chuck, never mind after the fact, not entirely a lie. As this campus visit wasn't entirely about eluding the national press corps. The single aspect of her life of late that *was* entire? The president's comfort with Dale's frequent absences of late from DC.

Rationalizations all around? Hell, yeah. But again, not entirely. Lots of exciting science—her forthcoming appointment, for instance—had nada to do with Mars. She could, should, and, damn it, *would* support such research for as long as she retained influence. For however much longer that'd be. If, while she assessed funding candidates, she also stretched her mind, formed an idea or two about what she might do with her life once the axe fell? So much the better. Serendipity was a thing.

From behind Dale came the sound of doors closing. The handful of students schmoozing by the podium dispersed and found seats. The Biology department head (or so Dale gathered; the woman didn't introduce herself) launched into an interminable welcoming speech. Then a grad student, head of the local chapter of the Society for the Study of Evolution, launched into his own rambling introduction. It was a good fifteen minutes after the hour until Antonia Rinaldi, the guest speaker, began her talk on the emergence of life billions of years ago, early in what geologists called the Archean Eon.

Dale felt comfortable with the basic orthodoxy of evolution, or, anyway, what she understood that orthodoxy to be. Random variation. Natural selection. Inheritance. The great tree of life, with its many limbs, branches, twigs, and leaves, past and present, all descended from some unknowable LUCA: the latest universal common ancestor.

But beyond that? Blissful ignorance, other than that people argued vociferously over details and that those altercations seldom changed minds. Were intermittent bursts of biological creativity through the ages real or misimpressions fostered by gaps in the fossil record? Endlessly debatable. Did evolution have a direction to it? Sure, fish, dolphins, and ichthyosaurs were all streamlined, and not by having inherited that configuration from some common ancestor. A fancy name like convergent evolution didn't make the similarities, when they happened, any more meaningful. Sometimes, environmental conditions favored a particular bodily configuration. Intuitively, how could a process driven by random events, from stray cosmic rays to errant asteroid strikes, have direction?

Okay, maybe she *had* wondered about the possibility of convergent evolution since Ira Coleman and his damned pictures of flying squirrels and sugar gliders. Of cats and their marsupial doppelgängers. She'd read papers calling archipelagos natural experiments in evolutionary biology, read about convergences and divergences among lizard populations on neighboring Caribbean islands, and come out of it … conflicted. Then taken comfort in the memory of body shapes that *didn't* recur. Elephants. Giraffes. Penguins. Repeatedly tried (and failed) to grasp why PPL would care.

Maybe she'd spent too much time around politicians (a situation on the cusp of resolving itself) because this fruitless wrangling only reminded her of an anonymous Washington wag's take on another science. First law of economics: *For every economist, there exists an equal and opposite economist.* Followed by the second law: *They're both wrong.*

Not that Anonymous was the only oft-quoted economist. Also much beloved of politicians was a line attributed John Maynard Keynes: *When the facts change, I change my mind. What do you do, sir?*

Damned facts. Dale sometimes wondered if she should be changing her mind.

From what Rinaldi was saying, the Tree of Life might be another of those things conventional wisdom had long misunderstood, or, at least, that *Dale* had. Even today, Rinaldi reminded, bacteria and viruses often swapped genes. (As Dale knew too well. Hell, as *any* MD knew. Lateral gene transfer was a factor in the spread of bacterial resistance to antibiotics and touched upon her real purpose in Austin.) In life's earliest era, with robust cell membranes yet to appear, how much more would gene swapping have mattered? Wholesale gene migration might have driven the evolution of early cells far more than the occasional mutation of single genes and orthodox descent.

Which, if true, rendered the trunk of Darwin's Tree of Life wholly metaphorical. Which, if true, transformed that trunk into some messy, unknowable web. Which, if true, turned LUCA from a single cell with a unique destiny to an evolving community of promiscuous cells ceaselessly exchanging genes.

Which, however intriguing as a concept, must be forever speculative. When she'd been in the lab, and undoubtedly still, what drove medical research was how biology operated in the present. Not what might have transpired eons ago. Not what might unfold eons into the future.

But weeks and months from now? As more and more bacteria became resistant to antibiotics? *That* was an evolutionary development that very much mattered.

And so, her afternoon appointment ….

Everyone but Reuben, his ankle still iffy, was outside. Maia and Islah had hiked a few klicks west to collect yet more rock samples. Teri and the other guys were busy with routine chores. All of them … waited.

Me, more than most, Teri thought.

"Should be soon," Reuben radioed. "Its dash cam already sees *Burroughs* and *Bradbury*."

Not a minute later, the ill-fated SUV appeared over the nearby, serrate, eastern ridge.

"Well done, Reuben. Umm, park it alongside the NASA lander." Because SUV and trailers might well carry Paula's … traces, to be combined with the remains that no one, Teri perhaps least of all, could yet face unloading. One more duty weighing on her ….

Still, the SUV and trailers were essential equipment she couldn't write off. Teri looked around. The solar panels weren't all that dusty, and the guys were between inspecting hydroponics domes. "Julio, Keshaun, if you hadn't noticed, the SUV is back. Could you check it out?"

"Sure," Julio said.

"Do you want it or the trailers unloaded?" Keshaun asked.

"Inspect everything for damage. Inventory what's onboard. For now, don't unpack."

Because Mission Control had already hinted about a drive in the opposite direction, scoping out a path up Olympus Mons. For that, they wouldn't need a cable reel. (Because why in hell would anyone ever trust *that* again? But the trailer itself, sans reel, could still be useful.)

Intimations about getting back on the horse ....

It had scarcely been a *week*. Sick, insensitive bastards.

"Doctor Moskowitz, I appreciate you meeting with me on short notice."

"Phil," Dale's host countered. "Or 'Hey, you' works. We're informal here. As for explaining our project and giving you the grand tour, it'll be my pleasure. We don't get many presidential science advisers."

Phil Moskowitz was tall, pudgy, and stoop-shouldered. No matter his pressed khakis and blue oxford-cloth dress shirt—fancied up for the visiting dignitary?—bushy and unfashionably long sideburns had her imagining tie-dye and bellbottoms. Well, if anywhere was anachronism-appropriate, this would be the place.

"Dale for me, then. Since you brought it up, how many?"

He laughed. "Presidential science advisers? Counting you ... one."

Room 6140 of the Johansson Life Sciences Center could have been any biology lab pretty much anywhere. Rows of lab benches with tall stools. Stacks of petri dishes. Shelves of bottled chemicals. Microscopes and other lab instruments. Computers. Faded cartoons taped to the walls. Grad students in jeans and tees, coming and going. What might have been an ordinary chest freezer. The room's single overt idiosyncrasy was its wall display, reading 101,632.

However mundane, that chest had brought Dale here. Or, anyway, what transpired within. "So, the LTEE."

"The LTEE." Phil foot-snagged and dragged over stools from the nearest lab bench. He sat and gestured to her to do the same. "The long-term evolution experiment. A handful of new generations bred daily of E. coli. They'd reproduce much faster, of course, under ideal conditions, but an all-they-can-eat buffet is no way to sustain evolutionary pressures. I'll get around to explaining the daily routine, but the short version is that each day's samples exhaust their food in about six hours. As of around lunchtime today"—he pointed to the wall display—"we're somewhere around 101,632 generations since the original sample. You know why E. coli?"

Escherichia coli was easy to culture. Most strains, never mind E. coli's ubiquity in the intestines of most warm-blooded animals, were harmless. It had been studied for the better part of a century. However haggard recent events had her feeling, surely she didn't look as old as *that*?

She elected to take his question as rhetorical. "LTEE's run continuously since 1988?"

"More or less. The only major interruptions were several months during the COVID pandemic and a shorter hiatus for H10N3. The most recent pause, a few days, was for a move across campus into our new digs here."

"Restarting each time from samples you'd kept in the deep freeze."

"Right. E. coli defrost as good as new. I'd imagine you know most bacteria are like that. But freezing isn't just for such exceptional circumstances. We cryopreserve samples every 75 days, call it every 500 generations, in case there's reason to look or roll back. If we suspect a contamination problem. If we overlooked some interesting mutation and want to look for its earlier manifestations." He grinned. "We call those our frozen fossil record."

The hardiness of bacteria—and archaea and viruses—having been, until the Ares mission, perhaps Dale's biggest single job worry. Arguably, it should still be. Year after year, melting ice caps and glaciers released yet more ancient microbes against which people, animals, and crops might lack immunity. Sometimes, already had. Not three years before, an anthrax-precursor bacterium *had* popped up that way. Canadian authorities had sacrificed dozens of cattle herds to contain that outbreak.

If Phil noticed her attention wandering, he didn't comment. "When your office set up this visit, they said your focus was antibiotic resistance."

"Call it *a* focus. The whole experiment interests me."

"That's good. Our research is relevant, but it doesn't involve antibiotic resistance directly."

A young woman had been loitering nearby, expression anxious, datasheet in hand. "Phil? Can I get your signoff on this? You know Accounting."

"Indeed, yes." He took the datasheet, gave it a thumbprint, and handed it back. "Don't break this one, please."

Looking chagrined, she scuttled off. Dale wondered what the kid had broken. Followed by wondering since when a thirty-something was a kid.

"So, okay," Phil resumed. "Alas, research isn't cheap."

Hinting that a good word from her couldn't hurt with LTEE's five-year NSF grant up soon for a renewal. "I shouldn't comment."

"Understood. Okay, the tour begins." Phil stood and opened the chest. Air spilled out, as best she could judge at body temperature. A big incubator, then, not a freezer. Some mechanism within slowly moved two rows of stoppered flasks back and forth, left and right, mixing the contents. Fourteen flasks in all. He closed the chest. "Thus concludes the grand tour.

"Here's the drill. A grad student removes the flasks daily. He or she, whoever has that day's duty, transfers a one-percent sample—which is millions of cells—from each old flask to a new flask. The new samples, with a fresh but limited supply of glucose, go into the incubator. Whatever's left in the old flasks—whether that grew or failed to grow, whether or not any of it mutated—is fair game for study. Some, as I'd said, goes into our frozen fossil record."

"Big picture first, Phil. What's happened over the years?"

"Big picture? *Evolution* happened. Larger cells across all lines. Not the same increase in every line of descent, but the same *trend*. Faster cellular reproduction, the extent of increase again varying, also across all lines, in the race to exploit scarce food while it lasted. Atrophy of metabolic pathways for nutrients other than the standard glucose we give them.

"The E. coli genome has not much more than 4000 genes. Statistically, every last gene has mutated many times by now. Of all those mutations, maybe a hundred have been persistent. Maybe a quarter of *those* are obviously beneficial." He tipped his head, scratched his chin, frowned. "Let's see, what else? Six populations developed what might be considered defects in their DNA self-repair mechanisms. The standard repair mechanism was maybe too rigorous for the starvation diets on which we keep the critters, such that faster adaptation is favored."

"All of which tells you … what?"

"Well, the repeated emergence of a few characteristics is striking. I'd expect the pattern to extend to antibiotic resistance."

Bringing to mind, well, not that morning's seminar as much as her mind's wanderings *during* the lecture. Ira Coleman. Sugar gliders and flying squirrels. "Repeatability. Are you suggesting evolution has … direction?"

"I could use a Coke. You?"

"Anything diet and decaf."

"Decaf? You *have* been out of the lab for a while." With a shrill whistle, he caught a grad student's attention. "Joe, would you mind grabbing us a Coke and a bottled water?"

"Sure, Phil." Joe was out the door, then back with their beverages, within seconds. "Doctor Bennigan, I *have* to say, I'm *so* interested in the Mars expedition. Do you—"

"What'd I tell everyone?" Phil chided. "No waylaying of our guest."

Joe studied his scuffed sneakers, mumbled what might have been, "Sorry," and hurried back to his workstation.

Phil popped the tab on his Coke can. "Direction? I wouldn't use that word. Direction somehow has a connotation of *intent*. Evolution has no volition, doesn't work to any goal beyond survival. Still, there's no denying LTEE has shown identical populations, faced with identical selection pressures, often evolve the same basic adaptations. Adapting to antibiotics fits the model as surely as adapting to food scarcity or, in a colleague's lab, to hothouse temperatures."

"Okay, not direction. How about convergent evolution?"

"Closer." He took a long, somehow thoughtful, swig. "To be clear, there's no inevitability here, just tendencies. There can be multiple ways to adapt to environmental pressures. Not a bacterial example, but consider a prey species faced with a new predator species. You have mice, and so you bring in a cat. The competition might favor faster mice *and* better-camouflaged mice. Your mice populations might well *diverge*."

"Cleo does her job well. I don't have any mice."

"Or so you'd like to think. Anyway, another thing. Some physical adaptations require multiple genetic mutations. That alone makes it improbable that two populations will evolve those adaptations in identical ways. Convergence is even less frequent when the order of multi-gene mutations matters."

Everything Phil said made sense, and yet … something nagged at the back of her brain. Something, some *way*, in which experiment and … nature differed.

"You look troubled," Phil said.

Yeah, she was. Except she couldn't explain *why* beyond, "This is a lot to think about."

People of Earth! All life is to be cherished, and so we join others in mourning the recent deaths on Mars.

And yet, our sadness is tempered by other feelings.

By anger. However sincere NEP's protective measures might have been—measures of which we were already skeptical—those precautions have failed. Literal trillions of bacteria, fungi, and viruses colonize every human being. The recent incident has now *twice* unleashed that microbial contamination upon any native Martian life.

By disbelief. In full recognition that conditions on Mars are harsh, we do not, and cannot, accept bland, unsubstantiated assurances that every bacterium, fungus, virus, and human cell set loose in the incident has perished. The tenacity of terrestrial life—even deep in Earth's rocks, in the darkest abyssal depths, high in the stratosphere, and clinging to the exterior of space stations—mocks such assertions.

By apprehension. The Mars missions have experienced failure upon failure. These deaths offer yet another demonstration that the hastily conceived missions are primed for disaster. We cannot expect them to be any better prepared for whatever Martian life they might encounter and—by intent or otherwise—carry with them.

Finally, by *resolve*. We hereby renew our pledge to defend Earth. We will stop any return of material or personnel from Mars.

—*Communiqué of the Planetary Protection Legions*

May 7, 2034

The survivors, as Teri had begun to think of them, gathered at the planet's first cemetery. Reuben and Julio had dug graves (on the far slope of a gentle hill, out of daily sight, while remaining a short walk from camp) and lowered the tarp-wrapped remains. Islah and Keshaun had carved headstones, laser-etched with names and dates. Maia had pressed beautiful ferns—they had no flowers—and sealed two bunches of the greenery between sheets of clear plastic.

Teri had eulogies queued up in her helmet comp to read from her HUD. Sincere? Yes. Grief had washed away the anger she'd carried for so long. But were those remarks *adequate*? She knew better. In the best of times, words seldom came easily to her. Yet, somehow, she had to speak, had to get through this. She took two paces, turned to face everyone—

Except the survivors weren't everyone. Not even close.

Only *now* did the true audience for this sad occasion register. The video recording they made would inevitably become public. To friends and colleagues, past and present. To countless impressionable girls and boys aspiring to careers in space. To the Phobos people, who'd asked if they might link in and pay their respects. To every know-it-all and naysayer, every Luddite and prophet of doom, eager to exploit the tragedy—and thereafter, to their gullible audiences. So much for all she needed to express. That must wait till the six of them were truly in private.

Teri began, somehow, past the lump in her throat. "Jacob Walker and Paula Kelly were taken from us far too soon. But no matter how much we miss them, we're here today to *honor* them. To admire their bravery, determination, and boundless talents. Not to dwell on the lives cut short but to remember the amazing accomplishments of their remarkable lives. Not to ...."

She even kept it together through a couple of anecdotes—until a surge of memories overcame her. Of the early days, the fun days, the great days with Jake. She managed to get out, "Who else has something to share?"

One by one, people offered other reminisces. There were tears but also laughter. If not catharsis, some easing of the pain.

Until lobbing the first handfuls of sterile Martian regolith into the open graves once more rendered Teri numb.

After listless hours in the dark of her cubby, Teri accepted the inevitable. Sleep wasn't happening. She slipped on a robe, slid back the curtain, and swung feet to the floor. If Reuben and Julio were asleep, she didn't want to disturb them.

She paced for a bit in the dark. Considered and rejected exercise. Tried and failed to work up any enthusiasm to ... try anything. Decided to be her own best friend and get something, anything, off the to-do list she'd let grow these past few days. Ideally, an item that didn't require interacting with anyone.

By GMT, and so Phobos, it was also late. She'd leave a message. "Asaph Hall Base, this is Teri at Barsoom. We'll refuel your lander today. I'll send an update when the refueling—"

Her comm console pinged. She finished the message, "... is complete," and opened the connection.

Xander Hopkins, rumpled, peered out at her. It seemed she wasn't the only one with insomnia. "Hi, Teri. Umm, is everything okay?"

Not even close. "Just sorry we're taking so long getting the lander back to you."

"No apology necessary. You had ... other things going on." He looked away from the camera. "'Other things?' Please, forget I said something so stupid. I never know what to say. Teri, I'm so sorry for all that's happened, the loss of your husband especially."

Did the words ever matter? "Well, thanks. For the concern and for all your help. From everyone up there."

"If the situation had been reversed, I'm sure you guys would have done the same."

She liked to think so. "Of course. If there is something we can do for you …?"

"I … we're good. Thanks anyway."

A definite hesitation. "You sure?"

"Uh-huh."

"Anyway, we'll reach out after refueling, so you can run your pre-flight checks. I expect you're eager to retrieve the bots." He still (or was it again) looked embarrassed. "Right. Not firing on all cylinders here. You will have retrieved them already with another lander."

"Umm, we're leaving the rovers. Valles Marineris has tons of interesting geology they can explore."

The LED of enlightenment blazed like a nova. Those NASA rovers were ….

Her mind rebelled at completing the sentence, much less *picturing* the situation. The once sterile little bots were now … what? Tainted? Contaminated? Soaked? In human blood and gore. In human intestinal bacteria. In ….

"Teri! Are you okay? Is someone there with you?"

Not only the rovers. The lander that had returned Jake and Paula must be as useless. "Do you even want the lander back?"

"Yeah, we do." Spoken with eyes once again averted. The lander, too, must be relegated to secondary purposes.

"Xander, that's all I had. Have a good whatever's left of the night. Maybe one of us can even get some sleep."

"Yeah. Goodnight, Teri."

She dropped the connection. Shuffled back to her cubby. Where, instead of sleeping, she lay awake, staring, trying to imagine what favor Xander had decided *not* to ask.

June 6, 2034

Survival came down to *ice*.

The vastness of Utopia Planitia, at least everywhere Kai and his colleagues had drilled and drilled and *drilled*, yielded only scattered, small pockets of buried ice. As for recycling the water they had, no process was ever 100-percent efficient. Water rations could only be reduced so far. All the while, the relatively nearby, kilometers-thick, north-polar ice cap beckoned. The math shouldn't have been difficult. The math—eventually—trumped the politics. Because the reek of unwashed bodies and the dwindling level of even recycled piss could only be ignored for so long.

Hence, weeks after they *should* have headed north, they had finally set out. After, even in Beijing and Moscow, the possibility of total mission failure outweighed the—who gave a fuck?—likelihood they might confirm scandalous American intimations of water shortages at Fire Star City. Rumors that, in fact, were true. That had been true all along.

Kai stared out the Mars Buggy windshield at a boundless red expanse. His shoulders, arms, and hands ached from clenching the steering wheel. His eyes stung from peroxide fumes and regolith dust, more of each brought into the tiny cabin at every stop. But for all his aches and exhaustion, he felt satisfied. Never mind the thousand-plus kilometers still to go, this trek had been a success. Beneath silvery tarps, the trailers in tow were piled high with blocks of ice. Some of that, to be sure, frozen carbon dioxide, dry ice, but the rest precious water ice. Given recycling—and perhaps, still some rationing—they brought enough water to last for months. They might even be able to expand their aeroponics capacity.

Zhao Jin had fallen asleep in the seat beside him, and Kai had to smile at the trail of drool at the corner of the colonel's mouth. In the (tiny) back area of the (tiny) cabin, Chen Xiuying and Ivan Vasiliev had given up bickering over how some football match might have ended had the star Russian goalkeeper not been injured (fouled, Vanya would have it) late in the first half. A glance over his shoulder showed Kai that they, too, had nodded off. Well, they were all tired. Apart from the drone of the ventilation fan and the faint hum of their vehicle's electric drive motors, the cabin was blissfully quiet.

Outbound, they'd stopped every night, erecting and camping in portable inflatable shelters. Now? Eager to deliver the bounty of ice, they'd chosen to drive straight through. Three-hour shifts let anyone not behind the wheel get in a good long snooze. Sitting up, but still.

Kai's latest three-hour stint had come and gone, but rather than wake Xiuying to relieve him, he kept going. She'd have wanted to talk—because the good doctor *always* wanted to talk—which would have interfered with his brooding.

No taikonaut could be described as traditional, but Kai remained conventional enough to dutifully report to his parents. Even from Mars. He kept his emails respectful, upbeat, and short. He mentioned nothing that might cause them worry. He aspired to modesty, even in describing the adventure of a lifetime. Perhaps their usual disinterest should not have surprised him. Their immediate reaction to the NEP tragedy definitely had.

"I hope you're keeping a diary," Father had recorded. "Especially after those foolish Americans got themselves killed, there will be a market here for such chronicles."

Kai had said nothing, hoping that would be the end of the matter. It wasn't. After the customary paternal well-wishes, the message forwarded that morning from Fire Star City became pointed. "Despite our disappointment that you did not respond to our suggestion, I inquired on your behalf to a literary agency. They agree this is an opportunity. They can arrange a writer to work from your notes and recordings."

269

Because if a thing didn't make money, his father saw no purpose to it. As if anything on Mars were for sale.

Well, Father, it would appear there will be more disappointment in your future.

With anger and frustration—and yes, a touch of guilt at his disrespect—roiling Kai's thoughts, sleep seemed impossible and civil conversation untenable. So, he kept driving. He was too wound up for sleep, and the task was mindless enough.

It didn't matter that windborne dust had mostly filled in their outbound tire tracks. He needed only to stay pointed more or less south. He needed only to keep the afternoon sun to his right. Should his attention wander with some crevasse or big rock in the way? Worst case, lidar and emergency braking would kick in.

And so, he drove ….

Kai jolted awake.

He half-sensed, half-remembered a bump, what any small pothole might have delivered. To his side, the colonel hadn't even stirred. Glancing over his shoulder, the two in the back seemed likewise oblivious. As for Kai himself, well, his heart was racing a bit. From suddenly waking, he presumed. He wondered when he'd drifted off, how long he'd been out. Not long, surely, but still careless. And—

The Mars Buggy was driving into its own shadow! Headed *east*!

Kai took a deep breath, tried to shake off a fog of confusion. He had a headache. His heart continued to race. He braked the vehicle to a stop. "Xiuying." She didn't react. He tried again, louder. "Xiuying!" Still nothing—and no one *else* stirred, either.

The colonel's wrist had a rapid but erratic pulse. Kai poked Zhao's shoulder. No response. Well, not *none*. Zhao toppled against the far wall of the cabin.

Kai sensed he himself was dizzy. Confused.

Something had gone wrong, and yet every dashboard indicator shone green. Well, *people* were sensors, too. Three of them were unconscious, and Kai felt crappier by the moment. So ….

Ah. He slid up a sleeve cuff. Stared at the tattoo-like, sweat-powered biosensor on his forearm. *It* wasn't green. Meaning … he struggled to remember. Meaning ….

Low oxygen saturation. Hypoxemia. Meaning …?

Rapid pulse. Dizziness. Headache. Confusion. It was almost like … almost like … the final, brutal kilometers of a marathon. Which only confused him further.

With a sudden shudder, Zhao explosively vomited.

There was a moment of shocked lucidity: *carbon-dioxide toxicity!* Kai slapped the emergency oxygen release.

And blacked out.

A bracing rush of cool air returned Kai to awareness. How long had he been out this time? "Anyone, can you hear me? *Anyone!*"

No response.

He checked Zhao again. Breathing, but with a weak and erratic pulse. He tugged the colonel upright, grabbed the man's shoulders and shook. Nothing. Slapped his face. No response.

Meanwhile, the two seated in the back had yet to stir, much less respond to Kai's shouts. Kai reached over the seatback. Xiuying looked blue and felt cold to the touch. She had no pulse. Ivan, at least, was breathing.

They needed a doctor—and Xiuying *was* their doctor. Kai pulled the AED, automatic external defibrillator, from its locker. Like an automaton himself, he hooked up Xiuying according to the device's voice prompts. After long, scary seconds, the AED decided her heart had stopped—as though the absence of a pulse hadn't already told him as much!—and directed chest compressions.

CPR in the small cabin, with Kai draped over the seatback, was all but impossible. He tried anyway. No good.

Ivan mumbled incoherently. No, in Russian.

"English, Vanya!"

"What … what's happening?"

"Unclear." Kai grabbed Ivan's arm, checked his pulse. Steadier and slower than Zhao's. He slid up Ivan's sleeve. The biosensor showed green. "Something's wrong with life support." The CO_2-to-O_2 recycling, if he had to guess—though guessing could get them *all* dead. "We're on emergency oh-two."

Ivan turned his head. "Xiuying?"

"We've lost her." Kai dropped back into his seat. "I think the colonel's in a coma."

"Shit."

In a word. Kai jacked a spare datasheet into the vehicle's console and handed back the datasheet. "Run diagnostics. Find out what's wrong." *Before we run out of oxygen.*

"While you do what?"

"Get medical advice." *From the only doctor closer than Earth.* "Then I'll contact *your* colonel. We might need an evacuation flight."

Ivan was already poking away at the datasheet. Also, frowning. "You must know neither colonel nor their superiors want us dealing with the Ares mission."

"If Zhao lives, he can complain." *If any of them survived.*

Consulting an ephemeris table in search of a comsat in view, Kai saw that both natural moons were overhead. He could contact the Canadian doctor on Phobos without leaving any tracks. Assuming no one up there chose to crow about this.

"What do you *mean*," Kai demanded, "in a few days? We could be dead by then." If their final catalyst cartridge for the Bosch/Sabatier recycler degraded as quickly as the one that had almost killed them? They *would* be dead by then. "Oxygen regeneration aside, Colonel Zhao needs help *now*." What type of help? Assisted ventilation? Cardiac meds? Sun Ying, on Phobos, could only speculate until they got Zhao to an infirmary with decent instrumentation.

Colonel Antonov, in an irritatingly placid voice, said, "It does no one any good if I die flying an unprepared ship."

"Either ship has more than enough LOX and LH2 to retrieve us," Kai persisted. "They carry emergency supplies, too. The mission commander"—reminding Antonov who was in charge here—"confirmed this before we set out." Because the contingency plan had always been a rescue flight. Even though no one had ever imagined *this* contingency.

"Fuel matters," Antonov agreed, "but there are also diagnostics to execute. Preflight checklists to perform. Simulations to run. The inevitable anomalies to chase down and resolve."

Simulations to run? There were no simulations for this specific scenario. There'd been no reason even to imagine flying to this exact spot. How could there have been?

The bastard is *stalling*, Kai decided. Happy Colonel Zhao might not survive. Happy the CMSA contingent could be all but wiped out. Even at the cost of Ivan as collateral damage.

Hard on the heels of those misgivings came an even darker intuition: Antonov might somehow have *caused* the accident. ("Always remember, Major. Should anything happen to me, you become the senior PLA officer." Zhao's earnest, prelaunch warning—as from another life, another era—now felt prescient.)

Four people used half the water of eight. Too late for Kai and Ivan, Antonov could swoop in with more oxygen, catalyst cartridges, and a driver or two to bring the Mars Buggy and its precious ice—and four corpses—the rest of the way to Fire Star City. Whereupon Roscosmos—and the Kremlin—would assert Antonov was the senior officer among the survivors.

"Colonel." Ivan grabbed the microphone. "Nikolai Mikhailovich, there must be *efficiencies* you could exercise. Some prudent expedients."

"I will look into it," Antonov said. "Meanwhile, I suggest you resume driving with all possible haste. Good luck."

The Chinese ground vehicle slewed to a halt during *Bradbury's* final descent.

Teri was out of her ship's airlock, a satchel of oxygen tanks clanking on her back, as soon as the landing area had somewhat cooled. Three spacesuited figures—two haggard men supporting/dragging a third—were already stumbling toward her. She didn't want to think about how they'd managed to wrestle a limp and unconscious figure into vacuum gear.

"Thank you for coming," one radioed in Chinese-accented English. "I am Carter."

She bounded to them. "I'm Teri. Here, let me help." She shrugged off her satchel strap, squeezed beneath an arm of the man they helped. The Slavic-looking guy, looking not much healthier than the patient, staggered aside. Frowning in concentration, he retrieved the satchel and started dragging it to his vehicle.

Carter said, "Please, Teri. As soon as you can, get my colonel to your infirmary."

"Not to your base? It's closer."

Carter shook his head. "Yours. Sun Ying will be more familiar with your Western medical equipment."

Sonny being the last doctor alive among all three missions (and at that, thousands of miles distant). So: plausible. As it was plausible that a technical glitch had kept Carter's colleagues from swooping to the rescue. Both explanations together? *Barely* plausible. Trouble at home, Carter? Interesting, but just then not relevant. "Okay."

Teri and Carter carried the colonel to her ship. Reuben and Julio were waiting inside, armed with a medical oxygen mask, ready to buckle the patient into an acceleration couch.

Teri asked, "Will you and your Russian colleague be all right? We could fly you to your home base."

"We need our vehicle and its cargo. With the oxygen tanks you provided, Ivan and I will be safe driving the rest of the way."

Not long ago, after an earlier disaster, it had seemed important to recover another ground vehicle. Damned, awful, deadly excursions.

"Teri!" Reuben called from the bridge. "Ready as soon as you are."

"We should go," Teri said. "Be careful, Carter."

"We will. Thank you."

As soon as Carter withdrew to a safe distance, *Bradbury* took off.

Ten minutes after they got Zhao into the infirmary, he had some sort of seizure. With Sonny giving frantic, remote guidance on things to try, their patient went into cardiac arrest.

He didn't make it.

June 8, 2034

If Zhao Jin had never made leading the expedition look easy, he had made it appear possible. Only now, with the colonel's former responsibilities thrust upon him, did Kai marvel at even that accomplishment.

Enough self-pity, Kai told himself. *You're lucky to be alive.* Never mind how *un*lucky his life looked to be going forward.

Across the Imperial Palace, behind a drawn curtain, Kai had Mingmei and Oorvi taking an inventory. They chatted, even chattered, with a natural ease he sorely missed. Not so long ago, he'd had that kind of friendship with both women. And could no more.

Since his unwanted elevation to mission commander, Kai had a new appreciation for the late colonel. *What would Zhao Jin have done in this situation?* Whether or not to act the same, Kai found it helpful to ask himself the question. And so, much of what had felt like busywork had come to make sense. Like the updated inventory he didn't need but had ordered anyway. In both shelters.

Because he *did* need time alone with his thoughts—without seeming like he did.

Oorvi had relocated to this shelter when Kai and the rest had set off for the ice cap. Officially, the shift had been by Zhao's edict, lest Mingmei be left alone. Unofficially, the colonel had been giving Oorvi a break from Antonov. Since the accident and the survivors' return,

Oorvi had asked to make her move permanent. "As a chaperone for you two," she had joked. As though anyone found humor in … anything these days.

Still, residing three and three in their shelters made more sense than four and two, and the Russians were happy to have their Winter Palace to themselves.

Marking Kai's first, and maybe last, popular decision.

You're lucky to be alive, Kai again reminded himself. An outcome that—between Mingmei's teardown of the Mars Buggy's life-support systems and Kai's consultation with Sonny on Phobos—he began to understand.

Electrolysis split water into oxygen to breathe plus hydrogen. Human respiration involved inhaling that oxygen and exhaling the carbon dioxide that cells produced as a metabolic byproduct. Carbon dioxide plus hydrogen—in an *extremely* endothermic reaction powered by waste heat from the buggy's radioisotope thermoelectric generator—produced water to close the cycle, ejecting carbon as its byproduct.

Even with 600 °C or more of heat, a catalyst was required. Any elemental carbon not immediately captured slowly contaminated the catalyst. Life support monitored carbon-dioxide levels, signaling when to replace the catalyst cartridge—and it was that CO_2 sensor that had failed. Leading to the gradual and insidious accumulation of odorless, invisible carbon dioxide in the cabin, and hence, also in their blood, until toxic concentrations were reached. At which point, the four of them had passed out.

After that? The colonel and Xiuying had died of apparent cardiac arrest. Excess CO_2 in their blood would have suppressed, and finally stopped, breathing. Sonny had volunteered to do autopsies if the bodies were transported to Phobos. Once automated blood analyzers had confirmed highly toxic CO_2 levels in both victims, Kai had seen no point in inflicting further indignities on his departed colleagues. It sufficed to know their deaths were consistent with that CO_2 excess.

If a sort-of pothole hadn't jolted Kai awake—a bit of pure luck—everyone in the Mars Buggy would have died. As for why he alone, however groggily, had come aware? Kai had his theory, and Sonny had hers. He believed endurance training for marathons had given him increased tolerance for CO_2. Sonny thought it more plausible that marathon runners self-selected from the population of those with genetically above-average CO_2 tolerance.

He'd accept either reason.

Leaving unanswered how a bad sensor had gotten into the vehicle. Russian meddling? PPL fanatics meddling? CIA machinations? Random misfortune, such as—so the after-action report read, anyway—had befallen the fuel depot aboard Tiangong and delayed the mission's departure?

Likewise shrouded in mystery: whether the CO_2 sensors in the shelters were any more reliable. Whether they could make catalyst cartridges from local resources, substituting frequent replacement of those for faith in untrustworthy sensors. What further unsuspected perils—he never doubted there were more—loomed over the mission.

Most perplexing of all to Kai: on whom he could rely. Not Antonov. Not after, by every indication, the Russian had abandoned everyone on the polar expedition. Even less after Beijing's too-clever ploy of double-bumping Kai above Antonov's rank to general. Moscow had quickly matched the men's ranks—but if only by hours, Kai had seniority. Until the Kremlin decided they needed another field marshal.

Their respective military ranks shouldn't matter. That the Russians now outnumbered the Chinese three to two shouldn't, either. Only China had the capability to resupply this mission. So, anyway, Kai assured himself, finding none of this reasoning as credible as the Russian proverb he'd somehow picked up along the way. *If you invite a bear to dance, it's not you who decides when the dance is over. It's the bear.*

Not So Glad: Storm Sinks City

Hurricane Galadriel, stalled for more than twenty-four hours above the metro area, continues to deliver destructive winds, torrential rain, and catastrophic flooding. Cumulative rainfall since the storm's arrival has passed sixty-two inches, already exceeding the previous U.S. record set by Hurricane Harvey in Texas in 2017.

Consolidated Edison reports widespread power outages throughout its service area, affecting 2.1 million households. Con Ed has requested repair-crew assistance from power companies in unaffected areas.

Travel across the region has virtually ceased. The Port Authority has closed all tunnels within its jurisdiction, its pumps unable to stay ahead of the flooding. Port Authority bridges and airports are closed by reason of near-zero visibility and fierce winds. The Metropolitan Transit Authority initially suspended operations on its A, B, and D subway lines, with standing water reported to be waist-deep or deeper in many stations along all three routes. This morning, "Out of an abundance of caution," the authority took the complete subway system out of service. Surface travel is all but impossible due to near-zero visibility, widespread street flooding, and wind gusts often exceeding 120 miles per hour.

Mayor Watkins attributed the city's implosion to, "A month's worth of rain falling every hour, hour after hour. As much as we continue to invest in preparations for extreme weather, climate change is a global problem beyond even our great city's capacity to mitigate."

New York's current travails are reminiscent of extreme-weather events that, in recent years, have hobbled Chicago, Dhaka, Mumbai, Paris, Montevideo, and Shanghai ....

—*New York Post*

DMV Hacked

An anonymous whistleblower claiming to work at PennDOT disclosed the compromise of data servers hosting statewide records for all registered car owners and vehicles. A PennDOT spokeswoman confirmed the breach, adding, "The department deplores this premature and unauthorized release of information while our security team continues to assess the situation. On a timely basis, the department will, as required by law, make full disclosure of the data breach."

Knowledgeable sources indicate that the sensitive personal information of millions of vehicle owners were exposed, to include names, dates of birth, physical addresses, email addresses, and phone numbers ....

—*The Philadelphia Inquirer*

"*Bradbury* calling Fire Star City. We're about fifteen minutes out," Teri radioed.

The announcement that Kai had awaited—and dreaded. "Fire Star City, copy. Hello, Teri. There's a flat expanse a kilometer north of our structures. We'll meet you there."

Midway between that spot and their modest encampment, two empty graves awaited.

"Copy," Teri acknowledged. "Carter, may we join your team at the ceremony, whether in person or by Zoom? Only to observe, of course. We will not intrude."

Zoom funerals. As though, during the COVID pandemic, he hadn't known enough of those for two lifetimes?

"We will be honored." Also, shamed. He had not thought to extend an invitation after the aid so selflessly given. The aid even then continuing, with *Bradbury* bringing Zhao Jin's remains. Further shamed not to have reached out to Teri and her people weeks earlier when they had suffered tragedy. "We will meet you soon. Over."

"Over and out."

Kai told everyone in both shelters to proceed to the cemetery. Mingmei and Oorvi—as both had requested—would bring poor Xiuying on the improvised stretcher. He ended with, "I'll join you soon."

Because he needed first, however belatedly, to invite his Phobos neighbors and to grab a camera and tripod for Zoom.

June 15, 2034

Sonny and Xander were once again in the biolab, she engrossed in the latest lifeless rock core, he engaged in zoning out. He had nothing to contribute until something IT-ish went wonky. That hadn't happened in weeks.

The lab's intercom crackled. "Guys," Cat said, "not to worry, but something's come up that I'd like to consult with you both about. When you can take a break."

"At your service," Xander said.

"Over comms or in person?" Sonny asked. "This process has become routine enough I can talk and work at the same time."

Hell, yeah, it's routine, Xander thought. At least when, whether or not you admit it, you no longer expect to find anything.

"In person," Cat said.

Sonny's brow furrowed as she silently estimated. "Assuming the current sample offers no surprise, fifteen or twenty minutes to finish. Can it wait till then?"

"I think any of us would happily have a surprise take precedence. Barring surprise, sure, twenty minutes or so. See you guys then."

"Twenty minutes," Xander repeated, confident the odds of a discovery were between Fat Chance and No Way. He wasn't disappointed.

Straight out of the habitat airlock, helmet removed, he asked, "What's up?"

Cat was on the treadmill, loping. "Remember your outreach to our Chinese friends about trading for iron-oxygen batteries and drill barrels? Well, I heard back today from General Wang."

"Who? Oh, Carter." Xander set down his helmet. "Yeah, what, seven or eight weeks ago? Carter sounded inclined, but then we never heard back."

Cat grinned. "Carter wasn't the boss then."

"Interesting," Sonny said.

"What'd he say?" Xander asked.

"He said we helped out Teri's bunch after their unfortunate accident. That you, Sonny, and Teri's bunch helped him. He felt it was his team's turn."

"Nice," Xander said.

Cat laughed. "Who says I believed him? My business experience is nonexistent, but my dad was in sales. I don't know if either of you bothered to read personal profiles of the other groups, but Carter's father is a gazillionaire, owner of one of China's largest steel manufacturers. Let's assume your buddy Carter picked up even a tenth of Daddy's business smarts."

"Nice or not, what, exactly, did he propose?" Xander asked.

"Nothing specific. He wants detailed specs of what we'd like, location data on where we'd want it, and what besides beamed power we might care to trade."

Xander started shedding vacuum gear. This didn't strike him as a quick conversation and back to the biolab. "I can gather specs. I'd leave the *where* to Sonny and Giselle. Trade goods? I guess we review our inventory for anything both surplus and light enough to transport by lander."

Sonny cleared her throat. "I have an ask of my own. If those guys haven't already melted all their polar ice, let's get a few chunks. I've coveted that since we saw them trekking north."

"Good idea," Xander said. Because the polar caps had been inaccessible. Rocket exhaust from a lander would melt ice, apt to refreeze over the landing gear faster than ice cores could be collected. Not that he'd hold his breath for life signs in the polar ice, but at least they'd be searching somewhere *new*. "Once we've done the inventory review, shall I get back in touch? I could be ready by midday tomorrow."

Cat blotted her face with a towel before slowing the treadmill's pace. "Yes to the review, but wait a few days to contact him. We don't want to seem eager."

By then, Xander had his arms and torso out of his counterpressure suit. He sat to extract himself from boots and suit legs.

Sonny said, "Xander's input? I get you wanting that. Trading for drill barrels and all was his harebrained idea. What puts me in the loop?"

"Umm, Sun Ying, isn't it? You're my expert on all matters Chinese."

Sonny snorted. "Me? I'm from frigging *Toronto*. My folks and I left Hong Kong when I was *three*, well before the Brits ceded the territory to the PRC. I have no memories of the place."

Cat countered, "You must have picked things up from your parents."

"You're *really* reaching. Aren't there experts back home to consult?"

Xander intervened. "I, for one, would rather leave the discussion mission to mission. Let's not risk this leaking."

Cat grinned. "Ah, the easier to get forgiveness than permission principle."

Xander didn't argue.

Sonny said, "On the other hand, I *have* taken psych courses. On that basis, I'd say you're on the right track being skeptical of noble motives. Carter trading with us when the former guy wouldn't? He's demonstrating he's now the man in charge. For the same reason, he'll prefer any arrangement be settled mission to mission, without involving higher-ups in Beijing. It means he'll want to make a deal. He'll want to show his team he's a tough negotiator, but not at the cost of failure. Approaching us and then not making a deal would have the opposite effect, especially with his Russians, of what he aims to accomplish."

"Or," Xander said, "he is sincere. Either way, we should be able to come to an arrangement."

"If even one of you is right, we'll get something done. Ergo, you guys should get to work. List things we can use and their relative priorities. What we might offer in return. How we can best approach the general. Loop in anyone here if and as you feel the need." Cat brought the treadmill to a halt. "As for me, I'll be in the shower."

June 30, 2034

Teri picked at her locally grown salad. Nibbled from a roll made with locally grown wheat. Studiously ignored the slab of "meat" printed from a blend of local and recycled resources. People really *could* live on Mars. Chinchillas, too. She still didn't get the attraction.

Reuben leaned across the table. Julio had opted to skip lunch and keep working, so they had Helium to themselves. "You okay, boss?"

"Sure." Because *okay* wasn't a high hurdle. It was right down there with *adequate*. Or *coping*. A notch above *apathetic*.

"I'd like to believe that."

"You don't?"

He set down his fork, his plate empty. "I miss them, too. But ...."

"But *what*?"

"But you don't talk about it." *It*. The deaths. Jake. "Not with any of us. You know, we're all here for you."

Because she *couldn't* talk about it. Once she opened the floodgates, who'd ever again take her seriously? So, no. Not going to happen. "I'm getting there."

"I—make that all of us—want you to know you can talk to—"

From her pocket, her datasheet: a highest-priority chime. The Blake Wagner chime. Under the circumstances, she almost appreciated a message from him. Almost. "My boss." Who seldom reached out except with an impatient demand. "Excuse me."

She withdrew across the shelter, put in earbuds, and started the low-res vid streaming.

"Hey, Teri. I know this is a hard time for you. All the partners do." Blake sat in his Dubai office behind a huge, empty desk. He looked … apologetic. Huh? "But the thing is …."

Here, Teri anticipated, is where he stops hinting and demands we start laying out a route up Olympus Mons. Because only a year remained till Earth's next launch window, and Blake had half-gigabuck tickets to sell to people with way more money than sense. Mom had sent pics of the ads. *Be the first to climb the Solar System's tallest mountain.* As if any of the extinct volcanoes of Tharsis Montes, each of them days' drive closer to Barsoom, weren't almost as towering as Olympus Mons and every bit as spectacular. Also, every bit as daunting.

Except—once Teri recognized her mind had wandered, and she rewound a bit—that wasn't it.

"The thing is, we've done some recalibrating. The partners do want you to check out Olympus Mons one of these days, but it's not your top priority. Expanding your infrastructure should come first. More ambitious construction with local brick, marscrete, and steel. More extensive agricultural experimentation. On the exploration front, scoping out the Tharsis Bulge for lava tubes that could be rendered livable."

Maybe the sudden interest in habitability and expanded capacity proved that NEP *did* mean to go after Croesus and its mineral wealth. Maybe they really intended to use Mars and its moons as their base. She'd be okay with that.

Unless the talk about asteroid mining were blowing so much smoke. Unless the alarmist press weren't being alarmist at all, and Earth's climate *was* turning to shit.

Unless Blake and his cronies thought they might someday need to move in.

July 28, 2034

If only with one painstaking step after another, Kai thought, they *had* gotten here.

First had come proofs of concept: a small, trial rectenna array deployed near Fire Star City, receiving microwaves beamed from Phobos. In exchange for that trickle of power, his people had hand-loaded a few drill barrels, iron-oxygen batteries, and rectennas made per NASA specifications onto one of their landers for testing on Phobos.

Next had come the serious haggling. Of exchange rates between the various physical goods and delivered kilowatt-hours. The premium to be paid in kilowatt-hours for every kilometer Kai's people traveled to make deliveries. The tradeoff between physical goods and deep drilling that NASA robots might undertake for Fire Star City, any water or ice thereby discovered being welcome to Kai's people. The sterilization protocols to be followed for handling the trade goods.

Not even that bastard Antonov had complained (much) as this process had unfolded. Water-recycling losses were inevitable. Kai had succeeded in fabricating new CO_2 detectors, but that didn't mean he or the Russians were eager for a return trek to the northern ice cap.

Once a nearby water supply was assured, Antonov would undoubtedly make baseless assertions to his superiors. That any cross-mission collaboration had been unnecessary. That had *he* been the man in charge, *he*, on his own, would have found enough ice or tapped into a deep aquifer—without doing the Westerners any favors. But the fall-out from that inevitable betrayal was a matter for another day.

This day, there was honest labor to be performed.

Kai stood with Oorvi on the outskirts of Fire Star City, in early morning sunlight, a NASA lander due at any minute. Ready to load it with enough equipment that the Phobos expedition could begin serious, deep drilling where *they* most wanted. Ready to deliver two blocks of polar ice. Ready to feel less indebted.

If Oorvi were correct, if their cooperation with the other mission betokened good karma? Kai would take the win.

Sonny, waiting on the sun-blasted surface of Phobos for the long-awaited polar-ice samples, reminded Xander of nothing as much as the proverbial kid in a candy store. Waiting by her side, he felt something like that, too. For the first time in a long time.

Of course, the Stickney Crater area wasn't sun-blasted *now*. True, the ice had been wrapped in silvery, insulated blankets. Wrappings could slip. Any momentary lapse while holding, carrying, or manipulating the packages might tear those coverings. Even though direct sunlight on Phobos couldn't quite melt the ice, sublimation was another matter.

Anyway, what mattered a hundred or so degrees Celsius *below* in a good cause? If Marslight alone didn't suffice for unloading the precious cargo, they had helmet headlamps.

Seconds after Xander spotted the glint of the returning lander, Cat's voice came over the radio. "Lander on final approach. Y'all will have your ice cubes real soon." As good as her word, and with a mere few gentle puffs of rocket exhaust, she set down the lander a short guide-wire slide from where they stood.

"After you," he said.

Sonny glided hand-over-hand toward the lander. Xander followed. They each used short tethers to secure the lander to convenient pitons. He opened the cargo hatch, removed one of the wrapped ice blocks, handed it to her, then took the second for himself. He followed her awkwardly, tugging with his free hand, along a guide wire to the temporary workstation set up near the biolab.

Handler One could have done much of that—but not with this lander. Not after it had carried human remains. Not after Carter and his people had unloaded and loaded it several times. Anyway, Sonny trusted herself (and *maybe* him, under her eagle-eyed supervision) more than a robot to transport these unique samples.

She'd made clear she trusted *only* herself to unwrap and prepare the samples.

They'd ventured outside this time with layers of fresh rubber gloves, rather than their usual sturdy (and filthy) surface work gauntlets, over spacesuit hands. She peeled off her topmost pair before unpacking the first ice block. Peeled off the next pair of rubber gloves before meticulously shaving millimeters from each face of the block with a sterile saw. With another sterile tool, she scraped the letter A into the top facet of the more-or-less cube. She moved that block, label up, to the far end of her work area. "Handler One, deliver the block marked *A* to the Mars side of the biolab. Store the block at minus 100 degrees Celsius."

It radio-clicked acknowledgment.

While the robot completed its assignment, Sonny processed the second ice block.

Throughout the procedure, Xander had waited nearby. Available if she should request help. Silent not to distract her. But the next steps—rinsing the freshly exposed ice surfaces with near-pure ethanol, then sloooowly rinsing off another few millimeters with barely-above-freezing, sterile water—was an undertaking for another day. Maybe another several days.

Wadding up the discarded wrappings for their keep-it-who-knows-what-might-be-useful-pile, he decided it was okay again to talk. "How do they look? Any impressions?"

"They look like … ice," David chimed in. (Xander presumed the man had been watching from the habitat through their helmet cams. That's what *he* would have done if he hadn't accompanied Sonny.) "But good job not sawing off a hand."

"I'll second the latter comment," Cat said.

"You know," David continued. "This could be any old ice. Water drained from their recycling tank and then frozen might be Carter's idea of humor."

"Doubtful," Giselle said. She must also be watching from the habitat. "To be certain, I need less glare. Sonny, Xander, back off a little from block B. Good. Now, turn. Let your headlamps strike the ice more obliquely. A bit farther. Farther. There. Good. David, you cynic, this is real, polar ice. I *thought* I'd seen seasonal layering. Without glare, the layering is unmistakable. Oh, and notice the trapped gas bubbles."

"Visible layers. Then you can date these ice samples?" Xander asked.

"I wish." Giselle sounded wistful. "Global and regional ice chronologies have been established for Earth. Getting to those involved huge numbers of samples and several date-approximation techniques, reliant on knowing *much* more about Earth's climate, geology, and biology than we begin to understand about Mars.

"To even begin defining a Martian ice chronology, I'd need many cores, all drilled down from the top of the ice, hence starting with the newest deposits. Layers seen in *these* blocks, and if I'm both careful and lucky, atmospheric samples trapped in the tiny bubbles, will provide glimpses of past climate, except I won't know how far past."

Mars's ice caps being kilometers thick, their two blocks had come from near ground level. Carter had provided video of people sawing chunks of ice from low in the rippled wall of a wind-and-dust-carved niche.

Xander said, "Makes sense, Giselle. Pardon my ignorance."

"Not your field."

"*Anyway*," Sonny said, "I hope no one expects to naked-eye see life signs in the blocks. If this ice has anything of biological interest, I'm confident that'd be single-celled. Microscopic. Scattered bacteria, or their Martian equivalent, or more likely microfossils of the same, wind-carried to the ice cap in some bygone era. The same sort of microbes we've looked for in rock cores. Even if, before the oceans dried up and the atmosphere blew away, Martian life had advanced as far as stromatolites, *those* weren't going to be blown long distances."

"Stroma-who?" Cat asked.

"Stromatolites. Microbial mats. Bacterial colonies. Not uncommon on Earth, even found in some ancient strata. But enough chitchat. My work here is done. Once Handler One has this second block stowed, Xander, let's head inside."

"Who's up tonight for *The Thing*?" David asked.

A suggestion that made Xander hoot. How could they not watch the classic horror movie about a homicidal, shape-shifting alien defrosted out of polar ice? "I'm not only in, I'll make the popcorn."

August 8, 2034

NASA to Drop Lunar Biolab: PPL "Outraged"

Ten months after three missions arrived on Mars and its moon Phobos, with no signs of past or present life to be found, NASA is reportedly scaling back its plans to quarantine samples and returning astronauts. Senior administration officials, speaking candidly on condition of anonymity, indicate a lunar biohazard facility is no longer deemed necessary. "Literally hundreds of samples have been studied from across the planet," one source said, "with no indication of biological activity *ever*. There's no justification for a lunar quarantine facility. Not for the inconvenience to the returning explorers. Not for the difficulties in recruiting specialists to work in such austere and remote facilities. And frankly, not for the huge cost a lunar biolab would entail."

Invited to comment, a spokesman for Planetary Protection Legions, a prominent public-interest group concerned with possible interplanetary contamination, expressed outrage. "Exploration of Mars has touched only the tiniest fraction of a world whose area rivals the land surface of Earth. Moreover, what few studies have been undertaken have literally just scratched that planet's surface. It is far too soon to conclude that world is lifeless. PPL objects strenuously with this change in NASA direction. Our position remains unchanged: nothing and no one can be allowed to return to Earth from Mars."

—*The Washington Post*

Dale had scarcely a moment to exchange questioning looks with Rebecca Nguyen before an aide ushered them into the Oval Office. Lance Kawasaki passed them, on his way out. He favored them with a cryptic wink.

The president and the NASA administrator sat on facing sofas—highball glasses in hand, grinning. Dale knew—at least she thought she did—the reason for her summons. Rebecca being here had only reinforced that belief.

But their bosses' high spirits? The high-proof spirits? Those confused the hell out of her.

In any sane universe, they'd be mad, furious, about that morning's ridiculous story in the *Post*. Reporters had waylaid her three times merely walking across the White House grounds. She'd had nothing better to offer than, "I don't comment on anonymously sourced stories."

"Madam President," Dale began, the door scarcely closed behind her. "I have no idea where this rumor came from. It wasn't from me."

"Or me," Rebecca added in a soft voice.

"Have a seat," Cruella said. They sat, Dale next to the president and Rebecca beside Van Dijk. "Relax. As for today's big story, it's not a problem."

It wasn't?

Dale murmured, "I imagine we're here about damage control."

"You imagine wrong." Cruella smiled. "The story *is* the damage control. Matt and I are the senior administration sources."

"What? There's been no decision to …." Dale's objection trailed off as she remembered to whom she was speaking. "*You* decided."

Rebecca crossed her arms across her chest. "May I ask why?"

The president ambled to the sideboard. "Can I get you girls anything?"

Dale felt … ill. "No, thanks."

"Nothing for me," Rebecca said.

"Suit yourself." Cruella returned with a topped-off glass. "It's simple. Mars is and, it seems, always was dead. Hundreds of samples collected from all across the planet, and not the first hint of life found. Matt's peers at JAXA and ESA know it, too. Seeing as how, Rebecca, you gave their people a free lift to Phobos, Matt and I let our counterparts know we expected them to pick up the tab for the lunar biolab. Knowing what we now know? Privately, they're balking."

Van Dijk took a long sip. "Hence, we leaked a change in plans before they did to force our hand. Now, when the news becomes official, it's our idea."

Dale found herself speechless. After long seconds, she came up with ... something. "Surface rock cores aside, there are the recently obtained samples of polar ice. *Those* contained traces of organic materials, which I consider cause for cautious optimism."

"There are," the president echoed. "Love the passive voice. Never mind that the Phobos crew took it upon themselves to negotiate a swap with the Chinese. Wu's bunch got a well dug for them, the promise of power ever after for the well pump, and an end to their water rationing. *We* got a bit of dirty ice, plus some batteries and pipes. Not the most astute trading. It was all in the PDB."

Presidential Daily Brief: the nation's most exclusive newspaper. Super-classified, and nothing the likes of which a mere science adviser would ever glimpse. As for how the provenance of that ice made its way into the PDB ...?

Dale had long suspected the NSA would eavesdrop. It seemed she could stop wondering.

Except she knew herself better than that. *If* having been resolved, *how* would gnaw at her. Had the NSA been reading her email? Compromised NASA's Deep Space Network? Hacked the relay satellites orbiting Mars? Penetrated a Chinese network (which, looking back to how the Mars race insanity began, seemed more than possible)? Deployed some espionage technique she was too innocent to imagine?

Uh-huh. This was the worst conceivable time to indulge her curiosity.

However dismissively, the president knew about the mission's new drill barrels and batteries. (Where had Xander mentioned trading for batteries? In private emails, yes, but Dale thought he'd kept matters simple in the official reports: just drill barrels and polar ice.) Her boss had to know about plans to probe deeper in the search for life signs. Did the woman not care?

"About the organics?" Dale hesitantly reminded.

"What about them?" Van Dijk countered. "Do those prove anything?"

Dale was *so* tempted to … what? Not *lie*. But shade the truth a tad. Perhaps, exaggerate a bit. Integrity won out. "Prove? No. Basically, 'organic chemistry' means chemistry with carbon. Life as we know it relies on such chemistry, but some molecules produced by living cells may also form in other ways. The organic molecules recovered from the samples of Martian polar ice are in that ambiguous category."

As astrobiologists at NASA and elsewhere had cautioned her. As they also reminded Dale that every manner of organic molecule, from simple sugars to the full set of nucleotide bases—key components of DNA—had been recovered from inside meteorites. A tiny, retrieved sample of the asteroid named Ryugu—as old as Earth itself!—had contained examples of twenty-some amino acids: about the same number as made up all earthly proteins.

Nor were tantalizing organic traces detected "only" in the Solar System. Radio astronomers had observed absorption spectra of several organics in nebulae thousands of light-years distant. Diethyl ether. Methyl fromate. There, too, some amino acids.

Were otherworldly molecules the precursors to life on Earth? To life on Mars? To life, well, on many worlds? No one knew. At least not yet ….

"Maybe," Van Dijk said, "the traces are accidental contamination from handling the ice."

Cruella said, "Or this new Chinese general is having fun at our expense."

"Yet, maybe they *weren't* contamination," Dale insisted. "We need more ice, more samples from around the planet. More *time*."

"Getting back to the biolab topic," Rebecca said, "I'm puzzled. Compared to what we've already spent, and more when the next outbound window opens, a lunar lab is small change."

"Everett Dirksen, anyone?" Van Dijk said.

"Right, but well before these kids' time." The president turned to face Rebecca. "For that matter, well before our time, but still a DC legend when Matt and I were first coming up through the ranks. Dirksen was Senate minority leader for a good ten years. 'A billion here, and a billion there,' he's famous for saying, 'and soon you're talking about real money.' You see, Rebecca, some of us would find it unfortunate to waste even a few billion to build and maintain a pointless lunar biolab. Everyone has better uses for the money."

Dale said, "The thing is, Madam President—"

"Enough. While we act paralyzed with fear about nonexistent germs, we're ceding an entire fucking planet to the Chinese and the fat cats."

"Respectfully, Madam President, Administrator," Rebecca said, "you'll remember that Article IX of the International Outer Space Treaty obligates us to curate and contain samples returned from a restricted celestial body at a proper facility. Mars is one of the restricted bodies."

Cruella raised an eyebrow. "Respectfully? In the history of the English language, no sentence begun that way was *ever* respectful. As for remembering an obscure treaty, it says nothing, my lawyers assure me, about labs on the fucking *Moon*. I'm told the NIH operates a BSL-4 facility in darkest Wyoming. We'll use that."

"Montana," Van Dijk said. "Hamilton, Montana."

The president waved off the correction. "The decision *has* been made for reasons above your pay grades, but you deserved to hear it from me first. You have, and it's time to salute the flag. By now, Lance will have rounded up a gaggle of press vultures."

Geese gathered in gaggles. A bunch of vultures, for whatever reason, was called a kettle. Uh-huh. Dale told herself, you're not focused on the Big Picture.

Here goes.

Cruella snapped, "Stop right there. I know that furrowed brow. I know the deep, centering breath that goes with it. Before you resign in a huff, answer me one question. Who would you rather have determine that the biolab in Montana is locked down tight? That their quarantine protocols are as rigorous and as ironclad as possible?"

Deflating Dale in an instant.

"I'm glad that's settled. Now the two of you go out there and announce our new policy to the vultures."

"Irony alert," Rebecca offered sotto voce on the short walk to the Briefing Room.

Just then, Dale couldn't give a damn for irony, or for anything past surviving the imminent ordeal. "What's that?"

"Ever been to Idaho?"

Huh? "No. Why do you ask?"

"Well, the Rocky Mountain Laboratories, that's the BSL-4 facility in Montana, is maybe two hundred miles from a national monument in Idaho. Picture ancient lava flows, cinder cones, every kind of volcanic remains."

"Picturing. What's the irony?"

"We won't get our lunar quarantine facility," Rebecca said, "but the park so near the lab is named, after its most prominent features, Craters of the Moon."

August 10, 2034

Two days stymied by an intractable problem could drive a person crazy. At the least, that impasse had sufficed to drive *Dale* crazy. After hours of tossing and turning (and the occasional spousal grumble), she got out of bed, put on her favorite, tattered robe, and went downstairs to make a cup of tea.

Rebecca had sworn up and down that—until the Oval Office summons—she'd not mentioned the trading with CMSA to anyone but Dale. For her part, Dale knew she'd discussed the matter with no one but Rebecca. Both women were determined to warn the Phobos bunch that NSA was almost certainly somehow monitoring their comms.

But *how?* Without saying so. Without disclosing national-security secrets.

(For that matter, when? Mars had entered a comms blackout. From Earth's perspective, it was almost directly behind the sun. Rebecca said the planet wouldn't recover decent angular separation from the sun—and so, from intolerable radio interference—until the end of the month. For some time thereafter, the DSN's priority would be synching up with the mission and processing the inevitable comms backlog.)

This wasn't rocket science. Rocket science, NASA did every day. This was a thornier problem. How does one slip an electronic confidence past the world's premier interceptor of comms and cracker of codes? Then, suppose she somehow, miraculously, found a way.

Would anyone on Phobos even recognize her clandestine message, much less know how to decode it?

Dale took a sip of tea, gone luke-tepid as her thoughts had churned. Gnawed at frozen chocolate chip cookies she had needed like a hole in the head. Rocked back and forth in her (non-rocking) chair. Rolled an end of her robe tie around a finger. Unrolled the tie. Began to reroll it—

And stopped dead.

The secret requiring protection? That the NSA tapped into comms with Mars. Maybe *it* wasn't the thing that needed saying. Everyone on Phobos was scary-smart, or they wouldn't be there. Smart enough to read between the lines.

Given the right lines to begin with.

Xander's private messages about trading for polar ice and the other things had had three addressees: herself and Rebecca, with a cc to Cat. He'd asked that the details go no further. Doubtless, he'd trust his longtime friend Rebecca to comply. Assuming it was fair to believe Xander had come to trust her ….

Dale dug the datasheet from her purse and started an email to Xander—not that the DSN would send it till the blackout ended. After the usual pleasantries, after routine comments about the latest set of abiotic rock cores, she added, FYI, THE GRAND POOH BAH IS UNDERWHELMED BY YOUR NEGOTIATING PROWESS. I HOPE YOU GOT A *LOT* OF BATTERIES AND DRILL BARRELS.

Because Cruella and Van Dijk had said as much. Because, coming from a presidential adviser, "Grand Pooh Bah" should be unambiguous. Because any foreign power intercepting Dale's message (and weren't the Chinese and Russians as likely to read this as the NSA?) would learn nothing useful from it.

Because—always assuming Xander did trust in her discretion—he was quite savvy enough to deduce how the president had gotten details of his negotiations with Wang Kai.

October 16, 2034

Teri gazed into the distance, the *far* distance. Agog. Wonderstruck. Speechless.

She stood with Islah at the summit of Olympus Mons. This was the highest peak on Mars—more, the highest, the grandest, in the entire Solar System. Wherever the gentle, undulating slope of this vast mountain itself did not intrude, she saw for hundreds of kilometers. If only in her imagination, the remote horizon exhibited a curve.

She had to say something. Didn't she? She came up with, "Wow."

"Wow," Islah agreed. "Worth every klick of the drive."

Around 3200 klicks, even discounting the many detours along the way. An epic trek to an epic location. Blake, damn him, was correct. People *would* pay a fortune to experience this. A hotel near the base of the mountain seemed in order ....

Tearing themselves away from the view, they climbed back into the SUV. However many eons dormant, Olympus Mons was a volcano with a truly spectacular caldera. Eighty kilometers wide. In places, kilometers deep. Within, crater layered upon crater, whether from successive eruptions or meteorite impacts or both. Offering, all along its rim, remarkable vistas.

At their third stop, early in mapping a scenic circuit around the abyss, Teri sighed.

"Incredible, right?" Islah said. "How can a person not be awed?"

"I know." But in the presence of such inconceivable grandeur, what Teri truly had been thinking was, *Lord, Jake would have loved this.*

"In the fields of observation chance favors only the prepared mind."

—*Louis Pasteur*

"Good luck is another name for tenacity of purpose."

—*Ralph Waldo Emerson*

"Mistakes are the portal of discovery."

—*James Joyce*

DISCOVERIES

November 9, 2034

Once more, the Law of Unintended Consequences had bitten Xander on the ass.

The ability to drill deeper meant rovers stayed put longer. So much for his sometime diversion of planning and overseeing lander missions and bot redeployments. With rare exceptions, his recent "work" days seldom went beyond playing vacuum-safety buddy for colleagues with actual tasks to perform.

From the earliest core samples retrieved from formerly inaccessible Martian depths, Giselle had reveled in fascinating new geological esoterica. Hideo had experimented with ways to exploit the exotic minerals some of the deeper core samples had revealed. David and Cat stayed busy helping those two.

No new signs of biological activity, present or even distant past, had emerged, but Sonny at least had renewed hope some *might*. The mere possibility kept her as engaged as when the mission had first arrived. Had her extracting at least as many sections per core as then, to be examined in even more excruciating detail. "No longer just looking near the proverbial streetlamp," she'd cheerfully declare several times per shift. While he dispensed snacks and wisecracks, fighting a losing battle against tedium and impatience.

His recent off-duty hours were as dull. Because the couples were ... coupling. Because Hideo, nice guy though he was,

was … quiet. The man had raised introversion to an art form. Also, for the foreseeable future, he'd be immersed during his off-shift hours in drafting the opening chapters of the memoir he had under contract to a Tokyo publisher.

Leaving: another evening to stare alternately into (figurative) space and at the datasheet with his notes about the damned, nagging puzzles he should long ago have abandoned as pointless exercises. Would have. If he weren't so damned *bored*.

The first mystery Xander couldn't get out of his head was how, two months prior, the president knew things—like homemade batteries as part of the trade negotiations—Xander hadn't disclosed officially. Because Cruella *had* known. He saw no other way to interpret Dale's "Pooh Bah" message.

Obvious possibility one: everyone on Phobos swore otherwise, but someone *had* blabbed. Still, whomever they'd told had not shared it to social media, much less with the press—because as sloooow as the search had been from such a long distance, Xander had done it. That being so, he saw no way any such indiscretion could have reached the president short of the NSA reading their personal emails.

Sure, their personal correspondence used standard public-key encryption for privacy. Arthur Schmidt wouldn't have bothered giving Xander a onetime pad if PKE was secure against nation-state-level snooping. If the DNI hadn't assumed (or known?) the Chinese, or the Russians, or whoever would monitor and crack open everything transmitted from Mars.

(Candidates for *whoever* turned out to be a substantial group. Every space agency ever to have dispatched an unmanned probe to the Moon or Mars had needed some deep-space comms capability. That swept up Japan, India, Europe, Brazil, Israel, and the UAE. Having first rented deep-space comms capacity from the UAE, plus backup from Brazil, NEP had begun building their own seventy-meter dish near their headquarters in the Emirates.)

Next came obvious possibility two: Carter, or someone in his mission, had talked. Given Arthur's concerns with security on NASA's DSN, of *course*, the NSA listened to other countries' equivalent deep-space networks and decrypted their messages.

Then came the less obvious, and scarier, possibility three: comms in the neighborhood were compromised. The skies above Mars teemed with satellites, and not only the birds that they used to relay messages to/from Earth. Most of these satellites dated to the earlier era of strictly robotic exploration. Networking all the satellites, whatever their provenance, had seemed an unambiguous asset. Any of those satellites might have been in the loop while he and Carter negotiated—then relayed those "private" conversations to someone back on Earth.

The damned thing was, Xander could prove or disprove none of these possibilities.

At least, he consoled himself, he'd eliminated scary possibility four: a bug or hack in the habitat's comm gear. He'd invested hours that would've been better spent sleeping in decompiling its actual executables and poring over the reconstructed source code.

With Hideo murmuring in Japanese—to himself, or his datasheet, or perhaps testing out his latest would-be deathless prose—Xander sighed. He took the two gliding steps to the habitat's galley. Snickers had become scarce. He settled for a Twix and got back to brooding.

The information that had been revealed? It wasn't secret, per se. He'd just seen no reason for people millions of miles away to be second-guessing as they'd negotiated. Things that Kai, Carter, had let slip suggested he felt the same way. Hell, it had been obvious Carter hadn't much wanted the local Russians second-guessing him. He'd used the public half of Xander's public/private key pair to secure their link.

Anyway, Xander *had* believed this local link secure.

Bringing him to his unrelated enigma: how to handle future trades. Because negotiations would recur. Because the additional power Ares might swap for more iron-based goods must derive from a dwindling stock of photovoltaic film. Even before they ran out of spare PV film, the power-for-iron exchange might reach a point of diminishing returns. If nothing else, Carter's folks might run out of uses for additional power before Sonny and Giselle—much less legions of biologists and geologists back on Earth—ran out of new places here they wanted to see sampled. One way or another, he needed something besides power to barter with.

Nothing was settled, but the odds seemed decent that Carter might accept payment in carbonaceous materials. If the CMSA bunch didn't choose to experiment with printing food from the stuff (not that Xander planned to volunteer this detail, but the *best* Sonny had achieved along those lines had been tasteless, oily glop), well, the

Phobian dirt had other potential. It was the closest approximation on or near Mars to petrochemical feedstock—and there were always uses for plastics. Besides, samples of the local regolith, after autoclaving for a month in what had surely been a superabundance of caution, had proven hospitable to earthly soil bacteria. The regolith so treated had, in turn, allowed several types of earthly seeds to sprout—which was more than could be said for Martian regolith so treated. The peroxides and perchlorates in the latter were, as long predicted, as toxic as hell.

Did seeds sprouting in the Phobian regolith count as successes? Unclear, at least so far. To his uninformed eye, the seedlings looked stressed and stunted. Again ruing that their genomic sequencers had arrived broken, he assumed chinchillas would have to fill in as guinea pigs.

Xander hoped such a swap could be worked out because fair was fair. Mars dirt for Phobos dirt.

Was there a way to negotiate without the U.S. government watching? Not if the leak was from Carter's side—or his own—reporting back through a channel the NSA had compromised. But otherwise ...?

Xander chewed on the candy bar, pondering. Without NSA-grade supercomputers at your disposal, "ordinary" public-key encryption was perfectly secure. The Ares mission had nothing like that. He couldn't imagine why the Red Dragon mission (or the NEP mission, for that matter) would have brought such equipment, either. So, if discussions could be had with no one overhearing ....

It *could* be done!

For half of each Martian day, the planet's rotation swept Kai and his people out of a line of sight with Earth. Several times every Martian day, Phobos, in its close-in, speedy orbit, likewise disappeared from Earth's view. And when such occurrences coincided? If the two missions communicated point-to-point, *not* via a possibly compromised comsat? If they used PKE? As long as both parties kept the conversation confidential, they could keep *everyone* on Earth out of the loop. The same precautions would work, should a reason arise, for him to interact in private with the Barsoom contingent.

What about Fire Star City and Barsoom dealing privately with each other? Trickier, Xander decided, but doable by bouncing high-powered signals off Deimos. Way back in the Sixties, NASA's first "comsat" had been nothing but a big orbiting balloon. If Barsoom and Fire Star City chose times with Deimos in the sky but Phobos set, they'd have complete privacy.

Across the habitat, Hideo turned, glowering. "What are you chortling about?"

Chortling. Had he been? Yeah, maybe so. "Planning ahead to establishing the Martian Common Market."

"You *do* have an imagination."

Xander finished off the last bit of his candy. "There are worse things."

December 21, 2034

NASA Declares Independence

Celebrating an achievement long in the making, NASA Administrator Matthias Van Dijk announced that his agency has crew-rated the Boeing-Mitsubishi Mars Clipper for deep-space missions. "With today's announcement," Van Dijk said, "NASA and our friends are no longer second in line for spacecraft after the New Earth Partners consortium. Starting in January, we'll introduce Mars Clippers into the rotation of our ongoing lunar program. In June, when the next launch window to Mars opens, our mission to that planet will proudly fly Mars Clippers. I call this an early Christmas present for the nation."

Sources within NASA indicate that beyond resolving issues of priority and trust, the new source for crew-rated spacecraft will also save the agency $70 million per mission over Moonships purchased, when available, from Interplanetary Enterprises ...."

—*Space Coast Daily*

January 16, 2035

The Ares mission lacking paint to watch dry, Xander whiled away his latest vacuum-safety-buddy shift in the likewise scintillating pastime of observing seedlings grow. Some of the latest experiments had mixed fecal matter with the local regolith, adding an olfactory dimension to the activity.

By no stretch of the imagination could his day be considered fun.

Sonny was rapt in her usual, too familiar, slice-and-stare routine with yet another Martian core sample. The latest batch came from deep beneath Jezero Crater. All sorts of water had been there. Long ago. Make that long, long, *long* ago. In some Slavic languages, supposedly, *jezero* meant *lake*.

A Scott Joplin rag streamed from his datasheet. Sonny whistled to herself, in a superhuman feat neither in tune nor in sync with the music.

He sipped tepid water from a drink bulb. Pondered whether the present miasma would forever ruin whatever he might eat. Went back to watching the plants grow.

The biolab's intercom clicked. "Guys!" Giselle called. "Not an emergency, but you'll want to hear this. Whenever you're ready."

This shift had another two hours or so to go. "Now works for me."

"Okay," Hideo and Cat announced almost in unison. They were across Stickney Crater, gathering ice from their local mine. David didn't bother to answer; he was in the geolab with Giselle. Supposedly troubleshooting a hiccough on the LAN, so far without any progress.

"Gimme a second." Sonny finally set down her instruments, arms left in the sleeves of her glove box. "Done. What's up?"

Giselle said, "Just the biggest discovery *ever*."

The images Giselle netted from her lab looked to Xander like chalk. Seconds later, she confirmed it: They *were* chalk. Calcium carbonate, in any event. He'd never gotten his head around the many mineral forms $CaCO_3$ could take.

Xander frowned. "Why all the excitement?

Because calcium carbonate had been seen on Mars often enough. Back to NASA's *Phoenix* lander, at least, while he'd still been in college. Chemistry had never been his strong suit, but he recalled those finds had been explained as some reaction of atmospheric carbon dioxide with liquid water flowing over calcium-rich surfaces.

"Tell them where this sample is from," David said.

"One of the Jezero Crater deep cores." Was there a bit of *gloat* in Giselle's voice?

Sonny extracted herself from the glove box, then the top set of latex gloves worn over her spacesuit hands. She stared at the wall screen displaying the chalk or whatever. "Do you have a closeup?"

"Here's the microscopic view. Call it 200-nanometer resolution."

In the new image, Xander could, barely, discern tiny compartments. His overall sense was of bubbles. If that impression was accurate, most were, in one way or another, squashed.

At his side, Sonny took in a deep, sudden breath. A … gasp? "What about with the electron microscope?"

"Coming up," Giselle said. Definitely gloating. Whatever this was, Sonny had missed it. Biology took first crack at all core samples. "10-nanometer resolution."

The new image zoomed in on a handful of the bubbles—only at this much greater magnification, the tiny shapes were much, *much* more than that. The mashed-together shapes offered lobes, pores, ridges. He couldn't characterize the shapes beyond … beautiful. Evocative.

"What *are* those?" Cat asked. "They remind me of shells."

"Because they *are* shells," Giselle said. "Or were. At least, back home, that's what we'd say. The White Cliffs of Dover? The Cap Blanc Nez, across the Dover Strait? Møns Klint in Denmark? Those, and places like them, are the remains of ancient microscopic, sea-dwelling organisms. Their shells eventually ended up on the ocean floor and were compressed over the ages into sedimentary rock. You've heard of the Cretaceous Period? Well, 'creta' is the Latin word for chalk. That's how widespread calcium carbonate is in marine beds of that era."

"Wait," Xander said. "Ancient, microscopic sea-dwelling organisms. Are you saying *these* are the remains of such things? On *Mars*?"

"I can't be certain, but it looks that way," Giselle said. "If I'm right, that's got to be Nobel Prize material."

January 26, 2035

Dale waited with Lance Kawasaki outside the presidential entrance to White House Briefing Room. He didn't want to duck questions about the day's topic. She couldn't set foot inside without her mere presence perhaps hinting at the topic.

Cruella did *not* want her thunder stolen.

Well past the scheduled time, the president emerged from the Oval with Matthias Van Dijk. She smiled. "Good crowd, Lance?"

"A very *curious* crowd, Ma'am."

As the swelling susurrus of voices from the Briefing Room made clear.

"Are you ready, Dale?"

As ready as I'll ever be, Dale thought. Also, what a damned shame it was that Rebecca Nguyen wasn't here to represent NASA. Dale could imagine a few reasons Van Dijk had excluded Rebecca, none flattering to him. At the top of Dale's list were his rumored presidential ambitions. The *why* of Rebecca's exclusion didn't matter. What did was that when questions turned the least bit technical, facing down the press hordes would fall on her. Of course, none of that rumination could affect her answer. "Ready, Madam President."

"Good." The president strode into the briefing room. Smiling broadly. Taking her victory lap. As Dale joined the West Wing aides seated along a side wall, the correspondents fell silent.

"I have a brief statement, after which I'll open the floor to questions. Almost forty years ago, outside on the South Lawn, a predecessor of mine spoke to your predecessors. Bill Clinton believed—because, at the time, NASA believed—that a meteorite of Martian origin had carried to our world proof of microscopic life. That evidence later proved to be ambiguous, much as the biological experiments performed even earlier by two *Viking* landers had turned out to be ambiguous. Leaving all of us as curious as ever whether Earth, and life on Earth, are unique.

"I'm here today to inform the world we need no longer wonder. Where other investigations offered only suggestive hints, the Ares mission, initiated by this administration, has found answers. The ancient, long-gone oceans of Mars *were* once the home of life."

Holy crap! Dale thought. *No* mention of NASA's partners on the mission. *No* suggestion that ESA's Giselle Delacroix had made the discovery, or CSA's Sun Ying had confirmed it. When Arthur had shared the super-duper-encoded message from Phobos about the big find—and Giselle's demand/threat therein—Dale had considered the Frenchwoman rude. Insultingly distrusting. The president had been livid.

Wise now seems the more appropriate adjective.

Cruella's high dudgeon notwithstanding, ESA and Élysée Palace had been brought into the loop. Thereafter, not to be seen favoring one ally, also the mission's other partners. Whatever confirmation messages Giselle expected must have reached her, because she hadn't emailed friends, family, and global media about her discovery. So even as Cruella swaggered *here*, concurrent press conferences would be happening in Brussels, Paris, Ottawa, and Tokyo.

"… looking forward to the return of our brave explorers with their extraordinary finds." Pregnant pause. Triumphant smile. "Are there any questions?"

The word storm that erupted must have included many questions. Not a one in its entirety was intelligible. Cruella waited silently, grinning, for the torrent to subside. When at last it did, she said, "I think it's most appropriate for my science adviser to take those. I'm sure you all remember Doctor Bennigan."

"Play nice, folks. Wait to be called on," Lance added.

So, it begins. As Dale, her hands sweaty, approached the podium, text popped onto its inset screen: ASHLEY TODD, WAPO. Lance had assigned a senior assistant to eyeball the crowd for prospectively friendly parties. Beneath the prompt, in a cartoon of the room's seating, a dot flashed. Front row, toward her far left.

Dale faced in the indicated direction. "Umm, Ms. Todd, *Washington Post*."

"Thanks. Nothing that's been found suggests current life on Mars. Correct? And I have a follow-up."

"Well, people and chinchillas on the ground there might disagree." The crack earned a few polite chuckles. "But native Martian life? No. Hundreds of samples collected from across the surface have encountered nothing living. What Doctor Delacroix"—giving the woman her due!—"found were microfossils from deep below the surface. Geologists don't yet have a precise stratigraphy for Mars as they have for Earth, but these fossils are likely billions of years old."

"Here's my follow-up. How do we know these *are* fossils? Mightn't some nonbiological process create such tiny structures? We've never before encountered Martian life, so what makes us believe we can recognize its ancient, microscopic remains? In short, isn't this another ambiguous situation, like those the president mentioned earlier?"

"Of course," Dale said, "anything this old will have undergone significant degradation. And yes, visual impressions of fossils alone might be inconclusive. So, I must emphasize, there's more than imagery that convinces me. Aside from the physical resemblance to microfossils found deep in chalk deposits on Earth, three things stand out.

"First, Doctor Sun detected complex organic traces in and near some of the apparent shells. Not every molecule was familiar, but some are. Fully identified or otherwise, those were assembled from the same chemical elements—mainly carbon, hydrogen, oxygen, nitrogen, and phosphorus—as familiar biology.

"Second, within a portion of the shells, the electron microscope captures occasional shapes reminiscent of features within Earth cells."

Portion. Occasional. Reminiscent. As weasel-worded as that sounded, it had to beat discussing organelles and cytoskeletons—or age-ravaged fossilized remains thereof—with White House correspondents. Dale hurried on.

"The final observation, which I find most compelling, merits a bit of background. Many elements exist in more than one atomic form, what chemists call isotopes. Isotopes of any particular element, such as oxygen, are chemically identical but have slightly different masses. Some organic processes favor specific isotopes, whether because the mass differences affect diffusion rates, or due to enzymatic quirks, or whatever.

"Long story short"—*too late*, mouthed a wise guy three rows back—"living plants and animals take in different isotope fractions of oxygen, carbon, and hydrogen than what's found in the air or water around them. These are all stable isotopes, I'll remind you. The intake ratios persist in a microbe's shell once it dies. The apparent microscopic shells on Mars show such isotopic imbalances relative to their surroundings. Is that clear?"

From the back of the room, to sincere laughs, someone called out, "I'll say yes, if there won't be a test."

FRED KEENAN, AP, with a different blinking light.

"Mr. Keenan, Associated Press," Dale called.

"Specialists around the world will be eager to study the evidence. When will it be made available?"

"Not as soon as people will like. We're dealing with super-high-def images, a lot of data." In scientific terms, a shitload. Dale kept that thought to herself. "Transferring those, with more evidence gathered every day, will take time. As it comes in—then gets archived, quality-checked, and annotated with appropriate metadata—NASA will share."

Keenan frowned. "Then for the foreseeable future, intending no disrespect to the crew on Phobos, we're limited to the impressions of just two scientists?"

Yes and no. Yes, Giselle and Sonny *were* the only geologist and biologist with full access to the data. But the mission planners had known upfront the limitations on sending data over such long distances. So, hundreds of experts had been consulted. At least, many thousands of their academic papers had.

In a manner of speaking. Wherein derived the *no* aspect.

Prelaunch, neural nets had been exposed to those thousands of academic papers. The catch was with the "deep learning" techniques that dominated modern artificial intelligence. It had been explained to her—or dumbed-down *for* her?—that neural nets trained themselves. Input by input (in this case, document by document), "learning" tweaked and nudged a mishmash of weightings assigned to

313

countless connections among a vast number of simulated neurons arrayed in many layers. That autonomous pattern recognition had created the mission's on-site AIde consultants for astrobiology, paleobiology, and geology.

Did these AIdes provide useful guidance? Unclear. Worse, unknowable. There was no algorithm to assess. No thought process to evaluate. No audit trail to review. Just the plethora of connection weightings among the myriads of simulated neurons. Whatever details the AIs had winnowed from among all the raw data available? Whatever conclusions they'd thereby drawn? Whatever had led them to follow-up measurements they'd suggested? In every case, mysterious.

To Dale, anyway. She liked to believe others had a better handle on AI.

"Psst," someone hissed behind her.

Lance, she expected, catching her lost in her own head. She hurriedly concluded, "We'll know much more once we get the samples returned to facilities and researchers here."

ERIN MURPHY, NYT, the podium suggested.

Dale bit the bullet. "Mr. Coleman, *Eco Herald*."

"Thanks, Doctor Bennigan." Coleman nudged horn-rimmed glasses up his nose. "Concerns of PPL and likeminded groups about sample returns may have seemed theoretical. With today's announcement, those worries became real. Will the administration reconsider the concept of a lunar isolation lab for curating and studying these samples? Better yet, will it consider *not* bringing back samples, instead sending additional experts and equipment to Phobos?"

The administration entailed a lot of folks. But the person who mattered? The president? No way. Dale had the figurative scars to prove it.

"Fuck, yeah," Cruella had barked. "When the return window opens, at least one of our ships will come home. Whether or not at that point anyone believes there's anything to study. To do otherwise, to show we're afraid of a return, is to cede an entire planet's resources to the Chinese and the cabal of centi-billionaires. That damned NEP bunch are already wealthier than most countries. We don't dare let them overtake us."

Which was no anecdote to repeat *here*.

"You'll recall, Mr. Coleman, that plans are in place to handle returned samples at the Rocky Mountain Laboratories in Montana." *Plans* being the operative term. The NIH and NASA had been frantic about prepping that BSL-4 facility *before* Giselle's discovery. Constructing such a lab from scratch on the Moon? No longer even an option. The clock had been run out. "You'll also recall that the discovery is of long-extinct life. There's nothing to fear."

Fear. The word had just slipped out. Through the back of her head, Dale felt Lance wince and the president staring daggers.

Dale had been told before, in this very room, by text displayed on this very podium, IF YOU'RE EXPLAINING, YOU'RE LOSING. That left changing the subject. "Let me repeat. There's no sign of anything *living* in these deep core samples."

"Because, with those hundreds of core samples, it's impossible for even one dormant microbe, one virus, to have gone unnoticed." Coleman sighed. "I believe that strains credulity. And if an overlooked microbe is brought to Earth, exposed to warmth and air and water ...?"

He shuddered dramatically.

Lance sidled up to the podium. "Such speculation isn't helpful, Mister Coleman. We'll take other people's questions."

The hell of it was, Dale shared Coleman's misgivings. Out of, as the trite expression went, an abundance of caution, she had recommended, she would continue to push for, the utmost precautions.

She said, "Even if a returned sample should contain such a surprise, we *are* talking about a BSL-4 facility. That offers the highest level of biosafety. We're also speaking of a life form unrelated"—scientific integrity compelled her to insert a qualifier—"in all probability, to Earthly life."

Because, just maybe, panspermia was a thing. Martian microbes coming to a young Earth aboard a meteorite. Or vice versa. Or both worlds seeded by microbes from farther away. The revived Carlsbad bacteria that Coleman had tried to bring up at an earlier presser had been in a stratum a quarter-billion years old. Rocks could drift between solar systems faster than that.

"*My* focus"—concern—"is with protecting Martian samples from contamination by *our* microbes. The risk you insinuate supposes microbes somehow alive, or revivable, in these most ancient samples. Then, that researchers fail to notice them. Then, that long-established safety protocols aren't followed. Then that, somehow, Martian and Earthly life are in any way compatible. Compounding remote improbability upon remote improbability."

"Or," Coleman countered, "that a spacecraft returning the Martian samples crashes, spewing stuff far and wide, bypassing those safety protocols."

"Speaking of spewing," Lance's voice boomed. To a ripple of chortles, he edged in between Dale and the podium. "Erin, you've been more than patient. What would the *Times* like to know?"

Ira Coleman, his face red, fell silent.

"Interest in the returned samples will be intense," *The New York Times* reporter began. "How will NASA and the other agencies decide which experts, from which institutions, have first crack? How and when and under what conditions will samples be made available for study outside the Montana facility?"

Lance stepped back. Dale returned to the podium and took that mainstream question. Then another, as straightforward. And another.

Wondering all the while how the lunatic fringe was taking the day's big announcement.

First and Final Warning

The once theoretical crisis of Martian exploration is now upon us. We need no longer speculate about the danger to our world from these ill-considered expeditions. Life assuredly did once exist on Mars. It would be beyond irresponsible to suppose that life does not remain there—and that we can hope to know how to protect ourselves against it.

Microscopic life can be found everywhere on Earth, from deep ocean trenches and subterranean rock to the stratosphere, from nuclear-waste cooling ponds to the extreme brine of the Dead Sea. Life is tenacious. Life adapts. Live *persists*. With the discovery that life once took root on our neighboring planet, only the willfully naive could expect life there did not also adapt as conditions changed.

We're told the "former" life on Mars involved the same basic chemistry as familiar biology. We *cannot* assume incompatibility between the two biospheres. In all probability, we have already contaminated Mars. We dare not cross-contaminate our precious Earth.

The Planetary Protection Legions and its ilk have repeatedly warned about such irresponsibility. They have protested. They have striven to awaken the world to the existential stakes of the Martian missions.

At least within the corridors of power, these counsels of sanity have been ignored.

In reluctant anticipation of the situation in which the world now finds itself, *we* have quietly organized and prepared. Today's boastful, self-satisfied pronouncements from the United States and its accomplices demonstrate the wisdom of our precautions. Because, more than ever, this is clear: Nothing and no one may return from Mars. Nothing and no one *will* return.

People of Earth, know this: Our assets are everywhere. Our resolve is unshakeable. For the world's safety, for *your* sake, we will do whatever is necessary to defend us all.

—Manifesto of the Earth Protection Front

Western Recklessness Condemned

President Wu today chastised the United States and its "cronies in reckless endangerment" for their intention to repatriate its Ares mission with a cargo of potentially catastrophic materials.

"The Chinese nation and its friends sent pioneers to live on the Red Planet. Our Chìdì (Red Dragon) One mission and its anticipated successors seek to expand the domain of mankind. We do not, like others, imperil what remains our species's only home."

—Xinhua News Agency

February 10, 2035

Teri sipped morning coffee, breakfast finished, skimming the latest news download to her datasheet. Earth was going to hell in a handbasket. Same old, same old—hysteria about imaginary Martian pandemics aside. Reuben sat across the shelter table, intent upon his own coffee and datasheet.

We're like an old married couple, she thought. Emphasis on old. Because Reuben's occasional overtures notwithstanding, sex wasn't happening here. As for the other habitat, her impression was the two couples humped like bunnies. Or chinchillas.

As the clock icon on her datasheet approached 8:00, she began psyching herself for suiting up, gathering everyone outside, and organizing the day's work: likewise, same old, same old. Sweep overnight dust from the solar panels. More bricklaying for the shed to become a cloth factory, the garments they'd brought all tattered, torn, and stretched from much wear. Laying pipe from a new well. Planning the next exploratory excursion. Mucking out the chinchilla cages.

Well, that *last* task must deviate from routine, taking special care around the new litter. Three days old, and the kits already bounced about their cages like Superballs. Beyond native Martian, they were second-generation native. The first generation born here was not only fertile but capable of bringing healthy offspring to term. She found herself grinning. Damn, if those little guys weren't adorable.

"You thinking what I'm thinking?" Reuben asked.

She had a good idea what *he* might be thinking. That the two of them were the only mature mammals within thousands of miles, maybe millions of miles, not having sex. (Well, that wasn't going to change. Never mind the associations his pilot-ness evoked, she'd never forgive his prelaunch conspiring with Jake and Paula.)

And her? *She* wondered if Maia or Islah would be so foolish, or careless, to get knocked up here. It'd be an insane risk even if both weren't, like her, well north of forty. Even if Paula were still among the living to monitor a pregnancy. And if, in a few months, they wouldn't all be headed for Earth, this time unable to tether their ships for spin gravity.

What might NEP's high muck-a-mucks think of a pregnancy? She was sadly confident she could guess. The instant this chinchilla update reached them, they'd want the final proof humans could colonize Mars. How soon till they dangled incentives for anyone pregnant to remain here to full term? A new mission with a doctor would be launching in a few months for January arrival.

She tore her eyes away from the kits, straightened in her chair, gave her empty plate a nudge. "If you're thinking you'd kill for fresh eggs, instead of the powdered, reconstituted crap, then we're on the same page."

Reuben flashed one of those charming, bad-boy grins. "Oh, I think that whenever we have eggs. I imagined everyone did." He tapped his datasheet. "No, I meant this."

She leaned forward to see what he'd been reading. EPF RENEWS THREATS. NASA: WE WON'T BE INTIMIDATED. "What of it?"

"Our return window opens soon." (In three months. Who among them *wasn't* counting the days? Even though, in an opinion she'd kept to herself, she didn't see a return happening. She could hope to be wrong.) "That's not a lot of time to determine who they are and what threat, if any, they represent. Whether their obsession with NASA's activities carries over to us. All of which leads me to ask if your buddy Blake and his pals will call EPF's bluff?"

Huh! If not at the same exact moment, they *had* been thinking about the same thing. "On the one hand, Blake, and I assume anyone like him, won't be caught caving to anonymous bloviating. On the other hand, he didn't get rich"—filthy, stinking rich—"by taking unnecessary risks. On the third hand, NEP can't acknowledge these people as a serious risk without chasing off the tourist trade.

"My bet is they'll tout other reasons for us to pass up the upcoming return window. We've acclimated. There are long-term projects we'd like to see through. They'll say we jumped at incentive payments, a million or three bucks apiece being a rounding error in the cost of sending new people to Mars."

Truth be told, she marveled the carrot hadn't already been dangled. Because no one could prevent them from leaving Mars. She was *almost* certain she believed that.

"Maybe so, but I'm going to keep training with the departure simulations. More so with the sims for remote control of *Burroughs*."

"As you should, Reuben."

He stacked their plates and headed with them to the tiny dishwasher. "Shall we get to work, Boss Lady?"

"We shall." Because, truth be told, there *were* projects here she'd prefer to see through to completion. Space Vegas had been a challenge, but lunar lodges and more orbital inns were already on drawing boards. To construct a proper hotel at the foot of Olympus Mons would be a logistical nightmare. It could take years. But being the one to do it? It would be legendary.

Emphasis on the conditional mood.

An adjoining park-dome, its plants rooted in the ground, would be a nice touch. So would a garden, for fresh veggies. Also, some flowers. The next time she could spare the energy, maybe she'd dicker with the NASA bunch for a few lander-loads of that good, nontoxic, Phobos dirt.

Teri slid back her chair. "Off to work we go."

Drought Enters Fourth Year

The Bureau of Meteorology expects Queensland's ongoing drought to continue through the summer. With levels in Lake Wivenhoe, source of fully half Brisbane's municipal drinking water, at historic lows, municipal authorities are said to be preparing significant new usage restrictions.

Bureau senior meteorologist Danika Cairns said, "The state, and indeed, all of Australia, should expect more drought, and more frequent drought, as global warming continues to worsen ….

—*The Queensland Times*

In the cramped confines of Col. Zhao's sleeping nook—become an office—Kai confronted his datasheet and the still-encrypted message from Earth. The MSS giving *him* a biometrically secured onetime pad as backup for Zhao's? It had felt paranoid.

Since the colonel's passing, it seemed prescient.

Kai decrypted and read. Read again. Read a third time, although the key passage was by then seared into his brain:

THE CO_2 SENSOR WHOSE INACCURACIES LED TO THE DEATHS OF YOUR COMRADES WAS MANUFACTURED BY THE NG PHI SEMICONDUCTOR COMPANY OF HANOI. PRODUCTION AND QUALITY-ASSURANCE RECORDS FOR MANY MANUFACTURING LOTS, TO INCLUDE THE FAILED SENSOR AND ITS SPARES IN YOUR INVENTORY, ARE UNAVAILABLE, SAID TO HAVE BEEN LOST TO A SLYBOTNIK GANG RANSOMWARE ATTACK IN APRIL 2034.

A COMPLETE SUPPLY-CHAIN INVESTIGATION OF ALL MISSION COMPONENTS IS UNDERWAY TO IDENTIFY ANY OTHER ANOMALIES ….

Said to have been lost. The implication was not wasted on Kai.

Fact: Roscosmos had supplied the Mars Buggy, one of Russia's paltry few material contributions to the mission. Fact: A Russian ransomware gang had destroyed data that might shed light on the sensor failure. Slybotnik was prominent among the hacker collectives operating with impunity within Russia as long as it ignored domestic businesses—and prominent *also* among the unofficial entities used by the FSB in deniable cyber operations against state enemies.

Did China fall into that category?

The damned Russian proverb Kai could never manage to forget reasserted itself. *If you invite a bear to dance, it's not you who decides when the dance is over. It's the bear.*

Once Kai's thoughts turned down that dark road, his suspicions only grew. How significant was it that Antonov had pushed, almost from their arrival, for the trek to the ice cap? That Antonov, uncharacteristically, hadn't demanded equal Russian participation when the long-distance trip happened? That Ivan, the lone Russian along for that trek, also happened to be an endurance-trained marathoner? That when Kai had revived, Ivan spoke out against contacting another mission for aid? That at the mission's start, the fueling of *Zheng He* had almost ended in disaster, not the fueling of *Gagarin*.

But for this scenario to make sense, Mars Buggy life support had to have been *expected* to fail. A known bad sensor alone wouldn't suffice—and upon returning, Kai had examined the vehicle, from top to bottom, without encountering anything else amiss.

Except there didn't need to be anything else. It would require only that life support's catalyst cartridge degrade quicker than was specified (lied about?) in the Roscosmos-provided specs. As long as the CO_2 sensor didn't flag the danger ….

Had Ivan, on that calamitous day, feigned unconsciousness?

It was easy to believe that, absent a fortuitous pothole jarring Kai awake, matters would have unfolded quite differently. That Ivan, sneaking surreptitious breaths from an emergency oxygen mask, would have let everyone else aboard the buggy expire in their sleep. That the plan all along had been for Ivan, sole survivor and sad hero, to soldier on with the cargo of lifesaving ice. To deliver that ice to what would then be a Russian-dominated base.

Even more so than the Russian Bear's den that "Fire Star City" had already become.

March 8, 2035

The depth from which samples were collected kept increasing. The evidence of onetime life had proliferated. The intensity of Sonny's testing expanded to match. Her humming reacquired upbeat qualities that had for so long been missing.

Only Xander's fifth-wheel idleness and the tedium of the biolab remained the same.

While Sonny examined yet another mass-spec readout, as cheery droning gave way to off-key whistling, Xander gave himself a stern, if silent, talking-to. *He*, more than anyone, had designed the Phobos mission. *He* had championed making an arrangement with the ground folks, had helped negotiate the trades. Without *him*, a discovery for the ages wouldn't have happened.

Taking up, maybe, thirty seconds.

He plodded through another chapter of the latest text she'd recommended, as though organic chemistry was ever going to make sense. (Had he wanted to deal in numbers beyond zero and one, he wouldn't have gone into computer science.) Scratched an itchy nose for her a couple times. Laid out a datasheet and started up the short highlights reel of his nieces' Little League season opener.

Xander missed the twins like crazy. He missed his sister almost as much. But the prospect of soccer uploads all season, of finding something in each match to comment about? Ugh. Personal vids sent across interplanetary distances were low-res to conserve bandwidth. Compressed for the same reason. Also rife with dropouts, from frequent lost scan lines to occasional entire lost frames. Accompanying audio could be as iffy. This was nothing like chatting to and from Earth orbit. Earth and Mars, at their *closest*, were four light-minutes apart. Requesting retransmission of lost or garbled packets? Being grossly inefficient, that was reserved for scientific data.

Around two minutes into the vid, over a background of parental cheering, he maybe heard something. A thoughtful *huh*? He paused the playback. "What'd I miss?"

"More of what looks to me like fossilized cells. None that I've tried to culture have grown." Sonny considered, brow furrowed. "The more deep-core samples I examine, the more organic traces I've come across."

"Enough to identify?"

"Chemically? Unambiguously? Not always. However …."

Was that a sly eyebrow raise? "Okay, there's *something*. What's up?"

"You know I've been characterizing various organic traces in the mass spec."

Which measured the masses of individual molecules. Sometimes that sufficed for an identification. That much, he knew. "Is it … DNA?"

"I *wish*. As if I could do anything with DNA if I had found it." She perked up. "Unless maybe you've figured out some way to repair the sequencers?"

After the job some oaf had done on both gene sequencers? He shrugged. "Then what?"

"Peptide mass sequencing."

"Gesundheit?"

She laughed. "So much for my recommended reading list. Look, it's simple." (Xander doubted that.) "I've identified some peptides."

"Short chains of amino acids?"

"Correct." She turned toward him, as far as arms still in the glovebox sleeves permitted. "Know the peptides that are present, do some statistical analysis, and voilà."

"Voilà, what?"

"I'll give good odds I've identified my first Martian proteins. Even if I encountered those in pieces. And they're *familiar* proteins."

"This merits a toast." The choices for which were water and water. He took in her expression. "I may be more enthused than you.

324

Why is that? You thinking about renewed levels of hysteria from PPL and such?"

"Water." She wriggled her arms free and accepted a drink bulb.

"What aren't you telling me?"

Sonny glugged down half the bulb. "The part PPL *almost* got right."

This was like pulling teeth. He tried to recall PPL's latest propaganda/clickbait. "What, panspermia? A *War of the Worlds* plague?"

"Umm ...."

"Okay, I get that on Earth proteins are the basic machinery of all living cells, and now you've confirmed a few proteins on Mars. I'll buy that microbe-bearing meteorites of Martian origin might have reached Earth, or vice versa, and so life on the two worlds might be *very* distantly related. Even so—"

"Don't get your knickers in a twist." Sonny drained her drink bulb and handed it back. "Forget about rocks bearing dormant whatever drifting over the eons between the planets. *I* got to thinking about life-bearing rocks, even dust, from Mars getting *here*. To Phobos. That any of us might be tracking into our habitat on our diurnal excursions."

Why in hell he had never thought that himself? "Oops."

His articulate insight didn't slow her down. "In that introspective frame of mind, I began wondering if any of the core samples I'd dispiritedly spot-checked and released to Giselle and David contained overlooked *active* biological traces. Because those guys' protocols for handling samples are nowhere near as rigorous as ours."

The inclusiveness was unduly generous. "Your protocols. Suppose you're right."

She snorted. "I *am* right, at least about anything blasted from the surface of Mars being way more likely to cross a few thousand klicks to land on Phobos than to go all the way to Earth. Also that, unlike a meteorite reaching Earth, no rock arriving here faced a fiery reentry."

If long-dormant Martian bugs were tracked into the presumably nurturing, nourishing environment of their habitat? He shivered. "So, what do we do?"

"*Now* it's we?" She started to grub around in the day's snack box. "Okay, *we* replace a slew of air filters—in the habitat, the geolab, and this lab, too—and then I check out the used filters for anything ... unusual."

March 13, 2035

While Islah scurried about—spray-painting a search grid, eyeballing the ground, tapping with her rock hammer at various outcroppings, putting the occasional stone chip or regolith sample under a portable mass spec—Teri … stood.

They were in an ancient volcanic expanse, deep within—and so, high upon—the Tharsis Bulge. Ascraeus Mons towered to the west. The peaks of both other Tharsis Montes seemed to peek over the horizon, but those had to be glimpses of smaller, closer features—plus her imagination running rampant. In every direction, in every imaginable shade of red and brown, stretched rolling landscape punctuated at random by craters. (Impact craters or volcanic or a mix? Islah would know, but Teri chose not to interrupt.) Their grime-coated SUV and trailer notwithstanding (not to mention the two of them, as mottled in their vacuum gear), the view here, about midway between Barsoom and Olympus Mons, was spectacular.

"What's the word?" Teri finally asked. "Should I set up camp, or will we be moving on?"

Islah straightened. "Oh, we should stay. Satellite observations had this one right, and I'm not surprised. Volcanic terrains are often ore-rich."

Teri headed for the trailer and their portable shelter. "In this case, ores of what?"

"Aside from iron?" (Because you couldn't swing a dead cat on Mars without striking iron. As for why swinging cats had become a metaphor, or why dead ones, Teri had no idea.) "Copper, for sure. Lead, zinc, and traces of gold. I may find others once I expand the search area."

Back in Barsoom, Islah and Julio had experimented with making basic carbon steel, but other steel alloys would come in handy. Stronger. More heat-resistant. Copper, if they found it, would mean *wire*, for which Teri could imagine endless uses. (Why the *hell* hadn't they brought along more wire? She blamed herself.) First up, once they had more wire: new electric motors. Retrofit those into the hubs of the cable-reel trailer—sitting idle because, after the accident, no one trusted the cable—and they'd have a short-range backup SUV.

"What's the bad news?" Because when wasn't there bad news?

"I'm yet to spot exploitable ore concentrations on or near the surface. Not short of strip-mining, which we're unequipped to do. Even then, it'd take smelting or major electrolysis to separate metals from the rock. Our only capability for *that* is at Barsoom, so we're talking about serious trucking."

Teri retrieved their deflated shelter. Toting it to a rubble-free candidate camping site, she took a mental note: request explosives, jackhammers, a bulldozer blade for the SUV, and (mass budget permitting) another smelter. Blake *had* said to focus more on infrastructure. "What about farther down?"

Islah glanced up at the sky, head tipped as if estimating the day's remaining sunlight. "I'll have a decent guess for you tomorrow, after a thorough survey with GPR." Ground-penetrating radar. A closeup survey of the grid with the handheld GPR unit would take hours. "For a certain answer, I'll need at least several test bores."

Teri unfolded the shelter and laid out its guy lines, then began hammering in tent pegs. Damn, this volcanic ground was *hard*. "Deep?"

"It'd be my guess," Islah said apologetically. "That's all I can offer ahead of a survey. Even GPR will only give me density discontinuities to suggest where ore seams lie."

Bad news, all right.

Deep drilling took time, and lots of it. Like so much of the work they did, this task would have been done better by robots—if they'd had bots other than the delicate toys that tended the hydroponics gardens. Bots they could have brought by the gross, had *Burroughs* and

327

Bradbury not been loaded up with food, and oxygen, and people. Of course, with NEP's whole purpose having been to prove people could live here, bots hadn't made it into their cargo-mass budget.

On the other hand, the Phobos expedition, with its different ambitions, had lots of bots and the capacity for widespread drilling. If they could be enticed.

People of Earth! The NASA-led Ares mission has been quick—in our opinion, rash—to declare its intention to bring newfound Martian biological samples to Earth. Does mere curiosity compel such recklessness? Or does this unbecoming haste come at the behest of the military, seeing unfamiliar Martian microbes as the basis for hard-to-counter bioweapons?

The motivation may be ambiguous; the dangers are not.

Remember last decade's COVID pandemic. By the most conservative estimates, the nations of the world went many trillion dollars into debt to battle that disease—not to mention the millions of lost jobs and lost *lives*. Those consequences, as unimaginable as they seemed at the time, could have been far worse. They *would* have been far worse if medical labs hadn't had the advantage of years of vaccine research on related viruses.

Only madness would rush to risk a pandemic for which medical science must be wholly unprepared. How many lives would such a plague take, and what urgent endeavors would it foreclose? Lifting some of the world's most desperate from poverty? Continuing the transition from fossils fuels? Mitigating some of the already horrendous climate change?

Let a billion voices speak: There cannot be a return!

—*Communiqué of the Planetary Protection Legions*

Xander flattered himself that he'd absorbed smatterings of biological lore from months of off-duty study. He stared, brow furrowed, at the wall display synched with a microscope's camera. The image crept across a smear of agar, common culture medium, on which sprinklings of dust and lint scraped from habitat air filters had had the opportunity to grow. Contamination of those filters with terrestrial microbes being certain, they'd borrowed the geolab for the day.

Giselle's suite of instruments overlapped only somewhat with Sonny's lab, but the skimpy dimensions were all too familiar. Also as in the biolab, Sonny worked with her arms inside glove-box sleeves.

Sonny cleared her throat. "Well? What do you see?"

"Umm, bacteria?"

She gave a melodramatic sigh. "That's it?"

"Not that I'm qualified to judge, but the little buggers look ordinary enough to me."

"To me, too. That said, 'look ordinary' and 'I recognize' are different concepts."

"Then what's Tony's opinion?"

Tony—as in Antonie van Leeuwenhoek, pioneer microscopist—being Sonny's AIde. No matter how rushed and Swiss-cheesed Xander's biology reading, he knew AI. If there was one thing at which modern AI excelled, it was pattern recognition. Train a neural network with many thousand representative microbial images, and it'd spot their germy kin without difficulty.

"Checking now." Sonny tapped at the datasheet also jacked into the microscope. "Tony says the same."

"No outliers?"

"Nope." Her nose crinkled, as though battling an itch. "Okay, next sample."

The dust-and-fuzz of the next sample struck the both of them—and Tony—as more of the same. As did the third sample. The fourth. The fifth.

"Okay," Sonny declared, "it's on to the mass spec." Which, in *its* turn, with a dozen separate samples, identified plenty of ordinary organic molecules.

She wriggled out of the glove box and turned to face him. "We're done, I guess."

"Meaning we don't need to worry about Martian buggies spattered to Phobos?" Not that Xander had worried. The few life traces retrieved from the planet below were seen only in deep cores. Were, however indeterminate their precise ages, *ancient*.

"Meaning," she rebutted, "that on the off chance Martian buggies do exist, they're much like life as we know it. Meaning also that, without gene sequencers, I'm out of ways to characterize them."

329

March 27, 2035

"**W**hat can we do for y'all?" came the thick, Texas drawl.

Of *course*, Cat Mancini was the one to answer Teri's outreach.

The atom-thin silver lining of recent deaths? The burying of past animosities. Cat no longer tried to get Teri's goat, and Teri reciprocated the favor. After all the NASA team had done following the accident, after dropping everything to help, to bicker seemed petty.

None of which meant Teri liked the other woman, even though she couldn't decide why. Not that her feelings mattered: She liked far less the snail's pace at which Islah's prospecting unfolded. Barsoomian accommodations, at least in misty memory, were luxurious compared to the little inflatable on the Tharsis Bulge.

"Hi, Cat. Teri Rodriguez here. Got a minute?"

"Sure. Two, even."

Jerk. "I understand you guys traded with the other base for drill barrels and other goodies. Are you in the market for more?"

"Then this is a business call?"

Teri sat in the SUV (suited up, except for her helmet, just in case) while, a few paces away, Islah fussed with the mass spec and her latest batch of samples. She twitched as a hail of windblown grit spattered, rat-a-tat, off the windscreen. "In a manner of speaking. I think we could help each another."

"Xander's our diplomat. Hold on."

As if a trade deal with NEP counted as foreign affairs. Well, whatever the reason, Teri would far rather work with Xander than with Cat. Maybe Cat grokked that, too.

After maybe a half minute, the man came on the line. "Me? A diplomat? I know people who'd find that quite droll."

"Diplomacy. Isn't that the art of lying without blushing?"

"That's mere tact. Diplomats can also keep a straight face …."

"You got a minute?"

"While picking your pocket."

She laughed politely.

"Thank you, thank you. I'll be here all week. All month, and, well, too damned long."

She knew the feeling. "*Anyway*, have you got a minute?"

"Can you tear me away from writing a lack-of-progress report? Any time." Pause. "How are you doing?"

"Good." A reflexive response. As was, "You?"

"Good. Well, I'd kill for decent meal, but otherwise."

"Glad to hear it. So, I was thinking—"

"Hold on a sec. You're linked in straight from the surface."

Bypassing the low-orbiting comsat network, he meant. "Do you always read packet headers? Or am I special?"

"Yes and yes. Don't ask me why, but I got to wondering if the three expeditions could communicate without the second-guessers far away, well, second-guessing us. Point-to-point radio seemed like a piece of the puzzle. As did talking only when Earth doesn't have a line-of-sight to either of us. Like now, for instance."

"Guilty. I'm also no fan of being second-guessed." She gave him a moment to ask how she thought they might be overheard. When he didn't, she wondered if that reflected discretion or knowledge. He must at least suspect someone listened in. Maybe he'd gotten his knuckles slapped, long distance, for his dealings with the Chinese. "Anyway, as I told Cat, I heard you guys traded with CMSA for drill barrels and such."

"Yeah, Carter and I reached an arrangement. Why?"

"I thought we might provide some of the same."

"Where by *provide*, you mean *trade for*. What is it you need?"

To the point, and she approved. "A couple of us are prospecting on Tharsis Bulge. Our SUV has a small, onboard nuke to provide power, which means staying onsite to drill bore holes. Before last year's dust storm, you offered us beamed power. Is that still an option?"

"You'd rather not stick around through a long drilling process." Pause. "Then besides beamed power, you'll want a few of our robots."

"If possible. As loaners. What do you think?"

"Hold on. I'm going silent for a bit."

"I'll be here."

Islah strode toward the windscreen, gave an exaggerated shrug—more inconclusive test results?—and loped back to her worksite. Teri watched the dashboard clock and her counter decrementing to when Phobos would drop below the horizon. Did a few deep-breathing exercises. Watched a dust devil skittering in the distance.

The radio connection gave a *click* as Xander unmuted. "You still there, Ter?"

"Sure thing."

"We've still got plenty of PV"—photovoltaic—"film. That said, it seems like we've achieved a decent balance among bots, drill barrels, and batteries."

"There must be other things you can use." Not because she knew it, but otherwise, they were done. Except that she *did* know. "What would six frozen rib-eye steaks be worth to you?"

"My firstborn child, if I had one. Though you could …." The innuendo trailed off into an embarrassed mumble. Men. "Umm, moving on, we're a scientific mission. So, we'd be interested in samples from places your team has visited. Ice cores from your mines. Everything geocoded, of course. Some metal if you do find it." His tone lightened. "And yes, you silver-tongued devil, a few steaks."

Never mind their audio-only connection, Teri caught herself nodding agreement. "I'll need to check out a few things, but we ought to be able to work something out."

"I'll wait to hear back. Well, good talking with you."

"Same here."

Zipped into her sleeping bag, peering into the dark at the inflatable's low ceiling, Teri reflected. About Islah (snoring in *her* sleeping bag) and the latest, again inconclusive, ore samples. The latest routine updates and minor glitches relayed from Barsoom. The prospect of outsourcing some of their drilling. The further possibility, if she and Xander reached an agreement, of moving to more ambitious deals. Because what Teri most desired, above the mere promise of power beamed from Phobos, was new power generation that she controlled. That she could rely upon.

So: NASA had ample PV film left. That flimsy stuff could no more survive where she and Islah camped, or much of anywhere on Mars, than it would have at Barsoom while the massive dust storm had raged. But at the highest elevations? *That*, it had come to her, would be another story altogether.

Throughout the weeks-long, world-spanning storm, satellites had shown the peaks of the tallest mountains ever serenely above the dust clouds. Maybe she could trade for a roll or two of PV film to deploy atop Ascraeus Mons, in the shelter of its caldera. Daylong power from PV deployed on the mountain would be more convenient than intermittent power from Phobos when that moon happened to be overhead and in sunlight.

Rather than erect an antenna tower to beam power downhill, with unavoidable losses in the conversion from DC to microwaves and back again, it'd sure be great if Islah was right about copper ore. And if NASA could be sweet-talked out of hydrocarbon feedstock to synth plastic insulation for cable made from that copper. And if Keshaun (assuming Barsoom's smelter and foundry would accommodate copper as it had iron) could extrude copper rod into wire, and also find a way to coat that wire with the hypothetical insulation. And if—

Quit it, she chided herself. *Get some sleep.*

Instead, her brain continued teeing up uses for the additional power they didn't (yet) have. Could excess power be used to produce additional energy sources? On Earth, most PV cells were manufactured in huge, sophisticated, power-gulping factories from super-pure silicon. Sure, Mars had plenty of silica, but it didn't matter. The team had nothing like the necessary equipment.

Sleep, damn it!

Instead, something vague about nonsilicon solar cells bubbled up from her subconscious. (Because her job—a key chunk of it, anyway—was knowing a little bit about, well, everything. Enough to know what sort of expert would know more. It was why so much of her so-called leisure time went to reading. Why she hadn't read a novel in at least ten years.) Manufactured with a simple printer on any kind of substrate. For practical purpose, just a special kind of ink.

If a faux memory weren't misleading her, this was the NASA tech behind those rolls of flexible, thin-film PV she so coveted. All based on … for long seconds, the word eluded her. Perovskites? If that was even a word, much less the word she wanted, was it a mineral? Or a family of mineral types? Teri had no idea.

But Islah would know, as she could speculate about the availability of the appropriate raw materials. She, naturally, oblivious to Teri's tossing and turning, remained soundly asleep.

With a sigh, Teri began scribbling notes in the dark.

It could have been planning that kept her thoughts churning. What, in the end, *did* keep her awake, what replayed over and over in her mind, was the back-and-forth with Xander. Amid their preliminary negotiations, hadn't there been—and if so, how very unlike her—banter?

Until, at last drifting off to sleep, Teri caught herself wondering: Hadn't she known at some level that they'd been flirting? They were literally on different worlds, so what was *that* all about? And finally: Which of them had been more inept at it?

April 6, 2035

As the sun neared the western horizon and the temperature plummeted, Kai brooded.

Not that his brooding was in any way unusual. Not since the accident that might not have been an accident. Not with Nikolai Antonov growing pricklier—and more of a prick—by the day. Not with the drudgery of existence in Fire Star City stretching endlessly ahead of him.

His afternoon's drudgery, shared with Oorvi, was offloading a stack of panes from their recently completed automated glassworks. Silica for glass, SiO_2, was more plentiful even than the iron oxides, rust, which gave this world its characteristic color.

The inflated plastic of their habitat domes, beneath the regolith-filled sandbags that blocked the ceaseless sleeting of radiation, was also protected from the just-as-unending abrasion of windblown dust. Of course, neither did that thick barrier permit through any natural light. The plastic aeroponics domes, exposed to sunlight— and so, to wind—were due, if not overdue, for a blowout. Sturdy glass structures to replace the weathered aeroponics domes couldn't be completed too soon. Double-paned glass walls, the gap filled with ice, would filter most radiation but not sunlight.

Kai grabbed one end of the next pane on the stack. Petite Oorvi took the other end. One meter wide by two long, a single glass slab was heavy even in mere Martian gravity. Or the bulk and weight of his vac-uum gear made the slab seem heavy. Or, more than he cared to admit, a year-plus on this world had rendered him weak. "And … lift," he said.

With a soft grunt from Oorvi, they did.

One by one they restacked the panes beside a marscrete founda-tion poured days earlier. Ivan and Masha attended to the ironwork, welding a water tank. Welding lengths of pipe. Erecting a framework of studs and roof beams. Mingmei trenched and ran power cable for heaters and water pumps from the solar farm to the site.

All while Antonov stood idle, ostensibly supervising "his" people's work. As though such oversight were needed. As though *he* were in command of the mission.

Prick.

Kai's self-appointed duty, however useful, was essentially mind-less. Was no impediment to the continued brooding that, as long as he kept it to himself, remained a harmless indulgence. Anyway, so he chose to believe ….

The NASA-led team had gone to Phobos to do fundamental re-search. More than *looking* for signs of extraterrestrial life, they'd *suc-ceeded*. The NEP team, as best Kai could tell, had had no purpose be-yond scouting out tourist attractions. Despite early tragedy, they had made a good start at that.

And CMSA's expedition? What had become, after enduring its own tragedy, *his* expedition? Beyond some of them surviving, what had they accomplished? What function had their trip to Mars served beyond the scoring of propaganda points—with even those devalued by a third-place finish in the Mars race?

If this mission was without meaning, what did that say about *his* presence here? What had his participation achieved beyond some-times driving Li's passing from his thoughts? If the expedition contin-ued along its current undistinguished path, who was to say the Party wouldn't abandon them in this lifeless desert?

With the fifth slab of glass staged near the foundation, with many more slabs to go and Oorvi already panting, Kai called a break. He pivoted slowly while she caught her breath. Surveying what had been built. Visualizing all that remained to be done if this tiny settlement was to endure. Frowning at the Mars Buggy and its trailer, which he must soon dispatch to the well for more water. Taking in the two ships that loomed over the horizon.

Two purposeless ships, given Beijing's command that the expedition remain past the return window that would open in the next month.

More and more, what the sight of *Zheng He* evoked in Kai's mind was *retreat*. Abandonment. After the admiral's death, on the order of a new emperor, China's overseas exploration had abrupt halted. The ocean-going navy, thousands of ships, was burned. For hundreds of years, the great man had been all but erased from history—as the admiral's namesake might now be forsaken. As this expedition was overshadowed by the other groups' successes.

No, Kai told himself. Promised himself. Just, no. There must, there *would*, be a point to his being in this place. He *would* advance the enterprise of Mars exploration, of human expansion into the Solar System.

But why should the other groups trust him to contribute? It wouldn't be because, to save his own skin, he'd allowed NEP to rescue him. Or because, rather than risk dying of thirst, he'd later traded with NASA.

He must offer something to *them*.

Did either other expedition rely upon the line of CO_2 sensors that had cost Zhao Jin and Chen Xiuying their lives? Kai didn't know, but he *could* be certain Beijing had held its findings close. If they had intended to share, they'd not have expended a key from the onetime pad to update him.

It was a small matter, Kai thought, but he could pass along the suspect sensor batch numbers. He could suggest that other mission-critical components might "somehow" have been compromised. Call it a start.

Which he *would* start as soon as, from his perspective: Earth had set. Phobos was in sight. Deimos was in a suitable position overhead to serve as a passive relay to Barsoom.

"If you're ready," Kai radioed Oorvi, "we should get back to work."

April 13, 2035

Same cramped habitat, blotchy with the same tracked-in soot. Same reconstituted crap for dinner. Same faces (who else?) around the too small table—though some faces struck Xander as more guarded than usual. Because everyone knew what was coming.

"Y'all good?" Cat began. Only a couple grunts came by way of response. "Well, let's have at it. Who should it be?"

Hideo cleared his throat. "If I may, I feel we should discuss first the prudence of a return flight at this time."

"The people we work for think it's prudent," Cat reminded.

Xander stood and began clearing the dinner trays. Before addressing the matter at hand, it appeared there'd be another round of the too familiar debate. As if this were Groundhog Day and not (somewhere on Earth, anyway) Friday the thirteenth.

"Perhaps they think it's … expedient," Hideo persisted.

Cat, to her credit, exhibited great patience. "Do you have any basis for questioning the motives of the governments that sent us? Because I don't."

"Apologies, Cat. Our agencies must believe the benefits of returning our samples outweigh the risks and that those risks are acceptable. I do not. We have only begun to study what appear to be microfossils. What if there is more to the samples than that?"

David jumped in. "I agree with Hideo. By the *next* return window, we should know better what we're dealing with. If anything native to Mars is still alive. If and how even dormant forms can be awakened. If such things interact with *our* biology."

The next window. More than two years off. Doable, given the ice they'd found, and hydroponics, and their food(ish) reserves. More than doable if the second-round mission launched on schedule, bearing fresh supplies.

Cat looked to Sonny. "Biology is your thing. Do you see any reason to delay?"

"Have I seen anything recognizable as a living cell? No. Or an intact, possibly dormant cell? Again, no. Or nonliving but with the potential to be dangerous, such as a virus? Still, no. Not as much as an intact protein. Has even one among the hundreds of samples I've attempted to culture, under a whole range of conditions, shown any evidence of biological activity? Never.

"*All* that I've found, in enough samples to discount the possibility of contamination, are the fossilized remains of ancient, disintegrated cells. Those, plus organic traces. Nor have I found a reason to question our containment protocols. Nor do I have reservations about the quarantine procedures planned for use back on Earth."

Xander filled a water bulb and reclaimed his seat.

"But *any* doubt?" Sonny continued. "I can't speak to every last microscopic speck of every last sample we've collected. That'd take more people than me and more equipment than what I have. Even then, it'd take years. Even if there were an overlooked, long-dormant cell, I can't imagine what might awaken it. If you ask me—" adding, with a chuckle, "well, I suppose you *did* ask me—a sample return is a more than acceptable risk."

Well put, Xander thought. He'd spent months watching Sonny examine endless samples with infinite care. Often enough, with her guidance, studied some of those himself. "Now that that's settled—"

"Wait," David said. "Can we talk longer about the dormancy thing? Yes, the samples are old, although we don't know how old." He glanced at Giselle, who nodded. "Hasn't long-dormant life on Earth been revived?"

Sonny hadn't just put Xander through biology boot camp. She'd also let him clone her research AIde on the habitat's main server, complete with its somehow familiar intonation and mannerisms. Tony did not *sound* like a Tony. Asked whose voice this was, Sonny had favored Xander with a wry grin. It'd taken him *days* to place the digital echo from their youth. Bill Nye the Science Guy.

So: Xander felt he knew this one. "From a seabed sample taken deep beneath the Pacific, dated to 100 million years ago. From deep underground in Carlsbad, a sample dated to 250 million years ago. *Nothing* like the eons since Mars had oceans."

"Well, to be complete ..." Sonny said.

"What?" David prompted.

"Samples have been recovered from almost billion-year-old salt beds with what *look* like intact microbes. Those are within tiny chambers, microhabitats, of the salt. People have debated for years how best to open those and attempt to revive anything within."

"Speculation," Cat said firmly. "Everyone's had their say, so let's move on."

David frowned. "I don't think—"

"Repetition *doesn't* lead to a different conclusion," Cat said. "Also, orders are orders. Starting tomorrow, our top priority is prepping *Lewis* and the cargo for its return flight."

"No," David said, "orders *aren't* orders. It depends."

Xander could have sworn that, as the pilots glowered at one another, the temperature inside the habitat dropped by a good ten degrees. Celsius.

Should he weigh in? Once Cat left in (gulp!) less than four weeks, he would be in charge. *It depends* would make a lousy precedent once he took over. His experience ran more in the direction of questioning orders and bending rules.

What in God's name had the president been smoking?

Regardless, he wasn't in charge yet. But while he hadn't absorbed the full treatise (anyway, CliffsNotes) on leadership Cat had compiled for him, he *had* internalized a few lessons. Like: BOSSES HAVE PREROGATIVES. YOUR BOSS INCLUDED. Meaning Cat. Meaning the president.

Meaning, Xander decided, he should keep his mouth shut. Cat had this.

"Explain," Cat snapped.

David crossed his arms across his chest. Straightened in his chair. Stared, unblinking, at Cat. At least he'd forgone King Kongian chest-pounding. "I have always followed your orders, Cat. *Yours.* You're here, not millions of klicks away. You know our situation."

Cat's eyes narrowed to slits. "And I'm the one giving this order. *Lewis* leaves when the window opens. Representative Mars samples will be aboard. All that remains to decide is who'll go with. A decision we *will* make tonight. If need be, *I'll* choose."

However decided, Xander knew, there weren't many options.

The president had decreed a triumphant Ares homecoming with proof of the expedition's epic discoveries. Once Wu reasserted that his people here would stay, Cruella had predictably also insisted upon an uninterrupted Western presence. BOSSES HAVE PREROGATIVES. Of *course,* she'd demanded that Cat pilot the lone returning ship. (If given a choice? Xander expected Cat would've taken the assignment anyway. She'd beaten herself up for a year already for being on fucking Phobos during her mother's mastectomy and throughout the ongoing hormone therapy. As though to lack clairvoyance were a character flaw.) Which led to Cruella's further insistence that the mission's *other* American remain on Phobos to assume command. Without as much as a courtesy heads-up to Xander. Because, again, BOSSES HAVE PREROGATIVES.

Bottom line: Any two of Sonny, Giselle, and Hideo could go with Cat. David, being their second pilot, would remain here with *Clark.*

For a miracle, no one argued further.

"Good, that's settled." Cat said. "Moving on, then. Giselle, you've been quiet."

Giselle shrugged. "What is there to say? We arrive home in November, in plenty of time for Oslo in December."

When and where Nobel Prizes were traditionally awarded. Alfred Nobel hadn't designated a prize for biology or geology, but Xander expected Giselle was right. Whether in chemistry, physics, or medicine, someone would find a justification.

"What about ... us?" David asked.

"Us? Really?" Giselle looked and sounded embarrassed.

"Really," David said earnestly.

"We had fun. That's all."

"*Okay*, then," Cat said. "We have one volunteer to go. Any others? Or for staying here a while longer? If not, we can draw straws."

"Don't you get it?" David's face reddened. "We *all* must stay. We can't blindly follow every order from Earth. Even stick-up-his-ass

341

Wang Kai figured out he had to take some initiative. That unenforceable orders are *suggestions*."

Cat snapped, "You do remember why we're here, right? I mean, you applied to be here."

"Sure, I did," David said. "I'm a pilot, damn it. Of course, I wanted to come. But never in a million years did I expect we'd find life. Not even traces of ancient life. That we *did*? That what we discovered might pose a risk to Earth, however remote the possibility? That changes everything."

"In fact," Cat said, "it changes nothing. To repeat, *Lewis* is leaving. You, Xander, and someone will stay. Which y'all already knew. So, let's wrap this up. Volunteers?"

"That'd be me staying," Sonny said softly.

Cat blinked. "You don't want to be on the flight? Jesus, it's half your discovery."

Not to mention, if none of Xander's business, that the two of them were inseparable.

Sonny flicked long bangs from her eyes. "I want to go, Cat. You must know that. But I can't. If anyone's going to need medical attention, it'll be someone who stayed. Not to mention, I'm the last doctor in the neighborhood. If only on call from the other expeditions, I'll be close."

Reminding Xander of Cat's pithiest aphorism: DUTY FIRST. For doctors, it seemed, as well as leader-draftees.

Cat took a deep breath. A second. A third. "Okay, I get it. I can even respect it. Hideo and Giselle, it appears we'll be shipmates."

April 18, 2035

Dale seldom slept well except in her own bed. Maybe Patrick by her side made the difference. Or the familiar lumps and sags in their old mattress. Maybe both. Whatever the reason, she struggled to get any decent rest on business trips. The half-pound bison burger and mound of fries, still undigested, she'd been egged into the evening before didn't help, either. None of it made getting up to an alarm this morning any easier.

So, she didn't.

When her datasheet chirped its damned, cheery tune, she managed, groggily, to bludgeon it into silence. Her gut unhappy at the mere concept of food, she called a NASA astrobiologist with whom she'd flown in, bowed out of the planned meet-up in the hotel's breakfast room, and told the datasheet to give her another hour.

Then didn't fall back asleep.

Because what weighed on Dale's mind—the main reason, if she was being honest, that she'd slept like crap—was this morning's destination: the Rocky Mountain Laboratories. Or, to be precise, the memories, the nightmares, of *past* experiences with BSL-4 labs. Of the angry protest outside Fort Detrick. Of the media mugging when she'd exited the facility in Lyon.

What madness would greet her this visit?

With a sigh, she got out of bed. Cancelled the datasheet alarm. Took a long shower, hot water beating down on her. Dressed. In the ten minutes remaining until their Uber convoy was due, skimmed preprints on recent outbreaks of antibiotic-resistant bacteria, finger-swiping to highlight key passages as she went.

Three Ubers were pulling up as she entered the hotel lobby. Two astrobiologists and two virologists from NASA made for the front car. Three molecular biologists and a geneticist from the NIH moseyed toward the second. Dale detoured for a to-go cup of lobby coffee—this week was her show; nothing would start without her—before striding to the final vehicle. The pair of CDC infectious-disease experts joining her nodded without any pause in their conversation. After dinner, after Dale had excused herself from the hotel's modest bar, it seemed the youngsters had gone back out for—what passed in Outer Montana, anyway, as—a night on the town. Karaoke.

Youngsters? No one Dale had invited to the sample-return readiness review would see thirty-five again. Well, young was a relative term. She wouldn't see *fifty*-five again.

"You should have come with us," Dr. Mbeke said.

"Clearly, you've never heard me sing."

Mbeke chuckled politely, then resumed her conversation.

The other vehicles pulled away. "RML," Dale told the car. "Main gate."

"Rocky Mountain Laboratories, main gate," the AI confirmed. After thirty seconds passed without correction, it eased into traffic.

This being the height of the morning rush, it might be a ten-minute ride. Dale was content to tune out the chatter and admire the scenery. The Catoctins and the Blue Ridge back home were pretty enough, but the Bitterroot Mountains were *mountains*.

She barely took note of her car braking. Not, when she glanced forward, that it had had any choice. The other cars from her hotel were queued up at the main gate, in among several other vehicles. Some would have brought the passel of academic specialists, lodging at more upscale hotels than the govvies, whom she'd also invited.

Dale had convinced the White House to forgo any announcement until *after* this four-day inspection and assessment. The entire point was to obtain an expert, independent, and unbiased evaluation of RML's readiness to handle precious and (in theory, anyway) conceivably hazardous samples. Because *she* believed the lab wasn't ready.

344

She believed that they couldn't get ready within less than a year. Which would mean, should sanity prevail, the entire Phobos team sitting out the imminent return window.

However the assessment turned out, why invite public speculation? Still, with invited experts from across the country, and a few from abroad, neither was this gathering a secret. She took the absence of protesters and media vans as a good omen.

Two men and two women in some kind of uniform stood by the front four vehicles, checking faces against photo IDs and IDs against clipboards. A man in a matching uniform, toting a mirror at the end of a long pole, seemed about to look beneath the second vehicle. Was entrance always so controlled, or was this security kabuki to impress the out-of-towners?

"We've arrived," Dale told her companions. "The tour will doubt-less be interesting"—as her Fort Detrick and Lyon tours had been—"as will the presentations. But those are only a start. The main reason we're here is to challenge everything." Because *no one* had ever curat-ed biosamples from another freaking world! "Unstated assumptions in particular."

"Understood," one said.

Their car came to a halt. And—

Flash!

There might have been an instant of ear-splitting din. Of unrelent-ing pressure. Of *pain.* Then there was … nothing.

Terrorism Strikes Hamilton

Twenty-seven people died today, and two were injured, in ex-plosions at the main entrance to the Rocky Mountain Lab-oratories. Five fatalities were Security contractors of the lab; the remaining victims were arriving government and academic visitors. The facility itself appears undamaged apart from the destroyed entry.

Hamilton police surveilling the scene attribute the explo-sions to devices hidden beneath vehicles. RML Director Dr. Enrique Gonzalez speculates that had the lab's Security per-sonnel been less diligent, the bombs would have triggered within the complex, and the loss of life been even greater. "Our people at the gate were heroes," Gonzalez concluded.

The mysterious Earth Protection Front released an untraceable communiqué claiming responsibility for the incident and deeming it, "Unfortunate, but necessary. Whether further actions will be required is up to those who would abet any return from Mars. They have been warned."

The federal reaction was swift. President DeMille, in her press conference, denounced, "this senseless atrocity, an apparent terrorist attack." The National Press Office of the FBI released a statement promising a thorough investigation that would bring the perpetrators to justice. The Bureau's field office in Billings has dispatched agents to assume control of what is sure to be a lengthy and complex inquiry. A Department of Homeland Security spokesman announced unnamed "heightened security measures" had gone into immediate effect at all federal research facilities. Increased security and a massive investigative presence are already evident at RML. The DHS advises that, "out of an abundance of caution," biologists should "exercise situational awareness, and bring any suspicious behavior to the attention of their local law enforcement."

Dr. Dale Bennigan, science advisor to President DeMille, and Dr. Frank Jaworski, a researcher at the CDC, sole survivors of the blast, have been medevacked to the Level II trauma center at Billings Clinic Hospital. Both are reported to be in critical but stable condition.

The incident's other victims and their affiliations are ....

—The Billings Gazette

The PPL continue to object, in the most strenuous possible terms, to the upcoming return flight from Mars. The perils of contagion from Martian exposure are by definition unknowable. To inflict such risks upon us all is unconscionable.

And so, while we do not condone violence, a preemptive strike was predictable—and even understandable. There were no innocent victims today at the Rocky Mountain Laboratories.

Everyone killed or injured was complicit in the reckless endangerment of all life on our world.

People of Earth! Demand the immediate cancellation of the irresponsible return flight.

—Communiqué of the Planetary Protection Legions

❖ ❖ ❖

@SaveThePlanet1815

Does anyone believe the Earth Protection Front isn't a wing of PPL?

April 20, 2035

From the narrow confines of a critical-care bed, Dale skimmed the *non*-bombing news. For … she didn't know what. Distraction, perhaps. A sense of perspective. An antidote for the anger, confusion, and yes, fear, gnawing at her.

Whatever it was, she wasn't finding it.

Patrick, as stubborn as, well, *her*, had at last stepped out. Adamant he'd venture no farther for nourishment than the hospital cafeteria, would be gone from her side for not a minute longer than necessary. Would call their "kids," and update both, while hopefully reinforcing that the best thing the girls could do for Dale was to stay home with and reassure their own children. Would remind hospital staff yet again to redirect the outpouring of sympathy flowers to the rooms of other patients. (The over-the-top floral extravaganza from the White House, the lovely, tasteful arrangement from their daughters, and the potted philodendron from, of all unexpected sources, Ira Coleman, more than sufficed for her little hospital room.) For even those few, modest requests, only a solemn vow to sleep had gotten Patrick out the door. As if his malnourishment and exhaustion could in any way benefit her.

As for her fingers-crossed promise to her husband, someone in the protective detail outside her room would acknowledge Patrick on his return, or Patrick would greet the agents, and then she'd feign sleep. In

Dale's defense, she'd left unspecified *when* she would sleep. Someday, somehow, it would happen again. She hoped.

If she ever made it past the worst of the horror at the bombing and her rage at those responsible. Past the ache of Patrick's worrying about her, as bravely as he tried to hide it. Past the nagging pain because— doctors being the world's worst patients?—she insisted her meds be kept to a minimum. Past the certain gauntlet of press vultures camped outside the hospital. Past shattered legs, and a twice-broken arm, and she didn't even want to think about however much PT. Past memories of colleagues slain and of the threats hanging over only God and the terrorists knew how many more. Past her guilt at having survived, it having been *she* who'd demanded and organized the fateful gathering at RML, *she* who'd invited everyone.

And so, desperate for … sure, call it distraction, she'd started catching up on affairs of the wider world, ignored for weeks as she'd obsessed over the procedural minutiae of sample return and curation and prepping for the ill-fated RML readiness review.

She surfed. Read. Doomscrolled like back at the height of the COVID pandemic. Because the state of the world looked as awful to her, if in a very different way, as back then.

Record heat across huge areas. For two weeks—this still being April!—highs throughout the Southwest had not once fallen below 100 °F. Between the drought and the heat, spring wildfires had already burned almost a million acres of New Mexico and Arizona. Lake Mead had dropped so low the Hoover Dam no longer generated any power, Los Angeles mandated water rationing, and the already meager agricultural allotments from the Colorado River were halved—with additional cuts expected.

Conditions abroad were worse, with temperatures in Madrid, Rome, and Athens often breaking 110 °F. Heat emergencies cascaded across the EU as much of the continent baked, as North Sea wind turbines spun desultorily for a lack of wind, and as authorities pleaded with truck and cab fleet operators to *supply* power to the grid from any vehicle batteries still holding a charge. Utterly unfathomable to her, temps had reached 127 °F in Delhi and 130 °F in Dubai. With infrastructure literally buckling, brownouts and, as often, blackouts rolled across the Middle East. Tropical Storm Deborah, stalled in the Caribbean, had so far dropped more than two feet of rain on much of western Cuba, drowning hundreds and inundating Havana. Around the globe, "tropical" diseases were spreading: Lassa fever. Ebola. Mpox. Dengue. Anthrax, for heaven's sake. Widespread crop failures were forecast, whether from too little rain or too much.

All that, and more, bringing far-flung misery. Spiking food costs and rampant hunger. Climate refugees in the millions. Mass protests. And death. Lots and *lots* of death. And ….

"Mr. Bennigan," an emotionless male voice announced out in the hall: one of Dale's Secret Service guardians, dispatched within hours of the attack, aboard the same government jet that had sped Patrick to Montana. Whatever the president's faults, she was taking the EPF terrorist threat seriously. Just too damned late.

"Please, it's Patrick. Agent Berger, Agent Griffey, I brought you coffees and stuff to doctor it with."

"You're a gentlemen, Patrick." A woman's voice this time. The second agent.

"Anyway, appreciative. How's the patient?"

"Not a peep," the woman said.

"Excellent." Patrick coughed. "But if you'll excuse me, I'm going to have a peek."

Dale tapped the datasheet into sleep mode and, closing her eyes, aspired to the same for herself. For Patrick's sake.

Certain that sleep remained impossible.

April 29, 2035

Feeling she should be holding a silver salver arrayed with canapés, Teri surveyed the hall. The delightfully *large* hall. Delightful despite the taint of fresh sealant. No, delightful because—the thought bringing a big grin to her face—this edifice was new. Not some flimsy shed erected to organize equipment. Not storage for ice or oh-two or fuel. Not even one of the minimalist glass constructions that sufficed for hydroponics. This sturdy structure, their largest and most elaborate to date, was for *people*.

A proper, permanent residence, with kitchen, bathroom, laundry, and decent-sized bedrooms. Not to mention, this charming common room.

Keshaun and Islah, laughing, stood in a corner a luxurious twenty feet away. Maia and Julio, drink bulbs in hand, chattered in another. Reuben, in a third corner, fussed over one of the room's frivolous touches: the regolith-and-pebble rock garden. Everyone wore casual sweats, their vacuum gear stowed in closets. Walls and floor remained, for the most part, free of regolith stains. Afternoon sunlight streamed in through double-walled windows.

The tableau was so ordinary and yet … exotic. Teri needed a moment to spot the novelty. These past two years, in flying tin cans, then in igloo-like domes, there'd been no corners.

Maia ambled over to Teri. "This is nice. Our own Martian mansion. Too bad we don't have much opportunity to enjoy it."

Teri could have deflected the observation with some evasion or even a neutral *hmm*. She could have stuck with the plan: holding her big disclosure for later in this impromptu party. After everyone had mellowed out on a surprise pizza, their last pizza, which she'd kept hidden at the back of a freezer beneath the peas and Brussels sprouts. But as her mom so often said, "Man plans, and God laughs." Never mind the contradiction with Mom-isms about the importance of planning.

How, then, to proceed? There wasn't a contest. She was with her best friends on *two* worlds. "Umm …."

"Umm, *what*?" Maia demanded.

Teri raised her voice. "Guys, could I have your attention?"

Reuben set down the miniature sand rake he'd fashioned from metal scraps. Islah and Keshaun shuffled closer. Julio joined Reuben by the rock garden.

"What's going on?" Julio asked.

"You guys know our return window opens soon. Okay—"

"Ten days," Keshaun and Islah burst out in unison. Reuben and Julio applauded. Maia whooped.

Of *course*, they knew. Even as they'd pushed to complete outfitting this building with electrical service, plumbing, and life support, the focus had been prepping *Burroughs* and *Bradbury*. Teri took a deep breath. "Okay, guys, here's the thing. NEP would like at least some of us stay on and continue developing infrastructure."

"Ah, *shit!*" Keshaun snapped. "I *knew* this would happen. It's those fanatics. PPL, or whatever they call themselves now. The moneybags back home are terrified what else the loons might do. Bomb their businesses. Maybe target them personally. They're going to leave us stranded here."

Teri shook her head. "That's not it. At least not that they've admitted."

Stony silence.

"They can *only* suggest," Teri reminded. "That and try to entice us. I mean, they can't stop us from launching on schedule."

Julio studied Reuben. "You being the exception, right? If you stay, the rest of us are stuck."

Reuben jammed hands into his pants pockets. "In a word? No. I was already going to remote-launch *Burroughs* into its Earth-transfer orbit. Someone at Space Vegas was always going to take control of the ship to dock it. Both ships could return that way, if I had any inclination to stay here. Which I *don't*."

Islah sidled closer. "If this isn't a reaction to the terrorist attack, what *is* it about?"

"My guess?" Teri began. "It's only a guess, mind you. I doubt even I'm entirely in the partners' confidence." Blake shared no more than he had to. "Establishing a permanent presence here is turning out to be a much bigger undertaking, a more expensive undertaking, than even multibillionaires can easily handle. Not telling you anything you don't know, but we've had our delays and our setbacks." If they didn't remember? The cemetery outside their north-facing window should remind them. "Plenty of things have gone slower than we might have liked. Completing this building, for one. For all we know, our sponsors are coping with some of the subtle sabotage the Chinese encountered.

"For certain, NEP has had few, maybe not any, takers for half-billion-dollar excursions. If they had, we'd have been pushed to pre-position supplies, maybe deploy some kind of shelter, near the scenic attractions." If that disinterest had registered earlier, maybe she could have dissuaded Jake from his damned stupid last trip. Maybe he and Paula would still be alive! The futility, the *waste*, of it still made Teri sick. "They'd have had less interest, Islah, in the mining opportunities you've discovered. Less curiosity about surfacing dust-storm-free calderas with PV film and distributing the dependable power from there. The next mission's cargo manifest would show less heavy-duty industrial equipment and more goodies to pamper the paying customers."

If anything, the more Teri had pondered it, the more harebrained "Mars tourism" seemed. An Earth/Mars round trip took too long! Blake was the single billionaire she knew at all, but *no* consortium partner struck her as apt to abandon their business empire for two-plus years on a lark. How many non-partner billionaires would?

The conundrum was: Blake and his associates were far from stupid. That left the bleak inference she'd been loath to accept—and unable to dismiss. For the fortune already poured into this expedition. For as much investment, or more, going into the second expedition as it neared July launch. For Blake having forfeited another fortune early on by withholding IPE ships from NASA. For an endeavor that must be decades, if not generations, from turning a profit. For what had seemed a prurient interest in chinchilla reproduction.

As Earth's climate continued its slide to almost literal hell, as its institutions and infrastructure crumbled under the strain, NEP was preparing Mars as its escape hatch!

Yes, climate trends were scary enough that humanity needed a plan B. Make that, a *planet* B. But by working together, damn it! Not hamstringing NASA and its allied space agencies. Not by aspiring to a private domain without governments and regulations, without oversight.

If her intuition was correct? Such selfishness and greed would be breathtaking.

It wasn't that Mars would be any less lethal, much less comfortable. Not within her lifetime, anyway, no matter how much wealth NEP might be willing, or even able, to put into terraforming—if such a thing were even feasible. Nor could settlements here be self-supporting for decades. However automated, a freestanding industrial base must require many thousands, if not millions, of people to sustain.

But whatever the hardships, however long the road to any kind of self-sufficiency, Mars *would* be far beyond the reach of starving, sweltering, disease-wracked, desperate multitudes looking for someone, anyone, to punish for the slow-motion train wreck of Earth's climate. And those many thousand émigrés necessary to transplant an industrial base and keep it humming? The price of their ticket, quite likely, would be years as indentured servants.

Dystopian worries for another day.

Teri said, "Guys, here's what I think. It's far cheaper to keep us onsite than to replace us. That's even before factoring in the irreplaceable experience we've gained and the leg up our remaining would give the incoming crews."

Maia said, "I've done my time and my job. I'm done with this place. I'm going *home*."

Concluded amid a chorus of me-toos.

"One thing." Julio hesitated. "Umm, what was that earlier about enticing us?

Bringing Teri to the *next* topic certain to put people's backs up. "Money. Our bosses offered twice what we've been earning, milestone bonuses included. I took the liberty of telling them to stuff it."

Double-takes. Blinks. Dropped jaws.

"Hold on," Julio said. "Not even double pay approaches the charms of a sunny Caribbean beach and a pitcher of piña coladas. Not given

354

everything we've already banked from this trip. I mean, none of us need ever work again. Still, that ought to be *our* decision."

Nor had double pay spoken to Teri. "Your decision, agreed, and it will be. But remember who signed up everyone in the first place. Did any of you bargain hard? Or at all? Uh-uh.

"I told the bosses what you said, Julio. We've already earned enough—and I stressed, *earned*—that we can retire in luxury. Also, that the longer we're here, the more accumulating balances become meaningless numbers. It's not as if we can spend any of it on Mars.

"*Then* I allowed as how, once everyone here had discussed it"— extending an arm, the hand raised, deflecting swelling murmurs of dissent—"that maybe, if they doubled the rates again, I *might* convince one or two of you to stay over. If they also immediately vested our few outstanding performance bonuses. That it'd help their case if the next mission would bring us creature comforts beyond mere replacement supplies. That for *triple* their opening bid, maybe more of you would consent to stick around for another couple years."

As she spoke, anger seemed to ebb.

"And?" Maia finally asked.

"They agreed. Make that, they *folded*. Six times what we've been getting paid, effective immediately—if we sign on. Plus, a personal goods allowance shared among whoever stays. Up to a half metric ton and two cubic meters, as long as the stuff is safe to carry, and we provide the wish list by week's end." That deadline was nonnegotiable. Launch windows were what they were, like them or not.

If anger seemed to have ebbed, avarice was also a facial expression.

"Talk among yourselves," Teri said. "I'll give you some space."

When she exited the kitchen a half hour later bearing pizza, all that her team wanted, apart from a steaming slice, was to know how and where to seal the deal. She was quick to collect and transmit their digital signatures. However good the new pay sounded? Soon enough, the daily grind here would trump any charm to be found in big account balances there.

Whereas what *Teri* most wanted to know was whether everything she'd squeezed out of NEP, plus Jake's back pay and the payout from his employee life insurance, would suffice, should worse come to worst, to bring her mother to Mars. That and whether the corporate-run dystopia Teri envisioned could yet be forestalled.

355

May 3, 2035

The past days (weeks?) were a blur. With *Lewis*'s planned departure less than a week off, Xander couldn't recall things ever having been this hectic. Even at the Lunar Gateway, kludging (in hindsight, still semi-crazy) the launch-late/land-early flight maneuver, they'd sometimes had helping hands. For sure, *he* had never before experienced such a time crunch.

No rest for the wicked … or the IT guys.

He'd supported Cat with her endless preflight sims, in his spare time sneaker-netting terabyte upon terabyte of data—*far* too voluminous to radio—from lab servers onto the ship. David, meanwhile, had run repeated diagnostics on all the ship's automated systems. In *his* spare time, taking a task off Xander's plate, he'd moved Cat's, Hideo's, and Giselle's AIdes from the habitat's main server to *Lewis*'s.

All that being the easy stuff, because Cat's concept of transitioning base command to him was to delegate coordination of *Lewis*'s departure. (Another aphorism from her parting treatise, in serious need of an irony alert: COMMAND ISN'T LEARNED BY READING. IT'S LEARNED BY LEADING.) She intended to launch on the ninth, early in the practical return window. (SHIT HAPPENS. WHEN IT DOES, ANYONE CAN FIND REASONS FOR DELAY. LEADERS FIND WAYS TO HOLD TO A SCHEDULE.) Sending off *Lewis* on time was his first big test. He refused to let Cat down.

356

And so, more and more, he stayed back, alone, in the habitat. Pulling the strings. Calling the shots. Herding cats. Juggling chainsaws. Mixing metaphors. Doing his damnedest to make this *work*. Through all that, left to introspect far more than he'd like. (TRUST THE TEAM. BUGGING PEOPLE FOR STATUS ISN'T LEADING.)

While Sonny and Cat inventoried, packaged, and labeled hundreds of samples from the biolab, then stowed those in the cargo hold's Mars-climate-controlled lockers. After months in that lab assisting Sonny, logically Xander should have been her junior packer. Instead, he pretended to believe Cat should, the better to oversee unpacking at the far end. Even without an aphorism (LEADERSHIP CAN'T ALWAYS BE LOGICAL, BECAUSE PEOPLE AREN'T), he'd have done it. Whatever time the women could spend together was precious.

While David, when not wearing his IT beanie, and Giselle gathered geological samples—or they had, anyway, until two days ago. Until (after nag upon nag that she remain with him on Phobos; after her many admonitions that he respect her decision, stay professional, and focus on the task; after her primal, open-channel scream to "Just shut the fuck *up!*") Giselle demanded that someone else, anyone else, or even no one else, help her complete the task. Friendship, much less benefits, was out the window. Leaving Xander, in his first command decision (NEVER CONFUSE CAUTION WITH INDECISION), to have Hideo help her finish packing.

While Hideo, aside from his new gig, squeezed in a final few experiments with utilizing Phobian resources.

While David, in what Xander *hoped* was the least worst decision, was now left to wallow. Even when he wandered alone to mope in whichever lab or ship was then untenanted. (Call that command decision three. They'd all become old hands at surface excursions. Once *Lewis* took off, continuing vacuum-buddy protocols would render the three remaining behind hopelessly unproductive. Lifting the rule a few days before launch didn't much matter.)

As for *what* David did alone, no one, least of all Xander, had the time or the patience to investigate. Amusing himself with new video hacks? Distracting himself with his own flight simulations, thinking Xander might prove more amenable than Cat to a Deimos excursion? Letting off steam blasting Bad Guys in some first-person shooter?

Nursing a broken heart? Once David got over his sulk and back to work would be soon enough to ask.

All the while, Xander *also* pored over official mission logs while Cat remained around to field questions. Those logs, plus the scattered glimpses she'd provided from her personal journal, made for a rude awakening. (LEADERS *DO*. QUIETLY. THEY DON'T KVETCH.) The frequent updates demanded by four space agencies—a major time sink even *after* her AIde got adept at writing first drafts. Running interference for the rest of them from the clamoring media. Monitoring every imaginable item of inventory. A week hence, every damned one of those tasks would be his responsibility. Then, in his "spare" time, because everyone took their fair share of the grunt work (A LEADER IS NO BETTER THAN ANYONE ELSE, JUST BUSIER), he'd reinstalled *Lewis*'s original micro-gee exercise equipment and helped restock the ship's larder.

And yet.

David, *clearly*, lacked the temperament to take charge. The man could, however, all snide video-game putdowns aside, take back flight control of the robot landers. As for Sonny, as long as the mission continued to collect samples, she'd have real work to do.

Leaving … him.

The funny thing? Being honest with himself, Xander had come to realize he wouldn't have wanted to go back—frequent tedium and complaints notwithstanding. As much as anyone, he'd been instrumental to the most monumental discovery … maybe *ever*. Only through his pushing and prodding and pretzel-bending of the rules had they gotten the tools to make that discovery possible. Any second act he could imagine on Earth seemed prosaic. If taking charge was the price of staying, well, he'd made peace with it.

Though he *did* hope David's sulking would pass sooner rather than later.

May 8-9, 2035

The evening was bittersweet, mixed bon-voyage celebration and sad farewells. Come morning, a separation of years began. Among the reminisces and laughter, before, during, and after David's unexpected montage of video clips, came more than the occasional tear.

Xander did his best to keep the mood light. (FEEL WHATEVER YOU WANT. SHOW ONLY WHAT YOU MUST. AS NEEDED, FEIGN CONFIDENCE AND GOOD CHEER.) With, to hearty applause, the rib-eye steaks from Barsoom. With Snickers long hoarded for the occasion.

No one could top the steaks, but it turned out everyone had planned something festive. Hideo brought out a stash of Kit Kats. Giselle, bless her, had saved up two week's worth of breakfast coffee—freeze-dried crap, but still, *coffee*. Cat and Sonny contributed dry-roasted peanuts. David, shaking off his recent funk, had suited up "for my own surprise," only to reenter the habitat, twenty minutes later, empty-handed.

"Umm, what was that about?" Sonny asked.

"In a minute." David even meant it literally. After popping his helmet, he'd made no effort to wriggle out of the counterpressure suit. The datasheet he took from a belt pouch, once unfolded, showed a pic of *Lewis*'s main cabin. A cooler door hung open. Within which ....

"Are those fresh *strawberries*?" Giselle asked.

"Harvested from hydroponics while the rest of you were otherwise occupied." David shook his head ruefully. "While I, I'm ashamed to say, was being, well, you know." (A putz, Xander completed, relieved the man seemed over it.) "That's the entire berry crop, and behind them is some fresh lettuce."

"*All* the berries?" Cat said. "Half belongs here."

"I freely donate my share." David began unsuiting. "Enjoy them while they're fresh. Anyway, we'll grow more."

"Ditto," Sonny said.

Xander made it unanimous. "Now if I may offer a few words ...." He waited out the melodramatic groans. "*Cat* has something to say."

Drawing a laughter-punctuated chorus of, "Speech. Speech."

Cat took a deep breath. "Unaccustomed as I am to public speaking ...." More laughter. "Seriously, and in just a few words, because tomorrow will be busy for some of us, I do have things to say. First, it's been the honor of a lifetime to be on this expedition with you. I couldn't be prouder of what's been accomplished. Thank you for all you've done. Second—"

"All *we've* done," Xander said. "You, included."

"Second, I haven't passed the baton yet." Renewed laughter. "No, *this* is the second thing. Forget the lunatic fringe back on Earth. Forget, even, the original Lewis and Clark. Years from now, *centuries* from now, people will name spaceships after *us*." Cheers. "And third, for you guys staying, I know you're in good hands. Now switching metaphors ...."

She tapped Xander first on one shoulder, then the other. "Even without a sword, I hereby dub thee ... Ares mission commander."

To animated applause, Xander felt his cheeks go warm. At least, thanks to the beard, no one could see he was blushing. He muttered his own words of thanks and appreciation, not nearly as eloquent as Cat. Damn, he had a lot to learn. "However reluctantly, I'm going to bed." Trying by example to give Sonny and Cat a few final hours alone together. David and Giselle, too, if they'd managed to patch things up. "Big doings tomorrow."

Sighs. Murmurs. Nods and hugs. A few more tears.

More with a whimper than a bang, the party ended.

❖ ❖ ❖

For the longest time, their return window had seemed impossibly re-mote. Then, having an actual departure to aim for, that same window had felt impossibly *close*.

Both impressions alike now disproved.

Suiting up, preparing to see off his friends, Xander could only marvel. Today *was* the day. A return flight *was* happening. Yet more amazing, six ships had taken part in the Mars race, but—at this window, anyway—only one would start back. Was this a second win? If so, did that really matter?

Knock it off, Xander told himself. Philosophize another time.

Giselle and Hideo had gone ahead to the ship. Sonny and Cat, heads close, held a final conversation. They donned helmets and were next out the habitat airlock. David and Xander were in the final phase of their suit checkout, helmets seated and sealed, electronics-module diagnostics run, comm checks complete, oh-two flowing, when—

PRESSURE DROP DETECTED. The warning throbbed, blood red, on Xander's HUD.

David had already started toward the habitat airlock. At Xander's tap-tap on an arm, David paused to look back. Xander raised three fingers.

David nodded and tapped his forearm keypad. "What's up?"

"A leak, damn it. Do you see anything?"

David circled him slowly, head tipping down and up, down and up. "Nothing." Circled Xander again. "Raise your arms." Xander did, and David peered at the suit's armpits. "Still nothing."

"Hey, guys," Cat called on the common channel. "We've got a flight to catch."

Xander put his mic back on that channel. "Be right out." I sure as hell *hope*.

"Happy to hear it," Cat said.

David, still looking for any obvious tear, shook his head.

A pinhole leak then, hard to spot? Or a tear out of sight entirely? Under the life-support pack on his back. Inside a heavy-duty boot. Beneath his Batman utility belt. A scratch or a worn spot in a compression seal. It could take *hours* to find and fix the leak, and as long again with the suit empty but inflated to confirm the fix. Double that if the initial repair didn't hold. "Cat, my suit has a leak."

"Copy that … Commander."

Emphasizing that, as of last night, *he* was in charge. *He* held final authority to approve—or postpone—the launch. Either way, she'd go along. Because ORDERS ARE ORDERS.

Getting to watch the launch in person was—of course!—no justification for delay. But then there was that final (final, *final*) systems check he'd meant to hop aboard *Lewis* to do.

SHIT HAPPENS.

Check.

WHEN IT DOES, ANYONE CAN FIND REASONS FOR DELAY.

Like choosing to re-redo the systems checks David, a pilot *and* Xander's IT understudy, had done twice already. Because, unlike this being-a-leader stuff, Xander understood IT?

LEADERS FIND WAYS TO HOLD TO A SCHEDULE.

"David's coming out," Xander radioed. "Sonny, David, if you'd be so kind as to record the launch on helmet cams, I'd appreciate it. Once they've released *Lewis*'s tethers and backed off to a safe distance, Cat, you're go for launch at will."

Jittery helmet-cam views. Bare-minimum thrust using only attitude jets, to edge off and away from tiny Phobos. Serious thrust deferred till an ultra-prudent two klicks of separation. The utter silence of takeoff in a vacuum.

Lewis's departure could not have been any more anticlimactic.

Almost as anticlimactic as—hours later, when Xander located it—where sturdy boot and ubiquitous Phobian grit must have abraded fabric-suit toe tip. What blasted timing! What damned, stupid luck! Doubtless fated, after patching, to provide the perpetual annoyance of a darned sock.

Xander assured himself, composing his first mission-commander log entry, that his luck could only improve.

"The world hates change, yet it is the only thing that has brought progress.

—*Charles F. Kettering (American inventor; holder of 186 patents)*

"The frontier in space, embodied in the space colony, is one in which the interactions between humans and their environment is so much more sensitive and interactive and less tolerant of irresponsibility than it is on the whole surface of the Earth."

—*Rusty Schweickart (Apollo astronaut)*

"Nobody ever figures out what life is all about, and it doesn't matter. Explore the world. Nearly everything is really interesting if you go into it deeply enough."

—*Richard P. Feynman (Nobelist in Physics)*

"For me the protection of planet Earth, the survival of all species and sustainability of our ecosystems is more than my mission, it is my religion."

—*Rajendra Pachauri, Chairman of the Intergovernmental Panel on Climate Change (2002-15)*

DESPONDENCY

May 20, 2035

Xander hadn't taken long to interpret Mission Control's hunger for information as a proxy for their level of trust. Meaning, the way they squandered precious DSN capacity, they were signaling *dis*trust. Cat's mission logs never showed her half so inundated with questions, so pestered for report upon report.

Yeah, well, he didn't blame them. Much. Cat had joined the mission as a seasoned astronaut. *He* was a political appointee. Twice now.

While Sonny plodded on the treadmill and David prepared their dinners, Xander tackled the latest long-distance interrogation. His AIde's draft responses remained too faithful to his style—too sarcastic—to forward unedited. The damned, dumb AI might take weeks, even months, of his handcrafted tweaks to acquire manners suitable to his new role. Becks wouldn't object in a personal exchange to his subtle digs or venting—hell, she'd laugh, then reply in kind. *This* was official correspondence for the record, alas, to be seen by scads of people who didn't know him or his sense of humor.

Leaving him again pondering new polite ways to report: landers still landed. Now and again, deep core samples still turned up organic traces and microfossils. Fruits and veggies continued to grow in the hydroponics dome. The three of them left behind on Phobos remained healthy. Old wine. New bottles.

Speaking of which ….

He'd love a glass (well, a drink bulb) of wine. Fine quality or vintage Tuesday, it didn't matter. Or Scotch. Bourbon. Tequila. Cheap beer.

While Xander murmured dictation and tapped corrections into a datasheet, Sonny hopped off the treadmill and joined David in the habitat's tiny galley. Sonny pined for Cat. David, in his own brusque way, never mind the arguments before *Lewis*'s departure, missed Giselle. Misery loved company, and their odd-couple bonding left Xander the odd man out.

His texting app popped up a notification. From Cat. They each re-layed messages through Earth, that being easier than repositioning their antennas before and after each contact. He'd asked for advice. How should he approach Mission Control about dialing back the questions?

To get, by way of response, all of: YOU'LL FIGURE IT OUT.

He'd gotten more helpful advice in fortune cookies.

Cat had been open enough the first week after *Lewis* launched. Not chatty, exactly. She never was. But not taciturn, either, especially (he'd asked) with Sonny. Not like the last few days. Giselle and Hideo had gone taciturn, too. Xander presumed they followed Cat's lead.

It dawned on him he'd been dense. She was cutting the cord. At least she'd left him the *Book o' Pithy Leadership Advice*. He wrote back, UNDERSTOOD, CAT. I'LL HANDLE IT MYSELF.

Feeling, for the first time since Cat left, the loneliness of command.

RML Resumes Preparations

(Hamilton, MT) The FBI, the Department of Homeland Security (DHS), the National Institutes of Health, and local law enforcement have completed their joint review of safety and security protocols at Rocky Mountain Laboratories. This review came in response to the April 18th terrorist bombing at RML's main gate. With the imposition of unspecified "heightened security measures," all parties have approved the facility for receiving and studying samples of ancient Martian life.

NASA's spacecraft *Lewis*, bringing those samples, is expected to dock at the Lunar Gateway on November 17th. Its crew and the much-anticipated samples will transfer to RML at a later date. NASA, its partner space agencies, DHS, and laboratory management continue to refine the details and timing of transfer ....

—*Montana Standard*

"Do you have a minute?" Teri asked.

Peering out of her datasheet, Xander Hopkins looked ... haggard. He rolled his shoulders, stretching. His habitat backdrop looked as tatty as Helium had become. Had her team not finished the new, roomy quarters, the next couple years would have been grim. A bedroom instead of a coffin-sized cubby? Nirvana. Even though her laundry room back home was larger. Also, setting aside how indistinct the concept of *home* had become.

"Sure." He raised a hand, semi-covering a yawn. "What's up?"

"How are you finding the big chair?"

"Less like a throne than I'd imagined." The image of his face jiggled as he walked to somewhere presumably more private, and his voice dropped. "More like a bed of nails."

Yeah, he looked about that well-rested.

"That's kind of why I'm calling. Having mission responsibility dumped on you? It could have been rough, and you can't vent to the remaining troops." Any more than she could vent to her people, and she was accustomed to the job.

He raised an eyebrow. "Uneasy lies the head that wears the crown."

"Something like that." In her case, *lonely*. Reuben would be more than happy to make a more intimate acquaintance. His intentions never went beyond deniable innuendo, but she felt more comfortable with the six of them living under one roof. "I'm here if you ever want to talk."

"Good to know." Yawn. "Sorry. For yawning in your face *and* if that sounded dismissive. I'd like that." Yawn. "Sometime when I'm more awake."

Since landing, her bunch had operated on Barsoom-local sun time, on which she'd finished dinner not long before. With Phobos orbiting Mars in less than eight hours, sun time would have made no sense—even without the complication of an eclipse every circuit. For Xander (quick downward glance at a datasheet corner) on GMT it was approaching ... one A.M. Oops. If perhaps not as much as him, maybe she needed sleep, too.

"Good, Xander. Any time."

Because, she could admit to herself, *I'd like it, too.*

May 25, 2035

On the road trip to and from the well, Ivan Vasiliev was positively chatty. *So* chatty that Kai could almost have believed that openness a sham: the faux friendliness of an abuser out in public with his battered wife or child. The faux friendliness of a conspirator who had bided his time for Kai, Xiuying, and Colonel Zhao to die on their calamitous arctic expedition.

Almost.

The big, gruff Russian had gone all stiff and formal at the well, as soon as he and Kai donned helmets to leave the Mars Buggy's cabin. As though that asshole Antonov would listen in on private suit-to-suit comm channels—which Kai found oddly reassuring. Maybe Kai's earlier, improvised bug sweep of the cabin, which hadn't detected anything, could be relied upon.

Unless the apparent candor were an act, so Kai would speak freely in the buggy. Unless Ivan, under Antonov's orders, schemed to draw Kai out.

Now *he* was the one all stiff and formal. Trying to reconstruct whatever unguarded thoughts had been expressed. Trying to anticipate how Antonov, ever a stickler for his perceived prerogatives, ever quick to take offense, might interpret those remarks. Resenting the snail's pace that was all the buggy could manage with its full water trailer in tow. Resenting the stubbornness of Beijing. "Abandon the Forbidden City and Tiananmen Square? Unthinkable."

No, the hours-long trek each time they needed more water was unthinkable. While continued drilling near the base—near so very many dry holes—was so much wishful thinking.

Around Mingmei and Oorvi, Kai didn't have to agonize over every word. With a shiver of uncharacteristic self-awareness, it occurred again to Kai to wonder. Since he had been put in charge, how comfortable did the women feel speaking around *him*?

"Are you all right?" Vanya asked. "You seem …."

Confused and conflicted? Frustrated? Paranoid? Yes. "I'm tired." Dissembling, but true.

Vanya gestured out the windshield to their right. "Then be of good cheer. That cluster of three overlapping small craters tells me we're almost back."

Fifteen minutes later, they drove into Fire Star City. Kai parked the Mars Buggy alongside the main water tank. He counted four people outside at various tasks. After asking Vanya and Oorvi to pump the water from the trailer into the tank, Kai went inside. Alone.

He needed to talk to someone, anyone, who didn't—in truth, or even in theory—report to him. To converse with someone, anyone, while not second-and third-guessing every word either of them spoke. Without, for at least a few minutes, any hidden agenda.

By a call relayed with a passive bounce off Deimos, he reached out to Teri Rodriguez. Because her mission hadn't intended to stay this long on Mars. Because her team might be running short of something useful that he could provide. Because, politicians be damned, rivalry between the tiny expeditions so far from home was pointless.

Even if that would-be altruistic offer was also a selfish act in service of his own mental health.

June 8, 2035

Mars Partners Pledge to Leave Earthly Disagreements at Home

Amid escalating tension between Russia and China over thousands of undocumented South China climate refugees daily crossing the border into sparsely populated Siberia, ISRO Chairman Indira Chakrabarti has reached out to her counterparts at CMSA and Roscosmos. Both partner space agencies insist that unrelated issues will not impede continued cooperation in the exploration of Mars.

"The Chìdi Two mission remains on track for July departure," Chakrabarti summarized her conversations, "with our native son, Pavan Gupta, confirmed among its crew.

—*New Delhi Times*

No one could be an expert in every aspect of science, and Dale knew better than to try. She had her strengths and staff for the rest. If she didn't even pretend to have insight into the subtleties of climate models and their projections, she had confidence in a deputy who did. She concentrated on "just" the health implications of climate change. Severe heat events. Increased asthma risk. Famine. Disease-carrying ticks and mosquitoes appearing earlier and earlier by the year, farther and farther afield. Ever longer allergy seasons. "Tropical" diseases spreading far beyond the tropics. The deplorable circumstances of climate refugees in their teeming millions—

Stop it! she instructed herself. Digging out after any absence takes time. Not that she'd ever been away from a job for half this long.

Uh-huh. Then why return at all? Patrick had asked often enough while she healed that she should have had an answer already. He'd asked again that morning, helping her into a Lyft (inspected first by a Secret Service agent!) for this, her first day back.

Why? That would have been a fair question even if the job hadn't almost gotten her killed. If she weren't just out of leg casts and into bulky orthopedic braces. But for the recent advances in electrical stimulation to accelerate the knitting of broken bone, she would *still* be home. Where, in the interest of a focus on healing and recovery, she would have continued to avoid news of the world. Worlds.

So, why *had* she come back? Why returned to work she'd learned to dread even before RML? Because quitting would have disrespected everyone who had died in the bombing.

Her office in the Eisenhower Executive Office Building, what President Truman once called "the greatest monstrosity in America," was altogether too apt.

"Stop feeling sorry for yourself," Dale muttered. But where to begin? For weeks, the office AIde had triaged the routine fire hose of reports from national labs and academia, the executive-branch requests for explainers, the updates from the Ares mission. As the backlog piled up, the AIde had done triage upon its earlier triage. The tip of the tip of the iceberg remained daunting.

Some topic had to come first, and climate-change issues won (lost?) the mental coin flip. If a coin could have, oh, dozens of sides. Merely a skimmed overview of recent climate-change news was overwhelming. Twenty thousand dead from monsoon flooding along the Bay of Bengal. A cholera outbreak in Liberia from earlier flooding. New, gloomy forecasts on the rate of Greenland ice cap melting.

Okay, she could have chosen a more upbeat subject. NIH research. DARPA's latest efforts in advanced robotics. Progress toward standards for a 7G cellular network. If none of those had the appeal of home and slippers, at least none was depressing. None was where her conscience told her to resume: preparations at RML since—

Her workstation chimed, and she glanced at the display. Her AIde's real-time interrupt icon flashed. She tapped ACCEPT.

"Excuse me," the AIde said. "You asked not to be disturbed, but I have an incoming call for you that falls outside normal screening parameters."

Did she want to talk with anyone? No, but neither had she decided how to get back into things. "Who's calling, and why?"

"Ira Coleman. He claims to have information about the Montana incident."

"Fine." Not even close. "Put him through."

Three rings and a vid window opened. Ira Coleman, all right. He looked ... conflicted. "Hello, Dale."

"Hello, Ira. Oh, and thanks for the philodendron. What's going on?"

"I was pleased to hear you were recovered and back to work."

Less than an hour into her first day back. Her first mug of office coffee not yet finished. "Do I want to know how you know?"

"It's called being a reporter." He hesitated. "I'm sure you've realized I have contacts among senior PPL people."

People well hidden behind anonymizing services and internet avatars. "Information you should share with the FBI or DHS. Or with me, and I'll pass along the names."

He shook his head. "Confidential sources, Dale. You must know I won't give them up. But here's the thing ...."

She took a swig of tepid coffee. "Yes?"

"One and all, they *swear* PPL had no part in the bombing. That they abhor violence."

"You believe them?"

"Yes." More hesitation. "That's not to deny the possibility PPL and EPF have some overlap in membership. I'd be surprised if there weren't."

"People you suspect, but you won't identify." Her voice cracked. "Mass murderers!"

Deep breath. "Not anyone I deal with. I believe that. But are there ... zealots in the movement? Fanatics? Hell, yes."

"Then why *did* you call?"

"To pass along, for whatever it's worth, PPL's message. And on my part ... to share their obvious concerns over what EPF might attempt next."

July 9, 2035

Gotham Gridlocked!

Life throughout the metro area continues at a standstill as the ongoing heat wave turns more and more tarmacs and asphalt roads into gooey, impassable morasses. Electric utilities, plagued by widespread, heat-induced failures across their distribution networks, continue to buckle under an unprecedented demand for power. Heat-stroke cases have filled hospitals to their capacity. Relief is not expected until next week, when daily highs may fall below 100°.

By emergency decree, Mayor Watkins has shuttered all nonessential businesses and ordered nonessential workers to remain home. Neighboring jurisdictions throughout the Tri-State area are taking similar precautionary measures. The mayor has directed city buses and ride-service companies to suspend operations across the five boroughs. "Saving lives in this crisis requires, above all else, conserving power for residential air conditioning and city-operated cooling centers. In view of these unprecedented demands on the power grid, thermostats should be set no lower than 85 degrees and nonemergency vehicles should not be recharged."

At press time, the city's official death count from the heat emergency stands at 97, but authorities expect the total to rise significantly ....

—*New York Post*

Sonny picked diffidently at her dinner. David methodically shoveled down his meal, his attention on his datasheet. While Xander, doing his best to chew and swallow without tasting his portion of reconstituted swill, fretted upon his shortcomings as a leader. (MORALE'S BAD? YOUR JOB IS TO FIX IT.) Except that at his every attempt to wrap his head around the problem, all he came up with was the punch line of an old joke.

The floggings will continue until morale improves.

Xander cleared his throat. "Thank you both for not mutinying and leaving me here."

Sonny stirred mashed potatoes with her fork. "Not that I'm a pilot."

"Then thank *you*, David."

That earned Xander a grunt. *Someone's* dour attitude clearly hadn't changed.

Something else then. "Sonny, how's Cat?"

"Moved on."

And wasn't *that* familiar? Xander started to inquire about Giselle.

"Don't ask," David snapped.

Leaving … what as a safe topic? The latest trace of another organic chemical he'd never heard of to crop up in a core sample? How riveting! A vid they might re(re)(re)watch together that evening? The micro-gee exercise regimen they were ever more cavalier at maintaining? Because who doesn't enjoy being nagged?

Over the past week, Xander had grown sufficiently discouraged that he'd tried again, never mind the supposedly firm resolution otherwise, to get Cat's guidance. She'd responded with another one-liner at the fortune-cookie level. This time, he'd persisted. UMM, CAT GOT YOUR TONGUE?

All the response *that* drew was MEOW.

He was, most definitely, on his own. What to make of that insight remained a work in progress. Except, being honest with himself, for any element of progress.

As long as he was being honest, he already *knew* the underlying problem. David and Sonny were depressed. Hell, so was he. They were stuck out here together for an extra two years so Cruella could make a geopolitical point.

Xander tried again. "You guys have an opinion on the big Dirtside news?"

David looked up from his datasheet. "That in six months we'll have company and some new supplies? You'll pardon me for not suiting up yet to greet them."

NASA *had* launched its second mission, on the Fourth of July, no less. Eight people this time, flying two of Boeing-Mitsubishi's new Mars Clippers. Days later, with launch support to Ares Two complete, B-M had dispatched its corporate expedition with a dozen crew. This very day—and so, actual news—CMSA had sent its second mission. It had *four* vessels: two ships with four crew each, the freighter delayed by the 2033 launch SNAFU, and a new Roscosmos freighter that RKK Energiya expected to crew-rate on upcoming lunar missions. Finally, before this latest window closed, NEP planned to send two ships with eight more people.

Come January, the neighborhood population would more than double.

Xander tried again. "That's not the only news."

David slammed down his fork. "What, that your NASA administrator has resigned? It is a matter of the utmost indifference to me."

"There's more to it than the resignation," Xander said. "Van Dijk, and pretty much everyone across the political spectrum, is calling Ares, calling what *we've* accomplished, a huge success. With the follow-on mission on its way, the main thing—"

"Is so much crap." Sonny shoved aside her plate. "Worse than this. On the basis of *our* success, *he* plans to run for your president. But you know Van Dijk. You know the current president, as well. Is he qualified to succeed her?"

Not in one ambivalent voter's opinion. "I do my best to ignore politics. What I can tell you, what *I* consider the day's big news, is that Rebecca Nguyen will be the acting administrator." Because Becks, unlike Van Dijk, deserved much of the credit for their mission's success. There was no one Xander would rather see lead NASA. For whatever weight his endorsement might carry, he'd use his backchannel to lobby the president to make the gig official. "I've known Rebecca for years. She's ideal for the job."

Sonny perked up. "She'll see to it the samples on *Lewis* get a proper examination? Even after the EPF bombing?"

"You can count on it," Xander said. "Not a doubt in my mind."

"Good to know," David said. He returned to whatever he'd been studying. Sonny went back to sculpting her mashed potatoes.

Leaving Xander to muse that taking Teri Rodriguez up on her invitation to talk wasn't the worst idea.

August 1, 2035

The blocky, newly completed structure remained nameless, New Beijing being unpalatable to the Russians and New Moscow as unacceptable to the Chinese, while Oorvi's facetious compromise of New New Delhi amused no one. Kai had imagined the standoff over names would be the only issue with their permanent residence.

How naïve.

Seething with rage, he studied the change that had transpired overnight. A sixteen-button keypad had replaced the standard airlock control panel. Familiar Arabic numerals marked ten keys, while the remaining labels were in Cyrillic. A digital display sat above the keypad.

An electronic lock. A Russian-made, electronic combination lock. Where simple bolts had secured the original controls to the frame, the new panel was welded into place. Even a six-digit code would mean a million possible combinations.

What other nasty surprises had the Russians brought? Guns?

Kai began a slow circuit of the building. Behind one of its thick, double-walled, glass windows, Antonov and his minions were suiting up. Willing himself calm, Kai continued around to the locked entrance.

Mingmei had accompanied Kai that morning from their igloo. He mouthed, "Radio off." Private channels were private only by convention. She nodded.

He leaned over until their helmets touched. "How quick to replace this with a spare control panel?"

"Maybe ten minutes. No longer, sometime we're not around, for them to re-replace it. I wonder who has the most parts."

As did Kai. He also wondered if the Russians' control panel had tamper detection. On second thought, he didn't wonder about this panel being alarmed. He'd bet on it.

Kai pointed at the Mars Buggy, early morning sun gleaming off the cabin windscreen. Control that vehicle, and you controlled access to life-giving water. "Let's have a look."

Overnight, it also had acquired an electronic lock.

Oorvi was still indoors, doing preventive maintenance on some of their printers. He could ask her to suit up and join them, make the numbers equal for the inevitable confrontation. Kai was still weighing his options when, back the way they had come, the airlock cycled open. The three Russians stepped out. Ivan had the decency to look embarrassed.

"Radios on," Kai mouthed to Mingmei.

"Good morning, General," Antonov called, his tone smug. "How are you today?"

A few long strides closed the gap. "Surprised to see that you moved in overnight."

"New Moscow was ready, as were we. Why wait?"

"I see," Kai said. "A name we never agreed upon"—and never will—"and a modification that we haven't discussed. Did you anticipate uninvited visitors?"

Antonov waved disdainfully. "No need to discuss, as it doesn't concern you. You see—"

"Doesn't *concern* us?" Mingmei burst out.

Kai shot her a warning glance.

"You see," Antonov continued, "Moscow has decided we go our own way henceforth. New Moscow will be a fine base for us and for our colleagues now on their way."

Now on their way. The impetus of this power play laid bare in four short words. Antonov had long chafed at being the junior partner. His government, too. With reinforcements (and weapons?) on their way, beyond recall, with the successful launch of the new Russian spacecraft, Antonov and his people were … mutinying.

Kai chose for the moment not to acknowledge the implication. "Of course, this new building offers ample room for everyone. We'll need the access code."

"That won't be possible. Consider us to have become two separate missions. You can, of course, build yourselves another." As Kai held his tongue, Antonov added, "As necessary, we have ... resources to sustain the division."

Weapons, that had to mean. "How separate, with but the single Mars Buggy?"

The Russian smirked. "I won't allow my mission to be held hostage by an artificial water shortage. That would be irresponsible."

But *my* mission can be held hostage? "Living in such proximity, with such limited resources, we must find ways to cooperate."

"I'm sure there will be ways you can help."

Assist. Serve. Take orders from. The situation was intolerable, and the man insufferable, but Kai managed a bland response. "By all means, we shall coordinate going forward." His restraint, in some small measure, came of intuiting the traditional counsel his father's father (or was it the Buddha?) would have offered. To be angry is to let others' mistakes punish yourself. But in the main Kai stayed silent because, whether from *The Godfather* or a *Star Trek* movie almost as dated, he had absorbed another lesson.

Revenge is a dish that is best served cold.

September 8, 2035

Patrick set a heaping plate in front of Dale. A tall stack of blueberry pancakes. Four crispy strips of bacon. A mound of scrambled eggs. Grits. Twice what she could eat.

Still, nothing beat a weekend brunch, and everything smelled delightful. She'd yet to regain all the weight she'd lost in the hospital, rehab, and endless PT, and the dear had made it his mission to put it back on her. She was contemplating an array of syrup options, one more of his unnecessary but adorable indulgences, when the folded datasheet beside her plate dinged.

The terse text was from Arthur Schmidt. YOU'RE NEEDED ASAP. CAR AND DRIVER WILL BE OUTSIDE WITHIN FIVE MINUTES. CONFIRM."

CONFIRMED, she tapped out with a trembling hand.

Five minutes. Maybe long enough, given her still limited mobility, to change from PJs and robe into proper clothes. All while reassuring her husband. Though who was going to reassure her? An abrupt summons wasn't without precedent, even on a Saturday. But on such short notice? With a *driver*? That meant bodyguard. Sigh. For the past week she'd reveled in the normalcy of *not* having a security detail hovering about.

What the hell could be going on?

Dale shoved back her chair and reached for her cane. "Hon, that was the White House." Loosely speaking. The DNI must appear somewhere on a White House org chart. "Guess whose presence is requested."

"Well, eat something first."

"Sorry. A car's coming for me. They'll be here soon."

"Remind me," Patrick grumbled minutes later, helping her out to the curb, "*why* you want this job?"

"You know why." Even though she continued to wonder herself.

Two SUVs pulled up in front of the house. Both were standard government issue: black; dark tinted windows; foreboding. She could only shrug—doing her best not to look (more) worried—at Patrick's questioning expression. Why, especially after RML, would *anyone* want this job? Did the second vehicle signify renewed protection for Patrick and the house? If so, Arthur had ordered it. The quickest route to answers was going for a ride.

As Dale's car merged into traffic and, craning her neck, she saw the second car staying behind, she gave up on maintaining a serene exterior. Her driver and a second Secret Service agent in the vehicle, alas, denied knowledge about, well, anything. Neither, once she was escorted into Arthur Schmidt's inner sanctum, did the DNI clarify the situation beyond that *Rebecca Nguyen* had summoned them both regarding something urgent "the boss" must know. Something Rebecca would not disclose except in person.

The protective details and armored SUVs? Precautions Arthur had ordered in the *absence* of information.

Well, Dale understood one thing: the boss. They three reported only to the president.

Her imagination ran wild. DNI, NASA administrator, and science adviser. What could this be about? "Aliens?" she finally guessed, yawning despite herself. A brief wait at the front desk and the trek through the building to Arthur's office had exhausted her. Would she ever regain any stamina? "Could NASA have found signs of *aliens*?"

Arthur shrugged.

Minutes later, Rebecca arrived. Her face was ashen. Her hands trembled. At Arthur's offer of coffee or water or whatever, she shook her head. "Thanks for meeting on such short notice."

Her armed escort left without speaking, closing the door behind him.

Arthur had risen at Rebecca's arrival. He suggested gently, "Maybe you should sit."

Rebecca dropped onto more than sat upon the office's short sofa. "Canberra forwarded a scheduled report from *Lewis*. The transmission arrived midafternoon today per GMT and ship's time, still morning for us, but—a rare bit of good luck—that's more like 1:00 A.M. Sunday in Canberra. The lone guy on duty had the presence of mind to skip past about a dozen levels of supervision and contact me directly. Which doesn't preclude lots of people, ours and at partner agencies, from happening upon it, because incoming comms are automatically archived at multiple, dispersed servers. Nor can I be confident just Canberra picked up the transmission." She shivered. "It came in the clear. It's *meant* to be unsuppressible. And that's …."

Bad, Dale completed. Very, very bad. "Canberra?"

"One of three ground stations in NASA's Deep Space Network. Between Canberra and the stations in California and Spain, DSN can always reach out to or hear from any spacecraft."

Arthur sighed. "I'm guessing the LOS"—line of sight, Dale interpreted—"between *Lewis* and Canberra means the Chinese, Russians, and Indians might also have received … whatever."

Was that last a get-on-with-it prompt? Maybe. Dale knew *she* wanted to know what this was about. Even as she dreaded what Rebecca clearly hesitated to reveal.

Rebecca nodded. "If any of their DSNs happened to have an antenna pointed toward *Lewis* and in receive mode? Which they might. It's not as though *Lewis*'s return trajectory is a big secret. Then yes, one of them could have received this. For another, also the UAE. They constructed a ground station back in 2021, in Dubai, I believe, to support their first Mars orbiter. NEP rents comms capacity from the Emirates, so *they* might be in the loop. To be complete, any decent radio-astronomy observatory on that side of the planet might have received it."

"Received … what?" Dale asked.

Arthur raised a hand. "Back up. How sure are you this troubling transmission is authentic?"

"Sure?" Rebecca nibbled her lower lip. "Almost sure. We wouldn't be here otherwise. As certain as I can be without bringing in specialists. Which would take time I don't know we can afford, in case someone else *was* listening. The metadata that accompanied the recording, as best I can judge, is what I'd expect, is self-consistent ... always keeping in mind my engineering background was propulsion. Call this one more reason I miss having Xander around."

"Okay," Arthur said. "For now, we'll presume this transmission is authentic. I have people who can check on that."

"But what *was* the transmission?" Dale urged.

"Words ... can't suffice. You'll have to see." A cheek starting to twitch, Rebecca turned. "Arthur, I knew better than try bringing a datasheet into this building." (As Dale should have. Instead, by reflex she'd tucked hers into her purse on the way out the door. That comp now waited in a locker by the Security desk.) "I assume you can open a secure connection to a NASA server. Oh, and I had Canberra encrypt the file before sending it to me."

After more machinations than Dale chose to try following, or could have followed if she had, about firewalls and air gaps and decryption, the video was ready to go up on a big wall display.

"Brace yourselves," Rebecca whispered.

The face scarcely seemed human. Scarcely seemed a *face*.

Bloated, purple-mottled flesh, the swollen lips almost black. Oozing pustules. Tissues peeling and flaking, even to scattered glimpses of bone. The nose little more than naked, pitted cartilage. Eyes, except for anime-sized black pupils, all blood-red. Had it not been for the snaky, sweat-soaked tresses, languidly adrift like some somnolent Medusa, even to speculate at a gender would have been impossible.

Dale had no doubt who this was. Not given the distinctive copper hue of that hair. Not given Rebecca's assurances the signal had come through the Deep Space Network, from a specific bearing in the sky, during *Lewis*'s latest scheduled reporting window.

As surely as basic physics, geometry, and the faintness of the signal established the video's origin, those long, coppery tresses identified Cat Mancini: *Lewis*'s pilot.

Beneath that gargoyle-ish visage, a bit of polo shirt, collar and shoulders, came within the bridge-camera's view. That garment might once have been white. Sweat-sodden, blood-spattered, vomit-encrusted, it was difficult to know.

"W-we ... w-what ... ghkgh," the apparition began. The slurred, faltering audio was all but unintelligible. In her struggle to enunciate, Cat displayed bleeding gums, missing teeth, a swollen, purple tongue, and glimpses of a pus-coated throat. Loud pounding on the hatch behind her didn't help.

Rebecca paused the playback. "I expect digital enhancement can clear that up, at least to an extent. That'll take time, though, and I think we need to get this to the president *now*." She swallowed. Hard. "In any case, the video speaks for itself."

Arthur nodded. "I'll put the NSA on it, but the process *will* take time."

"I can see why we have an audio problem," Dale said. "It seems a miracle that poor woman can speak at all. But why is the video quality so bad?" Which it certainly *was*. Grainy, like some rabbit-ears-equipped, pre-digital TV from her youth. On a stormy night. Staticky, like that, too. Jittery as well, with scattered horizontal swaths blank, and occasionally whole frames.

Rebecca said, "The hi-def transmission format we're accustomed to requires far too much bandwidth for interplanetary use. The quality NASA vids everyone loves? Accurate, but misleading. That remote imagery was first buffered on-site, then transmitted in chunks over the DSN at rates well below even pre-HD broadcast standards. Retries are often necessary, and every retry takes minutes to request and as long again to receive. We reassemble the chunks, once we have them all, to show at proper speeds.

"Bottom-lining it, real-time vid with *Lewis* has to be low-res. Any individual data packets, and sometimes even entire frames, scrambled beyond the capability of error-correcting codes are discarded. That's why we see gaps and skips. Oh, and the real-time audio subchannel will have similar gaps, aside from the ... other difficulties."

Rebecca removed her glasses, pinched the bridge of her nose, seemed at a loss for words. (Headache, Dale diagnosed. Well, she also had one coming on. A migraine, if she had to guess.) "Comms and IT are Xander's forte. I don't mean to play favorites, but still I'm relieved he's safe on Phobos."

As shocking as was Cat's ruined face on the paused video, Dale intuited things would only get worse. *Was* anyone on Phobos safe? Or anyone on Mars? "Should we continue?"

In a voice little more than a whisper, Rebecca said, "We must."

384

Playback resumed, with Cat shuddering violently, her inarticulate speech trailing off into a mucousy gurgle. Fresh sweat beaded on her face; more, shaken off, wafted in droplets. With jaws clenched and cheeks spasming, the seizure went on and on.

Hawking up gobs of bloody phlegm, she finally regained a measure of control, got out a few scattered, intelligible words and short phrases. "… sample e-e-escaped … aboard … can see." Behind the bridge hatch, the tumult only got louder. "… in h-h-hours."

It seemed Cat tried to describe symptoms. Maybe she'd said something about trying antibiotics or antivirals. If so, they'd been ineffective against … whatever. Dale *hoped* digital enhancement would clear this up. The few snippets she might have understood suggested many systems of the body under attack at once.

No familiar disease matched what Dale saw, could explain what she might have heard. Never mind how, approaching two and a half years among the same few people, Cat could have been exposed now to anything familiar. Leaving only the *un*familiar.

"Pause," Rebecca said. "Dale, do you have any idea what's happened to Cat?"

She'd been racking her brains with that question. "Not yet, but we can't rely on my memory. I need to do a search against combinations of her visible symptoms."

Arthur said, "Any database or medical AIde you could want is next door at NCTC. I'll call over to clear you in."

It figured the National Counterterrorism Center had such resources—this providing a new reason to be depressed. "Good, thanks. A basic question before that. Rebecca, when did NASA last hear from *Lewis*? Was anyone sick at the time?"

"A scheduled check-in three days ago. Seemed routine. Cat made no mention of illness."

"What about Phobos? Any recent contacts there?"

Rebecca managed a wan smile. "Yeah, yesterday. A snide text from Xander, because 'his' White Sox are almost a lock for the AL postseason, and 'my' Yankees aren't."

"Doesn't sound like they're experiencing a mystery plague," Arthur said. "That's something."

"But aboard *Lewis*, we're talking three days or less. Whatever Cat's got acts ungodly fast." Dale's mind raced, rummaging memories

385

for anything capable of progressing this *quickly*. Not the activated manifestation of any latent genetic condition or autoimmune disease she'd ever heard of. Not, despite the crew's unavoidable long-term radiation exposures, any form of cancer. Not the emergence of any familiar dormant infectious agent, such as shingles from childhood chickenpox. Leaving her, unless the NCTC med library offered up some esoteric condition she'd never heard of, with the unimaginable. Or the spontaneous mutation of a common terrestrial bacterium or virus, fungus or archaeon, so altered as to laugh at the immune system. Or …. "I know we're all thinking this. It seems like she must have some *Martian* disease."

"Yeah," Rebecca said. "Okay, resume playback."

As Cat's narration continued, somehow rendered all the more terrible by its very unintelligibility, as Dale assured herself *this can't possibly get worse*—

A hand—mottled flesh sloughing from bone; tendons twitching; knuckles swollen—rose into the camera's view. Awkwardly clutching a serrated galley knife.

To begin, as the comm session dropped, sawing at Cat's throat.

"It is a capital mistake to theorize before you have all the evidence. It biases the judgment."

—Sir Arthur Conan Doyle
(Sherlock Holmes, in A Study in Scarlet)

"Scientists are used to struggling with Nature, who may surrender her secrets reluctantly but who fights fair."

—Carl Sagan

DIAGNOSIS

September 8, 2035

From Arthur's call, asserting an "urgent security matter" required immediate presidential attention, to walking into the White House, not three hours had passed. He spent that time in consultations with a parade of analysts. Rebecca spent much of it poring over the same, horrific video—as though an nth viewing might offer some ray of hope, some less awful interpretation—and the rest leaving cryptic requests with people around NASA.

Dale used those same hours at the NCTC library, searching and thinking furiously. How, despite all the precautions taken on Phobos, this could have happened. What *this* might be. What could be done. What should be done. Only to nod off over her research. Again, on the short ride from Virginia, to be nudged awake as the car arrived. All too aware that her weariness was less a matter of convalescence than of avoidance.

Instead of the Oval Office, this time they were directed to the nearby, windowless Roosevelt Room. The president, her chief of staff, and the veep were already there, seated at one end of the long conference table, FDR's portrait gazing down at them. By some signal or vibe too subtle for Dale to notice, Arthur guided Rebecca and her to the table's opposite end. As though merely to have seen the *Lewis* vid might have rendered them deathly contagious.

Arthur got out only a top-level recap, along with hardcopies of his first frame grab, before the president erupted. "You're telling me those fucking *assholes* from PPL and EPF were *right?*"

"It would appear so," Arthur responded mildly. His pocket chimed, and he gave his datasheet a glance.

"Whereas *you*"—a presidential finger jabbed at Dale—"were fucking *wrong*."

Wrong? No. Martian life had always been a possibility. Which was part of why she'd pushed so hard for a lunar facility to receive samples— only to be overruled. Why she'd arranged the doomed RML readiness review, expecting support from it for deferring a return mission.

Who here had been wrong?

Dale knew Cruella well enough to anticipate how any response along those lines would go over. "Perhaps, but if this is a Martian contagion, I wonder why no one on Mars itself has encountered it. As far as I know"—Dale turned to Arthur, who nodded—"no one there has had any unexplained illness. Nor have our three people remaining on Phobos. Regardless, you can have my resignation at any time."

An offer that, were it accepted, would delight Patrick.

"Mine, too," Rebecca said.

The president glowered. "I'd have had Matt Van Dijk's resignation over this, if not his head on a pike, if he hadn't resigned a couple months ago." She laughed humorlessly. "For what, if any *hint* of this situation ever comes out, might set the record for shortest presidential campaign." (A prediction at which the vice president smirked. As if Van Dijk were the veep's biggest problem. As if anyone thought he had a shot at the nomination. Hope springs eternal, Dale supposed.)

"But you two?" The president thumped the table. "You're needed. You're not going anywhere. Now with that settled, who else knows what's happened aboard *Lewis*? Will this leak?"

"We must assume," Arthur said. "I've tasked resources to determine whether any other deep-space network happened to be monitoring *Lewis* at the wrong time. I should hear back soon."

Resources. Determine. Hacking? Or moles? Dale didn't know, nor did it matter.

Rebecca offered, "I've got people compiling a list of radio observatories who could've picked up the transmission, and my AIde is monitoring the internet for any relevant chatter. I've also tasked someone trusted at our DSN to reestablish contact, if they can, with *Lewis*."

"How serious is this Martian bug?" Cruella gave another ironic laugh. "Excluding the obvious. I mean, with the pilot dead, won't *Lewis* either sail by or burn up in the atmosphere?"

Rebecca said, "Barring surprises, yes, it'll sail by. If the ship hits anything passing through the area, that'll be the Moon, not Earth. Going about twelve klicks per second. That's"—she frowned, doing math in her head—"27,000 miles per hour. The ship would be destroyed, but still, chunks might … spatter. I wouldn't want to bet copies of the bug can't survive."

Arthur's dataset chimed again. He nodded approval at whatever he saw there.

Bug, indeed. Dale said, "By all indications, the pathogen must be extremely resilient."

"Well, then I have excellent news," Arthur said. "That last text was from NSIC. The National Space Intelligence Center out of Wright-Pat AFB. Space Force's long-range radars no longer detect *Lewis*, only dispersing debris. *That's* on a path that diverged from the ship's course about the time of Cat's last message. None of it comes anywhere near Earth. Remember how we heard pounding on the bridge hatch? I believe Cat planned to divert and then blow up the ship, that we heard Giselle or Hideo trying to break in and stop her."

Dale sighed. "I guess Cat waited"—in terrible torment!—"till she could call in a report."

So little of which was intelligible.

Except that the *imagery* spoke volumes.

The chief of staff, until that point a silent note-taker, asked, "Maybe this doesn't matter, but how does a ship coasting through the middle of nowhere blow up?"

"Disable cooling on the cryogenic tanks, till the fuel vaporizes and they burst." Rebecca mused a bit. "Or overfill the combustion chamber with LOX and LH2 before ignition. If anyone would know how, what sensors to take offline, and what safety measures to disable, it'd be the pilot."

The president said, "Cat was a hero. Unless the news gets out, we've dodged a bullet."

"God damn it, *no!*" Rebecca barked. "Apologies, Ma'am, but *no*. You can forget *unless*. This won't, can't, be swept under some rug. Even if

Lewis were said 'just' to have gone silent and been lost. There will be major inquests, same as after the *Apollo 1* fire, the *Apollo 13* explosion, and the losses of the *Challenger* and *Columbia* shuttles. The public, the media, Congress, will all insist on it. NASA people up and down the line will, too. If none of that were true, well, JAXA and ESA also had crew aboard. Those agencies, their governments, their publics and media, will all demand an independent inquiry."

Cruella glared at Rebecca, and at Arthur of the still-chiming datasheet, as Rebecca continued. "Then there's everyone on Mars and Phobos. They need to be warned of the danger! They deserve the best minds on Earth focusing on what happened, if they're at risk, and what can be done about it. And what about the four *new* missions en route to Mars? We can't allow them to proceed in ignorance. Madam President, this information must come out."

"For that matter," Dale said, "There's the 24/7 push to ready Rocky Mountain Laboratories. If no sample return is coming, let's take the pressure"—and EPF bull's-eye!—"off them."

The president said, "If everyone's done lecturing—"

"It's become moot." Arthur leaned forward, handing the president his datasheet. "Dale's buddy Ira Coleman has broken the story. Somehow, PPL already knows. Their latest communiqué, trending everywhere, is one *epic* I-told-you-so wrapped around choice screen grabs from Cat's final broadcast."

September 9, 2035

"**W**hy did no one *listen* to me?" David demanded. "It was *never* worth the risk." In the negligible gravity of Phobos, a person couldn't storm out of a room, nor did the habitat offer anything but curtain-off-able nooks to storm into, but David did his sticky-slippered best. He seemed close to tears. Sonny, as plainly, was stunned.

Xander himself wanted to scream. At the nightmare that had taken his friends. At the flood of guilt over, well, this entire accursed expedition. The Phobos mission had been *his* brainstorm. The improvised deep drilling, and the machinations to make that drilling possible, were all *his* doing. As far as he knew, everyone on Mars proper remained healthy, while he'd pushed and pushed until his mission delved deeply enough to retrieve the native pathogens.

NASA had uploaded a text summary with some frame grabs from Cat's final transmission. As if that imagery weren't proof-positive his friends had met gruesome deaths, there'd also been the Space Force announcement of *Lewis*'s diversion and self-destruction. After PPL's leak of the images, nothing less than that disclosure would have averted worldwide panic.

Good call, Cat, Xander thought. A leader to the end.

However morbidly curious he was to process everything for himself, he'd have to wait. For Arthur's experts, if they could, to clean up the video. For other specialists, if they could, to recover the audio.

Followed, after however long all that would take, with maybe *days* for the restored file to upload. DSN had to continue to support its lunar missions, the Ares Two ships on their way, and a good dozen or so deep-space robotic missions of NASA and its partners.

Knowing what little he did? Knowing it might be weeks, or *never*, till he learned more? That was unbearable. (Uh-huh. Well, IT'S NOT ABOUT YOU. Another of Cat's pithy observations on leadership.)

Xander had asked Sonny and David to the dining area to share news of the disaster. Now, only he and Sonny remained. She sat with elbows on the table, head tipped into her hands, dangling hair obscuring her face.

With a sudden shudder, she straightened. Professional detachment, or just its facade? "I'm going to the biolab. Give me a hand?"

"Let it wait a bit," Xander said. A day. A week. "This is a lot to take in."

"I love … loved Cat. And I *failed* her. I failed the *three* of them." Anguish spilled out in a torrent. "I was so sure every biosample was long dead. Yes, microfossils. Yes, organic traces. Nothing more. Nothing intact. Nothing alive, even in a dormant state. But I missed something. I *mishandled* something. How else could it have …?"

Mournful music began, drifting from David's sleep cubby. Mozart's Requiem?

Xander reached across the table, took Sonny's hands.

She glanced down at their joined hands, then up at his face. "Cat wanted me to return with her. If I had, maybe I'd have figured out what was happening. Maybe I'd have *stopped* it."

He squeezed gently. "Or you'd also be dead, and we'd have no hope of learning what got aboard. What we still must contend with *here*."

Because they *did* need to figure this out.

"You're right. I'll stay out of the lab till my mind starts working again." She managed a fleeting smile. "But soon."

"Okay."

"No, I mean it." Sonny reclaimed her hands, then stood. "But now, I need to be alone with my thoughts."

Thus leaving Xander alone with *his* thoughts. Did he want that? Not the least bit, as though that mattered. (IT'S NOT ABOUT YOU.) "Of course. Whatever you need."

She retreated behind the curtains of the exercise alcove. The treadmill motor started up, its drone competing with the dirge.

Xander went to the galley alcove for coffee and chocolate. Because: Feed a fever. Feed a cold. Above all, feed depression. Pacing in Phobian gravity was as unproductive as storming off, but, to the *thp-thp-thp* of walking with sticky slippers, he gave it his best shot.

Conspicuous by its absence from the day's dismal news was any mention of the follow-on missions. Risk horrific deaths from an unknown pathogen? Or abort the missions?

Not a difficult choice.

Still, nibbling (oh, the irony) on a Mars bar, he made his way through scenarios. Mission Control had time, entire months, to reach a final decision. If landing the ships then en route continued to seem unsafe, swinging *around* the planet to return the way they'd come would burn less fuel than landing. Well, not exactly the way they'd come—Earth and Mars alike having continued along in their orbits—but nonetheless back sunward. The ships carried more than enough food to last while they chased after Earth. Two years or so, Earth to Mars to Earth? He took out a datasheet to run the numbers—

Nope, no one *here* deflecting. No one *here* loath to imagine what it'd mean for the Ares Two ships to speed past with their cargo of food and replacements for worn-out gear.

Well, maybe they could land, offload, and then go on their way. Somewhere on the far side of Phobos, perhaps, remote from anything and everything his team had ever touched. Somewhere safe from life-bearing meteorite spatter from Mars. Or, to be super-cautious, somewhere on the far side of never-visited, also tidally locked, Deimos. *Clark* could fly there for the pickup once *Leif Erikson* and *Sacagawea* had come and gone.

Except either scenario was so much wishful thinking. Meteorite spatter from Mars sometimes reached Earth. Of course, such spatter, and more of it, reached Phobos. As, for that matter, Mars spatter must sometimes settle upon the back side of the more remote Deimos. Not that anyone would want a second possible plague ship to touch another moon.

Still, two of CMSA's four approaching ships, those only bearing supplies, *could* land. Perhaps Carter would share. His people could drive supplies to some remote spot on Utopia Planitia. Once they'd withdrawn, robots could load the donations onto a lander or landers, or even aboard *Clark*, without exposing anyone on the ground to contamination.

Uh-huh. With NASA's missteps, *his* missteps, being to blame for this mess, why would anyone give away any of what might be their last-ever resupply?

Leaving what?

Absent an understanding of events aboard *Lewis*, and how to prevent anything like it from ever happening again, he, David, and Sonny were screwed.

Emails from her mother and Xander clued in Teri before her employers could be bothered.

Mom, naturally, worried about her only child. She *wasn't* hung up deciding how best to spin the ghastly news which, in translucent text on Teri's HUD, with the wilderness of Mars as its backdrop, became that much more surreal.

Teri wouldn't be the only one getting a panicked note from home. If, for once, she were lucky, she'd been the first since that day's routine download to have an idle moment. Now to get everyone inside before their own scary, anxious emails distracted them. A moment of inattention here could kill as readily as disease. Also, faster.

She announced on the common channel, "There's important information, *not* a matter of safety"—in any immediate sense—"to discuss. Bring what you're doing to a convenient stopping point. We'll meet inside in fifteen minutes."

Sweeping dust from solar panels was interruptible. Teri completed the row she'd had half finished when the emails had arrived, then loped to the as-yet unnamed Mars mansion. She found Reuben and Maia already inside. The rest soon appeared.

"Okay, today's news from Earth," Teri began, only to grind to a halt at a loss for words. Suitable words, anyway. *Say something!* "There's no easy way to put this. You know three from the Phobos team headed back last May. They're not going to make it."

Once she'd started, the tale poured out in a torrent, with all the gory details from the AP article appended to Mom's email.

Keshaun broke a stunned silence. "Holy shit."

Teri nodded. "Yeah, that about sums it up."

"They don't know what did this? Or how?"

"If so, no one's released the information." If and when NASA knew, they'd tell Xander, and she felt confident he'd pass it along. If, by then, the bug hadn't wiped out Phobos, too, a prospect that made her feel sadder still. "I don't know much. The company hasn't weighed in yet."

"Jesus, we should have left while we had the chance." Julio put a protective arm around Islah. "Will we be abandoned here?"

Would they be? None of them had shown any sign of infection. Not that she knew that what had struck aboard *Lewis* had been an infection, but what else could it have been? "Short answer? I can't say. Again, I haven't yet heard from the partners."

Nor did Teri have any sense what they'd say when they did comment. Which drove them more, greed or fear? If the latter, fear of what? Plague that might erupt here or—if her suspicions were correct—the imploding climate of Earth?

"How about our neighbors?" Islah asked. "Will they be re-supplied? Reinforced?"

Following the *Challenger* launch disaster, and again after *Columbia* disintegrated high above Texas, NASA had grounded its space-shuttle fleet for more than two years. Teri couldn't imagine answers any sooner from whatever inquest *this* catastrophe spawned—with the inbound missions due in four months. Ares Two, she felt certain, would be waved off. As for the Chinese, she lacked intuition.

She said, "Once we finish, I'll contact Carter and Xander to ask what they've been told."

With every expectation she'd hear nothing encouraging.

September 20, 2035

"The m-medic AIde knows of n-nothing to remotely match it. It sn-sneers at broad-spectrum antibiotics. And at broad-spectrum antivirals."

Not to mention the immune system.

Dale paused the video so painstakingly enhanced by Arthur's computer whizzes. She couldn't understand why Xander and Sonny wanted to inflict the somewhat-repaired video on themselves, but they did. Okay, Dale *did* understand. In their shoes, she'd have demanded the file, too. That didn't make the insistence any less masochistic. In any event, she was determined to have something instructive to text before the laborious upload over DSN was complete.

Laborious, true, but nonetheless certain to happen within another few days.

She couldn't have paused playback at a worse spot, Cat's face frozen in a terrifying rictus. With a shudder, Dale swiveled to run queries on another datasheet. Both Ares One ships had left for Mars carrying a plethora of broad-spectrum antivirals and antibiotics, exploiting unrelated microbial vulnerabilities. *All* meds failing must say a scary lot about the pathogen. Then again, this late in the mission, the ship's pharmacopoeia might have been depleted.

"Fleming"—her AIde—"take a message for Sun Ying at Asaph Hall base. Start message: Which medicines, in what quantities, were aboard *Lewis* when it started home? Pause message. Strike 'started home.' Replace with 'departed Phobos.'"

References to the home Sonny might never see again? *Not* cool.

"I *thought* I heard you." (Patrick. She hadn't heard him padding downstairs and into the first-floor study. She swiveled the desk chair to face him. Barefoot, and as silent as a mute cat. Like Dale, he wore PJs and a robe.) "Why are you up, hon? It's three in the morning."

"I couldn't sleep."

He gestured at Cat's disintegrating face. "That won't help. Not to be a noodge, but maybe the point of having a staff is *not* to work round the clock."

The truer statement would be that her deputy had staff. They were how the Office of Science and Technology Policy monitored the vast federal research enterprise, how it churned out its many reports and recommendations. While her name topped OSTP's org chart, that was a polite fiction. Her primary job, often her *only* job, was serving as the administration's public face on science. Was advising the president on matters scientific, keeping her on the scientific straight and narrow. Responsibilities at which Dale felt she'd failed spectacularly.

All of which they'd discussed before.

"Here's a thought," Patrick said. "How about you chuck that thankless job before it kills you, and I mean that literally. You quit yours, and I'll quit mine. We'll do stuff together that's, oh, I don't know … fun. Also, safe."

"You love your job. Besides, rumor has it those beans won't count themselves."

"One, I *enjoy* my job. I *love* you. B, I've counted beans long enough, and we've saved enough of them, to know for certain that neither of us ever needs to work another day. And gamma, don't travel and spoiling the grandkids sound *nice?*"

"You're a dear, but I can't. Not with this situation unresolved. Not with our people, on Phobos and more on their way, in limbo. But you can go back to bed."

Instead, Patrick extracted heavy tumblers and a decanter of Scotch from the credenza. He splashed out generous portions, handed her the fuller glass. "A numbing agent, if I may presume to prescribe for the doctor."

"At least sit."

He did, in a leather wingchair across the study.

Dale restarted the vid, swiping the volume low in hopes Patrick would nod off.

"I doubt I could l-last even another hour. But whatever is killing us? Has already killed Hideo? It survived, even if d-dormant, the hard r-r-radiation and near-vacuum and the bitter c-cold of Mars. Maybe f-for eons. It will outlast *us*. It thrives … *in* u-us. It can't ever g-get to Earth. Ever g-g-get near other people.

"So, I'm making certain that w-won't happen. I've only waited this l-long"—for a scheduled DSN scssion, Dale understood—"so y-you'd know." A quick sideways-and-back dip of Cat's head seemed to indicate the hatch that flexed and boomed behind her. "Even though opinions differ. Call this my final command decision."

Dale killed the playback before its grisly finale, wishing a different verb had come into her mind. As she wished for something, anything, to give her, or any of the trusted specialists to whom she'd provided copies of the enhanced recording, a sense what they were dealing with.

"How many times of you watched that?" Patrick asked.

At least a dozen, and more appalling with each viewing. "I don't know. Several."

"Then tell me, what do you think happened up there?"

She took a cautious sip of Scotch. "I see several possibilities. A dormant Martian bug reawakened in the benign conditions of *Lewis*'s cabin. Or a mutated version of a Martian bug, given the hard-radiation environment the ship was in. Or a terrestrial bug, like a gut bacterium mutated into something unstoppable."

"Well, if that last one, it's no reason to blame Mars." The swig he downed was anything but cautious. "Or it's a reason not to go anywhere off-world."

"I offered that last possibility only for completeness. Astronauts, cosmonauts, taikonauts, and tourists have collectively spent hundreds of years in space. It's unlikely the mutation of a familiar bacterium or virus just happened for the first time. If one somehow did, it's unlikely ever to occur again."

But not impossible. Still, what was it Phil Moskowitz had said on her LTEE tour? They'd been discussing when—and when not—convergent evolution occurred among his E. coli strains, often in the context of antibiotic resistance.

The memory surfaced: "Some physical adaptations require multiple genetic mutations. That alone makes it improbable that two populations will evolve those adaptations in identical ways. Convergence is even less frequent when the order of multi-gene mutations matters."

Improbable did not mean *impossible.*

Around a yawn, Patrick said, "I don't get how life on different worlds can ever be similar enough to affect one another. I mean, isn't evolution the result of one chance occurrence after another? Maybe only the fittest survive, but I always thought the meaning of 'fit' changed. Like when that asteroid took out the dinosaurs. Random."

Not all the dinosaurs. Some survivors went on to evolve into birds. Also, not important. "Yes and no. Because it's also true that similar conditions can push evolution in a common direction." Like Ira Coleman's flying squirrels and sugar gliders, groundhogs and wombats. Or the frequent convergences among LTEE bacterial lines.

"Devil's advocate here." Yawn. "Wouldn't the basic chemistry have to be the same for one world's bugs to affect another world's life? Why would it be?"

Devil's advocate? At *this* hour? She knew he was trying to help. Told herself not to take out her fears and frustrations on him. Reminded herself of a lesson learned early in the academic phase of her career: To know that you understand something, teach it.

"You'd think." She took another sip. "We already *do* know Martian and Earthly life have biochemical similarities. I mean, our biologist-slash-doctor on Mars has seen it, again and again, with all sorts of organic molecules.

"How those similarities arose? We might never know." She'd *discussed* panspermia more than once with the president and often with a gaggle of West Wingers. The necessary repetitions implied she'd only tried and failed to *explain.* "Single-celled life might easily"—stretching a point—"have crossed between our neighboring planets aboard meteorites. Or drifted to both planets from much farther away. Either way, life on Earth and Mars might be related, and so based on the same chemistry."

Only it was deeper than "mere" biochemistry. Some essential mechanisms of cellular architecture dated way back. Ribosomes, for one. But before dawn was no time to try explaining protein synthesis

401

to an accountant. Not even a dear, sweet accountant doing his yawning best to help.

"Very distant cousins," he said stubbornly.

Aside from that whole convergent-evolution possibility, how different might conditions have been in early Martian and early Earthly oceans? Water was water. "You have distant cousins who manage to annoy you."

"Touché." He shifted in his chair, its leather squeaking. "Not the most compelling analogy, but touché."

She took a larger swallow of Scotch, the burn as it went down somehow soothing. "If you don't buy panspermia, try this idea for size. Astrophysicists claim one set of physical laws applies across the universe, across all time. Chemists say one periodic table characterizes the chemical elements and their possible interactions … everywhere. Maybe, and I'm spitballing here, universal laws lead in just one way to ensembles of self-replicating, energy-harvesting, entropy-defying mega-molecules. By which I mean …."

"At some basic level, only one type of life." He finished his Scotch, then stood to pour himself another. "Top off yours?"

"I don't know …." Even as Dale hesitated, something tickled the back of her mind. Some casual conglomeration of what they'd discussed and her random associations to all that. Possible biochemical similarities. Ancient origins of some critical cellular mechanisms. Panspermia. LTEE. Some of Patrick's more annoying cousins. Antibiotic resistance.

The fast-acting pathogen aboard *Lewis*, given Cat's last report, was antibiotic-resistant and antiviral-resistant. The human immune system seemed helpless against it. It must have involved a recent mutation, else whatever they had carried aboard would have struck earlier in the flight. Further, Dale thought it must have involved some improbable mutation. Otherwise, the people on Phobos, presumably exposed to the same pre-mutated Martian biota, would by now have suffered the same fate.

"Are you okay, hon?" Patrick asked gently.

"Yes. No. Maybe. I need a moment to think."

A fluky *set* of mutations? Maybe one in which intermediate stages were viable only with the individual mutations coming in a specific order. If so, breeding the pathogen had entailed improbability piled upon improbability: Horrible luck squared, or even cubed. The combination might never happen again! But even as Dale experienced a glimmer of hope, as she pondered how these hypotheses might be put to the test, that elusive memory continued nagging at her.

From her LTEE lab visit? Perhaps?

But no. The symposium where she'd killed time *before* her lab appointment.

The lecturer, for much of her talk, had dwelled on wholesale gene swapping among microbes. How such lateral gene transfer moved whole swaths of genes at once. How widespread the process must have been before robust cell membranes evolved. How, if to a lesser extent, such transfers still occurred, and from bacteria to viruses, as well.

She hadn't had any reason to speculate, as Dale now did, about long dormant Martian microbes perhaps yet to evolve that kind of robust cell membranes ....

With a shiver, Dale drained her tumbler. When Patrick poured her a generous refill, his brief presence scarcely registered.

Any number of pathogens might lie dormant in people. Mycobacterium tuberculosis sometimes hid for years in the lungs' air sacs. Human herpesviruses from long-ago mononucleosis or chickenpox also lurked. There were others.

Such pathogens might have shed genes that ended up incorporated wholesale into Martian microbes and viruses. Which might have combined a highly evolved terrestrial method of infecting human cells with—piling guess upon speculation upon surmise—a Martian-evolved mechanism fatal to ancient, ubiquitous, essential, cellular machinery. Perhaps a hybrid bacterium whose metabolites were toxic to ribosomes, stopping protein production and cell replication.

A chimera that might be—however precise and scary, there was no avoiding the word—so *alien* as to evade any immune-system response ....

Were these pieces of a puzzle? Or random synapse misfires, a mishmash of Scotch, sleep deprivation, and desperation for answers?

Suppose she wasn't making herself see patterns where none existed. Then what?

Then she'd glimpsed the recipe for an appalling hybrid pathogen. A recipe *independent* of improbable sequences of random single-gene mutations. A recipe that could occur over and over and over by lateral gene transfer.

A Franken-crobe against which terrestrial life might be—in fact, appeared to be—defenseless.

October 3, 2035

"**W**hat will become of us?" Mingmei asked.

Kai kept his eyes on the printer relocated (some might say snatched, but screw them) from the communal machine shop to their shelter. "You know what I know." Which was more than either of them would have been told were Colonel Jin still in charge. More and more, Kai wondered if ignorance *was* bliss. "Steel, please."

She retrieved a squeeze tube of powdered feedstock from a nearby cabinet. (Of course, the cabinet was nearby. Everything in the shelter was. Yet again, inwardly, Kai raged at that bastard Antonov, smug in his spacious New Moscow.) "Then what do you believe will happen to us?"

That we'll die here, the only uncertainties being how soon and how lingering the experience. Of a gruesome plague, perhaps, as had taken three lives on the American ship. By some new treachery on the part of the Russians. For the lack of crucial replacement parts, or trace nutrients, or any of a thousand items of cargo he feared would sling right past them.

Not that Beijing had conveyed anything about the disaster. Not that, if Moscow had volunteered information to Antonov, he had shared it. ISRO had its own DSN, but Oorvi was adamant her people had also been silent on the topic. *Xander Hopkins* had passed along information he'd received from his government. Because alerting others to danger was the moral thing. It was what neighbors did.

404

After weeks of official silence, weeks of mounting stress, *Kai* had broached the topic of the disaster with Mission Control, had demanded to know its impact on the Chìdì Two mission. Only then had CMSA acknowledged the crisis. Even that admission was vague and unhelpful, as they denied that any decision on further landings had been reached.

Only then did emails from family and friends begin to arrive expressing their worry. Of *course,* they'd known! Not even what the West mocked as the Great Firewall could keep unapproved Western news out of the country. It went to prove—as Kai had long assumed, anyway—that the State censored even the "private" messages sent to them over China's DSN. Doubtless personal messages he and his colleagues sent in the other direction were also censored.

Were the Chìdì Two crews still in the dark? Kai guessed yes. It wouldn't do for them to dwell on the risk they'd never signed up for—or that no one could force them to land on Mars.

The molecule (atom? quark?) of consolation? Antonov's delusions of Martian grandeur, of a Russian/Martian empire, would also be derailed.

With great care, Kai squeezed fine metal powder into a printer reservoir.

"Well, Kai?"

"I see no reason why the cargo ships shouldn't land. I expect"—hope for!—"at least that degree of assistance." Of course, he also expected that the Russians would try to keep the best parts of that delivery to themselves. Somehow, he must prevent that.

His answer seemed to satisfy her because she changed subjects. "Is Oorvi safe?"

Safer than *they* were, that being another thought he'd keep to himself.

When another visit to the well became necessary, he and Antonov had spent hours arguing who would go. Antonov didn't want to send two Russians. "Being fair," he'd said, not that Kai believed a word of it. Two Russians away in the Mars Buggy would've left three-to-one odds against the lone remaining Russian. Kai had been as averse to send two of his people. Not that much remained here for Antonov to steal.

"Oorvi and Masha are friends," Kai finally offered. Had been friends, throughout training and the flight to Mars. Remained close on Mars, in the months before Antonov's treachery. He could hope they still were. Overriding every other concern was that they *all* needed water, and no one dare travel unaccompanied as far as the well. Pairing Oorvi and Masha seemed the least bad option. "*She* feels safe."

"I still worry."

No more than I, Kai thought.

They waited in companionable silence while the printer slowly deposited and fused layer upon layer of metal powder.

Mingmei hadn't asked how long the uneasy détente here since the plague announcement would last. Good, because how should he know? *Beijing* remained conflicted.

True, Beijing had counseled everyone, Russians included, to exercise "good will for the safety of all." They'd *also* sent Kai command files, onetime-pad-encrypted, to print parts for their own electronic combination locks. More tellingly, they'd forwarded files with which to construct electromagnetic coil guns. Mars was seriously deficient in nitrogen for synthesizing nitrocellulose or nitroglycerin or even simple gunpowder to propel conventional bullets.

And so, before his eyes, the handgrip and barrel for their first weapon was taking shape. If barrel was even the proper term, that emergent rod being solid rather than a tube. By any name—combined with a control chip, mini-fuel cell, a trigger mechanism, and a hand-wound coil of copper wire—the coil gun would blast out steel washers. But if the situation ever descended to gunplay, they must all be doomed.

Near-vacuum and projectile weapons did *not* mix.

Again and again, Kai had assured himself there was a better way. Ever wondering what that might be ....

B-M Revises Mars Mission

Following the recent *Lewis* tragedy, Boeing-Mitsubishi today announced Daedalus, its self-funded Mars mission, has shifted its sights from the planet to a Martian moon.

Mio Abe, corporate spokeswoman, explained, "The uncertainties surrounding the *Lewis* incident make further human activity on Mars unacceptably risky for the foreseeable future. Phobos having been a transit point for the deadly contagion, that moon must also be considered off-limits. Deimos, however, is expected to offer the same resources of ice and hydrocarbons, with none of the biological hazards, of its twin moonlet.

"Boeing-Mitsubishi has therefore re-tasked our vessels en route to Mars to establish a base on Deimos. For the safety of their crews, and to preserve Deimos as a resource for all humankind, we urgently recommend that all persons and spacecraft that have touched down on Mars or Phobos avoid Deimos.

"Over the coming years, Boeing-Mitsubishi anticipates using its base on Deimos as a jumping-off point for tapping the vast mineral wealth of the Asteroid Belt ...."

—SpaceNews

Terrorists Strike Power Grid

Synchronized attacks across the nation early this morning struck more than a dozen coal-fired power stations. Preliminary indications point to fertilizer bombs aboard rented tractor-trailers whose control and safety-override software had been hacked.

The stations involved have been removed from service pending a thorough assessment of damage and all necessary repairs. "As a precautionary measure" in response to lost generation capacity, the Ministry of Power invoked nationwide third-tier conservation measures. Minister Banerjee pledged close cooperation with the Ministry of Home Affairs on increased security at these and other critical infrastructure facilities. The prime minister plans to make a statement on the attacks at 8:00 P.M.

In a communiqué released moments after the attacks, the terrorist group Earth Protection Front took responsibility, labeling continued coal-based power generation in the Thirties "willful blindness at best, and ecocide by any measure."

The Central Bureau of Investigation is pursuing reports that at some targeted stations, allies or sympathizers of the EPF opened gates and lowered security barriers before the attacks ....

—Times of India

Call this my final command decision.

Xander wondered if he'd ever get those words out of his mind. If he'd ever be half the leader Cat had been. If the three survivors could avoid more tragedy.

"You're muttering again." Sonny never looked up from preparing another petri dish.

For weeks now, they had spent most of their waking hours in the biolab. The things to be analyzed, cultured, or otherwise processed seemed endless. Fresh sections extracted from every Martian core whose earlier samples had gone aboard *Lewis*. Daily blood draws from the three of them. Random scrapings of regolith: from smudges on every structure's walls, floor, ceiling, airlock, and air filter. From much-spattered spacesuits—and even speckles tweezed from their boot treads. From the much-disturbed ground alongside the surface guide wires.

All that effort having yet to suggest as much as a glimpse of a hint to whatever had gotten loose aboard *Lewis*.

At least while David collected surface samples, they were spared his bored advocacy for a flight to Deimos. As though—even before Boeing-Mitsubishi revised its plans—mere variety could justify risking contamination of *another* world.

As sullen as David had become, Xander had half-expected to exit the biolab one day to find *Clark* missing. He'd slept better after remembering it had taken two people to land each ship on Phobos: the pilot and someone suited-up in the airlock, wielding the launcher for explosive-tipped harpoons. The B-M crews must be improvising harpoons of their own.

"Mutter, mutter, mutter," Sonny reminded.

"Sorry," Xander said. "Just thinking."

"If only I were up to that."

"Time for a break, then."

"True." She completed some fiddly, fine-motor task, extracted her arms from the glove-box sleeves, and turned to face him. "Also, not what I meant."

There was more than enough guilt to go around. (GUILT IS USELESS. YOU FEEL BAD? BOOHOO. QUIT YOUR NAVEL-GAZING AND MAKE THINGS BETTER.) All he managed to come up with was refocusing her thoughts. "That you've yet to spot anything here must *mean* something. Could Dale's theory"—nightmare scenario—"be correct?"

"Let's call it one of several possibilities." Sonny slid off her stool, stretched, and got a bulb of cold water. "Suppose some long-dormant Martian microbe slipped past me. It got into the humid warmth of the ship, sort of like Mars in the good old days, feasting on dead skin cells, of which we each shed millions daily. Well-fed bacteria on Earth reproduce rapidly, some in as little as twenty minutes, so assume Martian varieties can, too. Pretty soon, there could have been myriads aboard. And then? Natural selection could do a lot.

"In Dale's speculation, they'd have started out harmless. However aggressive they were on Mars in some distant era, they'd never have evolved the ability to penetrate the membranes of living human cells. Never had the opportunity to."

"Hold on a sec," Xander said. "If a Martian microbe can't penetrate cell membranes, how are shed cells its food?"

"Those are dead. They fall apart. Or dust mites chomp them up."

"Okay." Also, gross.

"Now suppose that—whether by random mutations *or*, per Dale's theory, by lateral gene transfer from a pathogen one of us carried along—the Martian microbe acquires a membrane-penetrating skill …."

"We have Franken-crobe. Then, yes to Dale's idea?"

Sonny shook her head. "I'd call it feasible. That's a far cry from believing in it, much less confirming it."

"What's the alternative?"

"Mutation of some *Earthly* bacterium or virus. That could also involve some dormant pathogen any of us brought along, but it needn't be that. We're each host to kilos of bacteria. By count, though not by mass, that bacterial load outnumbers our human cells. The microbiome is benign—until it isn't. Until the balance among the myriad kinds gets out of whack." She shivered. "Until, by chance, some dangerous mutation occurs, and the altered strain takes off. In this case, the mutation would have had to be unusually virulent."

A theory to absolve them both of responsibility. A theory to render the tragedy a fluke, that might permit them, someday, to go home. "Is *that* what you think happened?"

She grimaced. "What I *think* makes no difference. For what it's worth, I came up with yet another scenario."

Wonderful. As though they didn't already have more possibilities than data.

Uh-huh. Well, LISTEN *BEFORE* YOU FIND FAULT. Not to mention a kick in the metaphorical pants Cat hadn't included but that he richly deserved. To be a smartass is *so* much easier than being responsible.

He said, "I'm all ears."

"Are you familiar with retroviruses?"

Only in the vaguest sense. "Assume not."

"No virus can reproduce itself. They all, in some manner, hijack cell machinery to make copies. Retroviruses burrow into a host cell's DNA, that being as good a strategy as any for selfish genes to get themselves reproduced. Our genome is replete with inert stretches of DNA. Many such snippets are believed to be ancient retroviruses, or what those later mutated into."

"Okay. I think I'm following you."

"I'll try to spare you the med-speak. Mutation from the radiation environment aboard *Lewis* could have activated a dormant retrovirus within some cell of anyone aboard. So might penetration of a cell by an original or mutated Martian pathogen. The affected cell then made copies of the virus. When that cell died, it spewed copies, maybe hundreds of copies, of the no longer dormant virus. The process then rapidly repeats."

"Oh, like HIV is a retrovirus. But HIV spreads between victims by"—Xander tried his best to be clinical while discussing her dead lover—"exchanging bodily fluids. That doesn't seem like anything that could have happened on *Lewis*."

"That's how HIV spreads. There are other such retroviruses, like human T-lymphotropic virus types one and two. But not all retroviruses spread that way. Such as …." She poked at her datasheet. "Right. Such as JSRV. Jaagsiekte sheep retrovirus is an *airborne* retrovirus that causes cancer in sheep."

"An unlikely occurrence, I take it?" If so, another guilt-relieving possibility. "Is there evidence to support an awakened-retrovirus theory?"

"*No*, damn it! I have no actual evidence to support *any* scenario. Nor any idea how it, whatever *it* is, spreads. Or what, if anything, can be done about it."

"We'll figure it out."

"You promise?"

"Promise?" CREDIBILITY IS YOUR SUPERPOWER. NEVER MAKE A PROMISE YOU CAN'T KNOW YOU WILL KEEP. "I can't promise. But if this *can* be figured out? I'm confident we will."

"You're sure about this?" Julio asked Teri.

Was she? The answer depended on the antecedent of *this*. Sure that what they were about to undertake was one hundred percent safe? Not even close. Sure this was the least worst course of action? Almost. But sure they had passed the time for second thoughts? Sure she must exude the confidence she did not wholly feel? "I am."

"Then we do it." He started across the crater floor toward a distant pile of equipment.

"Let's wait for the others," Teri called.

Because she and Julio had been the first off *Burroughs*. Given everything she wanted done here, this was an all-hands-on-deck effort. Given the amount of equipment required and the distance from Barsoom, doing this by SUV would have taken multiple trips, each trundling drive lasting days. Hence, they'd flown here—or hopped, as Reuben disparagingly called the maneuver. He'd landed *Burroughs* on a plateau within the volcanic crater of Ascraeus Mons.

Julio paused, a few steps downslope from her. "You're the boss."

True. The mystery remained: Why?

How did a title bestowed years before, by people a world apart, continue to carry weight? Every last person on the team was here because *she* had chosen them. Jake and Paula had died on *her* watch. When the opportunity to return home had approached, *she* got everyone to stay.

An opportunity that might never come again.

As Reuben finished his shutdown procedure, waiting for others of the team to emerge from the ship, Teri permitted herself a rare moment to savor the stark majesty of this place. They stood on a flat expanse near the bottom of an enormous bowl. The crater rim loomed kilometers overhead, and yet they were at one of the planet's highest elevations. This mountain was *big*—

If not as huge as the challenge of living on a hostile planet. Their survival depended on literal tons of high-tech equipment.

411

Some had already worn out. More was burning out, or simply erod-ing, from the ubiquitous windblown grit. If new equipment and replacement parts they'd counted on failed to arrive, if NEP wrote them off, they were screwed.

As seemed more likely with each passing day. Mission Control continued responding to queries about the situation with bland variations upon a theme. "We're studying how best to proceed." About as reassuring as, "Your call is very important to us. Please hold." Or, "Don't call us. We'll call you." Teri's more pointed questions—then, point-blank *demands*—sent direct to Blake elicited nothing more encouraging.

She was *not* happy.

No way could six people, or twice that, or a hundred, maintain and build all that was required. But what choice did she have but to try? As a critical first step—survival on Mars depending on uninterruptible power, dust storms or no—she had to assure them of that power.

Three people emerged from the ship. Keshaun whistled in awe. "Do you realize that till today I haven't been more than a few klicks from home base?"

"Nor I," Reuben called from the bridge.

Islah smiled. "I wasn't kidding, was I?"

"Nope," Keshaun agreed. He turned to face Teri. "Where do you want the portable?"

Shelter, that meant. For a quick up-and-down flight, six people shoehorned aboard *Burroughs* had been mere inconvenience. But for the days of toil ahead, they'd need more living space than the ship. Any decent-sized plain near (but not too near) the ship would do. "I leave choosing a campsite to you two, but don't go just yet. For now, enjoy the view."

Reuben, after methodically completing the shutdown procedure, was the last to leave *Burroughs*. They allowed him, too, several minutes to take in the scenery.

"Okay," Teri said. "Enough lollygagging." She reviewed their as-signments: Reuben and Maia to scout out accessible locations along the crater rim with a view downhill toward their future strip mines. (Left for another day: how they'd improvise a bulldozer blade.) Ke-shaun and Islah to erect the portable shelter and offload Mars-made ironware. The four of them to begin delivering those beams and struts, the framework of a power-beaming antenna tower, to the chosen construction site. (Toting it all like pack mules. No one, Teri least of all, trusted what remained of the cable that had slaughtered Jake and Paula. Cable and its motorized reel had been left at Barsoom). She and Julio to roll out, in the bowels of the crater, like the universe's most fragile carpet, acres of photovoltaic film—

Donated by Xander, on the basis that "Times have changed," and "You can owe me one." Delivered by NASA lander. Offloaded by NASA robot. Sterilized—she had to hope!—in the days since, by solar wind, solar UV, and cosmic radiation.

As people dispersed and Teri started deeper into the crater, Julio cleared his throat. "Do we dare handle anything from Phobos?"

Hadn't they just discussed this? "Of late, I've spoke two and three times a day with Phobos. On video, sometimes. Xander sounds and looks fine. Sonny assures me they're healthy." Also anxious as hell, same as us.

Never mind that the three aboard *Lewis* had also been healthy—until they weren't.

"Our one doctor, and she doesn't make house calls." Pause. "Okay, boss."

As Teri and Julio trudged toward the waiting rolls of PV film, no matter the days of hard labor ahead of them, she couldn't stop thinking of everything *else* needed to make this a more permanent, more survivable, base of operations. Locate a nearby source of ice or an accessible aquifer. Disassemble and relocate the brick kiln, the iron foundry, the fuel plants, and so much else laboriously deployed in Barsoom. Construct new hydroponics facilities, transporting intact plantings from the old ones. Liberate Helium and Zodanga from their radiation-shielding sandbag cocoons, deflate the shelters, and reverse the process at this end. In time, construct a new Mars mansion. Scavenge everything useful out of any structure that wasn't portable. Bring the stinking chinchillas, those being their closest approximation to canaries in a coal mine. Or maybe for chinchillaburgers.

However many cargo hops by *Burroughs* and *Bradbury*, and however many refuelings, all that required.

Unless a terrible pestilence killed them first.

November 4, 2035

UNHCR Declares Global Emergency

Zainab Ali, the United Nations High Commissioner for Refugees, made official what for months has been obvious: the worldwide crush of climate refugees has reached crisis proportions. "All nations," she said, "must acknowledge the scope of this problem, make provision for humane transit and resettlement, and allocate the necessary resources. Barring such action, many thousands, perhaps even millions, will die unnecessarily."

With the latest change in seasons—in the ever-decreasing interval between unbearable summer heat and the threat of fierce winter storms—the annual wave of northern-hemisphere climate refugees is now in full swing. From Sri Lanka and southern India, northward. From India, Pakistan, and Bangladesh into Afghanistan, Nepal, and China. From southern China into that country's northern provinces and increasingly on into Russia, Mongolia, and Kazakhstan. In the western hemisphere, the United States is experiencing record influxes from Mexico and Central America, even as internal refugees, in numbers unlike anything that country has experienced since the Dust Bowl of a century earlier, swarm into the Midwestern states ....

—BBC World News

As the last of the bioterrorism experts straggled from the CIA conference room, closing the door behind her, Arthur Schmidt arched an eyebrow at Dale. As in: What do you think?

Almost two months into the crisis, she less thought than was *mired*. In the blur of so many such reviews attended. Symposia audited. Reports dutifully slogged through. Simulations studied and tinkered with. Freewheeling sessions of much storm but little brain. At the CDC. The NIH. With her own, OSTP, staff. At more universities and biotech companies than she cared to count. This day, at CIA headquarters in Langley.

"Umm." Now wasn't *that* insightful? "Every scenario they floated seems improbable."

Putting it mildly. Every last hypothetical bandied about that day—at a morning meeting that had stretched almost to 2:00 P.M.—involved multiple mutations to one or more common human-gut symbiotes, or the lateral transfer of long segments of DNA among symbiotes, or mutations to a dormant virus embedding itself in the genome of a symbiote or symbiotes. Or even more far-fetched combinations.

It wasn't that anyone discounted *Martian* microbes, but lacking genomes, those couldn't be factored into the CIA's beyond-top-secret simulations. And so, even cascading improbability upon improbability, starting only with known microbes, this group had failed to reconstruct Cat's full catalogue of symptoms.

Not that anyone else considering the problem had, either.

Arthur rapped on the tabletop, tap-tap-tap, tap-tap-tap, in what she took for impatience. "When all you have is a hammer, every problem looks like a nail."

Maybe not impatience with *her*, then.

Absentmindedly, Dale wound a strand of hair around a finger. Like too many fidgety tics she'd imagined long broken, hair twirling had re-manifested itself. Could nail-biting be far behind? "The thing about low probability events? They're only low probability until they happen. Then they're certain."

"Or they're low probability until someone makes them happen."

She twitched. "You believe this was a *bioweapon*?" Because if it were, how in God's name had it gotten onto *Lewis*? If such a thing were aboard, what could have set it off?

415

He made a wry face. "Believe? No. Still, you can't be surprised when the people who worry about bioweapons for a living speculate that way."

Her stomach rumbled. It had been a long meeting. "Then what? I mean, what's left?"

Because if they *didn't* sort this out, what hope remained for the people on Phobos and Mars? What chance that, in desperation, they'd someday fly home despite orders to stay put?

"The executive dining room here is surprisingly good." (Meaning he'd heard her gut. How embarrassing.) "To which we will repair in a few minutes. First, bottom-line it for me."

"Today's meeting?"

"Everything. Do you have confidence in any proposed explanation for events on *Lewis*?"

She forced herself to untwine the strand of hair. "Truthfully? No. We must keep looking."

"Of course." Arthur stood. "As discouraging as the search to date has been, I've begun looking on my own. When you have eliminated the impossible, et cetera."

Then what remains, however improbable, must be true. Sherlock Holmes. They were reduced to channeling fictional Victorian detectives. God help them.

She stood, too. "Lunch, then?"

"Sure. One thing first. It affects nothing you're doing, but I expect you'd like to know we're pursuing every avenue."

We? Who else was there? The ghosts of Watson and Crick? "Go on."

Arthur ran splayed fingers through his hair. (When had it gotten so thin? It would seem she wasn't the only one stressing out.) "When in doubt, we look for more data. We look in new places. One of those places was comms to and from Mars. Because—"

"Computer viruses aren't viruses. It's an *analogy*!"

"Peace. That's not where I was going. When I tasked the NSA to look, I had nothing specific in mind. But here's the thing ...."

Her stomach rumbled yet again, louder than before. She could only smile and shrug.

"Lunch soon. That's a promise. But here's the thing. This is classified, by the way. The archive of the Japanese DSN has a handful of outbound encrypted emails the NSA can't crack. The most recent of those went out this past April."

The NSA were hacking allies? Maybe she shouldn't have been surprised, but she was. Anyway, that wasn't her strongest reaction. "You imagine *Hideo* is somehow involved? He *died* aboard that ship."

"No. Well, not necessarily Hideo. JAXA, like NASA, allocates spare bandwidth on their DSN to unofficial comms. Family and friends on any mission's whitelist can queue up private—that's pronounced, encrypted—messages to Mars. But civilians use standard commercial encryption, nothing your average supercomputer can't crack, or none at all. As for anyone not on a whitelist, whether journalists, space junkies, or school kids, *only* messages in the clear get past a security gateway to the DSN."

"So the suspect message or messages. Addressed to whom, Arthur? Sent by whom?"

"Addressed to someone in the AresMissionOne email domain. The username within the domain, to the left of the 'at' sign? That's 'spaceman42.' Who, it turns out, might be almost anyone. I'm sure you know how easy it is to register yourself for an email address on, say, Gmail. People on the Ares project could do the same in their email domain, as you might set up different addresses to use with friends, close family, work, and online shopping."

"So, the mysterious messages went to one of six on Phobos. You just don't know who."

"You'd think, but likely not." Arthur grimaced. "Two reasons. First, prelaunch, *lots* of people used the mission-specific email domain. NASA, partner agencies, and contractors. Keeping the mission correspondence together was convenient, especially given the hurry we were in. Postlaunch, most non-astronaut accounts were closed, but, it turns out, not all. Loosey-goosey, but understandable, everything considered.

"Second reason. That an email to Mars specifies a particular email domain says almost nothing about who receives the *transmission*. Half the planet can hear it. Maybe more, maybe the entire planet, depending on the routing protocols hardwired into the non-NASA comsats out there. Think of sending to the spaceman42 email account as a sneaky way to transmit unattributable messages to the Chinese. Or to the NEP bunch."

Spy stuff confused Dale, even when watered down for television. "Then closing this spaceman42 account, here or on Phobos, will do no good?"

"More likely, it'd do harm. Now we know to monitor that account. Short of cracking the encryption, we won't know what they, whoever *they* are, are told—but even knowing they've gotten a message is a tip-off of sorts. Were they to discover the account had been closed, they could tell their Earth-side cronies to switch to another email address, maybe one in a non-Ares domain, that we wouldn't know to watch."

"I've lost the thread, Arthur. What's cyber have to do with an unrecognized"—and unrecognizable—"illness aboard *Lewis*? Especially if the cyber doesn't involve Ares?"

"Maybe nothing. Maybe we have two unrelated mysteries. I'd be remiss not to speculate, though, about connections."

"You must know who's sending the messages. Ask them."

"Purportedly, Giselle's grandmother, who struggles to read emails, much less send, let alone encrypt, one. Nothing in her email history suggests she originated the messages in question. Dollars to donuts her email handle and IP address were spoofed to get encrypted messages past the JAXA security gateway."

About then, five dollars for a donut wouldn't have phased Dale. "And even the NSA can't read the attachments?"

"Correct, and not for any lack of trying. I expect those were encrypted by OTP, like the one I gave Xander." (Her doubtless blank expression bought her more than she'd ever want or need to know about onetime pads.) "You ready, Dale? I'll admit to feeling a tad peckish."

But rather than move to the door, he kept talking. "One last thing. I've shared this latest conundrum with Xander, using our OTP. Given his proximity to Martian comsats, maybe he can figure out something."

November 7, 2035

In the dark of his sleep cubby, Xander stared at vague shapes all too familiar from hundreds of nights in the coffin-like space.

A *lack* of clarity? It couldn't have been more fitting.

Paranoia had to be an occupational hazard in Arthur Schmidt's line of work. Paranoia *and* an openness to convoluted ploys. This was, after all, the guy who'd come up with radar-spoofing drones to disguise the arrival date of *Lewis* and *Clark*.

For a few scary seconds, that errant memory had Xander fretting about the decoys. One had run smack into Mars. Seismometers on the ground and imagery from Mars orbiters left no ambiguity about its demise. The second decoy, though, had sped past the planet. Could a nefarious actor have (somehow) taken control of the surviving decoy, used it to spoof *Lewis* on its way home, as part of some new chicanery?

Not that such scheme, had it happened, would explain the loss of contact with the actual ship. Still, Xander spent anxious minutes in back-of-the-mental-envelope calculations, convincing himself the idea was absurd. Neither the decoy's fuel capacity nor the many months elapsed since the decoy passed Mars could accommodate such deception. Not even close.

The fact remained that Arthur suspected some new type of shenanigan. By whom? To what end? The DNI's secure note posed an assignment. It offered no answers, or even hinted at them.

Xander woke his datasheet. Two in the morning, and his mind wouldn't shut down. He might as well do something useful. First up: Ascertain if someone so in need of coffee could pull off making some.

The habitat's mail server indeed showed an account for spaceman42. As sysadmin, Xander had access to all accounts. This one's inbox held a few messages, sent months apart, their headers matching Arthur's description of what had been found (never mind how) in JAXA archives. The *attachments* were as clearly encrypted. Since NSA supercomputers hadn't cracked them, Xander saw no point in trying. The SENT folder was empty, consistent with their true recipient on Mars monitoring transmissions from Earth independent of the Ares email server.

He banged out a script to flag any future activity in the spaceman42 account. It was something he *could* do. Not a big thing, but he'd be alerted when someone on the planet below got another of these messages.

Coffee implied food—and a new reason to worry. The eve of *Lewis*'s departure, they'd each eaten a steak from Barsoom. Unlike the dirt and ice samples examined in the biolab, the meat hadn't undergone a rigorous safety protocol. (Hadn't undergone. How very blameless. *He* had lacked the sense to ask Sonny to inspect those steaks.)

Still, that was back in May. No one here had gotten sick. No one aboard *Lewis* had fallen ill until September.

Making Steakgate another harebrained idea inspired by Arthur's unhelpful message.

What further improbabilities could sleep deprivation conjure?

Sipping from his third coffee bulb of the night/morning, Xander stared, yet again, at the digitally enhanced version of Cat's final message. Something beyond the obvious continued to nag at him.

Arthur had been his cards-close-to-the-vest usual self about the restoration. Still, from his few, grudging admissions, and reading between the lines of emails from Becks, hints of the repair process had emerged. Interpolations and statistical models had replaced many of the lost imagery bits and improved the overall resolution. Other statistical legerdemain had approximated, then backed out, much of the in-transit interference.

Given the time, Xander might have done as much himself. The remainder of the enhancement wowed him. Pounding on the bridge hatch, digitally muffled. Semantic analyses made to fill in the audio gaps. For whatever reason, anatomical modeling of the vocal tract to (maybe) match the disease's outward manifestations had only made inarticulate speech worse; that effort had been abandoned.

Details aside, whoever had done the file restoration knew their stuff.

When Sonny, yawning, still in her sleep sweats, emerged from her cubby, he closed the replay window. The gruesome death of her lover was no way to start her morning.

Striding for the lav, Sonny just waved at him. She stopped on her way back. "No offense, but you look like crap."

That good? "Couldn't sleep."

"Something going on? I mean, something new?"

Aside from everyone being a suspect? But a suspect for *what*? That detail eluded Xander. How could he know when America's top spook didn't? "As if I need something new."

"That's fair." She studied his drink-bulb collection. "Any coffee left?"

"Should be some, and it's yours." Because she'd come over to the dark and caffeinated side. Because however much his *head* craved caffeine, his *stomach* fervently disagreed.

"Be right back."

While Sonny decanted coffee dregs into a bulb, he did his best to act serene. (KEEP WORRIES TO YOURSELF UNLESS SHARING CAN HELP.)

"Been up long?" she called from the galley.

"Is that a friend or the doctor asking?"

"Friend, for now."

"Well, yeah."

She came and sat next to him. "Anything you want to talk about?"

"Maybe another time." If only. "How are you?"

"Is that a friend or the mission commander asking?"

"Friend."

"In that case, I'm frustrated. Stymied. Clueless what else I can look for in biolab."

No more thwarted than he, trying to suss out whatever the *hell* it was about the *Lewis* video, their only hard evidence, that gnawed at him.

Apart from the obvious.

IT COSTS NOTHING TO BE POSITIVE. JUST DON'T *LIE*.

Xander patted her hand. "I have confidence in you, Doc. As your friend and wearing my mission-commander beanie."

November 11, 2035

A glum, silent, dinner.

Uh-huh, Xander thought, sliding back his plate. When had they last had any other kind?

MORALE'S BAD? YOUR JOB IS TO FIX IT.

Damn, but he missed Cat, more even than he missed someone else being in charge. How much more did Sonny miss Cat? Or did David miss Giselle?

Cat hadn't offered an aphorism for his next thought, but his mind's ear nonetheless served up one in her voice. ("What's Hideo? Chopped liver?")

"So," Xander began, "big plans for the evening?"

"A movie, maybe," Sonny said.

"Yeah, me, too," David agreed. "Suggestions?"

"I was thinking *Justice League: Retribution*." She looked at Xander. "You in?"

The 2030 remake, he supposed. With its six superhero leads digitally recast months ago. Because such had been the nature of their choices since word came of the disaster.

How was this healthy? Then again, who here was the doctor?

MORALE'S BAD? YOUR JOB IS TO FIX IT.

Heard you the first time, Cat. Anyway, he had bigger fish to fry. Alone. "I think I'll pass in favor of a walk in the park." Their aeroponics dome. "Enjoy the greenery, maybe do some mindless pruning. From outside looking in, it looked like there's some leaf lettuce to harvest."

He stood and started clearing the table. This was his night to clean up.

"Two out of your three qualify as work," Sonny said. "I'll get the dishes. Shoo."

Xander took his time suiting up, dawdling until Sonny and David were settled in front of the big screen (two-by-two datasheets stuck to a wall partition, each displaying a quarter of the vid), the audio booming. Until both would be occupied for the next almost three hours.

Offering an opportunity to test whether a change of scenery and complete privacy—and, yes, maybe even some of that mindless pruning—could deliver what days of brooding had not. Any progress toward resolving Arthur's comms conundrum. Any concept of the irksome whatever it was in Cat's video that still mocked and eluded him. Any opinion whether those enigmas had anything in common.

Or even, Cat, whether morale *could* be improved.

Xander circled the main aisle of the aeroponics dome for a good quarter hour, mind careening from topic to topic, before anything close to an idea emerged. If, cumulatively, hours of studying the reconstructed video had left only the vague sense of something amiss, maybe watching the *original* video would shake loose something in his brain.

It didn't.

He played both vids side by side and *almost* saw … he didn't know what. He tried stepping through both, frame by frame.

And … maybe?

He cobbled together a program to test that flash of intuition. Cleaning up noisy, degraded-by-distance transmission involved, in the main, statistical analysis of the interference. When recognizable interference changed gradually from frame to frame, or in a predictable pattern, the averaged noise could be digitally subtracted. Much reduced, if seldom fully cancelled.

In essence, that algorithm presumed a single source of interference: the solar wind. What for days his subconscious had been sensing, what his quickie program had confirmed, was the overlay of a second, uncorrelated noise pattern.

Cat's clothes, the visible parts of her chair, and the bridge bulkhead *all* exhibited more interference than her disfigured face and hand. That contrast seemed clearest in the unretouched frames—which people had stopped using as soon as even the earliest-stage cleanups were available.

He fine-tuned the DSN's standard noise-reduction algorithm. Rather than approximate interference from dropouts throughout the raw video data, his tweak only worked from dropouts in the periphery of frames. By omitting Cat's image from the process, his trial reconstructions sharpened noticeably.

Rendering Cat's ruined face—and only her face—all but noise-free. Applied to the entire vid, this correction also improved the audio subchannel.

Natural interference would *never* behave like this.

The aeroponics dome had much to commend it.

There was quiet and privacy, leaving Xander alone with his (troubled) thoughts. The soothing sights and scents of greenery, so foreign to this little world. The circular aisles he could endlessly pace, thinking.

Presuming his plunge down the rabbit hole into tinfoil-hat territory counted as thought.

Set aside bit-diddling-driven speculations for the nonce. What did he *know*? Months into its return flight, Cat's ship had vanished. More precisely, it had diverted and exploded. Beyond Arthur's assurances, the world's press agreed. Xander had digested enough international news these past weeks to believe the radars of several countries confirmed those details.

He also knew the ship had made that final, terrifying transmission before its course change and destruction. Again, it wasn't only NASA's DSN claiming to have heard this. The UAE's lone deep-space ground station happened to have been pointed in the right direction. (Too coincidental? Or, as had been reported, were they tracking *Lewis* and listening for its telemetry as a simple training exercise? Either way, they'd independently confirmed the ship's final message.) Arthur claimed someone in the UAE had leaked the information to PPL.

But could anyone actually *know* those things? Someone might have hacked DSN *and* the UAE system to fake the transmission. That same someone could have hacked various space-force radars, such that all continued to track imaginary debris. Still, it was difficult to imagine even top-tier cyber forces of a hostile superpower pulling off such feats and all those hacks remaining undetected.

Difficult, but—Xander had to entertain the possibility, didn't he?—not impossible.

What else? Earth's best minds in biology and genetics had failed to explain the imagery in the final *Lewis* broadcast. Sonny, as bright as any of them, more motivated than all of them, had also failed. Nor had she once encountered anything like a living cell, a dormant cell, or an intact virus.

As though there never was a pathogen.

He completed another shuffling circuit of the dome. A second. Another, still.

And froze.

The least deranged scenario Xander could conjure was that something aboard *Lewis* had transmitted a deepfake. Not that—given the low res, the interference, and the apparent ravages to Cat's appearance and vocal tract—standard deepfake detection tools had a snowball's chance on Venus of proving it. That something had altered the ship's course and then somehow destroyed it. Or—his mind recoiling from the notion, his gorge rising—some*one* aboard had done all that.

He refused to believe Cat, Giselle, or Hideo would do such a thing. Would kill the others. Would kill themselves.

No. *Lewis* must have been hacked, its crew killed soon after launch lest they discover the tampering and take back full control. Killed by a hacked life-support system, Xander guessed. Peacefully of carbon-dioxide poisoning—he could *hope*. Because the explosive-decompression scenario was too awful to contemplate.

If so, he'd been swapping emails *not* with Cat, but with her personal AIde. As Sonny had been interacting *not* with her lover, but with another AIde. As David, presumably, had interacted with Giselle's. David hadn't talked much about Giselle since *Lewis*'s departure, but those two had always been secretive about whatever they'd had between them.

What an oblivious moron he'd been! They'd *all* been!

Had Xander done the ship's final checkout, would he have spotted the malware? He'd never know, and the possibility gnawed at him.

Three dear friends might have died because he had become lax about emptying grit from his boots.

More shuffling. A few sips from the water bulb he'd brought to the dome with him.

Who could have done this? And why? Wasn't this nuts?

A pocket of his utility belt chimed. He retrieved his datasheet. "What's up, David?"

"Your cute girlfriend's on the line."

Not his girlfriend. Cute, true, as if it mattered. He and Teri *had* worked their way up to chatting several evenings a week, at least when local sun time wherever she found herself and GMT/Phobos time hadn't drifted too far apart. Someone whose spirits he wasn't duty-bound to buck up? Someone to be candid with? The conversations helped keep him sane. Teri, too, he guessed. "Put her on."

"Will do."

Yet in the second or two until the transfer went through, Xander had misgivings. If sovereign states had the resources for the sophisticated chicanery he'd imagined, well, why not NEP? Teri's employers collectively controlled wealth to put most nations to shame. And they had their own ambitions for Mars ....

"Xander, you look beat. Did I catch you at a bad time?"

How could they have a civil conversation? Her employer had built NASA's repurposed spacecraft! Was a backdoor into *Lewis*'s code so far-fetched?

Suppose there *were* a backdoor. Suppose a major load of malware had been uploaded through it ....

"Xander?"

Were he on Mars proper, could he have opened the (hypothetical) backdoor? Yes! Ships, landers, rovers, datasheets—most everything electronic in the mission connected, at one time or another, over the Phobos LAN. So: Hack a NASA lander or rover. Then, tap remotely into the Phobos LAN, using the compromised bot as a relay. Once into the LAN, access *Lewis* and spring the backdoor.

Teri's team had had more than ample opportunity to compromise Ares landers and rovers.

Also: oh, *shit*. Carter's bunch had had similar opportunities. If a backdoor existed, who was to say *they* hadn't found it? High-tech companies throughout the West had complained for decades about MSS-orchestrated industrial espionage.

Even as Teri *ahem*-ed Xander, a slow-firing synapse was reminding him that NEP rented comms capacity from the UAE's deep-space ground station. The same station that confirmed NASA's report of *Lewis*'s final message. The source, per Arthur, of the disaster going public. Did NEP foreknowledge explain that station "happening" to track *Lewis* at the wrong time?

Looping Arthur into this inchoate mess of inferences and speculations would burn through a major chunk of their OTP—a bargain *if* the spook made some sense of things. If Xander was right—about a hoax, about *Lewis*'s destruction as a part of that hoax—he had not the first inkling who'd been responsible. Or why. Or, beyond speculation, how. Or what role, if any, the mysterious spaceman42 had played in all this.

Or he could forward just his refinement to the *Lewis* video, could let the spooks draw their own conclusions. Yeah, he'd send it on. That felt *way* healthier than airing his baseless suspicions.

Louder throat-clearing.

"The truth is, Teri, I'm kind of distracted. It's been a long few days."

Trundling every rover on the surface back aboard the nearest lander. Recalling every lander to Phobos. Only then had Xander been able to reset the password on the command-and-control network. Examining recovered bots, one by one, for signs of meddling—bypassing comms with a clean datasheet jacked in with a physical cable. Reviewing backup files and audit trails, for evidence of earlier mischief. Left to do: Plug the new comms password into the bots.

Hmm … his subconscious, somehow, *had* been clued into the possibility of a penetration through a compromised bot. But if such a penetration were the culprit, he'd found no sign of it. Nor had David seen anything suspect when asked to double-check.

"Xander … do you want to talk about it?"

More than she could imagine, except he couldn't. As much as he'd come to admire and trust her, he dare not risk that she, or one of her team, anyway, was involved. "Another time, if that's okay. I'll get back to you."

"Sure. I understand. Bye."

Not until deep into yet another restless night did the disappointment in Teri's signoff penetrate. As though *she'd* needed to talk.

November 14, 2035

Lewis Disaster Clouded by Spoofed Final Transmission

NASA today disclosed new evidence concerning last September's loss of the agency's Mars vessel, *Lewis*. Acting Administrator Rebecca Nguyen explained, "Radar telescopes of our agency and others, as well as military radars, continue to show that *Lewis* suffered catastrophic failure on September 9th. We have, however, recently determined that the ship's purported final transmission was a clever digital forgery. Investigations continue to identify the party responsible for this deception, their motive, and determine whether foul play led to the loss of the spacecraft.

"With the possibility of any pathogen aboard ship discredited, and following consultation with our international partners, the Ares Two mission has reverted to its original plan. Our spacecraft en route will proceed to Phobos for refueling and then on to Mars."

In response to a question, Nguyen thought it "reasonable to assume" other missions approaching Mars would reinstate their pre-hoax plans ....

—*Houston Chronicle*

Mars Pathogen a Hoax? Then What *Did* Happen to *Lewis*?

Cruella DeMille has egg all over her face this morning after pranking by parties unknown. Prank, alas, is far too frivolous a word for the seemingly vast conspiracy that destroyed *Lewis*, slaughtered its international crew, and threatened to put a halt to Mars exploration.

The sheer embarrassment of the situation has this reporter expecting that Chicken Little, the administration's chief science adviser, is destined to become chicken salad.

—*Globe Enquirer*

Dale was up early. *Again*. Wondering, as she had wondered nonstop since Xander discovered the deepfake, whether today was the day.

It was.

She had just begun skimming headlines, a mug of tea, untouched and grown tepid, on the dinette table alongside her datasheet, when Patrick shuffled sock-footed into the room. One glance at his face showed he'd also seen the headlines.

"This is bad," he blurted out. "Well, not discrediting an imaginary Martian superbug. That part's fine. But you're going to be the scapegoat, aren't you? For accepting the possibility *everyone* accepted. NIH, CDC, WHO … and who else?"

As though invoking agencies by name would help. Unbending a leg, she slid out a chair. "Absolutely, that there's no superbug is good."

He sat. "And the scapegoat part?"

The president was pissed out of her skull, and fair enough. Someone in the administration would have to take the fall. A mere two months before the Ares Two mission arrived, that wouldn't be Rebecca, and no one else at NASA had any public name recognition. It wouldn't be Arthur, not with the need so urgent to identify the entity behind the hoax.

Leaving the presidential science advisor as the obvious candidate. That Dale had long been the public face of sample-return precautions? Slam dunk.

"Will I be expected to fall on my sword?" Or fired if I refuse? "Yeah, I'd give good odds you're looking at the lucky winner."

Whatever it said about her, she'd far rather jump than be pushed. "You know what, hon? I'm fine with retiring. As someone, who shall remain nameless, has long been suggesting."

"But not this way," he grumbled.

Nor how she'd have chosen to leave. "Hon, take the win."

November 15, 2035

As they suited up for another day's construction of the slowly rising New Beijing, Mingmei turned to Kai. "It's good news, so why haven't we heard it through proper channels?"

He'd wondered that himself. Mission Control in Beijing had yet to share news already a day old among the Westerners. Nor had Roscosmos, unless in encrypted comms that Antonov had not deigned to share.

"Still nothing from your people?" Kai asked Oorvi.

She shook her head.

The authorities back home must suspect his people and Antonov's monitored NASA's in-the-clear news updates. Or expect that Xander Hopkins would share his findings now that the word was out on Earth. (Except Xander *hadn't* shared anything. As though he felt betrayed. Which he, or at least his mission, had been. As though he didn't know whom to trust. A feeling Kai had come to know all too well.)

"I wish I knew," Kai told the women, not quite lying. He only *intuited* Beijing's reticence to risk new tension with the Russians, here or on Earth, lay behind the silence.

"More must be involved than a fictitious disease," Mingmei softly insisted.

In fact, Kai saw three puzzles. Who was behind the hoax? How had they done it? Why had they done it? As for the first, the Americans would make no accusations without incontrovertible proof. As for

432

the second, they'd never disclose much. Even to hint at vulnerabilities that might again be exploited would be irresponsible. None of which logic, to gauge by the news so far received by the NASA and NEP teams, had stopped Western media from speculating.

Leaving Kai vexed by that most troubling question of all. *Why?*

"Suppose some entity wants to keep this world to itself. It may have intended the hoax to deter its competitors from landing here." *Entity. Competitors.* No one could argue that he'd blamed anyone in particular of duplicity. Of State-sponsored murder. The NEP consortium was also an entity. "The deception, had it continued even a bit longer, would have kept competitors from establishing or expanding a foothold on Mars for another twenty-six-month cycle."

With a final wriggle, Mingmei settled fully into her counterpressure suit. She began an inspection of her life-support pack. "Or this 'entity'"—the air quotes unmistakable—"intended the hoax to keep away *our* people." She shot a meaningful glance sideways. Toward, outside their shelter wall, New Moscow.

Given (another nugget available only in Western news) Moscow's anger over the worsening border crisis? Given that Roscosmos now had its own Mars-capable spacecraft? A Russian hoax to deter a second Chinese landing *was* plausible.

As much as it pained Kai to concede, neither could he dismiss a State hoax meant to discourage a second Russian landing. It pained him more to consider the human cost of such a scheme. As it pained him to remember earlier suspicious deaths in this and the NEP missions.

Must ancient rivalries defile this new world?

All of these dangerous thoughts. Kai changed the subject. "I find it interesting that PPL prepared the public to believe the worst. Were they involved in the hoax?" If nothing else, riled-up, fear-mongering hordes had served as so many useful idiots.

"Let's get to work," he concluded, hoping to fend off any further unanswerable speculations.

Mission Control had resumed business as usual, just as if they hadn't stonewalled Teri for the last two months. Well, screw *that*. It was past time to seek out options for her people.

She injected into the middle of an innocuous, chatty, see-you-never-had-to-worry-about-me email to her mother: REMEMBER THAT SHIT HEAD WHO ALWAYS BUGGED ME? LET HIM KNOW I'M READY TO TALK.

Shit Head being Teri's pet name for the senior executive recruiter at B-M, Boeing-Mitsubishi. The man had tried for years, even throughout the run-up to her launch for Mars, to poach her from IPE.

That scatological disrespect had always mock-horrified Mom—with any luck, she'd catch the reference. Shit Head himself would understand his outreach should come over whatever DSN B-M had made arrangements with for comms with its ships.

Teri's feeler should be secure as long as NEP wasn't using high-end supercomputers to crack open her personal correspondence. Or if NEP did snoop, as long as they mistook *shit head* as an affectionate name for a pre-Jake suitor.

The B-M folks might well welcome a team of *experienced* Mars hands to assist their noobs.

China, Russia Tensions Flare

Protests by detainees against reportedly harsh conditions in a Siberian climate-refugee camp near Khabarovsk escalated into violence. Russian authorities have not released figures, but witnesses who escaped the camp amid the confusion report dozens of deaths by gunfire and many more wounded. The International Committee of the Red Cross has as yet been unable to gain access to the camp.

Beijing has labeled the incident unacceptable and vowed unnamed "consequences."

—*London Evening Standard*

November 18, 2035

After a week's silence, Teri had had enough. She radioed Xander.

"Yeah, sorry." (Not sounding sorry. Sounding … aloof? No, she decided, *guarded*.) "I didn't get back to you."

He had big bags under bloodshot eyes. Everywhere the beard gone shaggy didn't cover, his face looked slack. Utterly spent. Still in shock at learning his friends hadn't just died—they'd been *murdered*. Plunged all over again into grief and loss.

She said, "Maybe it's none of my business, but I have to ask. Are you all right?"

"Yeah. Peachy. What's up?"

"You can't believe *I* had anything to do with what happened to your people? Or any of my team here had any part in it?"

"Believe? No." His voice cracked. "But still …."

But you can't avoid lingering doubts. However awkward those might make you feel. As she had the nagging, unsubstantiated worry that NEP might have been involved. As he must have pondered the implication that both their missions had flown in IPE-built Moonships.

She tamped down all that. "Xander, I get it."

"I haven't heard. Is a second landing back on for your guys?"

So, they wouldn't be discussing the elephant in the room. "Officially, the landing was never off."

A hand rose into view, finger knuckle rubbing the corner of an eye. "Then is the relo from Barsoom to Ascraeus Mons off the table?"

An oblique reference to the rolls of PV film donated in what already seemed a bygone, *we're all in this together*, era? An age of altruism now regretted? "To be determined as to any permanent relo. Site development continues regardless to support mining. The ores will come in handy whatever comes next.

"But I can see you're busy." Emotionally drained. Physically exhausted. Kept upright only by the near lack of gravity on Phobos. "I should let you go."

"Yeah, I am …. But no. I've missed this. Any thoughts about what happened? Any insights from your people?"

She'd missed it, too! "Insights from our Mission Control? None. As far as they've let on, they're as confounded as anyone. But Maia came up with a scenario"—a bonkers conspiracy theory—"I've not seen in Earth media."

"What's one more? Shoot."

"Disclaimer first. I *don't* believe this."

"Then for the amusement value. I could use some amusement."

More so sleep, by all appearances—but without an explanation, without certainty, how could he sleep? Jake's and Paula's deaths had left *her* sleepless, zombified, for months.

Ironic amusement was the best she could offer. "What if a disaster happened *before* the hoax transmission?"

His cheek twitched. "What do you mean?"

"Suppose some catastrophic accident aboard. Something with life support. A meteor strike. Causes unknown. In any event, not foul play. You're the NASA guy, not me, but wouldn't such an occurrence raise major concerns about the follow-on missions already underway?"

"Of course. After any mission failure with loss of life, protocol is a safety stand-down. How does a plague hoax enter into this?"

"Supposition two. The president doesn't want to cede Mars to her rivals. If they, too, can be waved off …."

"Implying the hoax was invented after the ship went silent. That the hoax video was later concocted and uploaded for retransmission." His brow furrowed. "Implying that some sick, *sick* individual thought to leverage PPL's germophobe stunts and protests, even EPF's threats and bombings. Oh, also uploading a second hunk of code to alter course and explode the ship."

"That's Maia's concept. As for remotely piloting the ship, not a problem. It's a standard Moonship feature for unmanned, cargo-only missions. Self-destruct, however, is *not* an option."

"Every chemical rocket is a repressed bomb. I'd be shocked if I couldn't destabilize a fueled-up Moonship, given full systems access to fly the ship." He paused, head tilted. "Caveat: given that I had the source code for avionics, or the time to reverse-engineer it. The other hack that I'm certain happened would be simple: linking crew AIdes directly into comms to respond to messages and queries."

"I'm pretty sure you'd be voiding the warranty." (Was that a flash of a smile?) "Anyway, Xander, that's the scenario."

"Uh-huh."

"That's it? *Uh-huh?*"

"I'm thinking." That process extended for long seconds. "Sad to say, I know people that devious." Dry laugh. "Witness how Ares achieved our sneaky, first-place finish. If there were such a cunning plan, my IDing the final *Lewis* video as a deepfake blew it. But I don't buy it."

"Too difficult to keep such a big secret?"

"For the government that faked the Apollo landings on a Hollywood set?" This time, a definite smile. "No, here's my objection. How would … the people behind such a scheme later excuse their hoax? Once they're prepared to reenter the fray."

The easy give-and-take had felt delightfully normal again. For maybe a minute. Up until that damned hesitation. Until he'd let slip that in his mind the *someone* responsible for the disaster might yet turn out to be NEP.

At least they were talking. "My bad. That's also part of Maia's scenario: an eventual 'discovery' through supposed simulation that the disease aboard *Lewis* had to have been a fluke. Caused by an entire set of mutations to some familiar bacterium, maybe a gut bug. Wildly unlikely ever to recur." She winked. "Here's where, in my opinion, the house of cards goes splat. To convince anyone, the recipe would have to be shown to experts. Right? So that independent labs could verify it."

"About that." Xander stroked his beard, frowned, stroked some more. "There's a simple answer. The government would classify that supposed simulation at the highest levels. They'd deem it too sensitive for even restricted release for peer review, lest it leak to become the template for a horrible biological weapon." Stroke, stroke. "If there were such a plot, of course."

"Of course," she got out. Because the longer they spoke, the less bonkers that conspiracy felt to her.

While the expression on Xander's face suggested she wasn't alone.

December 10, 2035

In caper movies, hijacking a security camera looked easy. Unplug the camera's output wire, plug in a datasheet to loop innocent, prerecorded footage, and done.

Could it be that simple? Sure—if the camera were placed somewhere foolishly accessible. In a security system so poorly designed that unplugging the camera didn't trigger an alarm. When neither human guards nor an AIde surrogate monitored the vid stream for suspicious gaps.

Whereas the cameras on the Ares landers and bots suffered from all *three* vulnerabilities. Also, as Xander brooded, a fourth. Natural atmospheric interference, as normal on Mars as Earth, injected random gaps into the radio uplink to obscure any quick skullduggery.

For completeness, there was even another out-of-bot exposure: the comsat network. Synchronous-orbit altitude above Mars fell between close-orbiting Phobos and Deimos; even their feeble gravitational tugs would dislodge satellites from what would otherwise have been areostationary positions. That left Martian comsats to orbit well below Phobos, with never more than a restricted view of the terrain as they raced past. Comm links between Phobos and a bot on the surface switched from one satellite passing overhead to the next to the next, just as a car rider's datasheet was handed off from cell tower to cell tower. When Phobos happened to be far around the planet from a bot, the comm session used an ad hoc *daisy-chain* of satellites.

How secure were the satellites? How secure the handoffs among them? What malware might have been snuck into a bot—or in the other direction, into base computers—during a compromised comms session?

If the hacking of *Lewis* had become a fixation, so be it. Xander would re-review archived video of every opportunity anyone below had had to meddle with a bot or lander. He'd reexamine at least a random sampling of bots and landers and other computers for malware he might have overlooked. Because what else remained to try?

But did he want more chiding about his fixation? No.

Sonny was back in her lab, relieved to be examining fresh, post-hoax cores. David was in the aeroponics dome, harvesting a bumper crop of leaf lettuce and tomatoes. Leaving the geolab idle—and a fine place to obsess in privacy. Or to navel-gaze, whichever way it worked out.

Xander radioed, "Guys, I'm done out here." *Here* being the bot garage, where he'd been doing routine preventive maintenance. *Here* doubtless also why the mystery was again vexing him. "I'll be in the geolab, checking on things there."

"Copy that," David returned.

Sonny offered a preoccupied-sounding grunt.

Xander settled in, helmet and life-support pack set aside by the airlock. The lab had six wall-mounted datasheets. He streamed old bot vids on five, reserving the last to search, sift, and sample metadata in the archive. Here and there vids stuttered, but no more than in his control samples: landings before direct dealings with the other expeditions, and remote from them.

"This is crazy," he muttered. As certain as he remained that *Lewis* had been hacked through the Phobos LAN, and it through a compromised mission bot, he had no proof. Barring some bright idea, no prospect of finding proof.

So, all he needed was a bright idea. Easy.

"Everything okay in there?" David's voice came from his helmet where it rested on the floor and from the intercom mounted high on a lab wall. "You're awfully quiet."

Xander answered over the intercom. "Quiet, yes. I take exception to awful."

"Okay. Resume silence."

Bright ideas, like spaceman42, continued to elude him. There had to be something he hadn't yet tried. He upped the fast-forward rate on the video replays. If going nowhere *faster* was progress of a sort, he took no comfort in it. Bright idea. Bright idea. Bright ....

Bright or not, he resolved to do something else. To do *anything* else. And that would be ... unmasking spaceman42.

Uh-huh. How?

Geolab was too small for useful pacing. He did his best, circling its pair of stools. All anyone knew about spaceman42 was that he, or she, got occasional encrypted messages. Orders from Earth, presumably. Except maybe not any longer, because after the *Lewis* hack had come out, the various DSNs had severely restricted who could send encrypted info.

Cut off like that, spaceman42 would be feeling anxious. Must wonder what to do next. Must ... must ... *must desperately hope his superiors could somehow reconnect!*

He'd give that bastard a message.

Xander had to wriggle halfway out of his counterpressure suit to extract the flash drive from his pocket. Biometric security notwithstanding, he kept the onetime pad *close*.

The OTP-encoded message he sent Arthur was brief. CAN SOME THIRD-PARTY DSN (UAE? BRAZIL?) WITH PLAUSIBLY BRIB-ABLE STAFF SEND SPACEMAN42 A ZERO-DAY, NO-CLICK, EMAIL EXPLOIT? IF SO, HAVE IT "PHONE HOME" TO US BOTH.

Followed by an even terser note, because a trojan might alert spaceman42 he'd been spotted and was being hunted. UNLESS YOU HAVE A BETTER IDEA.

Did intel agencies keep to themselves the security holes found in commercial software? So said the conventional wisdom. So said countless spy novels. In the dark net's black market for zero days—vulnerabilities the software vendor had had zero day's notice of—the CIA and NSA were reputed to be among the highest bidders. How better to penetrate an unsuspecting adversary's computer than through an unpatched, unsuspected vulnerability, using custom code no anti-malware software knew to look for?

How better to expose spaceman42?

December 18, 2035

HOOK BAITED IN 24 HOURS. YOUR UPLOAD TO MULDER@ ARESMISSIONONE.GOV. ACKNOWLEDGE.

Arthur hadn't written much. He hadn't needed to. Anyway, bonus points for *The X-Files* reference.

Xander created a Mulder account to receive any upload from Arthur's trojan, set a trigger to alert him to any incoming messages, and returned an ACK. He already had a trigger in place for messages to spaceman42.

And now to wait.

After three anxious days, Kai heard back by secure comms from Mission Control. Except not mere "Mission Control," but General Qian.

RECOMMENDATION RECEIVED. REFERRED FOR APPROVAL.

Above the general, head of the Strategic Support Force, were only the Central Military Commission and President Wu himself! Kai granted himself permission to hope.

If approval came, *Xuanzang* and both cargo ships would divert at the last possible moment to land near the well site. *Xuanzang's* crew would control most resupply and the lone developed water source for thousands of kilometers. Would put thirsty, upstart Russians in their place.

December 23, 2035

After four interminable days, with hope fading, the trojan phoned home.

Vibrating like a sonofabitch, Xander's datasheet startled him awake. Mulder had an email with the subject line BAIT TAKEN.

The "vid" attachment, when Xander opened it, was pure raw ASCII, scrolling beneath a blinking white-on-red banner: SPACEMAN42 UPLOAD. Here and there, an English-language word flashed past within the streaming gibberish, never enough to convey meaning.

Abruptly, the scrolling stopped. The banner quit blinking, its text updated to TRANSMISSION ENDS.

Damn, that was *quick*.

Whether the trojan had crashed the infected datasheet, or spaceman42's decryption app misfired while processing the trojan-disguised-as-attachment, or spaceman42 simply had an uncanny intuition, didn't matter.

Xander edged aside his cubby's blackout curtain to peek out. Sonny sat in night-shift dark at the galley table, flickering vid shining off her face, audio streamed to earbuds. David's blackout curtain was drawn. Well, it was nice *one* of them was getting some sleep.

Xander would've preferred to move to the table, but he had no intention of discussing the inconclusive investigations with Sonny. He let his curtain fall back.

Propped on an elbow, Xander checked for the spaceman42 alert he'd set on the mission's email server. He hadn't overlooked a notification; none had been triggered—as expected if the murderer was on the planet, monitoring all transmissions from Earth.

Now to ferret from whichever files the trojan had uploaded just who this bastard *was*.

Whoever had programmed the trojan couldn't have known file structures on spaceman42's datasheet. So: After establishing its surreptitious comm link, the malware had skipped past recognizable apps to start uploading files as it encountered them. Somewhere in the trove would be something to identify the perp.

In theory.

What little data the trojan had grabbed, in the seconds before its upload ended, matched part of an encrypted attachment sent months earlier to spaceman42. Xander's ruse had touched spaceman42—but not *IDed* him—perhaps tipping him off in the process.

Meaning Xander had learned nothing. Meaning this, too, had been an exercise in futility.

So much for theory.

December 24, 2035

Xander emerged from the airlock into the geolab, leaving the inner hatch open. He set down his clipboard to pop his helmet.

David looked up, his arms in a glove box. "Checking up on the amateur geologist?"

Xander retrieved and waggled the clipboard. "Inventory. I won't be long."

"I could have—"

"You work. I'll count." As Xander opened drawers, tallied supplies, jotted notes on the clipboard, David went back to studying some rock sample through a microscope.

Xander encountered David's helmet beneath a shelf and behind a wastebasket. With David's back still turned, Xander shifted the wastebasket, set the helmet out of sight within the airlock, and restored the wastebasket. He looked into a cabinet and took more notes, picked up his own helmet. "Done. I'll get out of your hair."

"Fine."

Xander exited the geolab with David's helmet in hand, held well below the level of the airlock hatches' glass ports. He bungee-corded the helmet to the nearest guide wire. Texted Sonny (in the biolab, unsuspecting) to eavesdrop on the intercom channel. Positioned himself at the airlock, with a view inside. Took several deep, centering breaths. The stage was set.

That play was a tragedy.

❖ ❖ ❖

After a long, hard day's work, Helium was re-inflated at the foot of Ascraeus Mons and partially re-interred beneath radiation-shielding sandbags. Sleep would be *so* good.

"You guys take the shelter," Teri told Maia and Julio. "I'll sleep in the SUV, give you some privacy." If they had the energy to use privacy? More power to them. Mainly the offer gave her cover for crashing as soon as she'd forced down some dinner, reviewed anything her AIde had flagged in the latest email downloads, and pinged the three in Barsoom for anything urgent *there*.

Among the highlighted emails was one from persistent@ spacephreaks.org. With a subject line like GLAD YOU REACHED OUT and that domain name? Obvious spam—except that encrypted attachments from strangers didn't get past DSN security gateways. (She expanded the message's header for the full routing. It showed Brazil's DSN.) *Especially* not since the pathogen hoax.

Teri grabbed a spare datasheet from an SUV locker to open the message and its attachment. Unless the latter had been encrypted using her public key, she hadn't a clue. But her matching private key did the trick.

MS. RODRIGUEZ:

I WAS PLEASED TO HEAR FROM YOU BY WAY OF YOUR MOTHER. IT'S BEEN A WHILE SINCE WE LAST SPOKE. I TRUST THIS COMMUNICATION CHANNEL WILL PROVE SUITABLY CONFIDENTIAL.

IN VIEW OF YOUR CURRENT LOCATION, I ANTICIPATE YOU HAVE SOMETHING UNUSAL IN MIND. BOEING-MITSUBISHI IS CERTAINLY OPEN TO DISCUSSIONS ON MATTERS OF MUTUAL INTEREST ....

As Teri continued reading, sleep became the last thing on her mind.

"Why, David?"

David startled at Xander's voice over the geolab intercom. "Why, what?"

Why shouldn't I override the safety interlocks and open both airlock hatches? Why shouldn't I let your blood boil in the vacuum and your eyeballs explode? "Why did you do it?"

"Rather an expansive question." David extracted his arms from the long rubber sleeves of the glove box. "Here's my question. Why didn't you ask about this, whatever this is, a minute ago, inside?"

You'll know soon enough. "Why'd you do it?"

David stood and faced the airlock. Whether at the hostility in Xander's voice or by chance, he started looking all about the lab. "Return my helmet, Xander."

"I'm afraid I can't do that, Dave."

"I don't understand."

The informality? The *2001* reference? Or whether he'd been found out?

It's the last one. "Yeah, you understand, David. Or should I say, spaceman42?"

If only for a moment, the man's eyes went round. "Who?"

"You were good, David. I'll grant you that. Savvy, in fact. I'd set a trigger on the email server, so I'd know if anyone accessed the spaceman42 email. No one did."

"I don't understand," David tried again.

"Here's the thing. When my trojan"—no need to drag Arthur and his people into this confrontation—"began streaming data from spaceman42's computer, I *didn't* have a concurrent notification from the AresMissionOne mail server itself. No indication that the booby-trapped message had been accessed as an email."

"I understand none of this. Not this spaceman. Not about malware. What I do know is that anyone on Mars with a line of sight to Earth can hear all its transmissions. They don't need our domain's email server to receive our inbound emails."

"Here's your problem, spaceman. This morning I realized the one thing I hadn't checked. Yes, the booby-trapped email remains unread on the mail server—but *just* before the trojan triggered, someone accessed the email backup archive. Which requires sysadmin privileges, and it wasn't me."

Beads of sweat had appeared on David's forehead. "Or whoever hacked our LAN before, whoever attacked *Lewis*, still has access."

Xander could feel Sonny on the link: bursting with questions but holding them in check. Or he read that into the faint sounds of her breathing. Or he imagined it. For all that, she was his witness. Of *course*, he was streaming A/V feed from his helmet to a datasheet in the shelter, but after "Cat's" final transmission, no skeptic would accept a mere recording.

"Well?" David demanded.

Xander kept quiet. Silence rattled some people.

David tried again. "What difference would it make if I were this spaceman? We all get personal messages from Earth."

"Not like this. Not with the sender spoofing Giselle's grandmother." Not with attachments even the NSA supercomputers can't crack. "I call Ockham's razor."

"Explain."

"Barring other information, the explanation with the fewest assumptions is—"

"I know what Ockham's razor *is*. What's it have to do with anything?"

What's the sweat on your brow have to do with anything? "There's been an elaborate scheme for secret communications with someone on one of the Mars missions. There was an elaborate plot to destroy *Lewis* and disguise the cause. The simplest explanation is they're part of a single conspiracy."

"Wait a second!" Sonny burst out. "Xander, are you saying David killed Cat and Hideo? That he would he kill *Giselle*?"

"David?" Xander prompted.

"I refuse to dignify this vile, hateful nonsense with an answer. Return my helmet."

Xander caught himself nodding as though Sonny could see him. "That *is* what I'm saying. David must have been preparing, at least for the eventuality, from Day One. The movies and even newscasts he was always so eager to digitally recast us in. Practice. The—"

"A hobby. It proves *nothing*." David said.

Yet it stinks to high heaven. "As for Giselle, David did his best to dissuade her from leaving. There might've been more going on than friends with benefits. For David, anyway."

David's face reddened. "Yes, I hoped she would stay, as if that's any of your damned business. If you're going to make accusations, why not at Sonny declining to leave with Cat."

"Because I was being *responsible!*" Sonny shouted.

"Moving on," Xander said, "no one here was more vocal about a sample return being premature than David."

"Here, perhaps, but plenty of people on Earth concurred. Anyway, if you'll recall, *Hideo* raised similar objections."

"Some," Sonny agreed. "Then, having spoken his piece, he went along."

"What's been eating me alive," Xander continued, "is that I might have spotted the malware aboard the ship. It *had* to have been a significant piece of code. Only I didn't get the chance. Because, out of nowhere, a suit leak trapped me in the habitat. You know who was the last one prelaunch to examine *Lewis*'s computers? Who saw no signs of the unauthorized code?

"The exquisitely ill-timed suit leak could have been a random event, or a first-time lapse in suit hygiene. My money's on a minute's effort in dark of night to scrape a toe of the suit."

"Then there's the fact that try as I might, I never found any intrusions on the Phobos network, yet we know *Lewis* was massively hacked. As though, perhaps, whatever datasheet you jacked into *Lewis* to 'check it out' loaded the hack. As though the hours you spent on *Clark*, supposedly amusing yourself with various simulations, were a different kind of preparation."

"Your inability to spot a hack isn't *my* fault," David shot back—but his voice quavered.

"Xander ..." Sonny pleaded, "help me. I've lost the thread."

"There *is* no thread," David huffed. Sweating buckets, but he managed to huff.

"Spaceman42 gets uncrackable messages via our email server from a spoofed source. Spaceman42 has sysadmin access to—"

"So do *you*," David shouted.

"... access to our server. *Lewis* was hacked, with David the last one to do a hands-on check before it departed. I *didn't* get to check, and only someone in our habitat could've mucked with my suit."

"This is *madness*," David hissed. "Coincidence upon conjecture. Give back my damned helmet!"

Something stirred in Xander's peripheral vision. It was Sonny, come to join him. "More of a *pattern* than coincidence," she said. "But surely, he wouldn't ...."

Wouldn't kill, especially not Giselle. Because Sonny had read David's ongoing dark mood as depression? Xander saw only guilt.

"Madness," David repeated. "Sonny, put my helmet inside the airlock. Please. I'm trapped in here."

She answered, "Fuck. You."

David tapped, with increasing frustration, on the geolab comm console.

"Didn't I mention?" Xander asked. "I've updated the base routing tables. Nothing from geolab gets off the LAN. Oh, and I rescinded your sysadmin privileges."

Meaning: No way to contact any accomplices. No appeals to Mission Control or ESA, his government or public opinion. No hope but his own powers of persuasion.

Good luck with that.

Xander said, "Here's your problem, spaceman. On top of everything else, you're arguing with basic physics."

"What the hell are you—"

"Do you imagine you can bluster your way out of this?"

The bastard might, in fact, not be wrong. Circumstantially, everything pointed at David. But absolute, incontrovertible proof? Xander lacked that. Which brought him to someplace between a hunch and a decent probability.

Over the course of the mission, David had gotten better and better with computers and software—but comms required different skills. Especially comms as complex as interplanetary networks. Especially when connections constantly shifted among hurtling comsats of differing vintages and manufacturers.

So, yeah. This was a bluff.

"When the trojan uploaded to my datasheet, Phobos was behind Mars from everyone on the ground. I know what kind of throughput a link to any of their sites could have sustained. I know what kind of latency is involved. You know what?"

David sighed. "Let me guess. The trojan's upload didn't take such a route."

Beyond a shadow of a doubt? No. Nor could there be certainty absent gory details about concurrent data streams through every link in an ever-shifting daisy-chain, including error rates and retries. All nuances David *wouldn't* know. "Hence ...."

Grudgingly, sullenly, "Hence the infected datasheet was local. On our LAN."

Gotcha. "You said it, spaceman."

"Doesn't mean it was me." From tone of voice, not even David expected that to fly.

"You sick, twisted, murderous *bastard!*" Sonny burst out. "Why?"

"Yes, I have a private channel with home! Xander does, too. It proves nothing."

We'll see about that. "Then under the circumstances, you won't mind sharing what's in those encrypted files."

"Again, those are none of your damned business. If I—"

"Here's a question, David. Once I report all we've discussed, all these *facts*, what limits do you imagine there'll be in investigating your life back to maybe kindergarten? Your every friend, relative, and casual acquaintance? How thorough the search for your traces on the internet and dark nets?"

Because however dark the dark nets, they weren't *opaque*. Not given the right tools, patience, and motivation—none of which would be lacking.

As by the flip of a switch, David … deflated. The bluster? The feigned innocence? The defiance? All gone.

"With enough motivation, search warrants, and subpoenas, I imagine even the BFV can find my internet tracks." (BFV? Xander wouldn't give David the satisfaction of asking. He took a mental note to look it up later and needn't have bothered.) "*Bundesamt für Verfassungsschutz.* German equivalent to the FBI."

"What will they find?" Sonny demanded.

"I tried to dissuade all of you from any return trip. You know that. I did."

"So what?" she said bitterly. "That was just *talk*. What you *did* was murder them."

"To protect all life on Earth. To force people to confront the dangers." David sighed. "Sometimes, sacrifices must be made."

"How noble of you," Sonny growled. "Let's say we sacrifice you."

David shrugged. Indifferent?

Because he'd once consigned himself—with Xander and Sonny as two more of his unwitting victims—to abandonment here. (Or on the planet below? Maybe *that* explained the many powered-descent-to-Mars simulations.) Had consigned the three of them to a lingering death as essential supplies ran out and irreplaceable equipment wore out. It just hadn't worked out that way.

From some long-ago English lit class, the stray quote surfaced. Shaw, maybe? *Self-sacrifice enables us to sacrifice other people without blushing.* Dead on, whoever had written it.

"The broken genome sequencers. That was you, wasn't it?" Sonny asked. (In shock, Xander supposed, or in denial, her mind recoiling from travesties too horrible to contemplate.)

David rallied enough to protest. "Suppose I hadn't. What could you have done with it but hand-wave away the risk of any Martian life you found? Arguing that what you sequenced was too ordinary to be a threat. Or that it was too unfamiliar, too divergent, to be a threat. As though anyone could intuit the perils of an awakened alien organism from merely its genome."

"Because you and your nameless accomplices know better?"

"Because my colleagues and I have the humility to acknowledge the danger from what we *don't* know."

"I could have understood the risks," she snapped. "Had there been anything *to* sequence."

"What's to understand? Earth is unique. Sacred. Endangering it is unacceptable."

Said the fanatic. "Back up, David. What's the BFV going to find?"

"My connections with PPL, since early in mission training. Through them, later, to what announced itself as the Earth Protection Front."

"Names," Xander demanded.

David laughed. "Names? Who uses names? Noms de guerre, sure. Internet handles. Avatars. I never *met* anyone."

As ISIS had massively recruited, back when Xander had first begun paying attention to the news. Thousands of foreign fighters had streamed into their "Caliphate," radicalized in this manner. As many domestic terrorist groups continued to operate, if on a smaller scale. EPF organizing and recruiting online fit the pattern. So did that everyone so far arrested for the Rocky Mountain Laboratories bombing, even tempted by plea deals, claimed ignorance of the organization's leadership.

The mission screening process should have discovered any questionable overt relationships. But anonymized interactions over the net? You had to know first to look for those.

"There was nothing dangerous in the samples," Sonny said. "Damn it to hell, David, you knew that. Microfossils. Chemical traces. All long dead. All inert. As you knew that everything would go straight into a full BSL-4 lab. So *why?*"

The bastard actually laughed. "The arrogance is breathtaking. Because in a few samples from a few cores *you* recognized only traces, you presumed there was nothing else to be seen. You presumed nothing might lurk, dormant, elsewhere in those same cores. You presumed nothing lurked in other cores among the cargo. You presumed reentry to Earth would proceed without a mishap. You presumed the transfer to the lab would proceed without a hitch. You presumed the lab would never experience a lapse in its safety protocols. You presumed that safety protocols designed from Earthly experience suffice for unfamiliar Martian pathogens."

"While you *presumed* the opposites," Sonny said. "All I hear is hand-waving, Luddite hysteria."

Xander heard a self-righteous, holier-than-thou murderer. *Self-sacrifice enables us to sacrifice other people without blushing.*

"If it's any consolation," David said, "I arranged peaceful deaths by carbon-dioxide poisoning, when life-support sensors showed everyone was asleep. It would have come early in the flight, with their AIdes configured to act for them."

Yeah, preflight David had ported the AIdes. Had, in fact, volunteered for the task. Call it *another* clue Xander had missed, along with the man's months-long phase of deepfaking the six of them into vids. For chrissake, he'd once cast them all as freaking, flesh-shedding zombies!

Xander said, "The final days before *Lewis* left, off by yourself, I'd believed you were sulking. That's not so, is it? You were rehearsing and recording 'Cat's' final message. Getting that abomination just right before deepfaking her zombified face and voice over yours in the vid file. True?"

"Your misguided value judgments aside, yes. The final touches, anyway. I'd scripted the basic version months earlier." David shrugged. "What now? Apart from whatever you report back, that is."

Forcing open both airlock hatches? It was tempting. Sonny's expression, as Xander glanced her way, told him she shared the urge. But no, damn it. *He* wasn't a murder. *He* wouldn't be judge and jury. But neither would he put anyone else at risk.

"For as long as I'm in charge here, David, that lab is your entire world."

Three hours later, Xander returned with sealed containers of food and water. Through the window of the airlock's inner hatch, he saw:

— David, unmoving, crumpled on the floor;
— jigsaw in one hand, wrist of the other arm jaggedly torn;
— in a pool of blood, its edges already brown and dried.
— beside a note written in bold block letters.

SOMETIMES SACRIFICES MUST BE MADE.

[Diaspora]

**E
P
I
L
O
G
U
E**

"The moon and other celestial bodies should be free for exploration and use by all countries. No country should be permitted to advance a claim of sovereignty."

—Statement of Lyndon B. Johnson, President of the United States, On the Need for a Treaty Governing Exploration of Celestial Bodies (May 7, 1966)

"For our generation, and those which will soon follow, Mars is the New World."

—Dr. Robert Zubrin, President, Mars Society

December 31, 2035

"**G**ot a few minutes?" Xander asked.

"Sure," Teri said, not that she did. Because the man looked weary. Not sleep-deprived. Not exhausted. Emotionally drained. If so, he'd come by it honestly. Again. "What's up?"

"I am?" He rubbed that scruffy beard. "Scratch that. Just on the market for a five-minute mental vacation."

"Happy to help." Anyway, prepared to help. She'd never forget his assistance and kindness after the accident. After yet another long day's labor by Ascraeus Mons—someday, they needed to come up with a name for the new settlement—a bit of downtime wouldn't hurt her, either. Ditto, any distraction from the chaotic mess within the resituated Helium. "No offense, you don't look up."

"In an effort to take my mind off of … stuff, I made the mistake of reading Earth news."

Stuff. His friends' murders. The perp's suicide. Just two of them left, at least for another few weeks—a maintenance nightmare, on top of everything else. Yeah, Xander had more than his fair share of *stuff* best not dwelt upon. "You don't find current events on Earth uplifting?"

He laughed bitterly. "It's so hard to decide what's worst. The cavalcade of climate-linked disasters. The escalating hostilities between Russia and China. Wondering if and when that spills over to this neighborhood. Snowballing revelations of EPF moles and sympathizers in the world's spacefaring agencies and companies. The frantic search for EPF sleeper agents within the Ares Two mission. Oh, I wasn't supposed to mention that last one. As though any semi-sentient individual wouldn't anticipate it."

"I rate as semi-sentient?"

She'd meant it as a *joke*, but his cheeks flushed. "Not what I—"

"I know. My peeps back home are engaged in a similar exercise."

He took a swig of something from a drink bulb. "Every day, it's clearer we, humanity, can't keep all our eggs in one planetary basket. If only we weren't collectively going about it so stupidly and parochially."

Aren't you the cheerful one?

"Okay," he declared. "Subject change. You guys have big New Year's Eve plans?"

Celebrate return to a random spot in an orbit? Teri had always thought the holiday silly, even living on the planet in question. But that wasn't the morale-boosting answer. "Wait for the bowl-game scores to come in." Not *watch* the games. Nobody's DSN had the bandwidth to stream football. She'd be lucky if they got a few short highlight clips. "How about you?"

Faster than he could wince, she regretted the words. How celebratory could they be on Phobos?

He said, "The night's big event will be flipping a coin for the last of our pudding cups."

"Easily as interesting as watching the ball drop in Times Square."

He glanced off camera at something. "I should let you go."

But I shouldn't let *you* go, she thought. Because you're a good guy. Because you've been through a lot, had too much dumped on your shoulders. Because you don't deserve being stuck up there, your talents wasted, practically alone.

"Xander, can you keep a secret for a couple weeks?"

"I think so." He gave a sour look. "It's clear that people can keep secrets from me."

She ignored the second part. "In that case, I have something for you to consider."

January 2, 2036

The president finished signing a bunch of papers in leather folders, handed the stack to an assistant, and emerged from behind the *Resolute* desk. Scowling.

At what? Dale wondered. Something about Mars, since Rebecca Nguyen had also been summoned. Again, something dire and ultrasecret, given that only Arthur Schmidt was also there.

The president settled on a sofa beside the DNI, facing the other women. "I gather we have a situation on Mars. Again. Arthur?"

Dale cleared her throat. "May I remind you, Madam President, I no longer work here." Because you threw me under the bus. Still, when the DNI calls, says you're needed at the White House, you go. Patrick's over-protective fussing notwithstanding. "My former deputy is more than competent."

"Yeah, well, I've yet even to meet the man. You, I know, so I understand Arthur asking you in. You'll tell me what you think, not what you imagine I might want to hear. *Especially* after you had to take one for the team. Trust me, I have no interest in disturbing your retirement."

"In a nutshell," Arthur began, "Xander Hopkins used our secure backchannel to serve up an ultimatum."

"What?" Dale burst out. "There's no way he's some kind of eco-terrorist."

459

Arthur shook his head. "Nothing like that. He and his Canadian sidekick intend to fly the coop. Take useful gear from Phobos down to the planet with *Clark*. Exact date unspecified, but before the Ares Two ships arrive. None of this, he says, is up for debate."

Cruella pinched the bridge of her nose. "Don't tell me he's defecting to the Chinese."

Arthur shook his head again. "That's one of the few details Xander does offer. He's going nowhere near Fire Star City. Where will he go? All he's saying is that he won't say."

"Epic insolence aside," the president said, "I don't understand this. How can *Clark* land on Mars now, when they couldn't at the start of the mission?"

Rebecca leaned forward. "*Lewis* and *Clark* approached Mars in 2033 with much of their fuel spent. What remained was more than ample to land on little Phobos, but not nearly enough to go down to the planet. The team has since produced fuel from the ice on Phobos. Refueled, it's quite possible for *Clark* to land on the planet. It's what their robotic landers have done all along. With Ares Two, the mission plan's always been refueling on Phobos and then landing this way."

"*Leif Erikson* and *Sacagawea* have experienced pilots," Arthur pointed out. "Xander has the landing simulation written by a suicidal sociopath."

"Hopkins has balls," the president said. "I'll give him that. Now what is it he *wants*?"

Arthur straightened his tie. Flicked an invisible speck of lint from a lapel. "He's offered us a choice. NASA can declare this *its* updated plan. Or it can try explaining why the Ares One survivors have gone freelance, taking a very expensive ship with them."

"Gone *rogue*," Cruella snapped.

"And his conditions?" Dale prompted.

More tie straightening. "That Dr. Nguyen be nominated as permanent administrator."

Rebecca twitched. "I had no idea."

Arthur gave the president a subtle nod that Dale took as *she's not lying*. Also as proof the spooks had no qualms about monitoring private conversations. At least the ones over DSN.

The president stared at Dale. "Okay, you're up. Can we spin this development as a good science thing? A safe thing?"

With an entire planet to explore, how could additional boots on the ground be a bad science thing? "Yes, of course, to the former." As for the latter, Dale marveled at finding herself dragged back into *that* conversation. "Regarding safety, the scenarios that most worried so many experts"—herself, included—"stemmed from the *Lewis* video. Of course, we now know that was a hoax. We're back where we started. That's me advocating for precautions to protect priceless specimens from inadvertent contamination and to guard against the seemingly low risk of any actual live sample or other surprise."

The president nodded. "Okay, I heard 'low risk.' I can work with that when your friends in the press come calling."

Friends didn't feel accurate to Dale. The rest of that prediction did. "The descent to Mars strikes me as far riskier than any biological danger."

The president turned. "And *you*, Dr. Nguyen?"

"I'm with Dale. A non-pilot attempting the first powered landing on Mars of a Moonship? Of course, it concerns me. But Xander is a straight arrow. If he said he's doing this, he *will*."

Cruella leaned back. Pursed her lips. Stiffened. Her eyes narrowed in thought. "I don't see a choice here. What can I do? Send in the Marines at the *next* launch window? Disavow the hero of last month and the month before? Wouldn't the party love *that*, a month before the primary season opens?

"Here's the deal. NASA provides these reprobates with what technical support it can. It brings aboard the partner agencies—in particular, the Canadians. It coordinates with Hopkins over what gear he takes, lest he compromise the successor mission. I give a confident speech about how we push past sabotage and tragedy to a bold next phase of Ares One. And Dr. Nguyen?"

"Yes, Madam President?"

"Congratulation on the promotion … *if* our guys make it down safely."

January 10, 2036

Kai was up before dawn.

Viewed from low orbit, Chidi Two ships' atmospheric entries would be spectacular. If Oorvi or Mingmei should notice his being awake this early, he'd attribute it to tasking observation satellites. That was the truth, if not complete. What he truly wanted to watch was *Xuanzang* and the two cargo ships touching down by the well, where the sun had already risen.

He was focused on scheduling those observations when faint vibrations shattered his concentration. Marsquake? Then he noticed a faint noise from outside. In *this* wispy atmosphere?

Even as Kai's mind raced, both phenomena faded. The sound … receded? He peered out the airlock-hatch windows. Where for so long two ships had stood, one glittered by starlight. He had heard and felt *Gagarin*'s launch.

Kai radioed Antonov in New Moscow. No answer. He tried again, hailing *Gagarin* with a widecast relay via a passing comsat. Again, silence. Redirecting an observer satellite, he saw what he'd most feared to see: *Gagarin* already completing the short hop to the well site. *Valentina Tereshkova* and its all-Russian crew were surely also headed there.

So much for taking charge of the water supply.

Xuanzang was about to streak into the atmosphere at almost 20,000 kilometers per hour, its computers in charge. The best Kai could do was radio a quick warning in rapid Mandarin.

That done, he shouted across the shelter, "Get up! *Quick!*" As the three of them donned vacuum gear, he recapped the situation. Wondering how, bearing their pathetic coil guns, they might reach the landing site soon enough to help. Wondering if the women, neither a soldier, would even go with him.

He wasn't a pilot. None of them were. By Mars Buggy, the well site was hours distant. Too distant. But New Moscow stood empty. Recapturing that structure might offer some leverage. They clambered out of their shelter to the first rays of the rising sun—

To discover the Mars Buggy parked flush against the outer hatch of New Moscow.

In the far distance, brilliant lights streaked across the sky! Four streaks. Four ships. Descending, as best Kai could tell, on parallel courses. "We're reclaiming the building," he said. At least then, they'd be doing *something*.

Mingmei was their best driver. He tapped her on the shoulder.

She glanced back at him, nodded, then climbed into the Mars Buggy's cab. A moment later, she radioed. "Motors won't start."

"Which one?" he asked.

"Motors. All four."

"Hold on."

Kai popped the hubcap off the nearest wheel. The electric motor in the hub was minus its rotor. He checked the other motorized drive wheel on that side of the buggy. Same. Then he noticed scuff marks, as if the buggy had been *shoved* the final meter to where it blocked the airlock. He guessed it had, and that the inaccessible wheels flush against the building also lacked their rotors.

Maybe he and the women could heave or drag the buggy far enough to expose the airlock. What further surprises did Antonov have in store for them if they tried? He'd been planning this stunt for a long time. Leaving what? Cutting through a wall with heavy-duty power tools, blowout and all?

No. They needed a better response than petty vandalism.

"That's not going anywhere, is it?" Oorvi asked.

"It's not," Kai agreed. "Come. We're returning to the shelter."

The first thing their return accomplished was getting them off the radio. Away from eavesdroppers. Then it allowed them to check on the landings.

All four Chìdì Two ships had landed near *Gagarin*.

Mars observers weren't spy satellites; at their best resolution, they would show only a handful of pixels for anything as small as a space-suited person. But even a pixel or two in Day-Glo colors so foreign to this world stood out. Especially creeping around the ships or hugging the undulating crests of ridges.

Spacesuited figures, forming skirmish lines.

Oorvi saw it, too. "That's a *battle*. I never signed up for a war. My government never signed up for a war. But a war is coming to us anyway."

Mingmei threw back her shoulders, "Nor have I, whatever the Party may think."

A *second* mutiny? No, Kai decided. Honesty. Rationality. Self-preservation. "Suppose I reach out to other expedition. If they can evacuate you, if they will take you in, would you go? I can make no predictions if, or how, or when, after that, you'd ever get back to Earth."

Mingmei frowned. "Take *you* in. That's what you said. Not *us*. What about *you*, Kai?"

He squared his shoulders. "I am a general of the People's Liberation Army. I stay."

"To do *what*?" Mingmei demanded. "Fight the Russians with your hands?"

With the coil guns they'd made, short-range and inaccurate as those had proven to be. "If need be. By the time the survivors come here, my presence could make all the difference."

The women exchanged anguished looks. "Contact the others," Oorvi whispered.

Kai did. He was still pondering tactics when an NEP Moonship swooped in to carry his friends to safety.

January 17, 2036

Xander's helmet radio crackled. "Ahoy, Asaph Hall Base. This is *Burroughs*. Coming into a hover near you. Are you both ready?"

"I see you, *Burroughs*." And what a welcome sight that was! But … *ahoy*? "Welcome to Phobos. This is Xander Hopkins." He looked to Sonny, who nodded. "Yes, we're ready." As we'll ever be, he silently completed.

Also, exhausted. From loading food and water, bots and batteries, med supplies and exercise gear, tools and lab instruments, all manner of stuff, aboard *Clark*. From dragging hoses to refuel that ship. From mining fresh ice to produce more fuel for today. Above all, from nerves.

"Reuben Ben-Ami. I'll be your captain today." The jocular tone vanished. "Let's do this."

"Aye-aye, captain." Xander triple-checked his triple tethers. He flashed Sonny a confident smile and, heart thumping, leapt. With an almost gravity-free world like Phobos, you didn't land. You *docked*. Without explosive-tipped harpoons, launchers to shoot them, and big motorized reels to wind tether, *Burroughs* had kept its distance.

He drifted past the vessel floating about twenty meters off. Spacewalks? One more thing he'd barely trained for. "Sonny, pull me back."

She did, and he jumped again. On his third try, he made contact with the ship. One by one, he transferred his tethers to clamps inside

an open hatch, reattaching himself with a carabiner. With three tethers set, he climbed down hand over hand. "Next up, fuel."

Returning hand over hand to *Burroughs*, towing the bulky hoses,
wasn't fun.

"Full up," Ben-Ami finally declared. "Glad that's done. Okay, if you
guys would wrap things up on your end, we'll move on to the fun part."

Pilots! Cocky smartasses, every one. Ben-Ami reminded him *so*
much of Cat. A wordless sniffle over the radio marked Sonny having
the same thought.

Step by step, they finished:

— Climbing back down, stowing the fueling hoses.
— Establishing a remote-control link between the two, very
   similar, IPE Moonships. (Because, given the choice, no one—
   Xander, least of all—put any trust in David's untested Mars-
   landing software.)
— Freeing *Clark* from the taut tethers that staked it to the moon.
— Climbing back up again to *Burroughs*, this time with Sonny.
— Casting off that ship's long tethers.
— Doffing and stowing their helmets and life-support packs.
— Settling into the passenger cabin while *Burroughs*, on gentle
   puffs of its attitude rockets, receded to a safe distance.

Abandoning Phobos and the facilities they'd built—and David's
corpse, as they'd found it—for the Ares Two mission two days away.

"Everyone comfy?" the captain called out through the open bridge
hatch. "Yes? Excellent. Then let's send *Clark* on a ride."

And damn if he didn't pull it off.

Mars!

Still trembling from the surreal experience of the landing, Xander unbuckled, staggered to his feet. After Phobos, barely a third of
Earth's gravity was brutal. "You okay?" he asked Sonny.

"I will be."

Reuben Ban-Ami exited the bridge into their windowless cabin. "It would appear you have a welcoming party. Shall we?"

"Sure," Xander said. He and Sonny followed their pilot from the ship—

Into sensory overload. The pink sky shading overhead to darkest maroon. Tiny crescent Phobos. The towering vastness of Ascraeus Mons. Undulating landscape that, after the freakish closeness of the Phobian horizon, seemed to extend forever. *Clark*, the ground beneath it still steaming. *Burroughs*, when he glanced behind him, wreathed in more steam. Farther off, ships of unfamiliar design that had to be Boeing-Mitsubishi's Mars Clippers. Sandbag-covered domes and a handful of more permanent buildings under construction. Antenna dishes and PV arrays. A hydroponics dome, with splashes of green. He didn't see *Bradbury*, perhaps already returned to Barsoom to await the second NEP mission, and where *Burroughs*, once refueled, would join it.

But what overwhelmed Xander was so many *people!*

The dozen in all-but-unspotted suits? Surely, the newly arrived Boeing-Mitsubishi contingent. The two … refugees? émigrés? exiles? defectors? from Fire Star City. In a shallow arc behind the rest, five—no, six, as Reuben Ben-Ami wandered that direction—survivors of the original NEP mission. Except they weren't NEP anymore, but rather B-M's newest consultants.

His head swiveling this way and that, taking everything in, the familiar voice on the radio took a moment to register. "Welcome to the Mars International Free Enterprise Zone."

Because—with sweat equity, and Boeing-Mitsubishi's backing, and (however reluctantly) NASA and CSA participation—this *was* the Mars International Free Enterprise Zone.

Amid all this over-stimulation, Xander sought out a familiar face. And there she was.

She smiled.

He smiled back. Raised a gloved hand, with two fingers extended. She nodded.

He said, "So, Teri, would you join me for coffee sometime?"

He took her broadening smile as a yes.

THE END

Acknowledgments

This book didn't just happen.

Okay, no book just happens. To write a novel is a major undertaking. That said, for *this* book I had more help than usual, contributions I deeply appreciate and wish to recognize.

Let's begin with Shahid Mahmud, publisher of Caezik Science Fiction & Fantasy. That I even tackled a near-future, Mars-centric novel was at Shahid's suggestion. Assistant publisher Lezli Robyn shared in those early discussions. Editor Cat (strictly a coincidence) Rambo helped shape the final draft. Thanks, guys.

The storyline (not to mention its obligatory red herrings) on which I eventually settled required a great deal of research. About: Mars and its moons. Living off the land in such hostile environments. Plausible near-future space capabilities of various countries and the private aerospace sector. Biology, astrobiology, and sample-return protocols. Earth/Mars transfer-orbit parameters. And so much more.

Without enumerating every book read or website visited (you're welcome), I'd like to acknowledge and credit NASA and the Mars Society for their wealth of invaluable studies and reports. As I'd like to acknowledge and credit Google Mars, the Marspedia, the Long-Term Evolution Experiment (indeed, LTEE is a real thing), and—shocking, I know—Wikipedia. To have embarked upon this project without these and many other online resources? I shudder at the mere idea.

When, after much research, plus that small matter of committing words to electrons, a draft novel emerged, it was time to engage a different type of assistance. On the science and medical fronts, I greatly appreciate the insights of my beta readers. Thanks herewith to Richard A. Lovett, Marc Mangel, Stanley Schmidt, and Henry Stratmann for their thoughtful and thorough feedback, both technical and authorial.

Last, but certainly not least, I thank my wife, Ruth. Beyond providing her usual eagle-eyed, yeowoman's duty as my first reader, she graciously handled deeper and longer-lasting authorial preoccupation than even my immersed-in-a-book norm.

As for the inevitable inaccuracies, oversimplifications, and artistic (or inartistic) license still to be found within these pages, all blame accrues to the author.

EDWARD M. LERNER
July 2023

About the Author

EDWARD M. LERNER worked in high tech and aerospace for thirty years, as everything from engineer to senior vice president, for much of that time writing science fiction as his hobby. Since 2004, he has written full-time.

His novels range from near-future techno-thrillers, like *Small Miracles* and *Energized*, to traditional SF, like *Déjà Doomed* and his InterstellarNet series, to (collaborating with Larry Niven) the space-opera epic Fleet of Worlds series. Lerner's 2015 novel, *InterstellarNet: Enigma*, won the inaugural Canopus Award "honoring excellence in interstellar writing." His fiction has also been nominated for Locus, Prometheus, and Hugo awards.

Lerner's short fiction has appeared in anthologies, collections, and many of the usual SF magazines and websites. He also writes about science and technology, notably including *Trope-ing the Light Fantastic: The Science Behind the Fiction.*

Lerner lives in Virginia with his wife, Ruth.

His website is *www.edwardmlerner.com.*

Printed in the USA
CPSIA information can be obtained
at www.ICGtesting.com
JSHW021917141123
52069JS00001B/1